LA SALLE'S GHOST

LA SALLE'S GHOST

A NOVEL BY **MILES ARCENEAUX**

La Salle's Ghost

© 2013 Brent Douglass, John T. Davis and James R. Dennis

Library of Congress Cataloging in Publication Data:
Arceneaux, Miles
La Salle's Ghost / Miles Arceneaux
1. Title. 2. Fiction. 3. Mystery. 4 Suspense

First Edition: September 2013
978-1-622880-27-0

Printed in the United States of America
Written by Brent Douglass, John T. Davis and James R. Dennis
Designed by Lana Rigsby, Thomas Hull, and Carmen Garza

Stephen F. Austin State University Press
PO Box 13007, SFA Station, Nacogcohes TX. 75962
sfapress@sfasu.edu sfasu.edu/sfapress

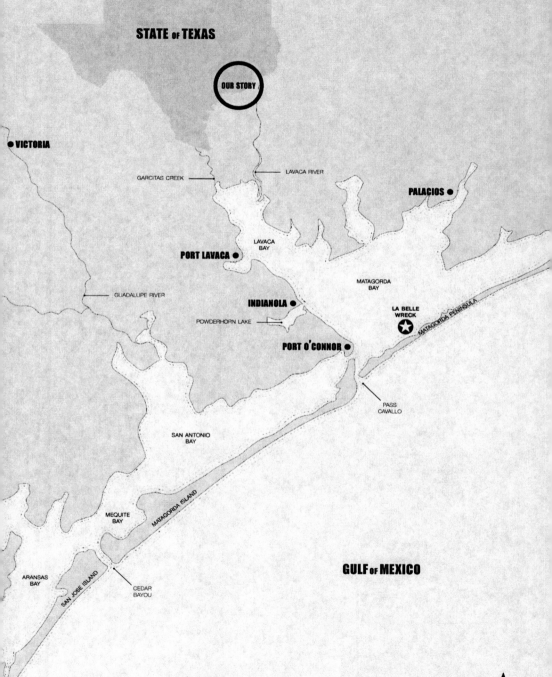

* MAP NOT TO SCALE

STATE of TEXAS

OUR STORY

● VICTORIA

GARCITAS CREEK

LAVACA RIVER

PALACIOS ●

LAVACA BAY

PORT LAVACA ●

MATAGORDA BAY

GUADALUPE RIVER

INDIANOLA ●

POWDERHORN LAKE

LA BELLE WRECK

MATAGORDA PENINSULA

PORT O'CONNOR ●

PASS CAVALLO

SAN ANTONIO BAY

MATAGORDA ISLAND

MEQUITE BAY

GULF of MEXICO

ARANSAS BAY

SAN JOSE ISLAND

CEDAR BAYOU

N

La Salle's sunken ship, *La Belle*, exposed on the floor of Matagorda Bay in 1997, as the excavation neared its conclusion. Hailed as one of the most important archaeological discoveries of the century. PHOTO BY: TEXAS HISTORICAL COMMISSION.

AUTHOR'S NOTE

Although this book relies on real events, it is a work of fiction. I have taken certain liberties in the retelling of the excavation of the *Belle* shipwreck and the discovery of the buried French settlement.

All of the 20th century characters and companies are products of my imagination, and any resemblance to persons living or dead is coincidental (with the exception of a certain governor with a signature white hairdo).

The Texas Historical Commission does indeed exist and was responsible for the world-class excavation it directed on both the *Belle* and the Fort St. Louis colony. I am not an archeologist, but I endeavored to capture the techniques and drama of their work. It is true that from 1996–1997, over twenty-five thousand people visited the cofferdam built around the sunken ship; just ask them if you don't believe me. The ship's fourth and final bronze cannon has never been found.

For the wealth of information I gathered on La Salle and his final expedition, and also on the excavation of the artifacts he and his colonists left behind, I am particularly indebted to three books: *From a Watery Grave—The Discovery and Excavations of La Salle's Shipwreck La Belle*, by James Bruseth and Toni S. Turner (Texas A&M Press); *The Wreck of the Belle, the Ruin of La Salle*, by Robert S. Weddle (Texas A&M Press); and of course, *The La Salle Expedition of Texas, The Journal of Henri Joutel, 1684–1687*, translated by William C. Foster (Texas State Historical Association).

— MILES ARCENEAUX

WHERE WAS THE TRAIL?

The explorer stopped and wiped the perspiration from his forehead with a ragged lace cuff. Ah, there it was, winding through a tangle of scrub oak and yaupon. He pushed through the brush, heedless of the thorns, following the faint game trail that led—he hoped—to the border between New Spain and the French territory of Louisiana. Earlier, he had crossed the river the Spanish called *Colorado,* the roiling brownish-red stream he had christened *Maligne:* "clever" or "cunning" in French, although it could also signify "devilish."

It was typical of René-Robert Cavelier Sieur de La Salle to affix his own titles on the natural world. He was a visionary, a great man by his own reckoning: a towering figure whom even his king, Louis XIV, *Le Roi Soleil,* must acknowledge.

Nonetheless, on this unseasonably warm day in 1687 he was leading a desperate group of sixteen men, a remnant of colonists who had once numbered three hundred, on a dash for civilization. La Salle intended to march all the way to Canada, if necessary, to reach French settlements.

His own base, Fort St. Louis, which he had built near a nameless bay on the Gulf of Mexico, had been beset by endless misfortunes. His mission, to establish a settlement on the mouth of the Mississippi River, had been a calamity. He grudgingly admitted he had overshot his target by many leagues, winding up in a treacherous and hostile land midway down the coast of the Spanish territory known as *Tejas.*

All of his ships had been lost—one to pirates, one to the blunders of a foolish navigator, and one to a vicious storm. The fourth had sailed back to France with a cargo of disenchanted colonists and a quarrelsome Captain.

Cowards, thought La Salle, then and now. It was he who was left to build an empire in the New World, he who would plant the flag of France in the northern reaches of New Spain, he who would thwart English schemes to control access to the *Golphe de Mexique,* and he who would bring lasting glory to *La Belle France.*

Never mind he was fleeing eastward now, leaving a tiny band of colonists to cope as best they could with disease and privation, and with the wild beasts and flesh-eating savages who infested that part of the coast. Fort St. Louis, the flyspeck colony he had cobbled together on the *Rivière aux Boeufs,* inland from the capricious bay, was just the first step on a road that led to riches, enduring fame and eternal acclaim. It was his destiny.

And if his men did not believe him, to hell with them.

He'd had to bully them, drag them and flog them every step of the way. *You do not believe,* he said. *You don't have the heart, the brains, or the balls to see what I see. I am La Salle and you are just the tools of my vision.*

He would return. Once before he had descended the mighty Mississippi River, claiming land all along the way for France. On this most recent expedition, he had penetrated deep into the wilderness of New Spain, marching as far west as the *Rio Bravo.* He was the greatest explorer of his age.

He strode ahead down the faint trail, never looking back.

The handful of men behind him did not share his blind confidence. In the forests there were bears, wolves, panthers . . . and Indians, of course. Nerves frayed by many months of stress, hunger and fear, they were on the ragged edge of collapse. They jumped as one when a whitetail doe crashed through the brush.

Worse yet, La Salle had split his party the day before, sending a small group led by his nephew, Colin Morenger, to reconnoiter for game and supplies. *We were few enough, and we are fewer now,* they grumbled.

La Salle is mad. The same thought echoed through the minds of the men from the hunting party who lay in wait for their leader, not far ahead, just around a bend in the trail. Morenger was already dead, the little shit, after presuming to dole out portions of the buffalo they'd shot, keeping most for himself. Just like his uncle, he was arrogant and overbearing. Well, they had seen to him, with an axe, just as they'd seen to Nika, the Indian scout.

Now for the "great explorer." He would explore them into their graves if he could. He had filled them with dreams of wealth and empire, but led them to death and starvation in the wilderness. *The madness ends here,* they swore to one another.

Voices on the trail ahead, just out of sight. The assassins crouched in the brush; one cocked a musket, careful to muffle the noise. The voices and the sounds of bodies moving through brush drew closer. It wouldn't be long now.

CHAPTER 01

SEPTEMBER 1995

It was the anniversary of my brother's death, and one of those rare nights on the Gulf when the wind fell slack and the sea was quiet and still. I lay on the roof of my Chinese junk, floating silently on the water about forty nautical miles southeast of Pass Cavallo, letting my mind wander. My eyes followed the stars as they wheeled toward an indistinct horizon, and I pictured my brother looking up at these same stars, floating on the same gentle current, and I wanted to believe his last moments were peaceful, too.

I wanted to empty my head and dissolve into the vast expanse of sea and sky surrounding me. It was these moments when I felt nearest to Johnny—or to his spirit, if that's what you want to call it.

Every September I returned to the same area—to the place where I imagined Johnny died fifteen years ago, knocked in the head and tossed overboard on the orders of an evil, low-down son of a bitch. I had put that part behind me, but something, a desire to be close to my brother I suppose, kept me coming back.

On this particular night, there were no clouds and no moon— as dark as it can get on the open sea. Only my mast light intruded upon the darkness as I drifted between sleep and wakefulness. Then I heard the splashing. Or was pretty sure I did.

At first I told myself I had only imagined the sound—the sound of a swimmer's stroke, faintly splashing off t he p ort b ow, a nd I tried to shut the noise out of my mind. Once, years earlier, I had been absolutely convinced I heard Johnny calling out to me in the distance, calling for help just beyond the arc of light from the masthead. But on that particular night I was drunk as a Mexican opal, and my senses were not entirely trustworthy.

The splashing grew louder.

I stood and stared intently into the darkness, still hearing the steady strokes of a swimmer propelling his body slowly, methodically toward my boat. Soon after, I saw a figure in the water, or rather the luminous outline of a figure, surrounded by a ghostly blue-green light, a faint incandescent trail following behind like a ship's wake.

When my eyes finally convinced me there was actually a man out there, struggling to reach my boat, I lowered the Jacob's ladder and climbed onto the edge of the gunwale, preparing to dive to his rescue. But where was he?

The sound of splashing had ceased, and the Gulf was totally absent of light—except for a dim glow under the surface, like an underwater docklight, drifting slowly downward, growing fainter.

I dove into the water.

When I reached the drowning man, he was still rotating his arms and kicking his legs in a slow, dreamy motion . . . winding down, sinking down, drowning . . . his movements haloed by the mysterious light surrounding his body.

He regarded me curiously with wide-open eyes before I grabbed him and kicked upward. When we broke the surface he gasped for air, thrashing momentarily and then docilely allowing me to tow him to the boat, too exhausted to struggle. At the boat ladder the swimmer hung limply on the rope.

"I do not have the strength, *mon ami*," he said, almost apologetically.

I climbed into the boat and then grabbed his arm to pull him up behind me. As he rolled over the gunwale, I looked down at the water and saw a massive oblong shape cruise past unhurriedly, surrounded by and trailing phosphorescence. Probably a fat tiger shark that had been following the swimmer in the darkness for no telling how long.

The man lay on the boat deck in the dim light, shivering and smiling up at me like a madman.

"Where in God's name did you *come* from?" I asked.

He waved an arm weakly to the north. "Out there," he said. "A long way. Since before the sun rise."

"That's a hell of a long time to stay afloat in the ocean, mister." I hooked my arms under his and pulled him up.

"Yes, a very long time," he murmured. His lips were cracked and blistered, his eyes swollen from the long immersion in saltwater. Even in the dim light it was clear he was sunburned and dehydrated to within an inch of his life. There were open sores where his saltwater-soaked clothes had abraded his chest and arms. I'd pulled cadavers out of the water that looked better than this guy. *Why are you still alive?* I wondered crazily, still thinking of spirits.

He staggered, and I guided him to a bench where he sat with his head down, his forearms resting on his bare thighs. After a moment he looked up at the mast light.

"When the night came," he said, "I swam for the only light I could see on the ocean. Your light. I thought I would never reach it."

He was grinning again, until his teeth started chattering uncontrollably.

"Let's get you below," I said, and walked him toward the cabin. He was shorter than me and of slight stature, but his arms were wiry and hard-muscled.

He looked around curiously. "What k-kind of b-boat is this?" he asked, as a spasm shook him.

"It's a Chinese junk."

"Ah, *oui*, of course. Then I am n-not hallucinating."

Inside the galley I wrapped the Frenchman (at least I assumed he was French) in a blanket, gave him some water and then administered some serious medicine—a tumbler full of Haitian rum. His hands shook so violently I had to hold the glass to his mouth.

He sat quietly on the cushioned bench while I changed into some dry clothes. Eventually his shivering stopped, and he sipped the rum. I made him some hot soup and strong coffee, and he accepted both gratefully, his aquiline nose disappearing into the mugs as he consumed the contents. A reddish, neatly-trimmed moustache and goatee boxed his thin lips, and he sported a stylish, close-cropped hairstyle.

"I could not believe my eyes when I saw your *jonque*," he said later. "I thought I swam all the way to Hong Kong."

"Well, that's where I found her," I said. "In the Victoria Harbor."

He nodded and smiled, which I took as a signal to continue.

"The previous owner was using the boat as a brothel until the city shut the business down. So, the madam agreed to sell me the vessel, and I sailed it here, to Texas. Over the years I've re-fit her to my liking."

"She is beautiful. And no longer a brothel, I suppose."

"No, I'm afraid not. Just an elegant *grande dame* these days, but she is named after a famous Chinese courtesan, I'm told."

"What is her name?"

"*Li Shishi.*"

"Well, I am glad to be aboard the *Li Shishi,* Mr. . . . ?"

"Sweetwater. Charlie Sweetwater." I leaned over, and we shook hands.

"Good to meet you, Mr. Sweetwater," he said. "I am Julien Dufay."

He gripped my hand firmly and sat back, looking at me expectantly. I got the feeling he thought I should know him, but I drew a blank. I nodded and repeated the name silently to myself. *Dufay, Dufay.* The name was vaguely familiar but I couldn't place it, so I just told him I was pleased to make his acquaintance and was glad he'd decided to swim over from the Côte d'Azur to pay me a visit.

When I asked how he'd ended up in the water, he shrugged as if it was of no importance.

"I suppose I fall. Or someone helped me fall. I do not know which."

"You mean *pushed* you? Are you saying someone pushed you into the water?"

"No, not exactly. I was standing on the deck of one of our crew boats, heading for the oil platform, when the boat swerve suddenly, very abrupt, and then next thing I know, *tout à coup,* I am in the water."

"The pilot didn't turn around and look for you?"

He shook his head. "There were only three of us on the boat. Maybe at first they did not realize I am overboard. Or maybe . . . ." He shrugged again. "Anyway, the current was very strong, and it carried me away quickly."

There was an offshore production platform about thirty miles to the northeast where I occasionally fished for red snapper and kingfish. I assumed Julien was a crewmember there, maybe a mud-logger or a data engineer. He seemed too refined for a roughneck.

"What about helicopters? Wouldn't the rig have called the Coast Guard?"

"Yes, later I hear the helicopters. But far away."

"I should radio in that you've been rescued, Julien."

He held up his palm. "No. We will wait until tomorrow. Let the bastards worry. I want to rest before I go back. Besides, it is so peaceful here on your—" he looked around appreciatively, "on your Chinese junk."

As Julien sipped his rum, a questioning expression appeared on his face. "Charlie, when I am in the water, swimming for your boat, the sea seemed to be . . . on fire, shining with light and life. I am sure I am out of my mind."

"Phosphorescence," I said. "The algae emit light when they're disturbed. I've seen it before, but never so intense."

The Frenchman nodded thoughtfully. "It was comforting somehow. I wasn't afraid."

"You did good, Julien Dufay."

Before long his eyes began to droop, and I fixed him a bunk. I'd be tired too after swimming for eighteen hours. He fell asleep almost instantly. I went outside and climbed onto the cabin roof to resume the annual wake for my brother. When the sun finally appeared, a perfect orange egg yolk at the edge of the sea, I dove into the water and floated on my back, drifting in the current and soaking up the morning rays. Eighteen hours in the water. I suppose it was possible if you kept your head and didn't panic—and if you were a damn strong swimmer.

——

Around noon, Julien surfaced from the master cabin. He bounded up the steps and greeted me in the wheelhouse.

"*Bonjour, Samaritain!*" he said cheerfully.

He was wearing a pair of my swim trunks and was shirtless, only a few thin hairs on his robust chest. He had recovered remarkably well after the long rest.

"You slept well, I see."

"Yes, very well. *Comme un loir.* Where are we going, Charlie?"

"We're heading toward the harbor in Port Lavaca."

"*Je vois,*" he said wistfully. Then his face brightened. "Can we sail her in? I would love to see this beautiful creature unfurl her wings."

"Not enough wind. It would take a full day or more to reach port."

"*Bon!* I am in no hurry."

For a moment I considered it, but thought better of the idea. The Coast Guard would already be aggravated that I had not immediately reported finding their missing person. I decided to change the subject. "Hey, I'll bet you're hungry?"

"*Oui,* I am very hungry. *Une faim de loup!*"

I cut the engine and let the boat drift while I went into the galley to fry bacon and scramble eggs. Julien wolfed down two full plates of chow and drank a quart of orange juice. After he finished eating, he leaned back in the booth and sipped his fourth cup of coffee.

"What is it that you do, Charlie Sweetwater? For a living, I mean."

"I'm a shrimper."

Julien grinned and kept looking at me, expecting me to say more. But that was about it when you boiled it down. My profession was shrimp. I either caught them or built and sold equipment that did. My sixty-five-foot gulf trawler, currently docked in Fulton Harbor, had been christened the *Johnny Roger* in honor of my brother.

"Well, of course we must have our shrimp!" he exclaimed. "It is sad to imagine a world without shrimp scampi, *n'est-ce pas?* Or shrimp creole?"

I laughed. "Yes, Julien. How could you make a proper paella without shrimp? Or a po'boy, for that matter? I have an almighty responsibility. But I do other things too. Think of me more as a *bricoleur,* a handyman."

Julien beamed. "Ah yes! The *bricoleur,* from *The Savage Mind,* by Claude Lévi-Strauss—a man adept at many things; a man who is good at putting preexisting things together in new ways. Am I right?"

"That's me, my friend. The savage mind."

Julien leaned over and slapped me on the arm. "Ha! Very good, Charlie."

I buttoned up the galley and we moved to the helm, where I started the twin six-cylinder Perkins engines (clean and quiet) and we pushed on toward the natural inlet known as Pass Cavallo.

On the way in, we talked about a wide variety of subjects, and in spite of my unfavorable preconceptions of the French, I found Julien to be forthright, interesting and irrepressibly optimistic—especially considering he'd almost drowned the day before, possibly with a little boost from somebody on his crew boat. I don't know what bothered me more, the fact someone might have tried to kill my new friend, or the fact he seemed unwilling to speculate on that very possibility.

I gave him the wheel for a few minutes while I brewed another pot of coffee. He couldn't seem to get enough of it.

He took the cup and gulped it with his eyes closed. "*Extra!*" he said. "Strong, black and made with a French press, just like the *café* my aunt would prepare. In fact, when I took the first sip this morning, it transport me back to her summerhouse outside of Paris. She would serve us coffee like this when we were children, not even twelve years. Now, over twenty years later, I drink *this* coffee and *voilà!* I have a flashback—triggered by the senses, in this case the taste and smell of your coffee—and I experience those wonderful childhood moments again. Have you read Proust?"

I admitted I had. When I'd enrolled as a philosophy major at the University of Texas, my dad, Dubber, a shrimper, just shook his head in dismay. "Son, I guess if you're absolutely committed to *not* having a job when you get outta college, then you're doing exactly the right thing."

Julien continued. "Ah, good! Then you know these are the ideas Proust explored in his novels: how what we choose to remember, and what we do with these memories, even the ones that bubble up unexpectedly—how they shape us and make sense of the world, no? *À la recherche du temps perdu—In Search of Lost Time.* A wonderful title to his masterpiece. Anyway, I have tried to capture this idea of involuntary memory in an exhibit I have curated at my museum. It is very powerful. What do you think, Charlie?"

I was thinking my guest should lay off the strong coffee for awhile. After six cups, Julien's high-pitched voice and animated gestures had begun to remind me of a hard-bop jazz improvisation, with a strong French accent.

Then, belatedly, it hit me. "You have a museum?"

"*Bien*, it is not mine, really. I like to think it belongs to the people of Houston, and of course, to the rest of the world. I just happen to work there."

"There, and on an offshore oil rig?"

Julien laughed. "I was scouting the rig for a film my wife is making. You really do not know who I am, do you?"

"Should I?"

"Well, considering you are a worldly man, I would think you have heard of DeBergerac Drilling Corporation. We are a *worldwide* company, you know. My grandfather was one of the founders."

Of course I'd heard of DeBergerac, the largest drilling enterprise on the planet. Privately owned by a French family of the same name, its corporate headquarters in downtown Houston pushed upwards like a gleaming knife blade above all other buildings in that skyscraper-besotted city. The DeBergerac executives looked down on the bustling blue-collar metropolis and its oily ship channel from their lofty perch on the 80th floor with Zeus-like detachment. They had punched deep holes in almost every county in Texas and in much of the Gulf of Mexico, equatorial Africa and the Middle East. If you chose to look at it that way, I'd rescued something like two or three billion dollars worth of equity from the saltwater.

"I wasn't aware you could find oil in a museum," I said.

"Hah! *Très drôle,* Charlie. But we have our cultured side, too. The family, or some of us anyway, believes it is important for people to know we are not interested only in the black gold, as you Americans call it."

Then I remembered—the Dufay Museum of Modern Art near downtown Houston. It housed a collection of paintings, sculptures and assorted avant-garde objects that rivaled any personal collection in the world. The building itself, designed by some celebrated French architect with two hyphens and an umlaut in his name, was a major city landmark.

"I'll have to visit your museum someday," I said.

"*Oui, absolument!* I will give you a personal tour."

"You're on, Julien. But right now, I think it's important that I announce your return to civilization. I'm pretty sure people are still looking for you. And besides, the Coast Guard gets seriously pissed off when they waste time looking for someone who's already found."

Julien sighed and looked toward the approaching mainland. "Yes, I suppose you are right. I would like to spend more time out here on your Chinese junk. What a magnificent anachronism! And so enchanting. I feel like I am in another time.

"I owe you my life, Charlie Sweetwater," he said, putting his hand on my shoulder. "And I am so happy I discover you and your sailing boat. It was good fortune, you know? A *sérendipité*." He closed his eyes and breathed in deeply. A fresh breeze from the southeast rocked the boat gently, and the teak hull creaked and moaned, seeming to exhale for him in response.

At dusk we reached the rough little commercial harbor in Port Lavaca. I had radioed the authorities two hours out that we were arriving, and there to meet us on shore was the Coast Guard, the local sheriff, a limo, an ambulance, an assortment of local wharf rats and two television crews. Julien became increasingly quiet and even sullen the closer we came to port. As we approached the dock, I asked him a question that had been bothering me all day.

"Julien, why do you think someone would want you to *fall* off your own crew boat?"

"What?" he asked, as if I were a stranger who happened to be standing next to him on a street corner, waiting for the light to turn.

I asked the question again, and he looked at me curiously and shrugged. "Because I am an asshole," he answered.

He left the wheelhouse and stood at the bow in the grey sweatpants and black windbreaker he'd selected from my sea chest, glumly observing the commotion on shore as we nosed into a slip. We eased up to the dock, and before I even threw a line over a mooring post, he climbed over the rail and jumped onto the gangway. With his shoulders hunched and his hands jammed into his pockets, he marched resolutely past the cameras and the crowd and disappeared into his limousine, never even turning back to wave.

FROM THE JOURNAL OF PÈRE POISSON

In the year of Our Lord 1684, on the 24th of July, we sailed from La Rochelle for the New World, seeking to spread the True Faith and the Kingdom of God. I sailed on the Joly, along with the Sieur de La Salle and two other Frère Menous with whom I planned to serve a settlement mission. Looking back now, I have concluded that despite my most fervent prayers, the angels did not see fit to protect this voyage or our ventures into this strange new land. I do not know why.

Père Poisson
Franciscan Recollect Friar
JULY 1684

CHAPTER 02

It was the following June before the cosmic tumbler clicked over another notch and put me on the path back to Port Lavaca—and to Julien Dufay. I hadn't thought much about the Frenchman since I'd plucked him from the sea and returned him to his rarified world, and there was certainly no reason to think our paths would ever cross again.

The day began with a sudden shower that dissipated as quickly as it had formed, leaving bright mirrors of water on the oyster shell roads and in the hollows of the rough wooden piers of Fulton Harbor. I was alone at my waterfront office, tinkering with an invention of mine and enjoying the ozone-infused air and the soothing sounds of a working harbor starting its day.

My office was a high tin warehouse, containing assorted tools of my trade, a rusty fridge that complained loudly about the incessant heat and humidity, and a mongrel dog named Quay. But the space was roomy and functional and suited me just fine. The large opening admitted the gulf breeze and offered a nice view of the boats in the harbor, including my Chinese vessel, which prompted many a double take from tourists who came to the docks to buy fresh seafood from the fishermen.

Sailing the *Li Shishi* into her new homeport for the first time had been one of the major-league treats of my life. My good friends and neighbors, the Vietnamese shrimpers who shared the harbor with me, thought I'd lost my cotton-picking mind. And not for the first time. From what I could tell from the little bit of pidgin Vietnamese I'd picked up over the years, I roughly translated their remarks as, "What has that crazy white boy gone off and done now?"

I decided to walk over to Charlotte Plummer's dockside restaurant to grab a cup of coffee. I needed a break from the recalcitrant contraption I was working on—something the marine scientists called a Turtle Excluder Device, or TED for short, but what we shrimpers called a turtle shooter. Federal law required us to attach one of these things to our trawl rigs, to spit out the occasional marine turtle that's swept into our nets.

When the TEDs became mandatory, there were a lot of pissed-off fishermen, because the large and cumbersome devices released many of the shrimp along with the endangered turtles—the latter of which we never had any use for in the first place. To be honest, most of us would just as soon run the EPA bureaucrats through the contraption.

Mostly out of frustration, I began playing with improvements to the basic TED design, and much to my surprise the government patented and approved my modifications for general use. This didn't sit well with some of the more militant shrimpers who resented the Feds telling them what to do, but it ended up making me a semi-big pile of money.

When I returned to the office with my coffee, one of my business partners was examining my latest TED design, which hung from a ceiling truss at the end of a trawl net. Although the device was basically just a mesh funnel attached to a metal grate, attached to the inside of the main drag net—a simple concept really—it was damned hard to get right. The funnel guided the turtles into the slanted grate where they slid out an exit hole back into the sea to, hopefully, make a lot of other turtles and one day render the TED obsolete. But if your materials, angles, gauges and diameters weren't calibrated exactly right, then either too many shrimp or too few turtles escaped.

"*Tío*, why don't you try regular bag webbing for the funnel? Instead of this expensive heat-set poly stuff?" said my business partner and nephew, Raul. "The fishermen down south can't get this fancy material."

"No they can't," I said. "That's why they buy ours."

Raul de la Rosa Sweetwater handled the sale of our TED technology to shrimp exporters in Latin America, and he brought back practical advice on making our design more commercially viable. He was my brother Johnny's son, by way of a Mexican sweetheart long since vanished. Raul had walked to Fulton from Tampico when he was fourteen years old, looking for his dad. I became his legal guardian after my brother died, and remained so until the boy turned eighteen. As a kid, he worked the shrimp boats, first for Johnny, and then for me. Now, we were business partners in Sweetwater Enterprises. After I put him in charge of selling our turtle shooter design to Mexico and Central America, our business tripled from his efforts. It was the smartest decision I'd ever made.

"But when our funnel net gets ripped, then what do they do?" Raul was saying. "They just take it off. If we design it to work with more common materials, they can repair it themselves and keep fishing legal. It will also make our unit less expensive to build."

"Sammy, will regular bag-webbing work?" I asked.

My second smartest decision was picking my other partner, Sammy Dang, the brains of the outfit. He had earned an advanced degree in mechanical engineering from Texas A&M and was skilled at turning my jury-rigged designs into a clean set of manufacturing specs. He handled sales in Asia, which was also a booming market for us.

Sammy was a serious kid, two years older than Raul. Quiet and purposeful, he served as a good counter-balance to Raul and me, who were happy-go-lucky and easily distracted, especially when the fish were biting. I'd met Sammy under rather desperate circumstances many years ago. A stand-up kid who'd grown into a stand-up man, betting on him had been a no-brainer.

Sammy looked up from the export documents he was studying. "As long as the polyethylene mesh is thermoformed and stretchable, it should be fine. And Raul is right. We could cut approximately ten percent off the unit manufacturing cost."

I concentrated on keeping a straight face instead of beaming like a proud paterfamilias. *Well, hell, boys,* I thought, *what do you need me for?*

Our executive meeting was interrupted when we noticed an attractive woman standing in the doorway. She wore jeans and a polo shirt with some sort of logo embroidered over the breast. She had the sort of natural athleticism Katherine Hepburn had once embodied. Something, maybe the casual disarray of her auburn hair and her sun-freckled skin, made me think she made her living outdoors.

"Hi. I'm looking for Charlie Sweetwater?" she said.

I stepped forward and extended my hand. "I'm Charlie. What can I do for you?"

"I'm Holly Hardin, from the Marine Archeology Commission. Jim Brannan told me I might find you here. I understand you're a friend of Jim's?"

Jim served as director of the Texas Historical Commission. I'd attended a few of his lectures, but mostly I knew him because he owned a house in nearby Rockport and drank at the same bar as me. He was an easygoing guy and didn't come off like a professor. He was also an expert fly fisherman and a pretty decent domino player. He'd skinned me at 42 more than once.

"Yeah, I guess you could say that. How do y'all know each other?"

"We're collaborating on a project. He recommended I talk to you." She glanced around, inspecting the warehouse. She didn't seem too impressed by the Sweetwater World Headquarters, which had its original incarnation as a Vietnamese seafood wholesaler. "Is there somewhere private we can talk?"

I introduced her to Sammy and Raul and told her she could speak freely around them, but she insisted on privacy, so I escorted her to an air-conditioned room built up in the corner of the warehouse. The office was sparsely furnished with a desk, phone and computer, and had a six-foot oil painting of a reclining Modigliani nude on the wall.

Quay, the piebald mutt we'd adopted, or rather who'd taken up residence in the warehouse and expected us to feed and shelter him like he was the finalist in the Westminster Kennel Club show, sat in the guest chair opposite the desk. He climbed down indignantly when I shooed him off.

Holly took the seat and examined the office dubiously. Her eyes landed on the painting.

"It's an original," I explained. "But also a copy. An original copy."

"Clearly."

She presented me with a cursory smile and folded her hands in her lap. Whatever I had been recommended for, she seemed to have reservations about me being the man for the job.

"Do you know much about the history of this area, Mr. Sweetwater?"

"I suppose I do. My family has lived and worked here for over a hundred years."

"Further back," she said, leaning forward in the chair. "Before your family was here."

As I rummaged through my brain for accumulated Gulf Coast history (Karankawa Indians? Jean Lafitte, the privateer? Civil War blockade-runners?), she watched me carefully with bright, observant eyes that were as blue as a marlin fin.

"Lemme guess," I ventured. "You've discovered a Spanish galleon buried in the Aransas Bay mud."

Her head jerked back, and she looked surprised. "How did you—? You've heard something? What have you heard?"

I laughed. "I haven't heard anything. I just guessed. You're a marine archeologist, working with the Texas Historical Commission, and most historical treasures found underwater once floated *on top* of the water. And unless sunken shrimp boats and scuttled barges are high on your list of wrecks with historical significance, I figured, why not a Spanish ship?"

"Not bad," she admitted. "But not quite right. We think we've discovered a French wreck—in Matagorda Bay."

"La Salle?" I asked, vaguely recalling the French explorer had once poked around the middle Texas coast looking for the mouth of the Mississippi. A pretty fucked-up venture, from what little I knew.

"That's right. René-Robert Cavelier de La Salle. He sailed to this area a little over three-hundred years ago with big plans to establish a colony. Two of his ships sank near Pass Cavallo."

"And your divers found one of them."

"Actually, I did. I found a cannon—almost six feet long with dolphin-shaped lifting handles and an insignia of a French admiral engraved in the barrel."

"A cannon. That's pretty exciting."

"In the muddy water I had to read the markings by touch, like Braille, but when we brought it up, the evidence was staring me in the face." She leaned forward, her eyes dancing. "We're positive we've found the wreck of La Salle's light frigate, *La Belle*."

She smiled for the first time, animated by the retelling of her discovery. I guessed for an archeologist, something like this would be a pretty big deal, and I said so.

"It will be the biggest historical find of the decade," she said, pushing a tendril of sun-bleached hair behind an ear. "Maybe of a lifetime. And what we need right now is someone to help us protect it."

"Protect it from what?"

"From amateur divers, careless trawlers . . . but mostly from treasure hunters. The last thing we need are a bunch of pirates screwing up our site. If word gets out, it'll be like the day after Thanksgiving at Wal-Mart."

"You want *me* to guard it?"

"Jim does. He says you're half-pirate yourself. I think he meant it as a compliment. Anyway, we don't want to hire a private security company. We're trying to keep the discovery quiet, at least until we figure out how to excavate the artifacts."

"And I suppose Jim said I was discreet."

"Well, he said you could be trusted. He also said you might be bored and looking for something to do since shrimping season is closed from June until mid-August."

"That's thoughtful of him." I sat back in my chair and stalled for time while I thought about it. "Things are pretty busy around here, me being, you know, Chief Executive Officer of a multinational business and all." I waved my hand around to remind her of my spacious and well-appointed executive office. Quay sprawled on the floor, chewing on a dried pig hoof.

"Your turtle release contraption, right?"

"Yes ma'am. We call ours the Texas Twister. It has its own patent and everything."

"Right. Well, if you're too busy, I'll try and—"

"I didn't say I was *too* busy."

The truth was, Raul, Sammy and Sammy's wife (who handled the books) pretty much ran the business themselves. We had farmed out most of our manufacturing to local shops scattered around the globe, and in return received royalties on our design, so there wasn't a whole lot for me to do. My job was to try out new design modifications and keep out of the way. When the season was open

I sometimes took the *Johnny Roger* out in the gulf and trawled for shrimp. But mostly I worked on my junk rig, did some light guiding for fishermen and hunters—friends mostly—and fished the flats, reefs and bayous around Fulton. It was an ideal arrangement.

"So you'll do it?"

"Sure. I'd love to be part of the biggest historical find of a lifetime."

Holly's face reddened. I guess my comment sounded more facetious than I intended.

"I'm serious, Holly Hardin. I'm your man. Trustworthy and discreet as hell."

She nodded once and shook my hand firmly, like she meant business and by God, I better mean business too.

"Okay, Mr. Sweetwater. Can you meet me at the Port Lavaca Harbor tomorrow morning? At ten o'clock?"

"You can count on it," I said.

She stood up to leave and had her hand on the doorknob when I stopped her.

"Ms. Hardin? What happened on that La Salle expedition? Didn't it end badly?"

"He lost all his ships, and pretty much everyone died."

"Damn," I said, shaking my head. "And he missed the Mississippi River by four hundred miles. Not a very successful operation, was it?"

"Not from La Salle's perspective, no."

"What happened to him?"

"He was murdered by his own men."

"Oh."

———

CHAPTER 03

That summer was a lot more interesting than I imagined it would be, and I liked to think I played a small part in the successful first stage of the project. In the beginning, I hung out on my shrimp boat near the submerged wreck, reading and watching out for careless shrimpers and plundering pirates—of whom there were none. Everything seemed stuck on high center. But when the project funding came in, I had a ringside seat to a remarkable engineering feat—the erection of a stand-alone, open-water cofferdam.

The structure emerged out of the murky water of Matagorda Bay like a colossal crown. It was just the damndest thing. When it was finished, it reminded me of one of those undersea lairs where James Bond's arch-nemesis sits petting his cat.

The objective was to enclose the entire shipwreck within double walls of sheet steel sunk deep into the bay bottom, and then to pump out the saltwater so the archeologists could conduct their slow, painstaking excavation work in the open air. They dumped twelve thousand tons of sand into a wide gap between the walls to press back against the crushing weight of saltwater that surrounded the dam, in effect producing a thirty-three-foot rampart around their hole in the water.

Building the structure required commercial barges to haul materials to the site, a huge crane to move and position the steel sheet pilings, industrial vibrators to drive the steel into the mud, and big diesel excavators with capacious clamshell buckets to dump the sand. Watching the thing go up, I felt like a boy with his first Erector Set. I probably took a thousand pictures. In the end, they'd constructed a watertight enclosure, which they pumped dry to expose the wreck—creating a mostly dry hole eighty feet across and twelve feet deep in the middle of Matagorda Bay.

For the first couple of weeks, Raul and Sammy gave me a break and handled a few of the night shifts for me. But they soon became bored with the job and returned to Fulton, saying that somebody had to mind the store at Sweetwater Enterprises. They weren't nearly as practiced at idleness as I was.

I didn't see too much of Holly during the summer months. Jim told me she would take her turn at bat once the actual excavation began. From Jim, I also learned the following: a) that Holly was a person of considerable standing in the field of marine archeology; b) that she was single, never married; and c) that she was completely and passionately dedicated to her work. He also told me I had about as much chance of sparking a romantic relationship with her as finding the treasure of Llanganatis under the gas pumps at the Sav-Mor in Fulton. I had to look up the reference. Llanganatis is a shitload of gold buried by an Inca general, supposedly in an Ecuadorian mountain range of the same name. Funny guys, those archeologists.

As the cofferdam neared completion, and the *Belle* was safely surrounded by a walled fortress of sand and steel, I began spending more time at a nearby marina owned by a friend of mine in Indianola. The joint was located on a narrow spit of land between Powderhorn Lake and Matagorda Bay, a short boat ride from the wreck site. Miguel Cantu Negron, the owner, head fry cook, bartender and bouncer, gave me free use of his boat slip. Beer, however, was not free.

"That'll be a buck, *cabrón*," he growled from behind his bar.

"I thought you were letting me run a tab," I protested.

"I am. It's a one beer limit, paid up front."

I slapped a dollar on the table, and he removed it with a dark, tattooed hand that looked like it belonged to a bare-knuckle boxer, which wasn't far from the truth. Before Miguel got out of the life, he was a mid-level enforcer in a Chicano street gang in Houston. Only a few people knew he'd done prison time, and even fewer mentioned it. Not to his face anyway. He'd kept his nose clean for almost twenty years and was as happy as a guy like Miguel could be, running his off-the-grid fishing marina and beer joint on this remote offshoot of the Texas coast.

He'd spent a good chunk of his adult life surrounded by gang-bangers, Aryan Brotherhood racists, hit men and big-stripe lifers in the TDC. The prison tattoos, including the inked line of tears near the corner of his left eye, and the ominous words *"Vida"* and *"Muerte"* inscribed between the knuckles of each fist, had mostly faded away in the years I'd known him. He now looked like the aging Mexican brother of Robert Mitchum. But there was still an air of slumbering menace about Miguel Negron. Most people instinctively left him alone.

No wonder Indianola—population approximately zero—appealed to his misanthropic tendencies.

Technically, Indianola wasn't a town at all, even though it showed up on some roadmaps. Back-to-back hurricanes in the previous century had leveled the once-prosperous community not once, but twice, and persuaded the mostly immigrant German townspeople they'd be better off scratching out a living in the Texas Hill Country than chancing another year by the lethal and unpredictable sea. There was nothing left but some ruined foundations and a granite monument stuck in the sand, marking the place where the township used to be. Indianola lived with its ghosts, a perfect spot for a man with secrets.

The nearest real town was Port Lavaca, fifteen miles away. Port Lavaca was a blue-collar community whose economy revolved around an aluminum factory, a plastics plant, and a vast oil refinery complex—all of which lit up the western shore of Lavaca Bay at night like a dystopian skyline. The community boosters welcomed big industry with open arms, but most of the shrimpers and sport fishermen I knew wondered why Lavaca was consistently the only bay on the Texas Coast where the fishing was always lousy.

In fact, one of the plants had dumped so much mercury into the upper bay that signs along the Lavaca Bridge warned fishermen it was not safe to eat anything that came out of the water—or else risk glowing in the dark and maybe growing a third foot. Alcoa was "inventing the future" alright.

"Miguel, when are you going to take a vacation?" I asked. "As far as I know, you've never once left this dive since you bought it."

"As far as you know."

"Where? Where have you been?"

"Maybe I've been to Palacios." Palacios was a small fishing town across the bay. "Maybe I know somebody there," he added.

"You mean, like a girl? Do you have a girlfriend in Palacios, Miguel?"

"None of your fucking business."

"Okay, Prince Charming," I said, holding my hands up in a *"no mas"* gesture. "I'm just tryin' to help you out . . . make a little civilized conversation."

Miguel snorted and walked off, wiping his hands on a filthy bar towel. To tell the truth, it was Miguel who had helped *me* out a decade and a half back. At least I think he did. All I know is that a real bad *hombre* wanted me and some people close to me dead. Instead, the guy wound up dead in a manner that had the hallmark of a certain Mexican ex-con all over it. But Miguel never admitted anything and I never asked.

I occupied one of the four stools behind the small in-store bar where Miguel sold beer, bait, fishing tackle, and soda pop. He had a fry grill in a small adjoining kitchen and a simple menu consisting of breakfast tacos in the morning, burgers and fried shrimp baskets in the evening. Miguel allowed regular customers to bring him their fresh-caught fish, and if they asked him politely, would broil, bake or fry it to perfection. He would also surprise you with unlikely side dishes; my favorite was his lemon and goat cheese risotto. I still don't know where he learned to cook, because I had never seen him read a recipe, or read anything for that matter, except maybe a tide chart or the Mexican wrestling magazines he received in the mail every month.

Attached to the store was a big wooden deck built out over the water. It had picnic tables and benches for the patrons and a pass-through bar for Hinkie, the reformed alcoholic who waited on the customers and helped Miguel with the chores. Of indeterminate age, Hinkie lived in a hail-pocked Airstream trailer behind the parking lot, right next to Miguel's hail-pocked Airstream trailer. He had a pleasant face and grinned a lot, like he was remembering a joke or playing a funny song in his head, but he rarely spoke. He seemed simple, as if the years of boozing had melted his brain. But maybe he was just canny.

A sizable crowd was keeping Hinkie and Miguel plenty busy tonight. It was mostly a proletariat clientele made up of commercial fishermen and industrial workers from Port Lavaca, some cowboys from a nearby ranch and a boatload of blue-collar kids who cruised over in their Whaler to drink some beer and enjoy the sunset. I was enjoying the sunset too, a little hypnotized by the low murmur of voices and the soulful baritone of Willie Nelson on the stereo system when the voices abruptly ceased, as a chorus of cicadas will suddenly do in late summer.

I sat up and tried to figure out what had happened and belatedly noticed that every head on the patio was turned toward the entry gate at the end of the deck. I couldn't see what they were looking at, but I heard the unmistakable voice of Julien Dufay, conversing loudly in French with an unseen companion.

He came into view, and I could see why people were staring. He wore tight grey pants and a black button-down shirt with pushed-up sleeves. On his head he sported aviator sunglasses and a Panama Ascot cap. He couldn't have looked more out of place if he'd ridden in naked on a unicycle.

Then I realized my fellow barflies weren't watching him at all, but the person behind him—a six-foot Amazon wearing platform heels and a white, fitted dress that was blinding in the slanted rays of the late afternoon sun. Her head was artfully wrapped in a colorful scarf, and she had a dusky complexion that was as smooth and creamy as mocha gelato. She glided over the deck and surveyed the crowd regally, like a queen selecting the evening sacrifice. On the jukebox, Willie sang about yesterday's wine and miracles appearing in the strangest of places.

A thin young man in a black necktie followed Her Majesty, holding a video camera and dutifully pointing the lens wherever the Amazon indicated with a nod or a slight tilt of her chin. Another young man followed the cameraman, frantically jotting down notes in a spiral notebook. Nobody in the unlikely group greeted or acknowledged the gawking customers at the tables.

"I know that guy!" I said to Miguel, who was also taking in the improbable spectacle. "He's the French guy who swam up to my boat last fall in the middle of the ocean, remember? I told you about that?"

Miguel and I watched in wonder as Julien, his Nubian queen, and her consorts continued their procession. Julien was gesturing toward the bay and gabbing theatrically with the zeal of an amped-up tour guide at the Louvre.

It wasn't long before I heard the first French joke from someone in the crowd, something about raising one hand if you *like* the French and two hands if you *are* French, and then a follow-up joke about a frog with a wart on its butt. The harassment came from two pocket-sized rednecks standing at the rail on the far corner of the deck. Both of them wore Western snap shirts and Roper-style boots and seemed to be carbon copies of each other, except one wore a straw cowboy hat that looked like a squashed roach and the other wore a gimme cap. Other than that, I couldn't tell them apart.

Julien stopped addressing his entourage, and it grew quiet for a moment, except for the sneering comments from the cowboy twins.

"They *are* monkey-looking fuckers aren't they?" said Cowboy Hat. He seemed to jitter in place, like he was running a race inside his head.

"You got that right," said Gimme Cap. "Hey, Ricky, you know how you separate the men from the boys in France?"

"How do they separate men from boys in France, Randy?"

"With a crowbar!"

The brothers snickered and spat into the bay. "I wouldn't mind gettin' me a slice of that colored gal, though," Ricky continued. "But hell, I'd need a stepladder to get to it."

"That's why they call it high-yellow, bro," answered the other.

Julien frowned and turned around slowly. He looked them up and down and smiled thinly. "Your humor is dreadful," he said. "Unimaginative, philistine and in poor taste."

Inside the store Miguel thumped my arm to get my attention. He motioned me to lean over the bar. "Those two *pendejos* are trouble."

"I can see that, Miguel. What do you want me to do about it?"

"If that *maricón* out there is your friend, you better figure out a way to stop this fight from happening."

"If he needs help with those two squirts, I'll jump in."

"It's not them I'm worried about," said Miguel. "It's their older brother sittin' at the next table."

I craned my head to see who he was talking about and saw a guy the size of a Frigidaire planted on a bench next to the twins. His massive head was almost square, with little ears stuck on each side like flesh-colored buds. The longneck beer bottle he held was engulfed by a fat-fingered hand that twitched in anticipation.

"I've heard of those guys," Miguel continued. "Ricky and Randy Sutton are the two sawed-off fuckers. They start the fights, and then their brother, Junior, steps in and finishes them."

"Well, I guess Julien might need some help after all, Miguel."

"Look, *cabrón* . . . . A fight happens in my joint, and shit gets broken that I gotta replace. It also clears out the customers, who leave without paying their checks. Someone gets hurt and then the sheriff comes, and me and my place get put on their county shit list. I don't want none of that, Charlie, *comprende?*"

I nodded. For Miguel, that many words constituted a Shakespearean soliloquy.

He leaned on the bar and watched me with his sleepy, deep-set eyes, still working a toothpick around lazily in his mouth. He was right. A fight would not be a good idea. Especially if Miguel got involved. I'd never completely gauged his capacity for violence, but I suspected it came down on the far side of lethal. I didn't want him back in the joint on account of Julien Dufay.

"Alright, chief," I replied.

I popped up from my stool and pushed open the screen door. "Julien Dufay!" I shouted. "You old sonofabitch! Come on over here!"

I walked straight up to him and gave him a big *abrazo*, turning him away from the Sutton brothers at the same time and steering him and his entourage toward the entrance to the store.

"I want to buy y'all a cold beer," I said, pushing them inside. "And I want to introduce you and your guests to the owner of this hallowed establishment."

I sat Julien down on a stool. "It's great to see you, Julien," I said, and then turned around and introduced myself to the woman. "Hi,

I'm Charlie Sweetwater, and I'm damn glad to meet you." She smiled and offered a smooth, graceful hand I regretted having to release.

"My name is Marguerite. I am Julien's wife."

Somehow I knew her name wouldn't be Betsy. Or Edna. Or Alma Jean. Marguerite sounded like she looked—luxurious, exotic and light years out of my class. My brother would have told me, "That's too much car for you."

"Charlie?" Julien exclaimed, finally adjusting to the change of focus. "It *is* you. I cannot believe it!"

He stood up and hugged me and began speaking rapidly in French to the woman and the two hipsters standing beside her. "He is the one who saved my life!" he stated in English, for my benefit.

"Saved your life?" I said. "I thought you were just out for a midnight swim and stopped by my boat for a towel and a cold beer."

Julien laughed. "I told you he was entertaining," he said to the group.

"Julien, what are you *doing* here?" I asked.

"Marguerite is capturing footage for the film she is making. Background material and some, how do you say? Local color. This is Laurent, the *directeur de la photographie*." Laurent was a fresh-faced guy with rosy cheeks and impossibly long eyelashes.

"And this is . . . ." He put a hand on the shoulder of the other foppish kid and looked at Laurent for help.

"François."

"Ah, yes, François." I had the feeling Laurent and François might be an item.

"*Bon,*" Julien continued. "So my driver tells me this marina is famous for the cooking and for the sunsets, is it not true?"

"No, you're right about that, Julien. It's, ah . . ." I glanced at Miguel who nodded his head imperatively toward the exit, "very true. But unfortunately, Miguel here has run out of fresh fish this evening. I'm afraid y'all will have to come back and try it another time."

Julien frowned. "Oh, that is too bad, maybe the shrimp—?"

"You came here in a car, didn't you?" I interrupted. "Because if you're game, I know another place we can go that has delicious, fresh-caught seafood. And it is covered up in local color. Perfect for your movie."

Julien thought about it for a minute. I heard Miguel clear his throat. Not a comforting sound.

"And I want you to be my guest," I added.

"No," said Julien, emphatically.

"No? Why not?" I saw through the door that all three of the Sutton brothers had stood up and were watching us closely, no doubt waiting for us to return to the deck. Junior looked restless, reminding me of a kid waiting for recess.

"Because I want you to be *my* guest," he said. "It will be *my* pleasure."

"Oh, well, okay then. I accept." I grabbed his arm and headed for the door. "Now, let's skeedaddle."

Outside the marina, a shiny black Suburban with tinted windows waited in the parking lot. A driver in a summer suit jumped out and opened the doors.

"Where to, Charlie?" Julien asked when we got settled. Laurent sat in front with the driver, Julien and I were in the middle seat with Marguerite between us, and the other kid, whose name I'd already forgotten, was crammed into the far back seat with the camera equipment.

As we pulled away from the marina, I tried to think of a restaurant in the area that didn't proudly feature the $4.95 "senior special" or an all-you-can-eat fried cod buffet, but Port Lavaca offered seriously limited options.

"I'm afraid there's not much to choose from around here, but if you don't mind driving, Victoria is only an hour away. They have a great steakhouse there, and the best wine cellar in South Texas. But it's up to you, of course, since you're buying."

Julien asked Marguerite a question in French, and she answered quickly and definitively. "I have a better idea, Charlie," he said. "It would be our pleasure to have you as a guest at our home, in Houston."

"In Houston?" I asked. "Tonight?"

"Yes. Marguerite thinks it is a grand idea as well, don't you, Marguerite?"

"We would enjoy having you," she said, placing her hand on my leg. If her husband noticed, or minded, he gave no indication. Marguerite smiled with something like anticipation in her eyes. "And you will enjoy it, too."

Julien leaned forward in the seat and addressed the driver. "Take us to the airstrip, Clarence, and call Philippe and tell him to ready the plane for the trip back to Houston." He sat back and smiled at me. "Champagne?"

He motioned to the kid in the back, who instantly opened a cooler and began pulling out crystal flutes and wiping the ice off a bottle of Perrier-Jouët.

"Sure," I replied, thinking of the beer and cheeseburger I'd abandoned back at Miguel's. "Why the hell not?"

———

When you first encounter a certain type of madman, he does not

seem like a madman at all. He seems like a completely different

sort of man; he seems like a visionary.

Père Poisson

SEPTEMBER 1684

CHAPTER 04

Less than two hours later, I was in the Houston penthouse of Julien and Marguerite Dufay, drinking eighteen year-old scotch and gazing out the window at a glittering cinemascope of lights that stretched to Galveston Bay and beyond. Julien pointed out some of the city landmarks, such as the 80-story DeBergerac Tower, which loomed off to the southeast. A savory aroma wafted from the kitchen.

"It's an impressive view, Julien," I said. "Maybe not as fine as your City of Lights, but not bad."

The enormous two-story apartment had vaulted ceilings and floor-to-ceiling windows on two sides. It was decorated with an eclectic assortment of fine antiques, unusual cultural flourishes from exotic places, and what I presumed to be priceless art, suggesting, but not flaunting, the couple's wealth and worldliness. Even the powder room off the foyer signaled their class, boasting a genuine Chagall hanging over the toilet. I had a picture of poker-playing dogs tacked up over my privy back in Fulton. To each his own.

"No, it is not *La Ville-Lumière*," he answered with a sigh. "I must admit I do miss Paris. But . . . *bon*, there is the family business." He shrugged and looked at me. "We try to make the best of it. Living here, I mean."

I heard a muffled groan from the living room where Marguerite lounged on a white leather sofa like an ocelot. I wasn't quite sure what to make of her yet. Her languid hazel eyes had been appraising me since we'd boarded Julien's plane in Port Lavaca, and I couldn't tell if she didn't trust me and was afraid I'd steal the silver, or if it was something else.

"My wife does not find Texas as interesting as I do," he said. "She gets bored here very easily."

"I know a roomful of people in Indianola who had plenty of excitement this evening," I said. "Boredom didn't seem to be an issue."

Julien laughed. "Yes, I suppose we present ourselves somewhat conspicuously. I do not think the footage Laurent taped will be usable—every head was turned to Marguerite. I wanted to capture the local people watching their famous sunset, you know, in *statu naturali*, casual. Not watching my wife."

I laughed. "Well, what did you expect? You had to know you weren't going to sneak up on the locals with a six-foot runway model and a camera crew."

"Yes, I suppose I should have known that, Charlie." As he looked at me, his expression changed, as if he were remembering something else. The smile remained, but there was a hint of irritation in his voice. "However, I do know what *you* were doing when you pulled me into the little store at the marina. You wanted to keep me from confronting those barbaric Sutton brothers. You think I cannot handle myself?"

"You *know* those guys?"

"Yes, I know the little bastards. And I know the big bastard, too."

"But how? Do they work for you?"

"No, no. They have never worked for the company as far as I know. I have been negotiating with their father for some leasing rights on their ranch—easement access, that sort of thing. They are all of them rather difficult."

"You're negotiating drilling rights on the ranch?"

"No, not that. I want access to a particular area for a project I am working on."

"What project?" I asked. I glanced at Marguerite, who was drinking something dark green in a lowball glass—absinthe, for all I knew—and thumbing through a copy of French *Vogue*.

Julien looked at me as if he were sizing me up for something. He put his arm around me and escorted me toward the kitchen. "First, let us eat dinner. You must taste my *Blanquette de veau*. It is not your Texas T-Bone, but I think you will be quite satisfied."

He was right. It was an exquisite meal, with wine pairings for each course and lively conversation that often had the three of us doubled over in laughter. Marguerite's reserve seemed deliquesced, melted by the wine and cuisine. And maybe a couple more of those green drinks. By dessert we were all pretty well hammered.

After dinner, Julien produced a dusty, hand-blown bottle of Cognac that looked like looked like Napoleon had been carrying it around in his saddlebag. We moved to the living room and Marguerite kicked off her shoes and laid her head on Julien's thigh, resting her long brown legs on the back of the sofa. They stretched about halfway to Beaumont.

As we sipped the expensive *digestif,* the conversation turned to the family business. Julien gave me a short history of the company and how he had landed in Texas. Initially, the DeBergeracs didn't drill for oil, but their mapping services, and later their proprietary software and logging equipment showed the people who did where to go and what was under the ground. Later they decided to vertically integrate and try their hand at drilling. Needless to say, they were pretty good at that, too. Houston was still the world capital of petroleum, no matter what those Saudi goatherds might say, so the French company left the Old World behind and, like Davy Crockett, were gone to Texas.

Julien's mother, Monique, daughter of one of the two DeBergerac brothers who founded the company, had married a rising corporate executive who eventually became CEO of the North American division. Julien had spent most of his life in France, but after his father died, he and Marguerite moved to Houston to be closer to his widowed mother.

Monique Dufay ran her late husband's company with flair and a good dose of Gallic iron. Since she gave every impression of living forever, Julien had never invested much emotional capital in the family business. He primarily participated in the business through his position on the company's board of directors. I got the distinct sense his heart wasn't in it, and I told him so.

"I will be honest with you, Charlie. My passion lies in the arts, not in commerce. I find tremendous pleasure in directing the Dufay art museum. The business of seismic exploration and extraction, it is . . . *héritage*, no? And, well, I am part of the family." Julien rubbed his temples with the tips of his fingers, as if the burden were pressing against his skull. "I must do my part, you know?"

"Julien tries his best to be a robber baron," said Marguerite with a smile (pronouncing it "bair-ahn"), "but he has a poet's soul."

"I would think the museum brings recognition to the company as well," I said. "And the family."

Julien looked up, his face animated. "Exactly! It is where I can best contribute. You understand completely." He beamed at me from the couch and leaned forward, obliging Marguerite to sit up. He glanced quickly at his wife and then put his hand on my knee. Clearly, he had something important he wanted to say.

"Charlie, I want to share something very exciting with you. I think it will be my greatest legacy to the family . . . and also to my country. Even to your great state of Texas."

"Lay it on me, Jules," I said, and took another swig of cognac, emptying the glass. Ol' Napoleon was whispering in my ear.

Julien poured another two fingers of cognac into my snifter and then added the same to his. "I have made an important archeological discovery," he said. "Perhaps the most important in many decades." He arched his eyebrows dramatically. "I believe I have found the Sieur de La Salle's Fort St. Louis, the first permanent European settlement in Texas. In fact, the first on the entire Gulf Coast between Florida and Mexico." Julien slapped my leg. "What do you think of that, Charlie Sweetwater, *eh?*"

I thought it was mostly a hell of a goddamned coincidence. Three months ago I had barely heard of this French explorer who died three centuries ago, and now he seemed to be everywhere at once. Underground, underwater and forty stories above downtown Houston. "What did you find?" I asked. "And where?"

"I find some French relics . . . up a river, near Port Lavaca."

"You do know they've found one of La Salle's ships, right? This summer in Matagorda Bay? The *Belle*, I believe she's called."

Julien waved his hand dismissively. "Yes, yes, I know. I knew it was out there somewhere in the bay; I have read the historical documents. But you cannot build a museum in the bay."

"A museum, Julien?"

"Yes, a history museum. Hopefully, an accredited international branch of the *Musée de l'Histoire* in Paris, built on the exact site of La Salle's colony. Imagine! An authentic reproduction of the fort and the colony, the reconstructed *barque-longue* they are excavating now in the bay, a display of the many artifacts that will be found in both locations, the wonderful documentary film my wife is creating—it will be a glorious monument to La Salle, and it will remind people of the important role the French played in the history of Texas and the United States. It will be something worthy of the *Musée de l'Histoire*."

"And of the DeBergerac family," I added, not unkindly. I was impressed by Julien's passion for the project. It was contagious.

"Yes! It will be *my* contribution. Perhaps not in bottom line profit, or barrels of oil, or market share, but a cultural and historic treasure that will honor my family just the same."

Marguerite watched her husband with admiration. There was a sudden lightness to him, a sparkle. And it expanded him, somehow.

"Will you help me, Charlie?"

"Me? How can *I* help you, Julien? I'm not an archeologist." I hoped he didn't have another guard duty position in mind.

"I do not know," Julien answered. "I will think of something. You are from that area. You know the native people and the ways of the region. And you have a demonstrated talent for saving me from misfortune."

He leaned forward and thrust his snifter of cognac toward me. "Tell me you will be a part of my project, Charlie — part of my grand vision."

I felt ludicrously flattered on one level and guardedly skeptical on another. Something told me there was a screw loose in the Frenchman's head. Yet, despite the load of misgivings floating around in my alcohol-soaked noggin, I was, at that moment, caught up in Julien's boundless enthusiasm. If nothing else, the project would be interesting.

What the hell, I thought.

"Count me in, Julien. I'll be your huckleberry." We clinked glasses and smiled like the pair of geniuses and visionaries we would undoubtedly prove to be.

"Génial!" he said. A baffled look appeared on his face. *"Mais qu'est-ce que c'est un* 'huckleberry'?" he asked.

"It's like an *amigo*," I said, flourishing with the glass (a dollop of thousand dollar cognac flying across the table). "A *partisan*, or a co-conspirator. Like, ah, Butch and Sundance, Ike and Tina . . . ." I tried to think of something culturally congruent. "Like Picasso and Matisse!" I said grandly.

Marguerite laughed. "Those two hated each other!"

"Well, let's just say Athos and Porthos, then. That would make you, Madame Marguerite, our Aramis—the third damn musketeer."

"Merveilleux!" said Julien. "The project has only begun—some necessary paperwork to be signed by the landowner—but I expect it to be, *euh, opérationnel* . . . full force, in one month. How can I contact you when it is time?" He was sitting on the edge of the couch, beaming at me with delight.

"Ask for me at Fulton Harbor. The town's a couple of hunderd miles down the coast, next to Rockport. Look for the *Li Shishi*. She shouldn't be hard to find. In fact, both of you should come, as my guests. I think you'll like Fulton. It's kind of like St. Tropez, except for the offshore gas rigs, stingrays, and bait shacks."

"It would be my pleasure to call on your boat," said Marguerite. "I have heard so much about it."

"One more thing, Charlie," said Julien. "I want to keep the project and the site a secret until I am ready to announce my discovery to the world. Can you keep a secret?"

"My lips are sealed. My word is my bond. All that shit."

Julien sat back and smiled. So did Marguerite. *"Bon,"* he said. "Then we have a deal."

We all smiled at each other until Julien set down his glass and stood up.

"You will be in the room at the top of the stairs," he said suddenly. "Marguerite has turned down the bed for you. It has been a long day." I blinked in surprise. It seemed an abrupt conclusion after so much bonhomie. Was I that drunk, or was it another one of Julien's mood swings?

We said goodnight, and I stumbled up the stairs and into my king-size bed. I think I fell asleep before my pants hit the chair.

Sometime during the night, I heard the bedroom door open and close again gently. I could smell Marguerite's perfume.

"Marguerite?" I asked the darkness.

"*Aimez-vous avec la lumière, ou sans?*" Her whisper was as smooth (and as French) as the Napoleon cognac we had enjoyed earlier that evening. "Do you want me with the light, or without?"

"Yes," I whispered back, "and yes."

A match ignited, and Marguerite's glorious backside appeared in silhouette as she lit a candle on the dresser. She turned around and slipped a flowing silk robe off her shoulders. It fell silently to the floor and, she stood looking at me, letting me *(Christ almighty)* look at her. *I take it all back, God,* I thought to myself. *You do know what you're doing.*

"But . . . Julien?" I asked, as a half-dozen moral considerations raced through my head. *Can you go to hell for screwing your host's wife? If you cuckold a friend, can he still be your friend? If a husband finds a guy in bed with his wife, can he legally shoot him in Texas?*

"He will not mind," she said. "I promise."

She must have sensed my hesitation because she sighed and spoke again. "Charlie, you must trust me. It is *okay.*"

"Okay," I repeated, as if in a trance. "In that case." I lifted up the corner of the bed cover, and she slid under the sheet next to me, her skin as soft as I had imagined it would be. She kissed me and tweaked my nose playfully.

"Besides, I heard you say you can keep a secret."

CHAPTER 05

The next morning, I wandered downstairs and found Julien preparing breakfast. If he knew about last night's tryst, he certainly didn't let on.

"*Bonjour,* Charlie. I hope you wake up with a strong appetite, because I am making *omelettes* with fresh spinach and Parmesan cheese." In his bare feet and black silk pajamas, he resembled a karate instructor. "Coffee?"

I sat at the island countertop and sipped the coffee, watching him glide around the gleaming kitchen like a pro. The kitchen sparkled with restaurant-grade pots, pans and knives, neatly organized around the stove and food prep area; it looked efficient and well-used.

"The secret is the dash of nutmeg," he said, sprinkling a pinch of the fresh ground spice over the omelet. "But just a dash. Too much of it is poisonous, but I suppose that is the way with many things."

"Like 150 year-old cognac," I said, rubbing my bloodshot eyes.

"Ah, you have a hangover? In French we say you have a wooden mouth—*la gueule de bois.* More coffee?"

"Please."

Julien placed two settings on the granite counter and poured two glasses of fresh-squeezed orange juice.

"Marguerite's not joining us?" I asked.

"Oh, no. She rises late in the day. I rarely see her until afternoon."

I hoped my relief was not apparent. It was too early in the morning to pretend not to be attracted to her, and at present Julien had such easy access to sharp knives.

"Today is a special day, Charlie," he said, pointing a fork at me. "Today I am going to take you to my museum and give you a personal tour. I want your opinion of my exhibit—the one we discuss on your boat, do you remember?"

"Something about the search for lost time, right?"

"Yes, you do remember!" he said, smiling.

The phone rang, and Julien left the room. When he returned, it seemed as though someone had flipped a switch on his disposition. I was getting used to his mercurial mood swings but was still at a loss for what triggered them.

"I must go," he said sullenly. "You can drive with me to the office. The car will take you to the airport from there, and my plane will fly you home." With that, he ascended the stairs and disappeared. Ten minutes later he reappeared, wearing a tailored pinstripe suit and a bright, silk Hermes tie.

We drove to the office in silence. Finally, I asked him if everything was okay.

He puffed out his cheeks and smiled ironically. "The company is only interested in looking forward, Charlie. The past is irrelevant." He turned away and watched the downtown skyline grow closer as we drove down Memorial Drive in the black Suburban. "Oil and gas is the only treasure they care about."

We arrived at the office building and passed through a marbled foyer that was as cavernous and cold as an ice palace, our steps echoing loudly in the lobby. The guard greeted Julien

"Good morning, Mr. Dufay."

Julien walked by the man as if he were invisible, so I said good morning for both of us. On the 79th floor, we were met by a polished receptionist who told Julien that Mr. Dufay was expecting him in his office. Julien nodded and turned down a wide, carpeted hallway. I leaned over the receptionist's desk.

"Which Mr. Dufay would that be?" I asked. "I mean, the expecting one?"

She looked at me suspiciously, like I was a fake Rolex hustler or a sidewalk hotdog vendor who happened to follow Julien up in the same elevator. I guess the *huarache* sandals, weathered khaki pants and Rockport Pirates T-shirt I'd worn since yesterday deviated from the standard dress code for DeBergerac employees.

"It's okay," I said, conspiratorially, tilting my head toward Julien. "He's with me."

Her impeccably made-up face tightened. "I see," she said, picking up the telephone. "Security, please . . . "

I smiled at her and hurried towards Julien's receding figure. When I caught up with him, he seemed surprised I was still around.

"Oh, Charlie, yes, I will have the secretary call a car for you. It will take you to the airport and fly you to wherever you want to go. You can wait in the lobby if you like."

Apparently the conversation was over because he began walking toward the double doors at the end of the hall. I was never a guy for lengthy farewells, but it felt a little like I was getting the brush-off.

"Okay, Julien. I want to go to Reykjavik."

He stopped and rubbed his temples.

"It's in Iceland," I said.

"I know where it is. Look, Charlie, I am sorry that I am—" The doors opened and a man, also in a tailored suit, stood impatiently at the entrance with his arms crossed.

"*Vous êtes en retard, mon frère,*" he said, pointing at his watch. He rattled off something else in French and made exaggerated gestures with his hands, shoulders and eyes as he spoke—gestures almost identical to Julien's. I figured this had to be his brother. When he finally noticed me, he stopped chattering and frowned, as if I'd just dropped a chilidog on the hand-stitched carpet.

"Hi," I said, stepping forward with my hand extended. "I'm Charlie Sweetwater, a friend of Julien's." At first, I thought he was going to turn his back to me, but he finally (and half-heartedly) offered a limp handshake in return. He craned his head to the side and looked around me at Julien.

"*Qui est ce?*" he asked with notable irritation.

Julien answered him in French and he grunted.

"You didn't tell me your name," I said, holding my ground. I was at least a head taller than him.

"He is my brother, Jean-Marc," said Julien from behind me. "VP of Energy Development, USA."

"We are very busy," said Jean-Marc. "And we have an important meeting in a few minutes. So, if you will excuse us?"

Without a word, the brother turned and disappeared into the office. Inside, I saw a massive conference table laid out with fruit, pastries and silver pots of coffee. The room was the size of a handball court, with a view encompassing most of Harris County.

"Goodbye, Charlie," said Julien as he walked by me.

The doors closed, and I was left standing alone in the hall, thinking for the thousandth time how lucky I was to be a shrimper with my friends in Fulton and not a VP of whatever, fighting my way up, and occasionally stumbling down, the corporate ladder. I looked out the big windows, floating high above the city. Like Mark Twain, I decided I'd take Heaven for the climate, and Hell for the company.

———

FROM THE JOURNAL OF PÈRE POISSON

Mssr. La Salle led a company of men to explore the Ile de Pin. On this island, they encountered many wondrous creatures, including a crocodile, wild pigs, many turtledoves, and parrots. Members of the crew have reported that parrots can be trained to speak, but I do not believe this. If they could speak, they would, of necessity, have souls. Holy Scripture teaches us that only men have souls, and thus it is clear that parrots cannot speak and the crew is distorting the truth.

I am not entirely convinced that all of the crew have souls.

Père Poisson
OCTOBER 1684

CHAPTER 06

I suppose if I had to raise a family, pay a mortgage, shop at the mall, and do other grown-up things on the money I made from shrimping, then I'd be shit out of luck. I took the *Johnny Roger* out when I felt like it, made only one or two drags each night and hightailed it home whenever there was the slightest chance of foul weather, which happens often on the water. I'd fire my sorry ass if I were in it just for the dough.

But the truth was, I enjoyed going out in the Gulf, and I liked having something moderately productive to do with my time. In my own lazy way, I was maintaining a family fishing tradition that had been around in one form or another for five generations. It wasn't the profession I'd imagined for myself when I was younger. In fact, my brother and I had wanted nothing to do with our dad's shrimp boats. But life has a funny way of spinning you around. Somebody once said maybe all we can do is hope to end up with the right regrets.

Of course, to shrimp these days you had to be part bureaucrat to deal with the state and federal paperwork, part U.N. translator to switch between English, Spanish, Vietnamese and Cajun French on a daily basis, and part monk who'd taken a vow of poverty. In spite of all that, the whole process of harvesting the bounty of the sea still held mystery and even beauty for me.

I'd seen it a thousand times, but every time I pulled the trawl net out of the dark water, the cod end of the bag bulging with catch, I felt a surge of excitement when I released the drawstring and watched the glistening mass of sea life spread over the deck—blue crab, grunts, catfish, rays, croakers, squid, and (hopefully) heaps of brown shrimp, all of it flipping and tossing and pulsating in a vibrant heap. The deck seemed alive with a mysterious aquatic energy. I felt like a voyeur, glimpsing a hidden world I only floated above in a clumsy, land-made vessel. All those myriad marine creatures, what did they *do* down there?

This last trip had been particularly fruitful. I'd run into a swarm of jumbos near the Aransas Banks and filled my holds with 11/16 count shrimp, fetching top market price. I'd just unloaded my catch, moored the boat in her Fulton Harbor slip, and was hosing out the bins below deck when a head appeared above me.

"Mr. Sweetwater?"

I shaded my eyes from the noonday sun and looked up to see Laurent's pretty face, his hair slicked back with mousse.

"Oh, hey, Laurent. What's up?" I climbed up the ladder and dried my hands on my khaki pants. He smiled at me nervously. Otherwise, he looked like a Banana Republic model.

"You here by yourself?"

"Yes, only me," he said. "Julien sent me."

I nodded and waited for whatever message he was bringing. In his shiny penny loafers, white jeans and teal-colored polo shirt, he looked as out of place on the shrimp boat as I'm sure he felt.

"He says for you to go to Port Lavaca right away . . . and to bring your motorboat."

I hadn't heard from Julien since getting the bum's rush out of Houston, and now it was "right away"? Julien had been vague about what my role would be in his La Salle project, and after Houston I'd halfway decided he'd been drunk, or bullshitting, or both. Although the way Laurent was talking, this wasn't really an invitation. "What for?" I asked.

"He didn't say. He just said for you to be at the site today."

"The Lavaca River, correct?"

"Yes."

"And you don't know why I'm going or what I'm supposed to do?"

"No, I don't. Julien, he . . . ." Laurent cleared his throat and offered a weak smile, "He doesn't really explain anything."

"He just gives orders."

Laurent nodded.

"And expects them to be followed."

"Of course."

"Right." I pulled the water hose up from the hatch and coiled it neatly on the dock. Laurent sat stiffly on the edge of the gunwale and waited while I finished tidying the boat.

"Beer?" I asked when I was done. Laurent shook his head no and watched with growing anxiety as I retrieved a sweating can of beer from the cooler, sat down on the hatch cover and popped the top.

"Mr. Sweetwater? Are you almost ready to go?"

"Look, Laurent. It's over fifty miles to the river by boat, and it's the same distance if I trailer the boat and haul it to the closest public ramp. I just got back from a week out in the Gulf. I'm tired, hungry and a little ripe, as you may have noticed. So here's the deal. After I finish this beer I'm going to drive to my house, take a long shower and then a short nap, and later this evening I'm going to burn a steak and drink at least a half-pint of bourbon on my porch deck. You can tell Julien I'll be there around noon tomorrow."

"He's not going to like that."

"You afraid he's going to shoot the messenger?"

"A little."

"Buck up, son. Tell your boss I'm an unreasonable and arbitrary asshole. He'll believe you."

Laurent sighed and turned to leave. "Okay," he said doubtfully.

"*Adiós*, Laurent. Thanks for delivering the message. I'll see y'all on the river tomorrow."

———

Early the next morning I hooked my 21-foot center-console fishing boat to the back of the truck and headed north on State Highway 35. As I crossed the Copano Bridge, I watched the sun struggle to pull itself up from Aransas Bay. It finally popped free and bathed the mosaic of saltwater, marsh grass and barrier islands in a muted yellow light fortelling the approach of autumn on the coast. And thank God for that. October already, and summer was still hanging around with the bite and tenacity of a snapping turtle.

When I reached Port Lavaca, I crossed the bridge and slid the boat off the trailer at a public ramp near Chicken Foot Reef, one mile from the mouth of the Lavaca River. The BP/Pemex oil refinery occupied the land behind me, imposing and menacing in the bright sunlight. Rainbow-colored petroleum vapors seemed to hover in the air. Even when I looked away, I could feel the plant's presence all around me and felt, more than heard, the low-frequency hum surrounding it.

The channel leading from the bay to the river was easy to follow, a ribbon of darker water cutting through the gray-green shallows. The trout fishing was good here. Over thirty years ago, I'd fished it with my brother, and we caught a bucket of trout in under an hour. I caught my limit first but Johnny caught the biggest, so we both claimed victory. I was happy to see the refinery complex hadn't fouled up the delta. Good for them, I guess. Other parts of the bay hadn't been so lucky.

I followed the main tributary into the river, which narrowed and widened and then narrowed again, like a rattlesnake digesting a pocket gopher. Six miles up the river, Laurent had said—a portable platform dock anchored to the western bank would mark the site. The shoreline was scrubby and low for most of the journey, with driftwood littering the muddy bank. Lots of cowbirds, egrets and red-winged blackbirds. An occasional alligator. But the embankment started rising at mile five, and I began to see hardwood trees growing in thick mottes above me.

A caracara hawk watched me sternly from the limb of a dead cottonwood as I motored gently up the stream, and further up, a blue heron wading near the shore was startled into flight, releasing a harsh squawk as he flapped away on long, gray-blue wings. The river looked remarkably pristine considering its proximity to the town and the factory complexes near its mouth. The only sign of human presence was the occasional piece of Styrofoam or strip of cloth lodged in the brambles high up the bank, evidence of the savage flooding that could turn the languid river into a raging, milky-brown torrent after a heavy rain.

I had real trouble picturing this backwater corner of coastal Texas transformed into Julien's cultural tourist Mecca. Then again, Disneyland had started out as a bunch of orange groves, and Six Flags Over Texas was just a glorified cotton patch halfway between Dallas and Fort Worth, so what did I know?

I passed Redfish Bayou and saw two red and white longhorn steers grazing on the shore, their improbable horns stretching more than six feet from tip to tip. A little piece of ambulatory Texas history there. I smiled at the sight.

Soon after, the river doglegged to the west and, up ahead, I saw three people standing on a floating platform anchored to the bank, each of them looking my way, shielding their eyes from the bright glare of the morning sun. A brand new Boston Whaler with a white Bimini top was tied to the makeshift dock.

I wrapped a line around a cleat and killed the motor. Marguerite's perfect teeth sparkled when she smiled at me. Laurent and the other guy were both hunched over their video camera staring at a small pop-up screen.

"Hello, Charlie. I am glad to see you," she said. There was a spark of merriment in her eyes that took me back to that penthouse bedroom.

"*Bonjour*, Marguerite."

"*Miraculeux!* The Texan has learned French since we met?"

"Nah, 'fraid not. That pretty much exhausts my vocabulary, unless *femme fatale* counts." She wore tight-fitting shorts and a white, button-front shirt knotted around her midriff. White on brown, *café au lait, ooh là là.*

"*Certainement*," she said with a wink.

"How is your film project going?"

"*Pouah*, it is a disaster," she huffed, flicking her hand impatiently. "This place is abominable. Nothing but mosquitoes and . . . what do you call them, Laurent?" (She put the accent on the second syllable of his name—Luh-RAW.)

"Ticks," he said, without looking up.

"Yes, ticks. They are hideous creatures. I found one attached to me yesterday, and when I pull it off, it leaves this terrible mark."

She rotated her leg to expose an angry red bump on her inner thigh, not four inches from her Venus cleft, which I happened to know was waxed clean and smooth as a peach. Yessir.

"Will you take us away from here, Charlie?" she said suddenly. *"Allez, s'il vous plaît?"*

The boys looked up quickly, their eyes flitting back and forth between Marguerite and me. I got the feeling they'd hop into my boat in a second if I started the outboard and she gave the word.

"Sorry, Marguerite. I need to talk to Julien first. Is he up there?" I pointed up the embankment where a well-traveled path zigzagged up the slope.

Marguerite sighed. "You disappoint me, Charlie. When I saw you coming, I thought you had arrived to liberate me." She smiled when she said it, but there was a hint of regret in her eyes. Then, in a low voice she added, "We could find an air-conditioned hotel room in town, and you can make sure I am completely free of the sneaky little Texas ticks."

Never in my life could I imagine such a statement would turn me on, but the thought of exploring her lovely body, inch by inch, even if I were searching for a blood-sucking parasite, was thrilling to imagine.

"It's a tempting proposal, Marguerite. It really is. But I've just got to see what your husband's digging up over that hill."

She made a flicking motion with her fingertips, shooing me away. *"Sauve-toi."*

When I crested the rise, Julien and another man stood in the middle of a cleared area the approximate size of a football field. They were gesturing and arguing in French. Narrow trenches crisscrossed a portion of the tract in a geometric grid, and beyond the trenches a group of six workers leaned on shovels under the shade of a pecan tree, watching the two men shout at each other.

Not wanting to get in the middle of a fight I knew nothing about, I walked over to the workers.

"Hey, guys. How's it going?" The men regarded me suspiciously, and a few of them seemed outright hostile.

"Who the fuck are you?" said a thick-set man with a square face and a flattop haircut. His neck and forearms were stout as fence posts.

"I'm a guest," I answered.

"Some kind of scientist?"

"Or a cop?" asked a rough-looking Mestizo wearing a "Metallica" T-shirt.

"Nope. Shrimper."

"Then why are you here?" asked a skinny guy with a ponytail and an acne-scarred face who looked like he'd enjoyed just about all the methamphetamine a fellow could stand. "There ain't no shrimp here."

"Friend of Julien's," I answered. "He invited me here."

Flattop huffed. "Well, welcome to fucking paradise."

I heard the arguing stop, and I turned to see Julien stomping away toward a small camp trailer located across the field. A little generator chugged away next to the trailer, which I assumed they used as their workroom and office, like the doghouse on a drilling rig. He went inside and slammed the door.

The man Julien had been fighting with stomped toward us, shaking his head. He wore a clean guayabera shirt and creased jeans, so I guessed he was management.

"Back to the shovels, men," he said. "There will be no backhoe." The men groaned and walked away, muttering and cursing. I could sympathize. Digging ditches was no picnic, especially in this heat and humidity. The guayabera guy noticed me remaining and lifted his chin. "Who are you?"

"Julien asked me to come here. I'm Charlie Sweetwater."

He studied me carefully.

"He told me about the project," I added.

He grunted. "Ah, well then, you are a privileged one. He has a strict rule about discussing the discovery with others. I am Antoine Gillette, the archeologist directing the project." We shook hands briefly. "Why are you here, Mr. Sweetwater, if I might ask?"

"I don't really know. Curiosity, mainly. That, and Julien asked me to come. Have y'all found anything worth putting in a museum?"

Antoine raked his fingers through a head of thinning hair and adjusted his glasses. "Yes," he said, "and no."

Evidently, that was the best answer I was going to get, because he turned around and walked toward a cook shed set up near the edge of the site.

Beyond the cooking area, I noticed two canvas tents set back in the woods that appeared to be barracks for the workers: one large rectangular tent and, closer to the trailer, a small square one.

About a quarter mile of hand-dug trenches lined the cleared area. A dozen men labored in the ditches, extending them foot-by-foot along a path of red survey flags planted in the ground.

Aside from the group of men I had talked to before, there was another group of workers that, judging by their clothes and their steady, methodical digging, appeared to be illegal immigrants. The Mexicans who crossed the river to work in the United States were without equal for this kind of backbreaking labor. They could sustain the pace for hours on end, seven days a week, even in the sweltering heat. I had tremendous respect for their stamina and resilience.

I could understand why the workers wanted a backhoe. In three days it could probably complete the pattern laid out over the site, finishing a task that would take three weeks by hand. Antoine Gillette stood in one of the ditches with an expensive-looking metal detector, probing a freshly-dug square of land with his instrument. A second technician, a fresh-faced guy who looked like a grad student, was also down in the hole with his own magic wand.

Julien stuck his head out of the trailer and eyeballed me. "You're late," he snapped. He went back inside, leaving the door open.

I supposed he expected me to follow him into the office, which, after a brief moment of deliberation, I decided to do. I'd already come this far; I might as well see what was on his mind.

Julien was leaning over a table, reading a field log. "I told you to be here yesterday," he said without looking up.

"Yeah, I got Laurent's message. And he was supposed to tell you I'd be here today. Is there some kind of emergency?"

"Every day is an emergency. I do not have time for delays."

I wondered if refusing to provide his crew with a backhoe qualified as a delay, but I kept my mouth shut. "Julien, why did you *summon* me here?"

"I want you to bring me a diesel generator and some barrels of fuel, and I also need a bigger water tank. I needed these things yesterday." He turned back around and began studying his papers again.

I crossed my arms and leaned against the doorframe. "Then why didn't you contract somebody local to deliver it? Why call a guy who lives fifty miles away? There must be three rig supply operations located within twenty miles of here. Hell, your company probably owns two of them. They could have a truck out here in an hour."

"We have no road access," he said, still studying the field log. "Problems with the landowner."

"Well, you have access to company supply boats, don't you? Why not use one of them?"

"You have boats too, don't you? Do you not know how to operate them? Is my request so difficult to understand?" He looked at me over his shoulder. "Do you want this job or not?"

We locked eyes and I considered his request. "No, I don't think I do," I answered.

His face reddened. "You told me you would help."

"That's right, Julien. I did. You asked me if I wanted to be part of your project, your historic project, for the glory of Texas and France. It sounded intriguing, so I said yes. What I didn't agree to was to be your hey-boy, or to be dragooned by a guy I thought I was helping as a friend—a guy who, frankly, right now is acting like a dick."

Julien continued to stare at me, pop-eyed. I suspected it had been two, or possibly three, geologic epochs since anyone had talked to him that way.

"I don't need the money," I continued. "It doesn't interest me. But what does interest me is helping you dig up 300-year-old French cannons and relics and whatnot. And, of course, being a film star in your wife's documentary."

The corners of Julien's mouth lifted slightly and he relaxed his posture. "My wife's films are shit," he said. "She makes them because she is bored and it gives her something to talk about with her artsy friends." He shrugged. "But I am happy to indulge her." He turned to face me. "I am sorry, Charlie. I did not mean to talk to you that way. It is because I am very stressed right now. Allow me to rephrase my question. Will you please help me get a generator to my work site? I would appreciate your help very much."

I took a deep breath. "Sure thing, Julien. Since you put it that way, I'll help you get your generator, and that other stuff, too."

Julien smiled. "Thank you, Charlie. I will be glad to have you as a colleague on my project. Yes, my collègue, eh? Someone who can appreciate its significance."

"Well, collègue, let's get to it. Let's start digging up some history."

"Bon. Antoine has the list of materials we need, along with information regarding the supplier I am using in Port Lavaca. I have a personal account there that I have arranged for you to draw on. I will trust you to handle the logistics."

"Fair enough. I'll get the list from Antoine." I started to walk away but paused. "You know, I could probably get you a backhoe, too. That is, if you wanted one. Or a trencher, even."

Julien looked at me pointedly. "No backhoe. The matter has been settled."

"Okay, no backhoe." It seemed senseless to me, but maybe he had a good reason for ordering his men to dig two-foot-deep holes the old fashioned way. Maybe a backhoe would tear the hell out of the site or disturb the artifacts somehow. As I reminded myself yet again, what did I know?

"One more thing." Julien said. "Please continue to keep the location of our site a secret. Can I trust you on that?"

I cocked my head and raised my hands in supplication. "Julien . . . come on."

"Okay, okay. I am sorry. Of course I can trust you. I have felt that from the beginning. Thank you again for your involvement, Charlie."

I saluted and clicked my heels together. *"Pour la France!"* I announced. And, once more to myself, *Why the hell not?*

CHAPTER 07

It took me most of the day to pull together the supplies. The manager of the supply company asked me a bunch of questions about the project, but I told him it was oil-related, which seemed to satisfy him. I leased a small barge to haul the gear behind my boat and arrived at the excavation site around sunset. When I climbed the rise, I was surprised to see the workers still digging the stripping trenches in the fading light.

I walked up on a cluster of men I recognized from that morning. "Hey boys, isn't it about beer-thirty?"

Flattop hocked up some phlegm and spat in my general direction. His pony-tailed sidekick looked up wearily from his spade. "Sure as shit oughta be," he muttered. "You bring any with you?"

"Nah, sorry. But I've got some Clove gum. Ya want some?" I shook a foil-wrapped piece of the aromatic chewing gum from the package and held it out for anyone who was interested. I'd been a fan since I was a kid. The three men looked at the gum like I'd just pulled it off the bottom of my shoe.

"A case of Bud sounds a hell of a lot better," said Ponytail.

I agreed with him and introduced myself. "I'm Charlie Sweetwater."

"I'm Vinny, Vinny Toussaint," he responded, and then he inclined his head toward Flattop and another man. "That's Clifton Sloan and Omar Camacho."

Clifton scraped some clay off the blade of his shovel with a scuffed, steel-toed boot, not even acknowledging the introduction. The other man, Omar, was a tall dark-skinned Latino with a one-inch scar running upward at the corner of his mouth, giving him a permanent sneer. Omar nodded his head almost imperceptibly, observing me with watchful, hooded eyes. He looked Mexican, but unlike most of the workers who crossed the border for work, he carried himself with a vaguely menacing swagger, like a *coyote,* or a drug-runner for one of the Mexican cartels.

As I'd already observed that morning, the trio looked like hard cases, more along the lines of ex-cons than blue-collar workers. The tattoos on Toussaint's stringy forearms looked like they might be jailhouse issue, and Sloan had the look of a habitual small-timer: mad at the world and blaming everyone but himself for his bad fortune. Granted, you don't meet a lot of ballroom dance instructors around a construction site, or in this case an archeology site, but I had a bad feeling about these guys.

A young man with sandy, well-barbered hair stood back from the group, tending to a metal detector. He couldn't have looked more different than his co-workers. Even in his sweat-stained jeans he looked like a frat kid holding a beer keg nozzle at a fraternity mixer.

"Finding any 300-year-old bottle caps?" I asked.

The kid started to smile, but it disappeared when he glanced over at his workmates. "No, Sir, nothing like that," he answered.

"Well, keep looking Mr. . . . . " I raised my chin inquisitively.

"Archer, Hoyt Archer."

"Well keep looking, Mr. Archer," I said, walking away. "Maybe ol' La Salle buried a case of Kronenbourg beer around here. You be sure and holler if you find it. I always carry a church key in my pocket, just in case."

I found Antoine in his office reviewing a stack of documents.

"Hey, Antoine. How's the earth-moving business? I brought you some power and light so you can brighten this place up a little." The trailer was cluttered and hot. Sweat beaded on the Frenchman's balding head. "Some AC would be nice, too," I added.

Antoine looked up, annoyed at first, and then his face brightened. "Ah, excellent. You have brought the supplies. They are on the river?"

"Everything from the list you gave me, even the lumber to build your, whatcha-call-it, your screening stations."

"Excellent. I think we need them very soon. I am finding very interesting anomalies in the northeast quadrant."

"Anomalies? You mean like Bigfoot droppings or something?"

"*Quoi?* No, they are magnetic disturbances. We find some iron readings, suggesting buried artifacts. Hopefully French."

"Because we're only interested in *French* artifacts, right?"

Antoine sighed. "Because Mr. Dufay is only interested in the French artifacts. As a scientist, I am impartial of course, interested in any object of historical importance, whether it is French, Spanish, Mexican, or even of the savages who lived here prior to the Europeans."

"You mean the Karankawa? Or are you talking about the Caddos or the Tonkawas? Because there were lots of 'savages' living down here before we either shot 'em, ran 'em off, or gave 'em smallpox in the name of civilization."

Antoine looked weary and annoyed. It's been my experience experts hate legerdemain in the hands of regular folks. Kind of brings 'em down to our level. "Yes, any of those tribes," he answered. "Even the Karankawa, although they were a vicious, thieving lot. La Salle might have succeeded in his mission had it not been for them, and today your Texas would be much different."

"More Frenchified? So to speak."

"I would think so, yes." Antoine looked over his glasses at me and then continued in a professorial tone. "These aboriginals were truly barbaric. Over six feet tall and naked but for their bone piercings and tattoos, and often covered with animal grease and dirt from head to toe. It is better they are extinct. Did you know they were cannibals?"

"You're kidding me!" I said, thinking Antoine didn't sound much like an impartial scientist to me. I had read quite a lot about the indigenous tribes of the area, and they seemed no better or worse than any other people who fought back against their invaders. The Karankawa had been extinct for almost a hundred and fifty years, the last one purportedly killed by a Comanche war party that cut his throat and rode off with his scalp. Rough justice, that. The Comanches made the Kronks look like the cast of a BBC miniseries by comparison.

"Well, I've always heard the Karankawa would never eat clowns because they tasted funny."

Antoine started to correct me but paused. "Ah, yes, American humor." He removed his glasses and cleaned them with a cloth. "At any rate, this area seems to have been a popular camp spot for many peoples, and for a very long time."

"So you've found a lot of these, what do we call them . . . artifacts?"

"Yes, we have." He pointed to some wooden bins stacked inside the trailer. "So far we have found pieces of pottery, musket balls, brass bells and rings, arrowheads, and many animal bones and shells—all suggesting centuries of activity on this hill."

Each bag was carefully labeled. I picked one up and examined it. "But, so far, nothing to suggest a French settlement was here?" I asked.

"Unfortunately, no. Not yet. And of course, that is what we must find. Mr. Dufay insists upon it." Antoine did not attempt to hide the derision in his voice. After witnessing this morning's argument between them, I didn't figure them for anything more than antagonists in an alliance of convenience.

"It's an ambitious plan, that's for sure," I offered in Julien's defense.

"Yes, Mr. Sweetwater. But sometimes his ambition is unrealistic. Reckless, even."

I think Antoine realized he had said too much, so he quickly changed the subject.

"*Bon alors,* I will review the provisions you have delivered and you can carry them up the hill." He began to collect the papers he'd been reading, carefully placing them inside a large metal lockbox. "My assistant, Reginald, will gather the men to help."

"Antoine, some of the items on the barge are heavy as hell, particularly the generator and the barrels of fuel. Are you sure you don't want to tackle this in the morning? When we can see what we're doing? We can just leave them on the barge 'till then."

"We will start now. Mr. Dufay will be here early in the morning, as is his custom, and he will expect everything to be in place." In spite of his disdain for the French tycoon, Antoine seemed duty-bound to follow his employer's orders, even to anticipate him.

But I was not. "If we start tomorrow at first light, I'll wager we'll have it knocked out by breakfast, before your boss arrives."

"Mr. Sweetwater. If you want to be a . . . *fainéant* while we work, I suppose that is your privilege, but the rest of us will start right now."

"Have at it," I said with a shrug. "By the way, where is Julien anyway? He doesn't stay at the camp?"

Antoine sniffed and made a face. "Occasionally. And when he does, he will spend all night working in the field office. But when he *sleeps,* his majesty stays at a hunting lodge on a nearby ranch, the Kestrel Ranch it is called—a six-bedroom mansion with a private cook and a helicopter pad. We, on the other hand, have this." Antoine swept his arm over the compound, smiling sardonically. "Now, Mr. Sweetwater, would you care to join us?"

I decided I might as well. I didn't want to be the guy who sat on his hands and watched others work when there was a job to be done. When we finished, I'd either go back that night and stay at a hotel, or I'd start back early in the morning. Either way, I was determined to make it back home in time to catch the Texas-OU football game.

"If you're waiting on me, Antoine, you're backing up."

It took us three hours to struggle up the hill with the supplies, using only flashlights and a lantern to guide us. We had to use chains and come-alongs to skid the genny up the hill, and rolling the 55-gallon drums of diesel fuel up the uneven incline in the darkness proved to be a particularly hellish challenge.

Vinny and Clifton cursed loudly, fluently, and often. The illegals (we weren't supposed to call them wetbacks anymore, but I'd always thought the word connoted a certain initiative) worked steadily and without audible complaint. They shared the fatalistic acceptance of circumstances that Mexicans everywhere adopt whenever *gringos* are involved in some incomprehensible idiocy.

Once the generator was set and I had it primed and purring, we strung up lights throughout the camp and soon had the place lit up like the Calhoun County Fair.

We took a break for dinner—chili and cornbread—cooked up by an older Cajun fellow who appeared to have a big toe grafted onto his right hand where the thumb used to be. Oilfield surgery, it looked like. Besides his role as cook, he was also the camp comedian. He was a gnomish little guy with the unlikely name of Dodo (pronounced, he was quick to point out, like the extinct bird) Desmarais. He had spent his entire life working around drilling operations and had the scars and missing fingers (and toes, I presumed) to prove it.

During our break he talked nonstop in a clipped, rapid-fire Acadian dialect that had even the wets and the two high-minded

French scientists laughing their asses off. He mostly told old Boudreaux-and-Thibodeaux jokes, including the old one about Boudreaux screwing Thibodeaux's wife—"He so dronk, he t'ink he's me!" Or the tale of young Boudreaux peering into the window of a whorehouse in New Orleans, and turning to stone just as his mother predicted. "Or part o' him, anyways . . . ."

After chow we began building the sluicing stations that would be used to sift through the mud for tiny artifacts. I assumed the half-dozen wheelbarrows I'd brought from town would be used for transporting the excavated mud and dirt to the sluices, and the industrial water pump on the barge would provide water from the river.

We finished around midnight and I decided to sleep over at the camp rather than return in the dark. The channels at the mouth of the river would be tricky to navigate in the darkness, and I didn't want to risk fouling my boat prop. Besides that, I was dog-assed tired.

I retrieved my bedroll from the dry bag I kept on the boat, and Antoine put me in the big tent with the workers. He and his French assistant, Reginald, had their own, smaller tent near the office, segregated from the laborers, I suppose, because they were learned archeologists, and we were, well, the "help."

A small lantern illuminated the big canvas tent, and I saw twenty cots lined up on the raised plywood floor. After a sixteen-hour day, the men were already asleep when I slipped inside the screen door. I saw six empty cots so I chose one, rolled out my bedding, and started taking off my sweat-stained clothes. The sides of the tent were up, and only a whisper of a breeze moved through the mosquito netting to cool the air. It was going to be a warm, sweaty October night.

Despite the hard work, I wasn't close to dozing off. All day I'd been thinking what an odd project this was. We were out here isolated and in the dark, living like we were on safari, but you could damn near throw a rock and hit Farm Road 616. Port Lavaca was only an hour's boat ride or a thirty-minute car ride away. Normally the roughnecks and chemical plant laborers who came through town set up shop at the Motel 6 or the Calhoun Motor Court, and enjoyed exotic futuristic amenities like ice machines and Big Macs. But these workers stayed here, in a stripped-down encampment that barely met Depression-era CCC camp standards. The whole situation seemed way off plumb to me.

Was archeology always this primitive? Always this secretive? It was hard for me to imagine nefarious tomb robbers coming out here at night to make off with a few pieces of broken pottery or a lead musket ball. In fact, I didn't see any reason for this kind of atavistic isolation, except for Julien's eccentric mania for control and secrecy. Unless, that is, Julien wasn't telling me everything. I lit a fancy French cigarette I'd bummed from Reginald and tried to puzzle it out.

In the dim light I belatedly noticed the guy on the cot next to mine was leaning up on one elbow, watching me.

"Hoyt, right?" I said in a low voice.

"Right. Hoyt Archer."

The kid seemed a little forlorn lying there in his expensive Eddie Bauer bag. The footlocker at the end of his cot had a Texas A&M sticker plastered on the lid.

"So what's a smart Aggie like you doing in a dumb place like this?"

"I don't actually start school until *next* fall. Me and my friend, Judson Strayhorn, decided to take a year off before we enrolled." He gestured toward a kid sleeping in a nearby cot.

"To see the world, right?"

"Well, that was the idea."

"But your dad thought this job would be a better way to spend your year off."

Hoyt smiled and looked away for moment, embarrassed. "My dad works for Judson's dad, at the same company."

"At DeBergerac?"

"Yes, Sir. Mr. Strayhorn thought this would be a good experience for his son, so he called Mr. Dufay and got Judson the job. My dad thought I ought to tag along to keep him out of trouble. He said we would build 'character.'"

I laughed. "Yeah, my dad thought the same way. He arranged for me and my brother to spend our pre-college year roughnecking on a wildcatter's drilling rig in Ozona. We spent three months hauling pipe as ginzels in that West Texas heat and decided to enroll early at UT and become philosophers."

"I wonder if I can last three months," Hoyt said, smiling weakly.

"Not the best of working conditions, I've got to admit. Who'd have thought archeology could be so grueling?"

"They push us pretty hard."

"I hope they're paying you good money for this."

"Yes, Sir. It's pretty good, alright. Better than we could make back in Sugarland. And since we can't spend any of it—"

"You're saving every penny you make."

"Yes, Sir. Even so, some of the workers decided they couldn't take it." He pointed to the empty cots scattered around the room. "I wake up every morning and look to see if anyone else has deserted."

That seemed a peculiar choice of words.

"Why not you?"

"Judson's father knows Mr. Dufay. I think he gives money to his museum. And my father . . . . Anyway, I just couldn't."

"No, I guess that would be awkward, for everybody."

I kind of liked the kid. But he and his buddy were swimming in dangerous waters out here, working with this rough-ass crowd.

"When's your day off, Hoyt? Maybe I'll show you guys some of my honey holes in the bay—take y'all out for some, you know, R&R."

"We don't get days off."

"What? Are you kidding?"

"No, it was in our contract. We only get paid if we stay on until the project is finished, and we get a big bonus if we find the ruins of the French fort."

"Damn, son. Y'all have been here, what, a month already? I thought the French put an end to serfdom after their little revolution."

I had noticed there was no means of transportation at the camp: no trucks and no other boats other than mine, and occasionally, Julien's. The only phone was a satellite phone in the office trailer. I wondered if being made to work for that long, cut off from the outside world, without time off, was even legal. The little pulse of apprehension I'd been feeling turned into a drumbeat. If the pay was so good, why were people "deserting" so readily?

"When do you expect to finish this little character-building experience?"

Hoyt shrugged. "I don't know. I guess when we find what Mr. Dufay is looking for."

Months of clearing thorny brush, digging ditches in the dense black clay, battling mosquitoes and ticks, and sleeping in a musty tent with a bunch of hard cases—probably not what young Mr. Archer had in mind for his gap-year adventure. Then again, what the devil was I doing here? I turned off the lantern and crawled into my sleeping bag, using my rolled up pants for a pillow.

In the darkness Hoyt said very quietly, "Did you know we found some bones?"

"Yeah. Antoine told me. What are they, bison?"

"They weren't animal bones."

He was talking so softly I had to lean toward him to hear.

"They were human bones," he whispered.

"Are you sure, Hoyt?"

"Yes, I think they were very old. We were told to leave them in the ground and not to mention them to anyone."

"Did they say why?"

"Well, they were speaking in French. But Dodo, the cook, he's from Louisiana and he sort of speaks the French language, he told me they were worried that if news of the bones got out, the sheriff would have to come out here to, you know, investigate."

"He might. You say they were old?"

"They think they were Indian bones."

I'd heard stories of construction sites being shut down by Indian groups if they didn't want a freeway or a strip center built on top of their ancestors, but this was private property. In Texas, landowners could build a house out of Kiowa skulls if they had a mind to, as long as it was on their own land. Maybe it was different in France.

"Sounds like management doesn't want to take a chance of anything interfering with their project, doesn't it?"

"Yes, Sir."

"So Julien put a gag order on the whole camp. That's why no one is allowed to leave?"

"I guess so, Mr. Sweetwater."

"I reckon it'd be awfully hard to enforce a rule like that. It didn't seem to stop the guys who used to occupy those empty cots."

"They probably went back to Mexico," Hoyt said. "And they didn't even speak English. I don't think Mr. Monroe would go after them."

"Go after them? Who is Monroe?" I asked, suspicious.

A cot creaked in the dark and Hoyt was silent for a moment. "Kind of like a security guard. He hired most of the crew, except for Judson and me."

"What else does the guy do?"

"I shouldn't talk anymore." I heard him roll away from me in his cot. "Good night, Mr. Sweetwater."

CHAPTER 08

I'd resolved to get an early start down the river, so I got up before dawn and slipped out of the dark crew tent. Frankly, the oppressive feel of the place was beginning to weigh on me, and I was anxious to be off. Dodo already had coffee on the stove and he handed me a cup as I walked up.

"*Bonjou,* Mr. Charlie."

"Morning, Mr. Desmarais." I set down my dry bag and took a sip of the hot coffee. It was strong enough to float a horseshoe. "Christ, Dodo! This tastes almost exactly like mud."

"Of course it do, man. It was ground just dis mornin'" He cackled at the joke, a vaudeville classic. "You want some *sucré* ta sweet it up, you?"

I took another sip. After the initial shock, the chicory-flavored blend was tasting a little better. "Nah. I'm startin' to get used to it now." By the time I finished the cup, I felt like I could bench-press the generator.

At the river I readied my boat for the trip back. A light fog lingered over the water; it would burn off quickly when the sun rose. Out of the corner of my eye, I noticed something moving about fifty yards upriver. A half-submerged shape was struggling to drag itself onto the shore. At first I thought it was a gator or some other animal, but in the dawning light, I realized it wasn't that at all. It was a man, writhing in the shallow water, and in obvious distress. I scrambled along the shore to reach him. It was one of the Mexican laborers from the camp.

"*Que pasó, hombre?*" I asked.

He looked up at me, his face contorted in agony. "*Me apuñala.*"

It stabs him? What stabs him? Then I noticed the dark flattened shape in the sand, as big as a manhole cover. The stingray was struggling too, trying to remove its tail and deadly barb from the man's ankle.

Most people have a strong visceral reaction to the sight of a stingray, and even after a lifetime on the coast, so do I. They look so damned *alien*. It was the same instinctive dread you encounter when you walk up on a rattlesnake.

Maybe it was because the ancient creature was almost impossible to see in the murky water of the Gulf Coast. Area anglers quickly learn to do the "saltwater shuffle" when they wade fish, sliding their feet along the bottom so they don't step on an unsuspecting ray. The consequence of ignorance is an excruciating sting that injects a nasty toxin. Occasionally, the barbed tail will stick in the victim, which apparently is what had happened to this guy.

"*Quitalo! Quitalo!*" he wailed, begging me to take it out.

The ray continued to lurch, flapping its leathery wings, fighting to separate itself from the intruder who had startled it in its river-bottom bed. Finally the spine broke off and the ray disappeared into deeper water, leaving a cloud of mud in its wake.

"*Como te llamas?*" I asked the man.

"*Nacho,*" he answered. "*Que clase de demonio es esto?*"

"It's not a demon, Nacho. It's a stingray. *Una mantarraya.*" I told him to stay calm while I went to get first aid. He was in his underwear, and his bathing kit was lying on the shore. The four-inch barb was lodged deep into his shin, probably stuck in bone. I wouldn't blame him if he never entered the water again. Hell, he'd probably never *drink* water again.

The Mexican moaned loudly and stared with disbelief at the savage barb embedded in his leg. I noticed with some concern that he was sweating heavily and his breathing had become irregular. All I could do for him right now was try to calm him and apply hot water to the wound—heat would help break down the toxin. But in the meantime, it would hurt like twelve kinds of bastard. I ran up the slope to grab some pliers to remove the barb, and I asked Dodo to fetch hot water *tout suite* and bring it down.

By the time I returned, Nacho's eyes were glazed and wild, and he was muttering unintelligibly. The crew gathered around their stricken co-worker as I worked the barbed spine out of the man's leg with a pair of channel-locks.

Several of the workers turned away, unable to watch as I wrenched out the spine, the blood flowing copiously onto the muddy bank. The man howled in pain and I didn't blame him one damn bit. Christ, what a way to start the day.

Dodo handed me the pot and I poured what I expected to be hot water over the red, puffy wound. The thick black coffee splashed over Nacho's ankle, and his face relaxed as the agony eased for the moment. I pulled back the pot and cast a sharp glance at Dodo, who shrugged. "You say *tout suite*, Mr. Charlie. Da coffee was handy."

Nacho looked up at me to ask why I had stopped. *"Mas, mas,"* he begged.

I continued pouring, shaking my head at Dodo Desmarais, Coonass M.D. When my patient finally glanced down at his ankle he jerked it away, asking me why I was pouring crankcase oil on his stab wound.

"You let dat good ol' chicory coffee do its work now," said Dodo. "It's an ol' swamp remedy." Total bullshit, but the laborer seemed comforted by Dodo's calm tone.

Stingray wounds were rarely fatal, but Nacho needed medical treatment. The labored breathing, puffy face and apparent delirium were signs he might be allergic to the potent venom. Deep puncture wounds like this one were also prone to a particularly nasty flesh-eating bacteria that thrived in the coastal waters. It was the kind of thing that could lead to amputation.

I gave instructions for some of Nacho's *compadres* to help me load him into the boat, and within minutes we had cast off. As we sped toward Port Lavaca, I positioned my patient on the stern so his ankle received a steady stream of hot water from the engine, providing some relief for the intense pain.

They treated Nacho at the emergency clinic, and after a few hours the venom had run its course and he regained his senses. The doctor informed him that he had a one hundred percent chance of full recovery. I volunteered to return him to the camp, but he told me that he was going to take advantage of his one hundred percent full recovery by finding new employment on down the road—somewhere a long way from the coast and its evil devilfish. Can't say I blamed him. I gave him a hundred dollars seed money, dropped him off on the shoulder of U.S. 87 and wished him well.

Before I trailered my boat and returned to Fulton, I decided to stop by Miguel's marina to fuel up and grab some lunch. It was a little out of the way, but I tried to trade with Miguel whenever I could. The marina business was barely a breakeven venture even under the best of circumstances, and in the best of locations. Yet the closest town to his operation was a mostly-submerged ghost town.

I was sitting at the counter talking to Miguel, watching him batter my shrimp and throw them into hot grease (to be more accurate, I talked and he pretended to ignore me, as usual) when I saw Holly Hardin out on the pier. She'd been on my mind quite a bit of late, even though I hadn't seen her since I retired as their official shipwreck sentry at the end of the summer. I suppose Julien's project had kept her on my radar. That and the way she looked in khaki work shorts.

"Throw in another handful of shrimp, Miguel," I said. "There's somebody I want to impress."

Miguel mumbled something unintelligible and, I'm pretty sure, shockingly profane, and then tossed a few more shrimp into the deep fryer. When they were ready, he dumped them in a red plastic basket and dropped them on the counter. "Six bucks."

"I'm gonna grab some beers, too. What does Holly drink?"

I walked to the cooler, pulled out a Lone Star and looked back at Miguel for confirmation. He nodded.

"Eight bucks," he said.

I gave him a ten. "Give the tip to Hinkie. He's the only one here who gives a rat's ass about customer service."

I tucked in my shirt and cradled the two beers and the basket of shrimp in my arms. As I kicked the screen door open with the toe of my boot I heard Miguel yell after me.

"You're too old for her, *cabrón*."

"Yeah, but I'm too vain to care," I yelled back.

A couple of crewmembers were helping Hinkie put fuel in the Historical Commission's research vessel, a 32-foot converted crew boat fitted with custom winches and specialized scientific equipment. Jim had christened the boat the *Anomaly*.

Holly sat on a piling at the end of the pier, looking out across Powderhorn Lake at the rafts of ducks gathered near the grassy inlets on the other side. A flock of pintails rose from the water in a flurry of spray and wingbeats, making several wide stately circles before splashing down almost exactly where they took off.

"They arrived early this year," I said.

"Oh, hi, Charlie," she answered cheerfully, as though it hadn't been two months since we'd laid eyes on one another. A THC patch was sewn over the pocket of her light blue work shirt. A red bandana partially restrained her thick mane of sun-bleached hair. "How have you been?"

"I've been fine and dandy. I brought you a beer and some of Miguel's famous fried shrimp." She smiled and grabbed one of the shrimp.

"Cold beer?" I asked.

"Oh, I never drink when I'm working."

"Oh, okay." *(Thanks for the head's-up, Miguel.)* "So how's it going at the site?"

Holly's eyes widened and she shook her head in wonder. "Better than I could have imagined. When was the last time you were there?"

"They'd just finished the cofferdam and were still pumping out the water. All I saw was a muddy hole with a few barrel staves poking up."

"Oh, it is *so* much more interesting now," she said. "You need to come see what we've uncovered since. You're part of the project, after all."

"More of a passive observer, I'd have to say."

"You did your part." She took another bite of the shrimp and then examined the tail, before popping that in her mouth, too. "In fact, what are you doing right now?" she continued, crunching on the crispy tail. "I could give you a quick tour . . . if you're interested."

I thought it over for less than a second. Suddenly, spending time with Holly seemed more important than the Texas-OU game. "Heck yeah, I'm interested. I just need to fuel up and then I'll meet you out at the cofferdam—in about a half hour. How's that sound?"

"There's a ladder and a place to tie off on the south wall of the dam." She hopped off the piling and walked toward the research vessel, which was readying to depart. "Hey, thanks for the snack."

I filled the twelve-gallon fuel tanks on my boat and ran inside to pay Miguel. I was as giddy as a junior high kid that'd just been asked by the head cheerleader to meet him after school at the Burger Barn.

"She never drinks when she's working," I said.

"Nope," he answered.

"You're a real friend, Miguel."

"She's too smart for you, *cabrón*."

As Miguel knew I knew, they almost always are.

Approaching by boat, the cofferdam seemed enormous on the still water—a trick of perspective and refraction, like the illusion of an oversized sun or moon when it's near the horizon. In the two months since I'd been to the site, they had erected a portable office building and a high, flat-metal roof to cover the excavation pit. The THC research boat was moored on the lee side of the cofferdam wall, which rose about seven feet above the waterline.

On top of the wide, sand-filled retaining wall, the place hummed with activity. Four screening stations, similar to the ones I'd helped construct on Julien's site, were set up nearby. Kids who looked like college students worked the stations, some emptying buckets of mud onto the screen sluices and others spraying the mud with pressurized nozzles and examining the artifacts that remained. The steady drone of diesel engines and generators filled the air with industrial white noise. I breathed in the pungent odor of wet sea mud and diesel exhaust.

Jim Brannan spotted me as he came out of the field office.

"Charlie! Welcome to the eighth wonder of the world!"

Jim was tall and lanky and sported a drooping grey mustache. In his baggy pants, work shirt and mud-spattered muck boots, he looked more like a Texas rice farmer than an archeologist. On the other hand, besides Jim and Holly (and perhaps Antoine), the only other frame of reference I had for this vocation was the *Indiana Jones* movies. Jim would have looked ridiculous with a bullwhip.

"You mean your hole in the water has replaced the Astrodome as the eighth wonder? Houston's gonna be pissed."

"Come see."

We walked to the edge of the dam and peered down into the pit. The spectacle was breathtaking. Twenty feet below, the unmistakable shape of the French vessel had been revealed beneath the dark alluvial mud. The emerging ship skeleton resembled the carcass of a hulking dinosaur trapped in a tar pit.

Workers in yellow waterproof coveralls swarmed around the site, digging, scraping and meticulously brushing away at indistinct objects within the exposed hull of the ship. Others hauled and raised buckets of mud to the screening crews above. Lying on long aluminum kick boards that spanned the breadth of the ship, a couple of archeologists leaned over the wreck, carefully picking at the contents below them.

"Amazing," I said.

Jim smiled at me, unable to contain his delight. "On so many different levels, Charlie. I honestly had no idea what to expect from the excavation, the wreck being submerged for so many years. I was afraid we might've built this impressive dam just to uncover some rotten wood planks and a few barrel staves. But this silty, mucky, oxygen-deficient Matagorda mud did a wonderful job preserving the *Belle*."

I shook my head in wonder. "The most interesting thing I ever discovered in this bay was an artificial leg."

Jim raised an eyebrow. "Well, we haven't found anything like that. But we're finding a remarkable number of artifacts."

"Like what?"

"Like gunpowder casks, lead shot, muskets, and a box full of some sort of spherical ceramic pots—we haven't figured out what those are yet. We've discovered iron tools, tackle for the ship, sailcloth . . . we even found fragments of rope in the aft cargo hold. It's astounding to find an organic artifact in that kind of shape after three hundred years."

His voice kept rising as he ticked more items off the list. ". . . cooking utensils, even a small cannon, also called a verso, a sort of swivel gun for close-range sea battles. Under every layer of silt there is another surprise."

I whistled. "That's a lot of stuff, Jim. And of course there's the bronze cannon Holly pulled out last June—the one that started all the excitement and got your picture in the local paper."

"Well, it's an important story."

"Of course, it'd be even better if y'all found a heaping chest of Spanish doubloons or *Louis d'or* coins."

Jim shook his head at me in disappointment. "Do you want to know how many times I've been asked the sunken treasure question by the local papers and by folks in town, Charlie? The value is in what the artifacts tell us, what we learn—"

I put my hand up to stop him. "Nah, Jim. I get it. I know this is a big deal, window to the past and all that." I rested my forearms on the rusty inner wall of the dam and surveyed the project appreciatively. "It's a damned impressive operation."

And so it was. Between the shipwreck and the buried settlement, and the flurry of excitement and energy surrounding La Salle's long-past expedition to the area, it was as if Texas was being invaded by the French once again.

"Let's go down to the excavation," said Jim, smiling, "and I'll let Holly explain how we shovel bums do it." Jim chuckled at his own joke and began climbing down the scaffold steps into the pit. "Slip on a pair of rubber boots, Charlie. And a word of advice. Don't start making lame pirate jokes or asking her stupid questions about treasure chests and gold. She has no patience for them."

The archeologists working around the wreck were young and earnest-looking. Many had ponytails and beards, wore hole-pocked T-shirts and had bandanas tied around their heads. The team reminded me of a roadie crew at a Grateful Dead concert, moving and working with practiced efficiency.

Holly was lying on her belly on one of the scaffold kick boards, examining some object in the mud below. She stood up when she saw us.

"Well, what do you think?" she shouted. It was quieter in the pit than on top with the gennys, but now there was the noise of the sump pumps as they sucked up seawater that relentlessly seeped into the hole. There was also a faint smell of sulfur, which Jim said was the result of French gunpowder stores mixing with Matagorda mud and brine.

"Y'all *have* been busy," I yelled back.

"Seven days a week, twelve hours a day. We're all working our butts off," she added happily as she approached. "And loving it."

Jim was right. Holly was dedicated to her work.

"What are you finding today?"

"We've found a wooden box that appears to be filled with all kinds of trade goods." She couldn't hide the excitement on her face, like she was barely suppressing a grin.

The hull of the ship was clear enough, but to my amateur's eye I couldn't discern many of the archeological treasures the crew was extracting from the muck. The contents of the ship resembled a lumpy stew, covered in brown gravy. "What kind of trade goods?"

"Well, we won't know for certain until we examine the artifacts back in the lab, but the box looks like it's full of colored beads, mirrors, finger rings, maybe even some wooden combs—objects the indigenous tribes here would have highly valued."

"Trinkets."

"Well, yes, trinkets to us, but not to someone who had never seen brass or steel, or even glass. These kinds of things would've had a lot more value than say, a crucifix or a treasure chest full of gold coins."

Jim and I exchanged glances. *She brought it up, not me,* I said with my expression. Jim laughed out loud.

"What?" asked Holly, looking from one of us to the other, her eyes narrowed in suspicion. She didn't miss a thing. Maybe Miguel was right. She *was* too smart for me.

"Nothing, nothing," said Jim. "Holly, would you mind showing Charlie around? He has lots of great questions about the project he's dying to ask you."

She looked at me dubiously. "Sure, Jim. Just give me a minute to speak with my guys and I'll give Mr. Sweetwater the grand tour."

As she walked away Jim patted me on the back. "Try to sound intelligent, Charlie."

"Thanks for the set-up, Jim," I said, already struggling to think of some befitting questions to ask the eminent, and attractive, marine archeologist.

Holly walked me through the operation, starting with a physical description of the *Belle,* a relatively small, fifty-two-foot, two-masted sailing ship. Holly planned to document and study the wreck *in situ,* then extract the parts and reassemble them later at the university.

I almost envied the ship, lovingly resurrected by Holly's competent hands. She pointed out the mast and the solid timbers of the hull protruding from the mud. Sturdy bulkheads, clearly visible even at this stage of the excavation, separated the bow compartment and the main and aft holds. As a sailor, I could appreciate the finer points of the ship's construction.

Without the benefit of the gulf breeze, it was stifling down in the pit. Holly had folded her rubber coveralls down to her waist and unbuttoned the top two buttons of her shirt. Beads of perspiration dampened her neck and throat. On her, it looked good. Me, I was sweating like a Bombay moneylender.

Holly said the crew had been working twelve hours a day, seven days a week, but the workers bounced around the site purposefully, laughing and joking, and oohing and ahhing at each new discovery. A marked difference to the crew of misfits at the Fort St. Louis dig site.

While my mind wandered, Holly patiently explained how sections of the wreck had been divided into one-meter squares with flags and striped PVC, similar to the grids I'd seen at the Lavaca River site, and how the exact depth and position coordinates of each object were carefully triangulated and charted using the latest high-tech tools.

" . . . so we piece-plot the artifacts with the TDS and the electronic field notebook to ensure that the provenance of the artifacts is accurately recorded in the computer."

I nodded sagaciously, and tried to focus, even though I only got about half of what she was talking about, a task made doubly hard because my attention had been diverted to a small gold crucifix suspended above her breasts. A bead of sweat ran down the valley beneath the cross and disappeared into some heavenly region below. Holly stopped talking and looked at me curiously.

"Charlie? Am I boring you?"

Uh-oh. "Of course not, Holly," I stuttered. "In fact . . . ." I looked around and spotted Jim and some of his staff up on the dam, smiling down at me like they knew I'd been busted, so to speak. "Uh . . . I was just thinking, that what y'all oughta do is um, open up your project to the public. Hire a PR person to, you know, spread the word." It was the first thought that popped into my head. "Bring the school kids out here on field trips so they'll want to become junior archeologists. Heck, invite the TV crews. Call *National Geographic,* or Lucas and Spielberg."

Holly cocked her head, her blue eyes boring into me, as though she was about to call me on my bullshit. Then she blinked. "Keep going," she demanded.

Emboldened, I went on. "You could build a big dock onto the side of the dam so the tour boats can tie up alongside . . . and put up signs for all the dock-building benefactors who will surely want to contribute loads of money to such a splendid project. They'll be competing with each other to sponsor you. It's all in how you present it," I said. "Kinda like Tom Sawyer persuading every kid in the neighborhood to pay *him* for the privilege of whitewashing his fence. Besides, who wouldn't want to watch a beautiful archeologist doing her thing in the excavation of the century?"

Holly grabbed me by the arm and marched me toward the scaffold steps. "We're talking to Jim," she said. I felt like I was being dragged to the principal's office for getting fresh with my teacher. Why could I never stop when I was ahead?

Holly demanded I repeat my "idea" to Jim (my desperate, grab-for-a-lifeline idea), and I tried not to act dumbfounded when he endorsed it wholeheartedly.

"Damn fine idea, Charlie! Absolutely inspired! We may yet convince people that this truly is the eighth wonder of the world." He looked at Holly. "I told you there was more to him than meets the eye."

"Under every layer of silt is another surprise," I said.

FROM THE JOURNAL OF PÈRE POISSON

I have finally had an encounter with the savages who inhabit this land.

The men wear no clothes at all, and the women only a skin from their waist

to their knees. Upon meeting me, both the men and women blew upon my

ears. Some of the crew believe this is a gesture of friendship, but I believe

(because the breath has always been associated with spirit) that they are

trying to infect my spirit with their own. La Salle had previously instructed

us that they were a deceitful race. We must begin our moral instruction of

these creatures, who apparently feel free to take our property.

Père Poisson
NOVEMBER 1685

CHAPTER 09

Early November is my favorite time to be on the Texas coast. Hurricane season is over, the summer heat has abated, and the damn-Yankee snowbirds haven't arrived *en masse*. For a few weeks, Fulton becomes the sleepy little fishing village that the Chamber of Commerce promotes on its billboards. We locals have the place to ourselves, at least for a little while.

Out on the water, it's even better. With cooler temperatures and calm weather, the water clears and the bay's underwater meadows—vast fields of turtle grass, shoal grass, widgeon grass—are suddenly revealed, along with the rich multitude of sea life thriving there. The sky ripens to a profound shade of blue that makes even the greasy wells on the bay somehow seem inoffensive.

The flounder migration begins as well. Raul and I had gigged a bucket of the flatfish in the sandy shallows near Saint Jo Island and returned to Fulton well after dark. When we hauled our stringer of fish to the dockside cleaning station we heard the office phone ringing. Someone—probably me—had forgotten to turn on the answering machine before we set out. Because we often worked on the boats or the dock outside the office, our phone was near the window so we could hear it.

"Should I answer it?" I asked Raul.

"It can wait 'til tomorrow," he replied, content as I was not to let anything intrude on what, up to that point, had been an idyllic evening.

Nu Dang, a fellow shrimper and long-time friend, appeared out of the darkness wearing his customary Vietnamese-style pajamas. "It ring for two hour!" He scolded, holding up two fingers and shaking them at me. "Very bad omen. Very bad luck! Two hour!"

Nu Dang was Sammy's uncle, and he still lived with his wife on their shrimp boat in Fulton Harbor, even though I'm pretty sure they'd saved enough money from their fishing and their bait shacks to buy one, or maybe two, of the high-dollar vacation homes on nearby Key Allegro Island. He appeared to be about seventy-five years old, but then he'd looked exactly the same since I'd first met him in 1979.

The phone rang again. The loud, insistent ringing echoed throughout the harbor. No wonder he was pissed off.

"Sorry about that, Nu Dang. Let me make up for it by presenting you with one of these beautiful flounders, for you and the missus." I grabbed the biggest of the pan-shaped fish and held it out to him, the two gelatinous eyes staring morosely into the distance from one side of the fish's head.

He vigorously waved it off. "No, no. Bad luck to take."

"Come on, Nu Dang. It's just a fish." Nu Dang was superstitious about most everything. I knew if I could convince him to take the flounder, he would repay me with something of similar value the next day—rice cakes or a bottle of fiery homemade *Nuoc Cham* hot sauce—just to cancel the debt and balance his karma.

His world was full of portents and superstitions that he constantly tried to interpret, offset, anticipate and navigate around. I'd really balled up his karma ledger sixteen years ago when I'd rescued his nephew after a boating accident near Cedar Bayou. Even though Nu Dang and I were friends, I could tell the debt still troubled him. Of course I believed in none of that balderdash, but when the phone started ringing again, I got a hollow feeling in my gut that it wasn't going to be the Texas Lottery people on the other end of the line.

Nu Dang glared at me.

"Okay, okay," I said. "I guess I'll answer it."

"*Merde,* Charlie!" said the voice on the telephone. "Where the hell have you been? I have been calling you for hours." Julien's voice raised an octave when he became excited, and he rushed the words, making him even harder to understand.

"So I've been told. What's the rumpus?"

"*Les vaches à longues cornes*—they say we shot them. They say they will shut us down—*le projet d'excavation. Quel désastre, putain de paysan!*"

"They shot the what? Slow down, Julien. And speak English, goddammit."

After a few minutes I was able to piece together the following: Mr. Sutton, the landowner who leased Julien the Lavaca River site, was convinced someone on Julien's excavation crew had killed his pair of prize longhorn cows, the *vaches à longues cornes,* and now he was giving Antoine and his crew two days to pack their shit and get off his land. The dead steers were found covered with brush in a ravine not a hundred yards from the camp, shot multiple times with a hunting rifle. Probably the same beasts I'd admired on my first trip up the river.

"That son of a bitch, Sutton, he comes to our camp with his ill-bred sons. Antoine tells me he carries a shotgun! I will call the police, *eh?* And they will arrest him."

"I don't think that's such a good idea, Julien."

"*Quoi?* Why not? He pulled a gun on my archeologist!"

I rubbed my eyes with the heel of my hand and sighed. It was easy for me to understand Old Man Sutton's response, and easy for me to understand how the law would side with him on the matter. Rural Texans viewed two things as sacrosanct: land and livestock. Going onto a man's ranch and shooting his longhorn steers—Julien was lucky Sutton hadn't called the law. They might have put the entire crew in the county jail. A century ago they would've strung them up to hackberry limbs and hung them as cattle rustlers.

"Julien, if you call the sheriff, he's going to tell you that it's a matter between you and the landowner, and there's nothing he can do about it."

"But I have a contract with that bastard, Sutton. We have a lease. It is our right to be there!"

"And the law's gonna say that it's Sutton's right to run you off. Trust me on this, Julien."

There was a pause on the line before Julien responded. "Then you must talk to this Clyde Sutton. Convince him that it was not us."

"Me? Why me? I don't know the man."

"You are a local, except you are intelligent and have some education, *oui*? You are able to communicate with these people. You can be my, how do you say it? My *médiateur*, my go-between."

I bristled at his implication that the people down here—people he'd never met or cared to meet—were all lower on the food chain than the evolved denizens of *la glorieuse France*. My dad always told me that there were two kinds of people in the world: those who thought there were two kinds of people, and those who didn't.

"Are you sure it wasn't any of your crew, Julien?" I thought of Flattop, Vinny and Omar. They had a mean streak in them every bit as dangerous as Sutton's three brawling sons.

"Of course I am sure. I have explicitly forbid the possession of firearms on my project. How could they shoot the cows without a gun?"

"So do you have any idea how those beeves ended up with bullet holes in them?" I asked, thinking how easy it would be for any of the crew to bring a gun into the camp, forbidden or not. "Judging by where you told me they were found, some of your outfit must have heard the shots."

"*Qui sait?* I think maybe Sutton cooks this up only to get us off his land, or to extort more money for us to stay. He has no honor in him. Go talk to Sutton for me. At least until my lawyers have a chance to prepare. We will destroy him in court."

"Julien, you might want to hold off before you call in the suits. This thing would end up in the local courts, and being accused of shootin' a man's livestock while you and your crew are guests on his land is not going to play well before a Calhoun County judge. Especially if you bring in a posse of corporate lawyers in silk neckties."

"The police, the courts. Is everyone corrupt down there? I have my rights, Charlie."

"And Sutton has his."

"Why are you taking his side? You know how important this project is. Who gives a damn about two cows?"

"Listen to me, Julien." Now my voice raised a level or two. "You're not going to make this go away by acting like a sanctimonious prick. Sutton cares a lot more about his newly-dead cows than he does a bunch of long-dead Frenchmen buried under his dirt.

I'm telling you the situation calls for a delicate touch. You go in hard and Sutton's gonna dig in. And he's gonna win, Julien, in any Texas court."

There was another long pause on the other end of the line. I could imagine him sitting in his penthouse, red-faced and popeyed, struggling to control his temper.

"That's why I need your help, Charlie," he said quietly, almost in supplication.

I closed my eyes and whacked the receiver on my head a few times. I should have let the sonofabitch keep swimming that night. He could be Castro's problem by now.

"I am asking you as a friend," he continued. "I know that sometimes I can be difficult. I become . . . *obsessed* with my work. But you must understand, Charlie, I cannot allow this project to fail."

After a few beats, I replied. "Okay, I'll drop by Sutton's ranch tomorrow. But no promises."

"Thank you. Thank you, my friend. I will not forget this."

"Julien, do you give me the right to negotiate on your behalf? Sutton's gonna want compensation for those longhorns, whether one of your guys killed them or not. And the longer this thing drags on, the worse it's gonna get."

"But we didn't—"

"It doesn't matter. If you want to get back to excavating Fort St. Louis, we need to work out a deal with this guy—and soon. Right now he's holding the cards."

Another long pause.

"Okay, Charlie. Do whatever is necessary."

"It may cost you some jack."

"*Quoi?*"

"Money, Julien. *Dinero.*"

"I have lots of money, Charlie. Like I said, do whatever is necessary."

"I'll see what I can do."

I thought we were finished talking but an instant later he was back on the line, "Oh, Charlie? One other thing. It is better that you do not mention the company to Mr. Sutton."

"Don't mention DeBergerac? Why not?"

"The man is suspicious of oil companies."

"Okay. Thanks for the heads-up." Then I remembered I also had one other thing. "Julien, speaking of the company, who is Monroe?

One of the crew mentioned him. Said he came around the site sometimes. Keeps an eye on the place, he said. Does he work for you?"

Julien hesitated. "He works for my brother."

"For Jean-Marc?"

"Yes. *Il est son conseiller,* his advisor. Is he bothering you, Charlie?"

"Bothering me? No, I haven't even seen the man."

"Well, please tell me if you have trouble with him, okay?"

That seemed like a strange statement. "Why would I have trouble with him, Julien?"

"*Ce n'est rien.* Never mind. Good luck on your meeting. Please call me after."

———

CHAPTER 10

The gate to the Sutton Ranch was marked by a cattle guard and a faded wooden board nailed to a fence post. A small tin sign announced the owner was a member of the Texas and Southwestern Cattle Raisers Association. A much bigger, more recent sign read PRIVATE PROPERTY, KEEP OUT. A dead coyote was draped over the barbwire fence.

The dirt road passed through a couple of big fields, overgrown with young mesquite, prickly pear and thorn scrub. Judging by the size of the saplings sprouting up everywhere, the fields hadn't been roll-chopped in years. The invasives had choked out the native grasses and erased the habitat. Before long the acreage would be impenetrable and worthless for grazing. Cattlemen like mesquite about as much as anthrax, but nobody had been keeping after this place. It had a forlorn, give-up look to it.

A couple of dozen Brahman cows grazed amidst the cactus. White cattle egrets, nicknamed "tick birds" because of the service they provide, perched on the backs of a few of the cows, searching the beasts for insects.

Soon the road entered a thick stand of oaks and dipped down through a dry ravine. When I emerged from the trees the main house was right there—a one-story cedar-planked building with a sagging front porch and curtained windows. I sat inside my vehicle and waited for one of the residents to acknowledge me—standard etiquette in ranching country.

A pack of snarling dogs appeared from under a rusty tractor and rushed toward my truck, jumping up on the driver door and scratching the shit out of the paint. Soon, an old man walked out of the house—a rough-looking bear of a man. But time and something, illness maybe, had whittled him down. His eyes were rheumy and mean. Thank God he wasn't holding the shotgun Julien had mentioned.

He whistled at the dogs and they trotted obediently back to their shade patch under the tractor. "What do you want?" he yelled from across the yard.

I rolled down the window. "I understand some idiot shot a couple of your cows."

Sutton (at least I thought it was Sutton) narrowed his eyes and glared at me. "What do you know about that?"

"I'm here on behalf of the idiot."

He motioned for me to get out of the truck, so I walked over and stood in front of him, keeping a wary eye on the dogs. "You Mr. Sutton?"

"Who the hell are you?"

"Name's Charlie Sweetwater. From Fulton. I run a little shrimp operation down there. I've visited the excavation site over on the Lavaca a couple of times. Saw those two longhorns last month when I motored up the river in my boat. Nice looking pair of beeves."

"They were a hell of a lot more than that to me. What do you want, Sweetwater?"

"I'm trying to figure out how to make this mistake right with you, Mr. Sutton."

"You work for those Frogs?"

"No, but the one in charge is a friend of mine."

"Dufay? That guy's an asshole."

"Yeah, I've seen that side of him, too."

"I'm not sure what there is to talk about. They're leaving and I'll be sending them a bill for my livestock."

"I respect that. There's not a court in the county that won't back you up, if it comes to that. It's your land."

"Damn right, it's my land."

I scuffed at the dirt with my boot. "I guess that 300-year-old settlement's going to have to stay buried on your ranch forever. Maybe it's better that way."

Mr. Sutton glared at me as he listened, but he didn't walk away. "What is it? Some kind of town or something?"

I shrugged. "They keep calling it a fort."

"You've seen it?"

"I've seen the trenches they're digging, but no buildings or anything. So far, all I've seen are bits and pieces they've discovered in the dirt. They don't mean much to me, but they sure get the archeology boys excited."

"Humph." He looked in the direction of the river and scratched at his beard.

"When did your wife pass?" I ventured. I'd asked around a little bit about Sutton before I came out to his place.

He scrutinized me a moment before he answered. "Eighteen years ago," he answered curtly. "What's it to you?"

"Just wondering? She get sick?"

"Cancer."

"It's a horrible way to die," I said. "I lost my mom to cancer when I was little."

Mr. Sutton nodded. "My boys were little, too." He pointed to the remains of a fenced area about forty yards from the house. "Near the end she liked to sit on the porch here and watch those two Longhorns graze in that pasture. They trace back to the first cattle my great-grandfather ever brought onto the place."

"Like I said, they were fine-looking animals. And I'm not saying that just because I went to the University of Texas." (A burnt orange longhorn was UT's mascot.)

Sutton pursed his lips, his expression more open. "That's where she wanted the boys to go to college. But after she died . . . ."

"They didn't go?" It was hard for me to imagine them in any college. Reform school, maybe. Picking up roadside trash in jail-issue jumpsuits, more likely.

His face hardened again. "No. After she passed I let the steers run wild . . . the boys too, I guess." He took a deep breath. "It's too late for any of that."

"Why's that, Mr. Sutton, if you don't mind my asking?"

He laughed bitterly. "The ranching business is not a money maker, Sweetwater, in case you didn't notice. And my wife's medical bills put me all the way under water. There's no money for college. Shit, there's barely enough to keep the cattle healthy—that is, the ones that ain't been shot."

"What if you did have the money?" I asked.

"Huh?"

"I'm just saying some careless fool took something of value from you, something of sentimental value. And I think you have a right to be compensated for that. But if Dufay doesn't go quietly and this thing ends up in court, it's gonna cost you a bunch of money to defend yourself . . . even if you're in the right."

Sutton looked at me sharply. "Make your point, Sweetwater."

"Okay. I think you not only ought to make 'em pay a fair price for those dead cows, but make 'em pay a fair price for their little treasure hunt, too."

"What do you mean?"

"Since Dufay and his archeologists are so interested in that ten acres of dirt over by the river, jack up the price on their lease, too. Believe me, he can afford it."

Sutton scratched at his beard, thinking it over.

The longhorns inspired me to take a shot. "Mr. Sutton, I'm a fifth-generation Texan. I'm no expert, but I've been interested all my life in the history that's played out here. Since you have—sorry, had—a couple of living artifacts of that history, I think you must know a little where I'm coming from. If Dufay and his crew were to finish digging up that French settlement, folks are going to want to come visit, take pictures, get a glimpse of the first and oldest settlement in Texas."

"I don't want a bunch of goddamned tourists driving across my place," he said darkly.

I nodded briskly in agreement.

"Sure. So have Dufay build you a private easement along the riverfront. Keep it fenced off from your place. He pays to build it and keep it up, he pays to lease it; but it belongs to you. You could put a good chunk of change in your pocket charging admission to visitors. Enough to send those kids of yours to college."

I grinned conspiratorially at him. "I don't think I have to tell a smart old timer like you the way to make a dollar off a Frenchman."

He cocked his head at me. "You say you're a *friend* of Dufay? Hardly sounds like it."

"He believes this Fort St. Louis project is important. I mean major-league, written-up-in-history-books important . . . and I think I agree with him. I think it's a story worth telling."

"What's in it for you, Sweetwater? Why are you doing this?"

I shrugged. "Honestly, I'm not sure why I'm doing it. I'm just a local who's into local history. But there's a way to handle this thing where everybody wins—a way that keeps the lawyers out of it."

"And Dufay still pays me for my cows."

"Oh, hell yes."

"He's gonna think he's bought a damn herd of 'em. Come on in and let's make some medicine. You like bourbon?"

—

Seated on a cracked leather chair in the living room and sipping Jim Beam from a highball glass, I received a history lesson from Clyde Sutton, the fourth generation to work the place and, besides his sons, the only remaining heir. Clyde's great-grandfather was a gambler who bought the ranch at the turn of the century with money he'd won at horse tracks throughout the South.

"Gambling man, hmm," I said.

"Yep. He became shot in Galveston after someone caught him trying to bribe a jockey. Just as well, really. He hated ranching. But goddamn the place musta been pretty back then," he said wistfully. "My granddad told me there was grass crotch-high, and big herds of pronghorn on the place. They even kept a few buffalo around for grins. My wife, she wanted me to buy a pair of 'em and put 'em out there with the steers. That would have been a hell of a wreck." His soft laugh trailed off and he stared down into his glass. "But that was a long time ago . . . ."

More recently, the Sutton family had been mired in a particularly nasty legal battle against British Petroleum and PEMEX, who had formed a joint venture and built a large refinery complex that pushed up against the southwest pasture of the ranch. After Sutton's wife got sick, he reluctantly agreed to lease a small corner of his land to them for their plant expansion. Her cancer treatments were ruinously expensive and, Medicaid or not, he needed the money.

Soon after the refinery project was completed, Clyde discovered the operators were illegally dumping benzene and sulfides into a shallow freshwater lake on his land. Dead fish and wildlife stunk up the area for months. Cattle sickened. When Sutton demanded they clean up the mess, their team of well-suited lawyers told him to piss off.

After months of rancorous and expensive legal wrangling, the suit was dropped when the EPA stepped in and declared the disputed site a disaster area, subject to strict federal guidelines that trumped all other legal claims. While the big foreign oil companies fought with the Feds over who would clean up the site, the inland lake sat on Sutton's land like a toxic stain, lifeless as a grease trap at the Dairy Queen. No wonder Clyde was suspicious of oil companies.

"For all I know, the shit they've pumped out over the years made my wife sick in the first place," he said bitterly, concluding his story.

The loss of his wife and the endless battling with corporate lawyers had apparently taken its toll on the man. From what I could see, he had withdrawn into his house, himself, and his whiskey. Meanwhile, his ranch and sons went to hell in a hand-basket.

Basically, Clyde Sutton's life had turned into a bad country song. The death of his carefully-nurtured longhorns was just the latest verse. Under the circumstances, I'd have sent Julien packing, too. Probably with a load of buckshot to help him along his way.

However, by our third triple-shot glass of bourbon (I had the feeling Clyde was way more practiced at all-day drinking than I was) we had settled on the tentative terms of an agreement. Perhaps the idea of doing something for his dead wife, maybe following through on her wish to educate the boys, spurred him to take action, to take a chance. He'd fallen out of the habit.

"Clyde, you have your attorney draw up the deal, and I'll deliver it to Julien myself. He's not likely to be very happy, but I know he'll like your offer better than walking away from his shot at making history."

Clyde leaned across the table and we shook hands and drained our glasses. I was fixing to leave when Clyde's sons pulled up in a mud-splattered supercab pickup. Through the window I saw them look long and hard at my truck before they walked in the door—the pint-sized twins and their gargantuan brother. Their eyes widened when they saw me in their living room.

"Boys, I want you to meet Charlie Sweetwater."

One of the twins snorted. "Are you jokin', Dad? He's friends with that faggoty Frenchman. I seen 'em together in Indianola."

"Watch your goddamn mouth, Ricky," snapped Clyde Sutton. "Me and Mr. Sweetwater have worked out a deal that'll reimburse us for those two dead longhorns."

The boys looked at each other in surprise.

"Why'd you do that?" said the other twin. "You can't trust this man. Besides, we can handle it ourselves. In our own way. We don't need no—"

"You shut up too, Randy. The deal we've worked out will bring in some money to fix this place up a bit, and hopefully, enough to send you boys to college like your mama wanted."

The boys gaped, and then looked at me with undisguised hate. Higher education was obviously not on their bucket list.

"What if we don't wanna go to college?" said Ricky, almost whining.

"Then you can go find a job somewhere besides here, and I'll hire a couple of wetbacks that'll be half the price of the three of you and will do twice the work."

The big fella hadn't taken his eyes off me since he'd squeezed through the front door. I felt like live wolf-bait on a tether.

The three boys huffed out of the room without a word. I imagined them going out to join the junk-yard dogs under the tractor, where the pack of them would sit panting in the shade, dreaming of tearing a chunk out of my ass.

Clyde Sutton walked me out to the porch. I surveyed the crumbling outbuildings and the Johnson grass-and-mesquite-choked pastures, and tried to imagine a once-thriving ranch, with fat cattle in the pastures and Mr. and Mrs. Sutton sitting in rocking chairs watching their youngsters play in the lush St. Augustine grass. *If you want to make God laugh, tell him your plans,* I thought.

"Clyde, one last thing and I'll get out of your hair. Could you give me permission to drive over to the excavation site so I can tell Mr. Gillette, the archeologist there, that the dig is still on? If Dufay welshes, I'll personally come back and help you run him and his crew off the land."

I hope Julien is reasonable about this thing, I thought. *If not, to hell with him. La Salle's buried settlement could rest in peace for another three hundred years for all I cared.*

"It's across the river. Gate's locked. I'll take you myself, Sweetwater. Jump in the truck."

No bridge spanned the Lavaca River inside Sutton's ranch, so we had to leave the property and re-enter on the west side of the river. After a kidney-bruising five-mile ride we arrived at the camp. Clyde said he'd wait in the truck while I informed Antoine about the stay of execution.

The Frenchman was ecstatic. Apparently he'd found more archeological treasures buried in the dirt, and it was "hurting his heart," to have to leave before he completed the excavation. I guessed he also had a big bonus coming if he found the fort.

I asked him and his assistant, Reginald, if they had heard gunshots the night the steers were killed, and they said they had not. Antoine said that once they'd received the new generator, they ran a big noisy warehouse fan in their tent all night long—to keep cool, to keep down the mosquitoes, and to drown out the untamed sounds of the South Texas boonies.

"It is better the cows are dead." Reginald added, careful to be out of Sutton's earshot. "They trample our excavations, yes? They come at night and make a big mess—*un chantier terrible*." His accent was even thicker than Antoine's. "Three times in one week they come!" He held up two fingers and a thumb. "Three times!"

"No shit," I replied, wondering who or what had encouraged the steers to make midnight raids on this exact place. I thought of the Sutton brothers. They told their dad they wanted to handle things in their "own way."

As I walked over to question the work crew, I searched the ground, not surprised to discover small amounts of grain scattered in the grass and pressed down into the dirt by boot soles and hooves. I picked up a few kernels and put them in my mouth, tasting the unmistakable flavor of molasses. Sweet feed—a mixture of oats, corn and barley, soaked in molasses. It's like crack cocaine to livestock. A cow will knock down a fence to get at a trough of sweet feed.

When I asked the crew if they'd heard the shots, the *mojados* said no in unison, an almost reflexive answer to anything that might lead to trouble or deportation, especially coming from a *norteamericano* they didn't know (no matter that this *norteamericano* spoke Spanish). The other group, including Clifton, Omar and Vinny, also claimed they'd heard nothing.

"I thought you said you were a shrimper," said Clifton. "Why don't you go fuck a shrimp and quit grilling us like you were a cop?"

I ignored Clifton and turned to Hoyt and Judson. "How 'bout y'all? Did you hear anything?"

They shifted their feet uncomfortably and wouldn't look me in the eye. They seemed to be moving stiffly, as though in pain. I noticed some swelling under Judson's left eye and dark bruises on Hoyt's upper arms.

"They didn't hear nothing," said Clifton.

"Hey, Judson?" I swiped my finger across my eye to indicate the bruise on his. "What happened?"

"Tree branch," he mumbled, not looking at me.

"That what put those bruises on your arm, Hoyt? A tree branch?"

"Yes," he said. "We were um, clearing a thicket."

I pulled at my ear lobe and took a deep breath. "Well, I'll tell you what, boys. If that tree branch hits you again, you be sure and let me know. Because I'll break that son of a bitch in half and toss it in the river." I looked at Clifton as I spoke, and he glared back at me.

Vinny slapped at a mosquito and jabbed a thumb toward Clyde Sutton, who watched us from his truck. "You friends with him?"

I smiled, big. "Vinny, I'm friends with everybody. Even ol' Cliffy, here."

I didn't tell Clyde Sutton about the sweet feed or about my conversation with Antoine and the crew. No use complicating things at this point. When we got back to the ranch house, I told him I'd look forward to receiving his contract.

I drove back to Fulton in the fading light, with Clyde's Jim Beam still pumping in my veins. I thought about the old man, and found myself singing every sad country song I knew—and hoping that the headlights in my rearview mirror didn't belong to a zealous state trooper. The car followed me all the way to the Rattlesnake Point turn-off and then drove on, a nondescript sedan with a single driver. Just a weekender going to his vacation house in nearby Copano Village, I guessed. I didn't think another thing about it.

FROM THE JOURNAL OF PÈRE POISSON

We have seen a Spanish ship pass our shore, heading toward Holy Spirit

Bay. Perhaps the Spanish have been alerted to our arrival. They may

be planning an attack while our defenses have been exhausted. We took

cover within our camp, which thankfully, the sand dunes obscured. We

could discern two Spaniards on the ship, but do not believe they saw us.

Père Poisson
NOVEMBER 1685

CHAPTER 11

That Sunday morning I was at my kitchen table tying flies, specifically my own variation of an Enrico Puglisi tarpon fly, with a Salt Shaker Black Death pattern. It was a real beauty. I wasn't expecting company, so a tentative knock at the door surprised me. Very few people happened by my small, weather-weary bungalow overlooking Copano Bay, which I suppose is why I liked it so much. The rattlesnakes, which were myriad (there's a reason it was called Rattlesnake Point), also kept random drop-ins to a minimum.

I opened the door to find Laurent: rosy cheeks, perfectly coiffed hair and a turquoise sweater draped across his shoulders. I didn't know whether to shake his hand and offer him a beer, or kiss him on both cheeks and make him a strawberry daiquiri.

"Hey, Laurent, come on in."

He peered into the house, reluctant to cross the threshold, still unsure he was at the right place. "This was the address the man at the dock gave me," he said.

"If you're looking for me, you're at the right place. Welcome to Casa Sweetwater."

I hadn't done much to the house since I moved in after Johnny died. I guess I was still trying to hold on to his memory. I'd added a few more books, a few more vinyl records, and I'd replaced the V-8 engine end-table with a gnarly oak stump I'd salvaged, sanded and lacquered after Hurricane Lana. A 1979 calendar from the local Tex-Mex eatery was still hanging on the kitchen wall.

"You want a beer?" I asked.

"It's ten in the morning."

"A screwdriver, then?"

"No thanks. I'm only here to tell you that Julien is waiting for you at the harbor. He wants to see you."

"Ah, merely the messenger, once again."

"I'm afraid so."

"Tell Julien I'll be over in a few. I want to finish tying this fly, and I feel I should probably change clothes too. I've got to look my best to hang with your crowd." I was wearing paint-stained karate pants and one of my brother's old T-shirts that read, "Fuck Art, Let's Dance."

I drove the six miles to Fulton wondering which Julien I would find at the harbor: the charming, magnanimous Julien, or the arrogant pudknocker I'd first seen at the river site. I hadn't heard from him since our phone conversation prior to my visit to Clyde Sutton's ranch. I'd tried several times to contact him, but each time his secretary waved me off. She told me the Sutton contract had been received, reviewed, signed and returned to Mr. Sutton, and that work continued on the project. She wouldn't comment about Julien's reaction to the terms of the agreement. Like most corporate secretaries, clever misdirection was an essential skill set. It still pissed me off.

Apparently, Clyde Sutton had sent the documents directly to Julien, and I had no idea if he'd held to the terms we'd worked out in his living room, or if he'd decided to channel all of his pain and anger into a punitive contract that nailed Julien's ass to the wall.

From Julien, I was prepared for anything from a histrionic tongue-lashing to a sincere atta-boy, but I was completely caught off guard by what awaited me.

I rolled up to the docks and found Julien and Marguerite standing in front of the black Suburban. Marguerite look achingly beautiful as usual, and Julien was grinning so big it made *my* mouth hurt. I wasn't sure if the smile was authentic, or if it was more like the death-grin Lee Van Cleef would flash right before he blasted the shit out of one of his Spaghetti Western antagonists.

"Hello, Charlie," he said, still grinning.

"Julien. Marguerite," I answered. She dipped her head regally in greeting. "So, what's shakin'?"

"It's about the Sutton contract," said Julien.

"Look, Julien, you said do whatever it takes, and I thought that under the circumstances I made the best deal—"

"*Arrêtez-vous!*" he interrupted. "I want to show you what I think of your *deal*. Come with me."

I followed them down the long pier until they stopped in front of my two boats, the *Johnny Roger* and the *Li Shishi*. I expected to see a phalanx of lawyers positioned on deck, armed with summons, writs and Montblanc pens, eager to sue me for willful misrepresentation. Or maybe I thought I'd find an obscene phallus spray-painted onto the white hull of my shrimp boat. Instead, I saw a sleek mahogany 26-foot Riva Aquarama speedboat, circa 1965, with bright red upholstery and a dashboard every bit as elegant as a classic sports car. No wonder it was dubbed the Ferrari of the boat world. Julien's new playtoy floated on the rippling water like a ruby on green velvet.

"Goddamn," I managed to say.

"You like it?" asked Julien, still beaming.

"It's stunning. You came here from Houston? In that?"

"It's for you, Charlie, a gift—to thank you for saving my La Salle project."

I was flabbergasted. The Riva classics were most frequently found in posh marinas on the French Riviera, or in films that featured Sean Connery behind the wheel with some bikini babe, tearing through the Mediterranean to evade SPECTRE's evil henchmen. Seeing one up close, floating next to the Vietnamese flathull shrimp boats, was like looking at, I don't know . . . a metaphor for something or other.

"Julien, this is crazy. It's too much." It was easily a $200,000 boat. "Why?"

"I just told you. Your help was well-timed. We have discovered some extraordinary things," he said in a low voice, looking around to see if anyone was listening. "We found muskets, Charlie! French muskets!"

"That's great, Julien. But this is not necessary. It's not . . . proportional." Part of me resented being put under obligation to him, as his lavish gift clearly positioned me. I wondered if I was being maneuvered. While another part of me . . . .

"Ah, but you haven't seen the muskets," Julien replied. "You do not like the motor boat?"

"Are you kidding? I feel like I've been promoted to Archduke or something."

Julien slapped me on the back. "I am glad you like it. I had my executive assistant do some research, and she said these motor-boats are the very best. I know how you like your boats, Charlie. She found this one in Saint-Tropez and we had it shipped over."

"I was worried that Sutton would be unreasonable, that you'd reject the deal."

Oh mon dieu! He fucked me good. It was highway robbery."

"What were the terms? We had agreed—"

Julien waved his hand insouciantly. "It doesn't matter, Charlie. The money is not important. I sign the agreement and told my lawyers to go find someone else to sue. The important thing is that we are digging again! And we are finding such wonderful objects." He clapped his hands together and pursed his lips. *"Alors,* Charlie, but I do have a request for you."

"Lay it on me, Jules," I said.

"Would you allow me to give Marguerite a tour of your Chinese junk? I want her to see the inside, so she can appreciate the beautiful craftsmanship. But more than that, I want her to understand how it looked and felt to me after you pulled me from the sea. It is like a dream to me still."

"I'll do you one better. If y'all have the time, I'd like to make you and your lovely wife a proper dinner on my boat this very evening. With napkins and silverware and, heck, I might even pull out a tablecloth. But first," I looked at the boat and then back at them and grinned, "I say let's take this splendid little motorboat out for a spin."

We climbed into the Riva and I checked the fuel, familiarized myself with the instruments, and then cranked up the twin 200hp Cadillac engines. The subdued rumble sent a tingle up my back. A convertible roof was hidden behind the rear seat, waiting for me to call it up with the flip of an automatic switch, but it was a warm fall day and we decided to cruise with the top down.

As I helped Julien and Marguerite into the boat, I noticed my neighbors, Nu Dang and his wife, Lua Xuan, watching from their shrimp boat. Nu Dang shook his head in disgust. To him, the mahogany and chrome work of art served no practical purpose whatsoever. It couldn't pull a trawl net, it wouldn't hold more than four or five crab traps, and there was really nowhere to land a fish. To them, it was a profligate folly. And where would the live-aboard kids sleep? He had a point. Sheer folly.

But oh, what a fine-looking folly she was.

We cruised down to Port Aransas feeling like privileged aristocracy, which I suppose is how Julien and Marguerite felt all the time, but for me it was a singular experience. When we docked in front of restaurant row in Port A, the boat drew stares from every direction, for once presenting something that could compete with Marguerite for attention. We returned to Fulton Harbor in time for happy hour on the deck of the *Li Shishi*.

In the spirit of my newfound kinship with 007 ("Bond, James Bond"), I mixed martinis for my guests while Julien showed Marguerite around the vessel and gave her an animated French play-by-play of his miraculous rescue from sea. He bounced around the boat like he was on a sugar high.

Marguerite showed great interest and great empathy for his story. After they finished the tour, I watched them embrace on the bow and turn together to witness the tangerine sun slipping quietly over the gothic turrets of the Fulton Mansion.

When the sun disappeared she leaned down and kissed him lightly on the lips, a gesture of surprising intimacy. I admit that I was puzzled by their relationship. Their affection for each other seemed genuine, yet she'd had no qualms about slipping into bed with me.

For dinner, I bummed three fresh-caught snapper from Nu Dang (still anxious to pay down the karmic debt I'd created for him) and seared them in a *beurre blanc* sauce. We dined on deck and drank several bottles of a fine California Chardonnay. When the evening cooled, I wrapped Marguerite in a camo duck-hunting jacket, the only winter clothing I had onboard. I'll be damned if she still didn't look elegant and alluring—like a *Vogue* runway model on the cover of an Orvis catalog.

A breeze picked up and we finished the night inside the galley gathered around the mess table, laughing, talking and sipping Grand Marnier. Around midnight, Julien and Marguerite rose to leave, graciously thanking me and making me promise that we would continue having our dinners at alternating venues; the next one was on them.

I almost felt embarrassed by their charm and generosity of spirit. They'd just given me a boat worth almost a quarter of a million dollars, for arbitrating with a crusty old rancher and facilitating a piss-poor agreement. Were they royalty tossing a florentine to a peasant, I wondered, or was there a bigger scheme I was too dumb to see? Maybe for a man worth hundreds of millions of dollars, a top-of-the-line motorboat wasn't that big a deal. I decided to accept their graciousness and return it in kind.

After they left, I cleaned up the dinner dishes and elected to sleep on the boat. I was about to crawl into the queen-size bed wedged into the forecastle when I heard footsteps on the wooden deck above me. Somehow I knew who it was before I even saw her. She appeared at the top of the steps robed in a white ankle-length coat, her slender figure silhouetted in the companionway by the soft harbor lights.

"Should I ask what you have on under that coat?"

She answered without speaking, descending the steps and throwing the long coat over the dining table and then languidly crawling on top of the silky inner lining, unclothed and uninhibited. With a long manicured finger she summoned me to join her. Had she been having the same erotic fantasies that I'd had while we sat at this same table not one hour before? In spite of my lust, which had become apparent under my white boxers, I had to answer to my conscience.

"Marguerite . . . about Julien? I can't—"

"He doesn't care," she said. "I promise. He is sleeping with Laurent tonight."

"Say what?"

"He is sleeping with Laurent. It is okay. We have both done this many times. We have a—*comment dire?* An understanding. Now come."

How could I refuse?

At Marguerite's suggestion, I lit a candle and then I thanked God for the bounty I was about to receive. I knew I would never be able to eat in the galley of the *Li Shishi* again without visualizing her nude body stretched across the wooden table, her long legs open, beckoning. Which was way the hell okay with me.

After we'd caught our breath, we moved to the master's cabin and buried ourselves under the covers. Marguerite talked openly about her relationship with Julien. She seemed to love the man despite their different sexual predilections.

"Appearances are important in the family," she said. "They know, but they never talk about it. And of course they expect us to be silent—*et conformist*, no?"

I nodded in agreement, although I was thinking that Marguerite and Julien were anything but *conformist*. "Speaking of the family," I said, "I've only met Julien's brother, Jean-Marc. A real prince of a guy."

Marguerite smiled. "Julien said his brother thinks you are a spy."

"A spy?" I wondered for a moment if the entire family was deranged. "For who?"

She shrugged. "For a rival oil company? For Sutton? For *the enemy*," she whispered dramatically. "He sees enemies everywhere he looks."

"Are all the Dufays and DeBergeracs as uptight as he is?" I asked.

"No, not all. But Jean-Marc is the worst of them, and he will do anything to rise in the company. He has no, um, *des scrupules*?"

"Scruples."

"Yes, that is the word. I hate him."

"I can't say I cared much for him either. It must have been difficult for Julien when he decided not to dedicate his life to the family business and all."

"Very difficult. In this family they start grooming their *progéniture* from very young. I think Julien's father realized his elder son would not be a corporate *commandant* almost from the beginning, and he withheld his affection as a result. And then when Julien decided to study art and literature instead of business, *ouf*, he stopped talking to his son altogether.

"What about Julien and Jean-Marc? Were they close when they were young?"

"*Non.*" She shook her head forcefully. "Jean-Marc has always been a heartless bastard. He was very cruel to Julien when they were children—always with the ridicule. He knew how to . . . there is a phrase—"

"Push his buttons?" I suggested.

"*Oui, c'est tout.* He is cruel even now. Thank God for Monique, Julien's mother. If not for her, his life would have been a complete misery."

"So, what does the family think of Julien's Fort St. Louis project?"

"*Pah,*" She flicked her hand. "Except for Monique, they give little attention to any of his projects. He has made a world-class museum in Houston, yet they hardly notice. *Hélas,* the Fort St. Louis project is Jean-Marc's idea from the beginning."

"Jean-Marc's idea?"

"*Oui,* he is the sponsor, even though he has no interest in *l'archéologie.* Julien was so happy when his brother brings him the project, you know? Very excited. But I think Jean-Marc is interested only in what is deeper underground."

I sat up. "Does he think there is oil on Sutton's ranch?"

"It is not the oil . . . it is *le gaz.* It is the only reason he pretends to care about the project."

"Because of the gas."

"*Certainement.* The land to the west is already profitable for DeBergerac. But the ranch of the man, *quel est son nom? Ah,* Sutton. It is there Jean-Marc thinks he will find the big pot of gold. But when he learns this man refuses to lease the mineral rights—he hates all oil companies I am told—then *voilà,* suddenly Jean-Marc has a great interest in French history."

"And he brings his brother onto the project."

"*Oui.* And I think he will use this *ruse* to get at *le gaz.* I do not know how he will do it, but I know Jean Marc. He is *so* concerned a rival company will get to it first. And he will screw Sutton, his rivals, even his own brother, to get what he wants."

All of a sudden Jean-Marc's suspicions of me made more sense. "Does Julien know this, Marguerite? About Jean-Marc, about the gas?"

She sighed. "He knows. But he wants to believe his brother will act, you know, like a brother. Julien is an idealist." She did not pronounce the word as though it connoted a desirable trait.

I was certainly no idealist, but I couldn't help but think of Clyde Sutton, and although I had no affection for the old man, and certainly none for his sons, I didn't want to see him get jacked around yet again—especially by a tool like Jean-Marc. It also seemed like a hell of a coincidence that La Salle's settlement happened to be sitting right over Sutton's gas, and I said so.

"Yes, that was lucky for Jean-Marc," she said. "But what he did not count on was that Julien would find so many of the *artefacts* on the site. He did not expect him to succeed. But my husband will succeed. He is very driven, you know?"

"Yes, I know. Just look at his museum."

"*Oui, quel bon exemple!* The family thought it was a place the mother could hide and protect her son, and then he transform it into a *grand a triomphe*—a treasure that contributes more to the legacy of the company than oil and *gaz* ever will. The people in charge of company *publicité* love the museum, even if the stockholders do not."

"Marguerite, what else is in this Lavaca River deal for Jean-Marc? I mean besides the *publicité* and the gas? I would think the gas deposits on that ranch are only a drop in the bucket for an outfit as large as DeBergerac."

"Yes, but it is a very large deposit, and it is right at his fingertips. Also he would be using a new technology to get the *gaz*. If it works, it would be very good for Jean-Marc, I think. It would be new business for the company, with very big potential—big enough to create a new division."

"And Jean-Marc thinks he'd be just the man to head up that new division," I said.

She nodded. "He wants to get his top executive position, and after that a chair on the board of directors."

"He's a grandson of the founder, and he's not on the board?"

"Only two members from each side of the family are allowed. It has been this way from the beginning. But Monique is the daughter of Jean DeBergerac, one of the two brothers, so she gets to choose the other member besides her. She chooses Julien. Jean-Marc *hates* it that his brother is a director and he is not."

She smiled. "Remember the soap opera, *les séries télévisées*, "Dallas"? I love that show, but when I marry Julien . . . I find myself in another family soap opera, you know? I supposed I was naïve."

As we lay there, listening to the gentle creaking of the boat, I thought about Julien and Marguerite. On the one hand, their world of money and privilege was extraordinary and incomprehensible to me, but on the other hand, many of their problems were so familiar, and no different from the ones faced, for example, by some of the impoverished Vietnamese immigrants living on the rusty shrimp boats moored beside us: the rebellious child, the aloof father, the scheming brother. I'd seen these dramas play out many times before.

"Marguerite? How did you and Julien meet? If I'm not being too nosy."

"No, it is okay. I enjoy the pillow talk. And Julien trusts you. You are one of the few." She laid her head on my chest. "We have to be careful, you know . . . who we talk to."

"Well, you won't find many paparazzi in Fulton."

"You make a joke, but it is a *big* problem when we live in Paris. Those people—*parasites!* They hunt us constantly—to catch us drunk in a club, catch me in the bed with a man, catch Julien in the bed with a man, always watching for the embarrassing situation, *eh?* Anyway, the first time I met Julien, at an art show in Montparnasse, I fall, how do you say? *Tomber follement amoureux?*"

"Head over heels?"

"*Oui!* Head over the heels. I want to protect him from the start."

"Yet you're here now . . . with me. I don't quite understa—"

"*Peuh!* You Americans! *Si traditionnels.* And your sexual mores—*si Puritains.* One can have love and affection without sex, no?" She leaned up on an elbow and looked at me with arched brows.

"I suppose you can." *Although I thought the other way had its merits, too.*

"*Oui,* of course you can. *En tout cas,* Julien knows I am here."

I thought about that for a moment. This was the part of the equation where firearms usually made their appearance in Texas.

She slapped me on the leg. "I am not going to have a problem with you, am I, Charlie? You are not falling in love with me?"

I laughed. "No, Marguerite. You won't have a problem with me."

I wondered how many times this had happened with previous lovers. Quite a few I'd bet. I patted her on the rump. "Unless falling in love with your *derrière* is out of bounds, because . . . ."

Marguerite laughed. "Enough talking. *Nous allons faire l'amour à nouveau.*"

I didn't understand her words, but her intentions were pretty clear when she hopped on top of me and pinned my arms against the headboard. For a moment I felt like just another stud in her stable, working from the neck down, so to speak. "We," meaning *she,* had "done this many times," she'd said. I felt cheap for about half a second and then decided I could live with myself for being her Fulton Harbor sex slave. It *was* a pretty nice motorboat, after all. A little second effort on my part wasn't too much to ask, was it?

"Do you have any soft rope?" she asked in an urgent whisper.

"God, I hope so," I answered.

———

CHAPTER 12

Wooden boats are needy, narcissistic things, requiring constant attention and never-ending care. And now I owned three of the damn things.

Just keeping the brightwork polished on these vessels promised to consume most of the rest of my waking life. I worked all day on the *Li Shishi,* the most beautiful and vain of the bunch, trying to keep the corrosive coastal environment from turning the Asian beauty into an old sea hag. Late in the afternoon, I noticed ominous-looking thunderheads building in the northwest. The radio said the first big cold front of the season was heading our way. Precipitation was expected.

When the initial draft of cool air washed over me, smelling of ozone and rain, I hustled to stow my tools and batten down the hatches. Raul and Sammy arrived to help me secure the boats with additional lines and fenders in case of high winds.

"This is going to be a good one, Charlie," said Raul as he hopped onto the pier from the stern of the shrimp boat, smiling as usual. He looked back expectantly at the dark roiling clouds that blackened the horizon toward Copano Bay. "A real golly-washer!"

"By gully, I think you're right, *mijo,*" I said. "A bonafide frog strangler."

Raul, like me, became energized by a storm. Some years back, the two of us had survived one of the worst hurricanes ever to hit the Gulf Coast—part of it out in open water, no less—so we were respectful but not fearful of inclement weather. Life-threatening meteorology gave life on the coast some texture.

"You guys want to stay here and watch the fireworks? I've got a twelve pack of beer iced down in the Igloo."

"Thanks, *Tío*," said Raul. "But I'm meeting some friends at Cooter Brown's for happy hour. It's dart night!"

I turned to Sammy Dang. "Sammy?" I asked, knowing beforehand he'd be heading home to be with his wife and two young daughters.

"Sorry, Charlie, but tonight is movie night: *The Little Mermaid*—for the tenth Friday in a row."

I slid open our warehouse doors and yelled to them over my shoulder. "Have it your way, *caballeros*. But I guarantee this'll be the best seat in town." As they trotted toward their cars, I dragged the beer cooler and a frayed and sagging deck chair to the building entrance and sat down to enjoy my own outdoor show.

It did not disappoint. The setting sun illuminated the front's advancing wall with a diffused yellow light, etching the muscular contours of the storm clouds in sharp detail. Towering thunder-heads, sheared flat on top, were rooted to the ground by a sodden base the color of peat. Soft, expectant light seemed to hang in the air, suspended over a bay that was calm for the moment but had turned a troubling shade of malachite green. I had never seen it that color before. It reminded me of the artificially-colored water on the River Adventure Ride at Six Flags Over Texas. The raucous gulls were silent and the omnipresent pelicans were nowhere to be seen. That worried me a little, too.

The tempest started with a powerful gust of wind, accompanied by fat globules of rain that splattered loudly onto the boat decks, pier and parking lot, and onto the tin rooftops of the harbor-side buildings, rattling a mad Gene Krupa drum solo. Then the raindrops stopped and the sun disappeared. Everything became still. I walked outside to see if the storm was skirting Fulton and moving on to another area, but without warning the sky seemed to come unzipped.

It rained nonstop for six hours, and was followed by another band of heavy weather that dumped still more water on the Texas coast all the way from Kingsville to Galveston. During a break in the storm I decided to head for the *casa*. Our lazy cur dog decided to follow me to the truck so I let him in the cab with me.

On the way home, I encountered a stalled car on the country road that led to Rattlesnake Point. The big monsoon had abated, but the slow, lilting rain still came down, making little paradiddles on the roof of my truck and causing a nimbus of moisture to form around a lonely streetlight that illuminated a sharp curve in the road.

Under the light, a man was stooped under the hood of his sedan, fiddling with wires or spark plugs, just like every jamoke who's ever broken down in the middle of nowhere. There wasn't another pair of headlights in sight.

I slowed down beside the stalled vehicle, leaned over and rolled down the passenger window.

"Need some help, mister?"

The figure straightened up from beneath the car hood and wiped his hands—big hands, I noticed—on his black jeans. He had on a short black leather jacket, with a white dress shirt underneath, and cowboy boots that looked like they'd seen a few rodeos.

"Oh, hell," he said, "just about all I can get."

Quay's ears pricked up when the man spoke, and he regarded the stranger with what I would have taken to be wary apprehension if I didn't know for a fact the mutt barely bothered to acknowledge most humans.

I put the truck in park and punched my flashers button.

The man walked closer. "Say, friend, you wouldn't happen to be going anywhere there's a telephone, would you?"

Well, what was I supposed to do? The guy was standing out there in the road getting wetter by the minute.

Besides the dog, my front seat was crowded with magazines, logs and assorted papers, so I hooked my thumb toward the rear seat of the crew cab. "Yeah, sure, c'mon, get in."

"Hey, I appreciate it," he said, making his way to the back door of the truck. He moved with a lazy economy of motion; he'd been ten feet away from the truck when I checked the rearview mirror, and the next thing I knew, he was standing at the door. Quay's upper lip lifted in the beginning of a snarl. I rubbed his head reassuringly.

The dome light came on as my passenger climbed in, and I caught a glimpse of an angular, almost rawboned face, pocked here and there with old acne scars. His dark hair was slicked back with rain.

Late thirties, early forties, I guessed. He reached over the back of the seat to shake hands.

"I thank you. Monroe Chambers."

In his handshake was the impression of power kept carefully in check. Even so, his viselike grip required me to pivot my body toward him for more leverage. His eyes, I saw, were direct and the irises were brown, but so dark a brown they blended fully into the black pupils. The impression was unsettling. Then the lines around them crinkled in amusement.

"Dog rides up front, huh?"

"He wouldn't have it any other way." I slipped the truck in gear and we began to bounce down the road back to town.

"Must be tough on your love life. Most girlfriends don't cotton to playing second fiddle to the dog." He had something of an East Texas twang, but it wasn't the flat nasal redneck patois of the Big Thicket backwoods. There was education there, and a sort of wry irony.

"Quay thinks I'm mostly cramping *his* style." The dog didn't take his eyes off the man in the back seat.

"'Quay?' That his name?"

"We're still working that out. He lives by the docks, so 'Quay,' you know? One of the guys in my shop calls him 'Key' like Key Largo. And I've got a Mexican friend who says it should be 'Cay,' pronounced like the letter K. They all mean the same thing, but it doesn't really matter. The dog doesn't answer to any of them."

"Well, he's a fine figure of a dog. Though I seem to be making him nervous."

I'd noticed that. Still no signs of other headlights on the two-lane road. I suddenly noticed that, too.

"Where were you headed this time of night, Mr. Chambers?"

"Aw, I was gonna meet this buddy of mine at Pete's Bend. He thinks we can do some good casting for trout around the docks and pilings there."

I raised an eyebrow at him in the rearview mirror. *Good casting for trout? Fishermen "fish" for trout. And there were no docks or pilings at Pete's Bend.*

"Trout don't usually rise when it's raining. They like it dry up top. And early in the evening."

"Well, my buddy's a lousy fisherman."

We rode along in silence and mulled that over for a bit.

Quay shifted restlessly. Monroe Chambers rode easily over the potholed road, his compact body swaying, his hands resting quietly on his knees.

I thought back to the "Monroe" Hoyt had mentioned at the camp, and remembered Julien saying he worked for his brother, Jean-Marc.

"For trout y'might try the oyster shell pads over in Italian Bend, or the grass over at Swan Lake if you're lookin' for a big yellow-mouth," I said. "Otherwise, the only thing the pilings will hold are sheepshead and tangled line from the last group of Bill Dance yay-hoos."

I could feel him looking at me from the back seat.

"Unless you're looking to catch snook," I added.

"Yeah, snook would be good."

We hadn't seen snook this far up the coast for at least a hundred years. I glanced at his reflection in the rearview mirror. "I'd say your chances of hooking one of those would be pretty slim, though."

"Like I said, my buddy's a lousy fisherman," he said after a pause.

I pulled up to the stop sign at the only intersection between my house and town and set the truck in park, and then I turned on the dome light and twisted around to face my passenger.

"I wonder if you and I might have some friends in common," I said. "Maybe of the French persuasion."

Monroe Chambers looked at me with mild inquisitiveness. "That might be the case. Texas is a small state sometimes."

"I happen to know a French fellow who's employed some security to keep an eye on his projects. You wouldn't happen to know anything about that, would you?"

"Nah. But I imagine if it was important, the fellow probably wouldn't hire a rent-a-cop. He'd hire a pro."

We regarded each other for a moment, and I tried to catch his pitch-dark eyes blinking, but couldn't do it. I switched off the dome light and faced the front, resting my hands on the steering wheel, trying to decide what to do next. A flutter of rain fell on the truck and abruptly subsided.

"That was a pretty good downpour we got earlier," I said. "Can cause a car to stall sometimes . . . . But give the distributor plugs a few minutes to dry out and it'll usually start right up." I glanced at Monroe in the mirror. "Do you suppose if we went back to your car, it might start right up?"

He looked back at me with an amused expression. "I think there's a good possibility it might."

"Yeah, that's what I think, too."

I executed a wide U-turn in the intersection and headed back the way we came. We rode in silence, the windshield wipers marking the time, the rain tapped on the hood. The man in the black leather jacket got out of the truck and stood haloed by the streetlight. The car sat by the side of the road, its hood up, looking like a yawning prehistoric creature. Monroe Chambers paused at my door and locked eyes with me.

"I just wanted a look at you, Sweetwater."

I hadn't given my name.

He rolled his shoulders and turned up the short collar on his jacket. "And I've had a look at you."

He walked away whistling a little snatch of what I recognized as Miles Davis's "Freddie Freeloader."

Quay and I were quiet on the drive back home. A couple of times the dog looked at me curiously, as if he were asking me to explain what had just happened.

"Beats the hell outta me, boy," I answered.

—

The next morning I wrapped a blanket around my shoulders and went outside to greet the day, inhaling the fresh oxygenated air, as delightful as a lungful of primo *sinsemilla* weed, and just as intoxicating. Under the bright blue sky, only the drooping Chickasaw plum that grew by my house, and the saturated cedar deck under my bare feet, indicated that a kick-ass norther had blown through the night before. The concrete cistern that supplied my water was full to overflowing.

I had not slept well—images of roadside serial killers, escaped mental patients and other urban legend boogeymen swirling around in my dreams. Why had Monroe gone to the trouble of faking a roadside breakdown? To threaten me? Scare me? Size me up? Why me? I drew the blanket tighter around me, thinking the best way to clear my head was to get on the bay and do some wade fishing. The trout would be active along Scotch-Tom Reef, same as always after a big storm.

Through the open door I heard the coffee perking and the TV weatherman droning on about cold waves, unstable air masses, record rainfall and hail. There had been massive flooding north of Port Lavaca, minor wind damage in Refugio. Wait . . . *what?* Massive flooding north of Port Lavaca?

I walked into the kitchen in time to see aerial images of a raging Lavaca River that had breached its banks and fanned out over the flat coastal plain. The weather guy mentioned a twenty-eight foot crest *(Holy shit!)* and that the flooding would continue over several days. I did some quick guesstimations in my head, trying to gauge if Julien's site was safely above the flood plain. If it was, it wasn't by more than a gnat's eyelash.

I decided to go to town for breakfast. I would learn more about the flood from the old-timers who drank their morning coffee at the cafe. In a small town, it's always the best place to go for breaking news. When I grabbed the car keys off the turntable dustcover, I noticed my Miles Davis *Kind of Blue* album sitting on the platter, still spinning in circles at 33 revolutions per minute. That son of a bitch had been in my house, listening to my records.

—

When I arrived at the office after breakfast, the phone was ringing.

"Sweetwater Enterprises," I answered.

"Charlie! *Mon dieu,* I am so glad you answer." It was Marguerite. "Please tell me Julien is with you."

"No, he's not. I haven't seen him since we all had dinner the other night."

"*Ô!* I was afraid of that. You must help me find him, Charlie. I must know if he is okay. Did you see the pictures of that river on the television? Terrifying! *Le fleuve était comme un monstre effroyable.*" She began chattering at me in French.

"Slow down, Marguerite. Did you call the satellite phone at the camp?"

"Yes, of course. The phone is not working since the rain. I call it a hundred times."

Possibly, the phone was out because of the weather. Hopefully, Julien or Antoine had evacuated the crew before the river rose. That would have been the prudent course of action. But something told me that didn't happen. So far, neither of them seemed predisposed to either prudence or foresight.

"What about the ranch house where he usually stays?" I asked.

"No one answers. I think the phone is not working there, also."

I suggested she call Julien's brother—he would have command of company planes and choppers. They could go to the ranch house. They could make a pass over the camp. They had lots of resources.

"*Bof!* Julien's brother—*quell con.* He thinks there is no danger and Julien is fine."

"He said that?"

"He talked to some people and they tell him the river is at the, *comment dire . . . ?* The *apogée.*"

"The river has crested?"

"Yes, that is it. They say *probably,* but they do not know for sure. But probably is good enough for Jean Marc. He tells me Julien is *probably* at the ranch anyway."

"Well, that's the first place I'd look."

"*Ô, merci, merci,* Charlie," she said. "Thank you for doing this. I knew I can count on you."

I started to tell her my comment was rhetorical, but I figured the Kestrel Ranch wasn't really that far, less than an hour away from Fulton, so it wasn't so difficult for me to make the trip. But if Julien wasn't there, I wasn't sure what the next step would be. Trying to get to the work camp—a camp that might be underwater—to check on a crew that might already have evacuated . . . that was a whole different proposition.

"I'll go to the ranch house, Marguerite, but if he's—"

"If he is not there then you must go to the camp, Charlie. That is the only way to know if he is safe. I am so worried for him."

I could hear her sniffling on the other end of the line.

I wasn't ready to commit to floating down a raging river, so I promised her I'd check the ranch and get back to her. I hung up the phone and sighed. So much for Scotch Tom Reef.

———

FROM THE JOURNAL OF PÈRE POISSON

We returned to our new encampment, only to find it in a desperate condition. Very few preparations had been made for our arrival, and little progress had been made towards the construction of even a rude shelter. La Salle refused to take counsel from anyone, insisting that he had no need of unsolicited advice. Several of us die each day, and this colony has suffered from various illnesses, including the malady of this land. The natives constantly harass our camp.

Père Poisson
NOVEMBER 1685

CHAPTER 13

A half-dozen locks interlinked the chain that secured the Kestrel Ranch gate, and I didn't know the combination to any of them, so I pulled my bolt cutters out of the toolbox and snapped one of the links. I told myself it was an emergency situation type deal. On the othe hand, I wouldn't have been surprised if I drove up to the house and found Julien in his pajamas, lounging on the veranda reading Rimbaud. The way Antoine had described the place, it sounded pretty first class.

I'd just pop in, say hello and then get my happy ass back to Fulton. But just in case, I had decided to drag my jon boat behind the truck. It had a shallow draft and could navigate in low water, but it was big enough to carry six to eight people at a time—if it came to that. But I'd cross that figurative bridge when I got to it.

Which was very soon. When I reached the ranch house, I found the place empty, locked up tighter than a whorehouse on Election Day.

I sat in the truck and considered my options, cautioning myself that not every damsel in distress, not every plea from a beautiful woman (even one with a seductive French accent) was necessarily a call to action. It was pointless and borderline dangerous to go to the excavation site, and I knew it.

But, strange as it seemed, I'd come to feel vested in Julien's project, and I truly wanted it, and Julien, to succeed. Hell, the guy was still my friend, in spite of his faults and eccentricities—and most importantly, I'd given my word that I would help him.

But it wasn't just Julien I was worried about. What about Hoyt and Judson? What about Dodo and the Mexican workers on the site? Even Antoine and Reginald? I felt especially responsible for the two college-bound boys. They were in over their heads, perhaps literally. For a moment I imagined the entire crew clinging desperately to the branches of a tree, the churning water trying to tear them loose and wash them away.

Whatever the reason, I decided to give it a go.

At the entrance to Sutton's ranch a patrolman pulled up beside me as I was turning the wheel on the gate's combination lock.

"What do you plan on doing with that skiff, mister?" he asked, almost yelling to be heard over the roar of the river.

The Department of Public Safety was always on the lookout for looters and crazies in a disaster situation, and I guess I looked a little suspicious, or a little crazy, getting ready to put in on a river that was raging through the brush country at 52,000 cubic feet per second— a thousand times more water than normal.

"I'm going to check on a friend. He's camped on a bluff near the creek, about four miles downriver."

"This is your property?"

"No Sir. It belongs to Clyde Sutton, but I have permission to be on this road, such as it is."

The officer regarded me skeptically and then looked out at the lakes and watercourses that had spilled over the riverbank onto parts of the road. "Mister, you take that little boat down there, and get swept into those rapids—you're on your own. You know that don't you?"

"I'll be careful."

He took my name and license plate number, as well as the contact information for my next of kin. After that, I saw him look me over and make notes on my physical description—things they could use to identify my body if they pulled it out of the drink. When he put away his note pad he shook his head and frowned.

"Mister Sweetwater, I saw an F-250 and a thirty-foot gooseneck stock trailer get pulled into the river this morning like they were kiddie-pool toys. I want you to keep that in mind."

"I'll be *real* careful."

He shrugged and tipped his hat. "You do that."

As per the agreement he signed with Julien, Clyde Sutton had opened this particular ranch road to improvement (with Julien's money), but so far, only part of it had been widened and graded. Not that it helped me much. After only a hundred yards the caliche road dipped down and became submerged under a vast sheet of standing water.

I parked safely away from river, unhitched the jon boat and dragged it down to the water. Two wooden paddles and a six-horse-power outboard would be useless if I got caught in any kind of current, so I'd have to keep to the edge as much as the terrain and water depth permitted. I strapped on a bright orange life vest and beseeched the patron saint of floods, whoever he or she was, to watch over my ass.

The little outboard coughed and sputtered but it propelled me forward as I navigated slowly and carefully downstream through the milky brown water, keeping a safe distance from the raging current to my left. The main part of the river rushed by at an alarming speed, throwing up six-foot haystacks when it encountered obstructions or barriers. Islands of flotsam formed, disintegrated and re-formed, and large uprooted trees passed me with the power and violence of a runaway 18-wheeler on a narrow road.

I edged timidly from one eddy to the next, on the lookout for strainers, snakes and collapsing walls of mud off the high, red-clay banks, and doing my best to steer clear of the islands of sticks and brush that drifted in the swirling water, many of them teeming with fire ants, ticks and leeches—all of them hungry and desperate for a host. It was slow going.

Three miles downstream from the gate, I bumped into a cow carcass, its bloated side rising up in front of my bow. I pushed it off with a paddle and tried not to breathe the fetid gas escaping from the drowned beast.

Before long, I was able see the bluff where Julien's camp was marooned; it was completely encircled by water. Another eight feet of rise and only the trees would have been visible. If the clear weather held, the river would recede quickly as the floodwater dumped into the bay. In the long run, these massive fresh-water injections helped flush ocean water from the bays, lower the salinity, and regenerate their rich biodiversity. But right now, I felt like I was circling the drain along with everything else.

I switched off the outboard and paddled through a thicket of submerged live oaks to a spot on the bluff that looked like a solid landing. Two unhappy water moccasins slithered into the bushes as my bow nosed into a muddy bank streaked with alligator slides. There was no telling how many critters had found refuge on this lonely little bluff. But there were no happy campers here, human or otherwise.

Over the rise, I ran into the crew tent and stuck my head through the canvas door, only to find empty cots, muddy bedding and damp, filthy work clothes. Boot prints crisscrossed the mud-covered floor, and the flies and mosquitoes were as bad inside the hooch as out.

On the ground outside the tent, pieces of broken liquor bottles were scattered about, and a faint odor of tequila hung in the air. Either I'd stumbled onto the aftermath of a wild party, or the Temperance League had come and purged the crew tent of the devil liquor. Turns out I was right on both counts.

At the dig site I was surprised to see the crew hard at work, most of them stripped to the waist and knee deep in mud, shoveling brown soupy muck out of the holes and into wheelbarrows. Julien paced up and down the trenches, yelling in French and English for them to keep working, quit slacking and hurry the fuck up or he would fire them all.

Antoine and Reginald were at the screening stations slapping at mosquitoes and working their way through buckets of mud, searching for artifacts exposed by the sluice boxes.

The crew gaped at me as though I'd been beamed down from the starship *Enterprise,* but Antoine only looked up wearily when I approached. "How did you get here?" he asked. With smears of mud on his glasses, and a shirt that looked liked it had been used to wipe down a dump truck, he didn't look much like the esteemed archeologist he imagined himself to be.

"I motored over in my jon boat. I'm surprised you guys didn't try to get out before the river rose," I said.

"Now there is a brilliant idea," he said sarcastically. "It *was* our plan to get out when we see the river start to rise, right Reginald?" Reginald, who looked worse than Antoine, if that was possible, grunted as he picked up a bucket of water and poured it over the mud. "But where is the boat, eh?" asked Antoine. "I tell you where. It is washed away, that is where is the boat. Along with the barge, the dock, the compressor and the water pump."

Reginald was nodding his head vigorously. "The men take turns watching the river to warn if comes the flood," he said. "But Vinny Toussaint—"

"But Vinny Toussaint, on *his* watch, is getting drunk with the other men," Antoine finished. "*Quel idiot.*"

"*Une imbécile ivre,*" added Reginald.

Behind me I could hear Julien shouting at the men in the excavation pit. "And that kind of pissed off the boss, did it?"

"He has gone mad," said Antoine. "He has been this way since early morning, since before the sun. First he breaks all the bottles of *spiriteux*—the uh, whiskey he finds in the tent, and now I believe he wants to break the men, too."

I turned and watched Julien pace around the pit, waving his wiry arms, pointing and gesturing in his jerky manner. The sleeves of his white linen shirt were rolled up and his pressed khaki pants were somehow unsullied by the dark wet clay. The men toiling in the pit looked like tar babies with shovels stuck to their hands. I felt like I'd arrived at the head of the river of darkness, at Kurtz's mad redoubt.

"Maybe he just needs some cheering up," I suggested.

Reginald huffed again. "*Bonne chance!*"

"Maybe he just needs you to take him away in your boat," said Antoine. "Maybe me too. I am this close . . ." he held his thumb and forefinger a couple of inches apart, "from leaving this . . . *merdier.*"

I thought about Antoine's suggestion as I walked up behind Julien. It wasn't such a bad idea, taking him away on the boat. It looked like everyone could use a break; this was craziness. And given the way the men were glaring at their fearless leader as he insulted their parentage and urged them on in less than diplomatic terms, it was only a matter of time before they threw down their shovels and walked off the job. Or walked off with his head.

I put my hand on Julien's shoulder and he jerked around.

"What!"

"Dr. Dufay, I presume?"

Julien stared at me through crazed, uncomprehending eyes, like it was the ghost of Charlie Sweetwater standing before him and not me, his flesh and blood *collègue.*

"Charlie?"

"At your service," I said. "I dropped by to make sure everybody's okay." There were dark rings under his eyes, and his face seemed to be stretched tight over his skull and pinned back behind his ears. I wondered when he had last slept. "Marguerite was worried, so I volunteered to check up on you."

Julien scratched at an angry red bug bite welting up on his neck. "Well, now you have checked."

He seemed distracted and agitated. I was about to speak again but he turned back to the crew. "Excuse me," he said, walking away. "There is much to do."

Evidently a worker had done something that displeased him, because he marched toward the man—one of the Mexicans—with arched brows, arms open in frustration.

"You! You there! *Qu'est-ce que tu fous?* What the hell are you doing? I told you to be careful in that area. You will damage the artifacts! Are you deaf? *Cuidado, machacho,*" he said mockingly, butchering the Spanish.

The Mexican laborer acknowledged Julien impassively and adjusted his shoveling to a shallower depth as instructed, his dark eyes betraying no emotion or surprise. But the way he sliced the blade of his shovel into the yielding, wet soil betrayed deeper feelings.

"You are careless because you are hungover, *eh oui?* Because all of you . . . " he swept his finger around the entire crew, "all of you are hungover. You feel like *sheet* . . . and I am *glad, ha!*"

Clifton and Vinny raised their heads and regarded Julien with bloodshot eyes. Omar kept working, but with the usual sneer on his face, as if he were imagining a punishment for his abusive French employer far worse than shoveling mud with a massive hangover. His shirt was unbuttoned and I noticed for the first time a leather sheath hanging from a ball chain around his neck; it was probably a fixed blade neck knife—a deadly weapon favored by criminals and Special Forces dudes.

"It is in their contracts, you know." I realized belatedly that Julien was addressing me. "Yes, it is. Each one of them signed a contract with me, that specifically forbid alcohol on the site. But nooo, they decide to have a big party, *se sauler la gueule!* And you see? *Bof!* The *bateau*, the *quai*, the *compresseur* . . . down the river."

Julien reminded me of one of those rubber dolls that you squeeze and the eyes pop out of the head. He needed to be off the work site quick, before someone bashed in his thick French skull.

I cleared my throat. "Julien, will you walk with me a minute? I have news for you . . . and a proposition."

"*Quoi?* What proposition?"

"I uh, I don't want to discuss it in front of the workers," I said *sotto voce*. I grabbed him lightly by the arm and walked him toward the river.

"You mentioned a proposition," he said after a moment.

"Yes, I did." I needed to come up with a plausible excuse to get Julien off the island, willingly. Would he leave if I said Marguerite was worried? Probably not. And then I thought of Holly Hardin and Jim Brannan and *their* La Salle project out in Matagorda Bay—as different from Julien's train wreck of a project as night and day. Julien needed to see it. Maybe Antoine, too. Maybe they'd learn something.

"Julien, the reason I'm here," I began, "is to deliver a special VIP invitation from the Texas Historical Commission, inviting you to come view the *La Belle* excavation site in Matagorda Bay. Jim Brannan, the director, wants to give you and your wife a personal tour."

Julien grabbed me by the shirt. "You told him about my project?"

I pulled his hand away slowly. "I told him that you are the director of the Dufay Art Museum in Houston, and that you have a personal and professional interest in French contributions to Texas history. Which is true, right? He said it would be his honor to share his discovery with you."

Julien stroked his beard. "He said that?"

"As God is my witness," I answered, hoping that God was too busy with other problems to keep track of my lies and blasphemies. "Jim is a big fan of your museum."

It took some doing to convince Julien to leave the site that same morning to visit the cofferdam across the bay, and even more convincing to persuade him to bring along Antoine as his "museum specialist."

"Antoine might pick up some useful techniques that will speed up our progress," I said. "Reginald can handle things for a couple of days."

———

Before we left, I ran into Hoyt.

"What's up, kid?" I asked. "Where's your buddy?" I hadn't seen Judson since I'd arrived.

"He left," Hoyt said with a shake of his head. "He said he'd built enough character for a lifetime."

"But you didn't go with him?"

"I thought about it, Mr. Sweetwater. I really did. But I kinda need this job."

"And Judson didn't?"

Hoyt shrugged. "Not as much, I guess."

"I thought your dad worked with Judson's dad?"

"He works *for* Judson's dad. My dad . . . my dad's a pipefitter. He knew Judson's dad growing up."

"Ah, I see. So, since you're still here, what are you going to do with all the money you're making?"

He gave me a sheepish smile and an upraised thumb. "Gig 'em Aggies."

I laughed. "College money, huh? You're alright, Hoyt." I looked over at Clifton, Vinny and Omar, who were leaning on shovels, smoking cigarettes under a tree. "By the way, have you had any more trouble with the three stooges over there?"

"No, Sir. They've mostly been preoccupied with those Sutton brothers. They've got some kind of feud going with them."

"A feud?"

"The brothers have been sneaking around here at night, stealing stuff, messing up our site, making weird animal noises, firing guns and stuff—to scare us, I guess. Clifton, Vinny and Omar take turns every night guarding the camp."

"If they're not too drunk, you mean?"

"Yeah."

"Well, they shouldn't have shot Clyde Sutton's steers. That kind of thing tends to piss stockmen off."

Hoyt looked surprised. "How did you know—?"

"You keep clear of all that nonsense, Hoyt. The feud, the drinkin'. Just keep your head down and do your job. This project will be over before you know it. It'll make for a good story some distant day."

I started to walk off and then stopped. "Hey, by the way, have you seen any more of that Monroe character you mentioned last time I was here?"

"He's dropped by once or twice."

"Was he here when Judson decided to take off?"

"No, Sir. Or at least I didn't see him."

I nodded. "Okay. You take care, kid."

"Okay, Mr. Sweetwater."

"Charlie,' I corrected. "Call me Charlie."

"Okay, Charlie." He smiled and then picked up the wheelbarrow, pushing it toward the screening station.

As I waited for Julien and Antoine, I stopped to talk to Dodo at the cook tent. He was busy peeling potatoes for lunch.

"Sorry we can't stay for lunch, Mister Desmarais," I said.

"Dat's too bad. I was gonna whip up some cottonmouth snake jambalaya an' red-mud cous-cous, me. Dis here is some kinda fuckin' mess. I bet Paul Prudhomme don' have ta woik in dese conditions."

"I don't know about that, Dodo. I've seen some Mardi Gras day-afters that would make this camp look like the Waldorf."

The little Cajun cook barked with laughter and made the sign of the cross. "You know, long time ago I had me a job up in Dulac. We rode out dat Hurricane Betsy. Dat storm, *mais oui*, gimme de *freesôns*—de goosebumps—like I ain't had again til' last night. Now, dis mornin', dat *coo-yôn* Julien like anudder storm all to hisself."

He cocked his toe-turned-thumb toward where Julien was exhorting his workers one last time. "*Bon chance* you turn up when ya did, you. You help tamp down dat storm da bossman's brewin', an' mebbe jus' in time, too."

Antoine came over and poured a splash of coffee into his cup from the pot Dodo had simmering on the camp stove. "Desmarais, you talk like you have a mouth full of *merde*," he said. "French is the most beautiful language in the world, but you make it sound like Pig Latin. You coonasses should stay in the swamp."

"You jus' don't appreciate da poetry of da Cajun tongue," Dodo replied.

Antoine took a sip of the coffee and dumped it out. "*Bah. Qui est terrible*," he said, shaking his head. "Julien likes having you around for some reason, for a mascot, maybe. But if you are going to walk around on your hind legs, you could at least speak the language correctly." He dropped the coffee mug on the table and stomped off.

I was too startled to say a word. Maybe the Frenchman was venting spleen he'd saved up for Julien. But still, in any camp I'd ever been in, be it a hunting camp, work camp or plain old family campout, the guy who did the cooking was customarily held in esteem. Pissing on the camp cook was bad form.

But Dodo just laughed and shook his head. "Dat boy," he said, "he jus' a *peeshwank* dat. I might have ta school him, me."

———

CHAPTER 14

When I called Jim Brannan from the Lickskillet Steakhouse in Victoria and requested he host a *Belle* VIP tour for Julien and company, he graciously consented—even agreeing to go along with the conceit that the Texas Historical Commission had instigated the idea. "Just call it doin' my part for Franco-American relations," said Jim. "But you owe me."

Julien called Marguerite, who was happy to hear that her husband was alive and well. She insisted on flying in to join us on the tour. She would meet us at Miguel's marina in Indianola the following morning.

At the restaurant in Victoria, Antoine complained repeatedly about the food, but I watched him revisit the lunch buffet twice to refill his plate, his mud-caked boots leaving a trail of terra-cotta chips from his chair to the steam table. Even in his filthy clothes he comported himself with a conspicuous air of superiority, completely disregarding the stares of the regulars.

We drove to the Kestrel Ranch, and a matronly Mexican woman laundered our clothes, prepared our dinner (a hearty cassoulet) and turned down our beds. Julien and Antoine acted like it was no less than their due. We dined on a screened veranda attached to the house.

I turned in early and, lying in bed listening to a screech owl, tried to make sense of the day: the feud between the Sutton brothers and the trio of troublemakers at the camp; Judson's decision to leave and Hoyt's resolve to stay; and finally, Julien's perverse camp confinement rule for all crewmembers. If they were worried about looters, why not hire a guard to be there when the crew was off the clock? If they were worried about secrecy, what could the men divulge that would be of any interest to anybody? What was Monroe's role in the project?

I thought back to what Marguerite said about Julien's brother and his single-minded quest to get at the gas under Sutton's ranch. It wasn't just a coincidence that the archeological site and the gas were on the same ranch. I suspected it was why Jean-Marc had steered Julien to the project in the first place. But how did he know where to find the Fort St. Louis site?

I also puzzled over Julien's current accommodation. Antoine said it was a hunting lodge of some kind, and maybe it was. But it wasn't being used for that now. There were plenty of trophy heads mounted on the walls, stacks of hunting magazines lying around, and even a stuffed bobcat crouched on the fireplace mantle. I supposed Julien had rented the entire house for the duration of the excavation project. But who else was using the house?

Julien stayed in the annex and had that building to himself, but in the main house I saw evidence in every room that the place had been fully occupied of late. All of the beds in the bedrooms appeared rumpled and recently slept in, and in the common areas I noticed office accessories and power strips plugged into the outlets. The place felt like a busy field office to me. I resolved to look into it some more.

On our way to Indianola the next morning, I asked Julien about the house, and he mumbled something about it being a company lease. He wasn't in a talkative mood so Antoine filled the silence with chatter, mostly French, until we pulled up to the marina. Jim and Holly were waiting at the dock when we arrived.

"That was one hell of a storm last night," said Jim. "Holly said there was major flooding on the Lavaca and Tres Palacios rivers."

"Noah would have been impressed," I replied.

"Well, you know what they say, today's disaster is tomorrow's archeology." He laughed at his joke, and I laughed too, even though I'd heard him say it at least a dozen times over the years.

I introduced my guests, and everyone shook hands. Marguerite arrived a few minutes later and, after an emotional embrace with her husband, said hello to her hosts. I had to prod Jim to respond when she offered him her delicate hand. Holly rolled her eyes at her infatuated colleague and called for us to board the crew boat.

The day was crisp and cool with a slight northerly breeze. A playful pod of bottlenose dolphins glided ahead of the boat's prow, leading us to the cofferdam. Marguerite watched them and squealed with delight, calling to them in her beautiful French.

"Aphrodite, born of the sea-foam," Jim Brannan said close to my ear.

We both watched her watch the dolphins until I felt Holly's eyes on me from the helm of the crew boat. I broke away and joined her in the wheelhouse.

"Lovely morning," I said.

"Yes, I noticed how much you were admiring it."

"Well I—"

"What's the story on these people, Charlie? Brief me."

I glanced out the back window and saw Julien and Antoine sitting on the stern deck bench seats. Antoine craned his head, searching the horizon for the cofferdam, while Julien sat motionless, staring at his feet. "Julien's the guy I rescued from the Gulf last year. I think I told you about that. He's the executive director of the Dufay Museum of Modern Art in Houston and part of the DeBergerac family."

"*The* DeBergerac family?" asked Holly.

"Yeah, same one. He's the grandson of one of the founders."

"Pretty rich company you're keeping, Charlie. What's his interest in our project? If he's here to write a million-dollar grant, he's my new best friend."

"French history. The guy's crazy for it. I think he'd like to reclaim Texas and the entire Louisiana Purchase for President Chirac and the *Musée de l'Histoire de France*," I joked. "But he'll settle for reminding people that the French flag flew over Texas soil, at least for a little while."

Holly immediately stiffened. "Has he said anything about reclaiming the *Belle?*" she asked.

I immediately grasped her concern. I suppose the ownership of a wreck could be disputed by, say, a sovereign government—rights of salvage be damned. Lawyers can dispute anything. I sure as hell hoped I hadn't put Holly and Jim's project in jeopardy.

"Jesus, Holly, I didn't think about that." I looked back at Julien. "But I really don't think that's what's on his mind. He's never mentioned anything of the sort, not once, in any of the conversations we've had."

Holly looked at me closely and nodded. I could tell she was not completely convinced. "And who's the other guy?"

"He's an archeologist. He works for Julien and the museum."

"They keep an archeologist on staff at an art museum?"

"I think he's more of an art historian with an interest in archeology," I said, lying only a little.

"The two have nothing in common."

"I won't let anything happen to your project, Holly. I'll ask them to keep it secret if you want."

She laughed. "That's very *galante* of you, Charlie. But the cat's already out of the bag since we've opened the project to the public. Thanks to your brilliant idea, *La Belle* is becoming more popular than a Galveston gambling cruise, at least for the moment."

"Well, every girl likes to be popular. Is that so bad?"

She laughed. "No, Charlie, I meant what I said. It was a brilliant idea. You have no idea the funding and free publicity we've gained from being 'popular.' Features in magazines, TV crews, kids saying they want to be marine archeologists . . . ." She shook her head in wonder. "Incredible."

Holly wasn't kidding. As we pulled up to the cofferdam docking station, a pontoon tour boat was tying off at the new public dock. People filed off the boat, led by a young female archeologist wearing a T-shirt that read "Midden Mama." Many of the tourists wore cameras around their necks and began taking pictures the moment they docked: a winch, a generator, a crew shack with a bunch of muddy boots piled up. It didn't seem to matter, they snapped away.

After the tourists disembarked, a very vocal schoolteacher rode herd on a group of young kids from a local elementary school. Our French guests watched the bustling operation in awe.

"Extraordinaire," I heard Marguerite whisper to her husband.

"Welcome to the excavation of the shipwreck *La Belle,"* Jim Brannan said grandly. "One of the most important archeological finds of the century, and also the first time a cofferdam has been used to excavate an underwater wreck *al fresco."* He walked us across the sand to the interior wall of the dam.

"Monsieurs and madam, voilà, the barque-longue, La Belle." Jim's French accent was appalling, but the effect of the spectacle on his guests was unmistakable. Julien had adopted his pop-eyed look, and Antoine seemed unable to close his mouth. Marguerite had a huge smile on her face and uttered a string of acclamations in French. This was, it was clear, their first exposure to the big leagues. It made their set-up on the Lavaca River seem slipshod and rudderless.

Jim launched into a description of the cofferdam and its construction, making a point to mention me and my "incalculable" contribution to the project—"protecting the integrity of the wreck after its discovery."

I tipped my battered Shakespeare Lures ball cap and bowed. "He makes being a night watchman sound pretty important, doesn't he?" I whispered to Holly.

Jim walked us to the public dock and talked about the tremendous interest the wreck had generated with professionals in the field of history and archeology, and with media groups from as far away as Germany and Canada. "We've even had a call from *National Geographic,*" he said proudly. And of course, there were many junior archeologists visiting from the schools. He waved to the Roscoe Wilson fifth-graders leaning over the rail on the other side of the pit, and they waved back.

"But so far, no film crews?" asked Marguerite.

"No ma'am, not yet. Not that I know of."

"*Super,*" she said, barely able to contain her excitement. It wasn't hard to see what she was thinking.

After Jim finished his part of the tour, he turned it over to "the eminent Dr. Holly Hardin, underwater archeologist and co-director of the *Belle* recovery project. She knows more about sunken ships than King Neptune." Jim thought that one was pretty funny.

Holly led us down the scaffold steps into the pit and began going through the excavation process step-by-step. She described the construction, compartments and components of the ship, as well as the treasure trove of artifacts *La Belle* was offering up. Today's big find was a remarkably preserved coil of anchor rope resting deep in the bow of the ship.

Throughout her detailed exposition, Julien remained uncharacteristically quiet, but Antoine challenged Holly at every opportunity. "Anchor rope is organic," he said. "I do not think it possible that it can be so well-preserved. How can you be sure this is actually *La Belle?*" And then he started challenging her on the methods they were using in the excavation. "The water you spray on the artifacts, it only makes them more fragile, more likely to fall apart. Also, you are using the wrong tools."

At first, I thought he was being gauche, or flexing his academic muscles. Then I concluded he was being a pompous ass because, well, because he *was* a pompous ass. As he continued his diatribe, Marguerite looked at him curiously, raising an eyebrow. Jim's commentary became strained and self-conscious, while Julien seemed to be focused inward, disconnected from what was taking place.

Me, I couldn't tell if Antoine was making legitimate points, but one thing I *could* have told him, and it came from experience: You don't mess with Texas women, hoss.

Holly smoldered and endured the interruptions for a while, but I could tell she was about one snotty critique away from mashing Antoine Gillette like a guacamole salad.

"Your method may work fine on dry land excavations, Mr. . . . what did you say your last name was again?"

"Gillette. *Doctor* Gillette."

"The method you describe may work fine on dry-land sites, Mr. Gillette, but not when the timbers and artifacts have been in an anaerobic state for three hundred years. We have to keep them moist to inhibit decay."

Antoine shrugged dramatically. "If you say so. But I think you are damaging the artifacts."

Holly's blue eyes turned stormy, and she folded her arms tightly across her chest, probably to keep herself from shotputting the Frenchman over the wall of the cofferdam. This was her life's work, and professional courtesy be damned.

"Perhaps you'd like to finish the tour yourself," she said icily. "Since you're obviously the expert."

"Perhaps I would consider it if—"

"*Tais-toi!*" Julien said sharply, seeming to zero in on the situation for the first time. Antoine mumbled something else, and Julien grabbed his arm. "Antoine. I said shut . . . up!"

Jim and I exchanged glances, glad Julien had said something. Antoine was being an asshole, and he seemed offended less by Holly's methods than by the fact that she was a woman. Antoine reminded me of a commercial airline pilot I knew who lamented the trend of women aviators in the cockpit. Each time a female pilot or co-pilot made Captain he would sigh, shake his head and mutter, "Another empty go-go cage."

"I apologize for my colleague," said Julien. "He forgets we are guests at your worksite. My wife and I are . . . " he searched for the right word, "*astounded* by the scope and execution of your project. You are doing magnificent work here, and we cannot imagine such important work in any hands other than your own."

He stepped forward and vigorously shook the hand of Holly and Jim in turn. *"Merci,* Doctor Hardin. *Merci beaucoup,* Doctor Brannan. It has been our great honor to meet you and to see first-hand what you are accomplishing here. Thank you for arranging this, Charlie. It has been a revelation."

As damage control went, it wasn't bad. When he chose, Julien could charm a Hindu into eating a cheeseburger.

When Julien finished speaking he turned and headed toward the scaffold. After an awkward pause, Marguerite thanked us as well and followed her husband up the steps. Antoine trailed sullenly behind.

"I guess the tour is over," said Holly.

"So it seems," Jim agreed, frowning.

I couldn't blame Jim for being aggravated. I'd put my good name on the line, vouching for the trio, and one of them had practically accused the two THC experts of professional malpractice. Holly probably found me about as attractive as smallpox. I wanted to crawl under the mud.

I was walking to the scaffold when one of Holly's assistants yelled for her to come quick. "You gotta see this!"

Standing over the pit, even I was able to understand what the excitement was about. A human skull had been discovered inside the bow of the ship. Holly and her assistant examined the partially exposed skull and carefully, delicately, almost lovingly, brushed away the mud and debris surrounding it. The skull was facing sideways, resting inside the coil of anchor rope, its eye sockets staring obliquely toward the hull of the ship. Other bones were situated around the head, suggesting an entire skeleton.

Was it a man? Perhaps a sailor? Had he drowned? Starved to death? Died of disease? What were his last thoughts as he lay there on his bed of rope, five thousand miles from home in a savage, unforgiving New World swamp?

These and a dozen more questions raced through my mind. Until now, the shipwreck had been something of an abstraction: fascinating, extraordinary even, but as benign as a chalky arrowhead picked up in a dry riverbed. Encountering the remains of a person somehow humanized the wreck, compressing the three hundred-year gap of time into an event that suddenly seemed immediate, personal and tragic.

While the archeologists gathered around the ship to get a look at their momentous find, I climbed the scaffold and boarded the

Anomaly. Wisely, Antoine had made himself scarce, but Julien and Marguerite sat together at the stern. She had her arm around her husband and was gently stroking his head.

"Julien, you're not going to believe this. One of your long lost countrymen has just been discovered inside the wreck. They've found what looks to be an entire skeleton in the forward hold of the ship. Just think, it's probably a member of La Salle's expedition. Tell me that doesn't blow your mind."

Julien looked up distractedly, his glazed eyes seeming to light up for an instant, but then they dulled again, and he hung his head.

"He doesn't feel well," said Marguerite.

"But . . . *one of the Belle's crewmen!*" I said. "Don't y'all want to see him? I mean, this person would have *known* La Salle!"

Julien looked up again. "The bones of a dead sailor. Who cares?"

I looked at Marguerite. "What's wrong with him?"

"Would you ask one of the workers to take us back?" she demanded. "My husband would like to leave now."

I wondered what had happened to the woman who was giddy with excitement over the prospect of filming the *Belle* project, and the man who only moments ago had graciously praised Holly and Jim for their spectacular success. It was as if someone had let the air out of both of them.

"Are you sure?" I asked. "Julien?"

He waved me away without looking up, as though I was a butler who'd announced a visitor and was no longer needed. They sat together, wrapped up in each other and wrapped up in their own world—a world that revolved around them exclusively, around their money and private schemes and projects. A world that apparently didn't admit or welcome classes of people they considered lower than themselves: like sailors or laborers or hell, probably shrimpers either.

I wondered if my special status was only because I'd saved Julien's life, or maybe because I had a Chinese junk that amused Julien and a soft rope that entertained Marguerite after midnight. Who knows? All *I* knew was that I was ready for a break from Julien Dufay and his whole fucked-up Fort St. Louis project.

"They will take you back when they're ready," I said, and climbed off the boat.

FROM THE JOURNAL OF PÈRE POISSON

I meant to write about the nights here. They are quite different from our nights in Rouen. There, within a few hours after the sun sets, all the world is still and quiet as it prepares for sleep. Here, the night is full of watchful anticipation. One waits for some creature to pounce, or slither, or awaken. Rather than repose, our nights are restless and uneasy.

Père Poisson

NOVEMBER 1685

CHAPTER 15

I was back in Fulton, tending to a hot and greasy job I'd been putting off for a long time, specifically tearing down and rebuilding the cylinder head for one of the diesels on the *Li Shishi*. The revs on one engine had been dropping off, and after the usual trial-and-error sleuthing, I had narrowed the problem down to a pitted cylinder head assembly and worn-out gaskets.

Since working down in the engine room of the venerable junk was a refined form of sweaty hell, I had (with Raul's help) detached and lugged the whole assembly into the big central workspace of our warehouse. Now I sat surrounded by packing material, staring at a parts manifest written in Chinese and hoping the replacement head and gaskets I'd ordered from Taiwan actually fit.

"This job is apt to harelip the Pope," I said to no one in particular. Raul was at lunch, and Sammy Dang was on his way back from Macau, courtesy of Tiger Airways.

The sun was dazzling through the doors I'd rolled open to create a little cross-ventilation, so the figure who appeared suddenly, backlit by the glare, was an indistinct silhouette.

As the man stepped inside, I could see his face was shadowed by the brim of a silver-belly Stetson. A stray shaft of sunlight gleamed off the polished cinco-peso badge on the breast of his starched white shirt.

I straightened up, mechanical travails forgotten.

"Well, whaddya know," I said. "O.B. Hadnott."

It wasn't fair to say that Hadnott hadn't changed. Hell, we had all changed. But, where O.B. was concerned, the overall remained pretty consistent.

His stomach was beginning to belly out over his silver belt buckle a bit, and the mustache he'd cultivated the last time I'd seen him—he and his wife's twelfth wedding anniversary—was shot through with silver. The faithful .357 revolver he'd carried as part of standard Texas Ranger issue had been replaced with a modern 9-mm Glock.

But the blue eyes in the lined face still shone with the same cool, stoic resolve. It was a gaze that many a South Texas badman had come to dread. And he still stood with the cadet-straight posture that made his six-foot three seem even taller.

I wiped my hands on a shop rag and bounded forward. "Long time no see, Sergeant! Or is it lieutenant?"

Hadnott's smiles were few and far between, but this one was genuine. "It's captain. And how the hell are you, Charlie?"

"I'm alright, I'm okay," I said, pumping his hand. I gestured to a pair of chairs positioned around a card table. "How's Trinny?"

"She's fine," said Hadnott, taking a seat. "She owns about seventeen nail salons between Corpus and Houston."

I tried to picture O.B. slipping off his custom Lucchese boots for a pedicure. Failed miserably.

"And the kids?"

"Ana and Joaquin? Doin' well. Busy."

Hadnott took off his Stetson Roper and placed it carefully, crown-down, on a clean spot on the table.

"Hey, Captain, can I interest you in a *cerveza fría?* I've got a couple in the fridge."

Hadnott glanced down at his badge. "Workin'."

"Yeah? What on?"

"I heard you were pitching in on some kind of archeological deal out near Port Lavaca."

"A fella I met a while back is running it. I'm just helping out."

"You know of a kid named Judson Strayhorn?"

I didn't like the feeling I was getting. "Yeah, sort of. He's working with the crew. He and a buddy. At least, he was. They told me he'd skipped the site. Went AWOL."

"He's AWOL, alright," said Hadnott, pulling out a pocket notebook and consulting some chickenscratch scribbling. "The Calhoun County sheriff pulled his body out of a snag downstream from the site two days ago. He'd been shot in the back with a high-powered rifle and ended up in the river. Coroner says he doesn't know if the boy was dead when he went into the drink. I'm sorry, Charlie."

The world dimmed down to a shade of gray.

"Aw, hell," I said softly.

"Yeah," said Hadnott. "That about covers it."

I wasn't fooled by the Ranger's laconic response. Over the course of his career, O.B. had been exposed to just about every variety of human misery and perversion, and it had marked him. He didn't *not* care, but the job came first. Staying frosty let him focus. And God help whomever he focused on.

"Doesn't *have* to be murder," O.B. mused after a period. "Kid left the job site, could have been cutting across the place, and the owner was out after a big buck, or maybe some hogs. Kid caught a wild round, fell in the river. Been known to happen."

"Maybe, but I don't believe it," I said, and I told him the tale of Julien and his La Salle obsession, the archeology dig, and the characters who had accreted themselves to the project. I also sketched in my encounter with the boys and Clifton Sloan before Judson disappeared.

"That bastard was already beating on those boys to keep them in line. If he found out Judson had skipped, he might have gone after him and put him down. He's enough of an SOB to do it."

"I'll look into it."

"Good. But . . . why are *you* looking into it? Isn't this a job for the locals?"

O.B.'s mouth turned down under his moustache, and he shrugged. "You know how it goes. Lucius Strayhorn, the boy's father, writes big checks to the governor every four years. Got himself appointed to the Board of Regents over there in College Station. Rich guy with a lot of stroke. He made a phone call to the capitol, the governor called my boss, and here I am."

"You don't really think somebody was out pig shooting, do you?" I asked.

"I do not."

"You think I should keep nosing around the project and maybe do some digging for you?"

"I do."

I thought about that young boy, looking forward to being an Aggie, for chrissakes. It was all ahead of him, but someone had pushed him out into traffic.

"I can go there in the morning."

O.B. nodded. "Maybe we'll cross paths. I'll be going out there, too." We both were quiet—a moment of silence for the Strayhorn kid, I suppose. Finally O.B. picked up his hat and placed it on his head. "Anything else?"

"Well, while you're here, there's this one guy who's been hanging around the job that I can't quite make. Works for Julien's brother, Jean-Marc Dufay. Julien said the guy is Jean-Marc's advisor, but to me he seems more like a union-buster type."

"He got a name?"

"Monroe Chambers. Supposedly, he wasn't at the site when Judson bailed on the project, but, I don't know, there's something about him that doesn't feel right."

O.B. wrote the name on his pad, snapped it closed and rose to leave. "Much obliged, *amigo.*"

"Any time. And by the way, congratulations on your promotion." I stood up, and we shook hands. "Hey, am I also supposed to salute or something?"

O.B. cracked half a smile. "Go to hell, Charlie."

"I'm on my way, Sir."

———

CHAPTER 16

The next morning was gusty, the bay streaked with frothy whitecaps—not unusual for late November. There's a reason the Fulton live oaks fronting the bay grow sideways, bent landward by the unceasing offshore wind.

I hauled my boat to Sutton's ranch, in case the new-cut road was still flooded or else too muddy to drive. Turned out, it was both. The river was high, but it had mostly settled back into its banks, a far cry from the monster that roared through a few days before. Beyond the gate I saw that the caliche road was saturated and undoubtedly slicker than all get out. Further ahead, I could see that at least one section was still underwater—no way I was driving to the site today.

I put in under the bridge, leaving my truck and trailer parked under the overpass. The strong, muddy current hurried me downstream to the site. I arrived without issue and fastened the bowline to the one remaining piling—the rest of the pulverized boat landing was probably halfway to Veracruz by now.

The embankment was slick and muddy, and I had to grab on to roots and bushes to pull myself up the bluff. By the time I reached the top, my jeans and windbreaker were covered in mud. Over four months on the site, and they still hadn't thought to build steps into the bank. I was already wishing I was back in Fulton, re-setting the motor on the *Li Shishi* or re-spooling new fishing line onto my reels—something practical, something that made sense. Instead, I was back on the doomed Island of Doctor Moreau, looking into a possible murder.

The excavation pits were mostly empty of water, but nobody was working in the holes, at the sluicing stations, or anywhere else that I could see. Maybe they were on break, although on closer observation it didn't appear that any work had been done since my previous visit. Dodo Desmarais was skinning a scrawny rabbit under the cooking tarp, standing in the same place I'd last seen him. I felt like I'd been away from the camp for four minutes instead of four days.

He lifted his chin and smiled, waving the bloody boning knife he clutched in his gnarly, misshapen hand. He swept the chunks of rabbit into the big pot, picked up a chef's knife and started chopping celery and bell peppers, looking up as he worked.

"*Bon temps,* Mr. Charlie. You like a rabbit Sauce Piquante? I gonna make some maque choux an' some plum cobbler. It's gonna knock yo' dick in da dirt, you."

I poured myself a cup of coffee from his eternally simmering pot. "Too good for these knotheads, Dodo. Where'd you find that rabbit?"

"It run up and jump in da pot when I call it."

"You speak jackrabbit, do you?"

"No, man. *Brer Lapin,* he speak dat Cay-jon, yessir. I t'ink he said he las' name were Robacheaux."

It was the first good laugh I'd had in that God-forsaken place.

I found Reginald inside the dark little field office, slumped in a folding camp chair. He was a pitiful sight. Papers were scattered around the room, and the floor was caked with mud.

"What's shaking, Reggie?" I switched on a light. "And where is everybody? It looks like the Prussians just marched through and raped and pillaged your camp. Hope they spared you boys the first part."

He looked up slowly, his bloodshot eyes widening in surprise at seeing me, then narrowing in irritation when my words registered in his brain.

"*Fous-moi le camp,*" he muttered. "Go away."

"Don't be like that, I'm here to help. Where's the eminent house archeologist, Antoine Gillette?"

"He is not with you?" There was an anxious edge to his voice.

"No, he's not with me. I came alone."

"Then where is he?"

"Beats me. The last time I saw him was three days ago, at the cofferdam." I looked around the office. "You mean he hasn't been here since then?"

Reginald stood up shakily. "No."

I got the feeling Reginald hadn't been all that comfortable playing foreman while Julien and Antoine were away.

"Reginald. Where is your crew?"

He looked down. "I . . . . In the *grande tente,* I suppose."

"On break? Why aren't they working?"

He tapped his muddy boots on the leg of the drafting table, knocking off a layer of dried clay. "*C'est une bonne question,*" he said weakly.

I sighed and glanced out the filmy window toward the crew tent. "What have y'all been doing since the boss left?" I asked.

"Well, it is so muddy, you know? So the crew stay in the tent."

"Doing what?"

Reginald shrugged. "I do not know. I think they drink, mostly. Smoke the marijuana—*vous savez.*"

"Uh-huh." It wasn't hard for me to imagine Clifton and his cohorts taking advantage of Antoine and Julien's absence, but it was strange the Mexicans weren't working either. I wondered if they'd been coerced into this little mini-strike. "Well, you know what they say . . . if the cat's away, the mice get hammered."

"*Quoi?* What cat?" he asked, nervously.

"Never mind." There was an aura of fear and helplessness around Reginald that was awkward and slightly embarrassing for both of us.

"Hey listen, Reggie," I said, wanting to change the subject, "Has anyone else been out here today?"

"Like who?"

"Like a Texas Ranger?"

"A Texas Ranger? What is this Texas Ranger? Like in the movies? *Les Westerns?*"

"Sort of. He's in law enforcement. A guy with a badge and a cowboy hat, wears a sidearm." Reginald looked confused again so I pulled an imaginary pistol from my imaginary holster. "You'd know him if you saw him."

"No," he said. "No Ranger is here. Why do you ask?"

"Just curious. I thought someone might have come by to check on things, that's all."

"No, no one comes. Only you. Since four days." There was an awkward pause. "But I have been very busy, you know?" he explained. "All the time I have been researching the historic documents and cataloging the artifacts." He walked to the papers stacked on the drafting table, grabbed a sheaf of documents and waved them at me. "It is important work, yes?"

"Of course it is, Reggie." It was pretty obvious that Reginald had retreated into his tin refuge after he'd lost control of the camp, and now he was trying to salvage a little dignity by maintaining the importance of his "research." I felt a little sorry for the guy.

In retrospect, it was a bad idea to suggest leaving him in charge of a crew made up of *mojados* who couldn't understand him, and a pack of ex-cons who would probably whip his ass or worse if he tried to force them to do anything they didn't want to do.

"Is everyone in your crew okay?" I asked. He didn't seem to know about Judson, so I decided not to tell him. Better to let Captain Hadnott ask the questions. I didn't want to foul up his investigation by being any more reckless than usual (although my first impulse was to march into the crew tent and beat a confession out of Clifton).

"The crew? Yes, I think so. *Pourquoi?*"

I was about to ask about Hoyt specifically, when through the window I saw him walk up to the cooking tarp, where he picked up a knife and started helping Dodo chop vegetables for supper. Thank God. The kid was okay.

"No reason," I said. As I stood at the window, looking out at the muddy camp, thinking about the miserable conditions and about Judson Strayhorn's tragic end, I wondered if the entire project was cursed. The first project, the one that played out here three centuries ago, certainly was. Jim had said that of the 180 colonists that came here to settle, only a small handful survived. Maybe it was better to leave the dead alone.

Or maybe this wasn't the Fort St. Louis site at all. I was beginning to harbor a few doubts about the authenticity of the site. Four months of excavation and no signs of the actual fort. No foundations, no fortifications—nada, zip.

I turned around and saw Reginald hunched over the drafting table, studying a small book with a magnifying glass. "Whatcha got there, Reggie?" I asked.

"A historic document" he said solemnly.

"Yeah? Would you mind showing me some of these documents?"

"I'm not sure Antoine and Julien would—"

"Sure they would. I just took your bosses to the *Belle* excavation site out on Matagorda Bay, and the head honchos for that project were more than happy to talk shop. Showed 'em everything they'd found except the dirty French postcards that ol' horndog La Salle hid under his bed in the captain's quarters. Now I'm giving you the opportunity to show me what you've got, Reggie. You're a professional. School me on some French history. And in return, I'll put in a good word for you with your bosses."

He pursed his lips while he considered what to do. Julien's senseless code of secrecy had infected the whole camp. It was pointless.

Apparently, the thought of my endorsement tipped the scales, because Reginald moved to the table and began describing the documents with great enthusiasm. He showed me photocopies of papers that Julien had obtained from the French Marine Archives and the *Bibliothèque Nationale de France*. The papers included correspondence between La Salle and King Louis XIV, authorizing the expedition; transcripts and maps from the diary of an engineer and cartographer named Jean-Baptiste Minet who had accompanied La Salle on much of his fateful journey; and even a ship's manifest listing all the contents loaded aboard the four vessels for their expedition to the New World.

The elegant handwritten documents were inked in 17th century French, but Reginald said the writing was legible to him and absolutely *fascinate* to read. I could make out a few words, but otherwise it just looked like fancy scribbling on a crinkly, discolored page.

He showed me pages from another diary as well, written by none other than the Sulpician priest, Jean Cavelier, La Salle's own brother. One of the pages inside the folder showed a crude map indicating a cluster of buildings on the bank of a river that fed into a bay.

"Is this the map you used to locate Fort St. Louis?" I asked. "It doesn't seem like much to go on."

"It is one of them, yes, but it is quite authentic. Mr. Dufay paid a very large sum of money to purchase the original document."

I wondered how the cost of the document had anything to do with its historical value or its accuracy, but I held my tongue.

I leaned over and pointed to part of the map. "What does this say? Is it the name of the river?"

"Yes. *Rivière aux Bœufs*—the River of the Beef, but they meant the bison, I think. They say they were quite numerous here in La Salle's time."

"So I've heard. And you boys landed on this particular site, set up camp, and started digging, based on this specific map?" I shook my head. "I gotta admit, I'm not seeing it, Reggie. It seems kinda . . . vague."

"Well, of course Mr. Dufay has other sources, to be sure. One is a very rare document—a journal from *un Père Franciscain,* a Franciscan father, named Pierre Poisson, that precisely identifies the site of the fort." Reginald tilted his head to a medium-size box safe beneath the drafting table.

"And where did this *pièce de résistance* come from?"

Reginald stroked his wispy beard reflectively. "*Docteur* Gillette mentioned that Julien receive the journal as a gift. I believe it was from his brother."

"Can you show it to me?"

Reginald stooped over to twist the combination wheel on the safe. The heavy door opened with a thunk, and he reverently removed a cracked and faded leather-bound journal about the size of a dime-store paperback. He opened it carefully, reverentially, turning the wheat-colored pages very slowly. Many pages were stained by 17th century raindrops, or perhaps tears, and some of the graceful calligraphy was smeared. He turned to a page with a hand-dawn map showing two rivers flowing into a bay labeled *Baie de les Veches.* French word, *veches* . . . Spanish word, *vacas* . . . Lavaca.

"Lavaca Bay?" I asked.

"*Oui.* And here is the fort."

Sure enough, an X bearing the label, *Le Fort Saint-Louis,* was marked on the west bank of the eastern-most river—the Lavaca River.

"Cool. A treasure map," I said. "When I was young, my brother gave me one of those too. Except the 'treasure' was bogus. It turned out to be my own coin collection that the sumbitch stole from my dresser and buried in the backyard. Took me two weeks to find it, and then my dad blistered my ass when he came back from the Gulf and saw three dozen holes in his St. Augustine lawn."

While Reginald locked up the documents, I wandered over to some of the plastic tubs and bins lined up against the wall of the trailer. "Are these some of your latest treasures?"

"*Absolument.*" Reginald then proceeded to show me some of the artifacts that they had discovered on the site. The pottery shards, hawk bells and finger rings I'd seen before, but also some new items: an ax head, a tin cup, a couple of belt buckles. And of course the musket that caused so much excitement last month. In its plastic wrap, the musket stock resembled a rotting stump of oak, the iron lock and barrel long since rusted away.

He moved to another plastic container, a large one filled with water. "*Ce trésor,*" he said with excitement, "is the verso, or the swivel gun. A movable canon that was no doubt mounted on *La Belle* for defense against enemy ships." An indistinct chunk of metal about three feet long lay in the bottom of the tub, and Reginald raised his eyebrows to communicate the significance of this recent find.

"Impressive," I said. "It looks like you've made some progress after all, eh? But you still haven't found the foundations for the fort?"

"No, but we keep looking."

"I tell you what, Reggie. I agree that this is important work y'all are doing here, and it's no good that you and the crew are stranded out here with no access to critical supplies, like mosquito repellent and toilet paper. It looks like you're low on groceries, too. Hell, your cook's resorted to chasing down supper in the woods. What do you say I make a trip to town and pick up a few things? If I run into Antoine, and he's already taken care of it, great, I'll give him a hand hauling back the supplies. He's going to need help anyway if he got another compressor and pump."

"That would be very good Mr. Sweetwater. The men cannot work without the supplies, no?"

"That's right," I said, although I knew a shortage of supplies did not explain or forgive the lack of work and the complete abandonment of discipline at the camp. "But here's the thing, Reginald. I need two men to help me with the supplies and the boat. Especially with the river running the way it is."

"But Mr. Dufay has forbidden—"

"I'll talk with Julien," I said, exiting the office. "Thanks for the history lesson. I'll pick my own guys."

On the trip down river I told Hoyt and Dodo about Judson's death. Hoyt did not take it well.

Dodo gave a low whistle and put his arm clumsily around the boy. "*Mo chagren,* podna. Dat's one damn sad t'ing."

Hoyt asked a few questions—When did it happen? Did his folks know? Where was he shot? Did they know who did it?—and then he went to the bow of the boat and sat cross-legged on the deck, facing forward, shoulders slumped. No crying. Aggies, even potential ones, are supposed to be tough.

I turned to Dodo and raised a questioning eyebrow. "Talk to me."

"Dat boy, Judson, leave by his ownself, him. Pack a bag one night, tell his buddy he don' need dis kind of work, no more, no. He try to get ol' Hoyt to go wit' him but Hoyt, he don't go. So Judson, he shake his podna's hand, tell him he'll see him back in Houston, and den light out inta da dark."

He sighed in either sadness or frustration. "Dat po' *p'tit,* he don' even make twenty."

"Who saw him leave?"

"Everybody be sleepin,' 'cept me and dose two boys, far as I know. Da three stooges, dey been hittin' da bottle pretty good dat night. I hear 'em snorin' like a buncha *cochons.*"

I shook my head. "*Cochons?*" Dodo was giving my smattering of coonass French a workout.

Dodo scratched a mosquito bite. "Like dem hogs, ya know?"

"You're sure somebody didn't go out after him, later in the night maybe?"

"Don't know fo' sure, me. But dey were all in dere beds when I get up to make da coffee in da mornin'."

"Seems like it would've made more sense for Judson to leave during the day. There wasn't anything holding him there—was there?"

Dodo spat into the river and became quiet.

"Dodo, I'm pretty sure Clifton and his asshole buddies shot Sutton's longhorns, so I know they're armed. I also know about the Indian bones y'all covered up at the site. Either of those things have anything to do with Judson having to sneak away at night?"

He nodded. "Clifton and dem others, they 'fraid dat boy gonna spill the beans 'bout who shoot them cows—and 'bout dem bones, too. They don' wanna see no sheriff out der, no sir. 'Fraid de might lose dere bonus money, too."

I recalled the bruises I'd seen on the two boys a couple of weeks ago when I'd questioned them about the dead steers. I didn't think it possible, but my opinion of Clifton, Vinny and Omar dropped a couple more notches.

"What kind of guns do they have in the tent, Dodo?"

He looked at me and smiled. "You pretty well informed fo' a part-time guest."

"I'm trying to figure if their guns match the caliber that killed Judson."

"Dey shoot da Winchester Model 70 . . . 30–06. An' dey got 'em an ol' handgun, too. A 9-millimeter Luger. Fo' snakes, dey say. Dey keep 'em both under a mattress."

"A thirty-aught-six killed Judson."

"It's a popular gun, fo' true. But I'm tellin' you. Dey were sleepin' da night he slip out."

"How about Monroe, He around during any of this?"

Dodo's eyes cut quickly to mine. He shrugged. "He don' come around much, but when he do, he make everbody real nervous. Even Clifton and dem. We don' never know when he gonna show up or why he's dere. Julien say he jus' keeping an eye on da place for his brudda, ya know, but . . . ."

"But what, Dodo?"

"But," He laughed, seemingly at himself. "I don't never see him blink. You notice dat? Just like a gator. Him stand dere, don't move, don't blink. But I get da feelin' he could bite you in half in a second, him. Whatever Jean-Marc's got him on da payroll for, it ain't his good looks."

—

We arrived at the Port Lavaca marina and asked around to see if Antoine or Julien had been there.

"Julien Dufay," said the old man reviewing the slip rental sheet. He pushed his glasses up on his forehead, squinting at the sheet. "The French guy, right?"

"Yep. The same. Wiry, high-strung little guy, with a big nose and a goatee."

"And a hell of a temper, too."

Uh-oh, I thought. "What happened?"

"He a friend of yours?"

I had learned to be careful with that question; being Julien's friend had certain liabilities. "Not really. I'm working with him on a project. My name's Charlie Sweetwater."

"Crenshaw," he replied, shaking my hand. "Well, Sweetwater, he came here three days ago with another Frenchman, that one a little older. Wore eyeglasses, startin' to lose his hair. Pushy fellas, both of 'em. Anyway, the short one, Dufay, he asked where he could buy a motorboat, and I told him about the two or three that were for sale here in the harbor.

"They asked me to show 'em the boats, so I did. Took 'em by each one: a little Hydra-Sport, an old Boston Whaler, and a 15-foot Tracker that needs a new outboard. And then the guy with the glasses, he started complaining about the boats and telling me they were pieces of crap. He used some French word for it, but I knew what he meant. Said I was trying to rip him off, can you believe it? And they're not even my boats. I'm just showing 'em what's for sale at the harbor. Who needs that shit?"

The old guy shook his head in dismay. I could certainly empathize.

"Did they buy a boat?" I asked.

"Oh, hell no, but hold on, it gets better. So the older guy keeps mouthin' off until finally, the short guy tells him to shut it, you know?

"They went rattling on to each other in French from then on, but I got the jist of it. They're getting louder and louder, until they're practically screaming at each other out on the docks, waving their arms like a couple of squirrels fightin' in a sack."

The marina guy demonstrated. They were givin' it this . . . " (he flicked his chin, fingers splayed outward), "and this . . . " (he made a fist and slapped his arm with his other hand), "and of course this . . . ." (the universal single digit). "Man, I coulda sold tickets."

French, I thought, the language of diplomats. "Those Frenchmen would bitch if you hung 'em with a new rope," I said.

Crenshaw gave a short laugh and then continued. "It sounded like the taller guy, the one with glasses, is giving the other one a list of demands. And Dufay, he keeps shaking his head, no, until the taller guy finally gets right up in his face. And then Dufay shoves him and brushes his hands together like he's through with him, you know? And the taller guy stomps his foot and pulls a credit card out of his wallet and throws it in the bay. I'm guessing it was a company credit card. Then he storms off toward the parking lot, madder than a puffed toad."

"Sounds like the two comrades had a falling out, didn't it?"

"Mister, if they didn't, they've got a strange way of gettin' along."

"Seen either of 'em since?"

"Nope. Couple of days ago another guy came in here asking about 'em."

"Who was that?" I asked with interest.

"Didn't give his name—solid looking fella, though. Black hair, had some old scars on his face, like zits, you know?"

Monroe, for a fact. Was he following Julien? Or was he two steps ahead?

"Hey, you know what?" Crenshaw pulled a clipboard off a peg and studied it a moment. "Yep. It says here their slip's still paid through the end of the month. Since y'all know each other, you're welcome to use it if ya want, 'though if you're a friend of theirs, God help ya."

"Thanks, but I'm just picking up supplies. In fact, I could do with a couple of 25-gallon tanks of diesel and some tie-downs and come-alongs to secure 'em."

Crenshaw not only helped us load supplies on the boat, but he loaned me his truck so we could pick up the other items on our list.

"Drive safe," he said. "But if you get a chance to run over one of them Francypants on the way, be my guest."

Hoyt waited in the truck while Dodo and I picked up a compressor and a water pump at the supply store. The kid seemed to be in a fog. I doubted he'd ever lost someone to violence before—let alone a friend.

As we loaded up, it occurred to me that the boy needed to check in with his folks. They would have heard about Judson, and they'd be worried sick about their son. I sure as hell would be.

I located a phone booth and sat in the truck while Hoyt called his mom collect. He slumped against the glass as he talked, his eyes closed tight.

"The funeral's day after tomorrow," he said when he got back in the cab. "In Sugarland."

"I'll stake you to a bus ticket," I said. "You need to be there, son. The job will keep."

"How can you be sure? Mr. Dufay—"

"Don't worry about Julien. He'll be cool with it. I promise." *Or I'll damn well twist his parrot's beak nose until he is,* I thought to myself.

At Port Lavaca's sad little Greyhound station, I told the boy he might think about finding another job before he started college. "There's plenty of other backbreaking jobs out there in the real world. Find one that allows you to let off some steam on the weekends."

"Yes, Sir," he mumbled. "I'll think about it."

Dodo lit a cigarette and regarded the boy. 'Tit' Hoyt, you in a *mal pris*—a bad place. Ya keep ya chin up, you."

Hoyt smiled for the first time, wanly. "Don't they have some kind of Cajun proverb for that, Dodo?"

The little cook smiled back. "Lemme drink a Jax beer and t'ink on dat."

——

CHAPTER 17

We returned to the site around lunchtime the next day. Dodo had convinced me to spring for twenty pounds of barbeque for the crew, along with gallon buckets of pintos, coleslaw and potato salad—he took his camp cook responsibilities seriously. "Dem boys be eatin' nutria if I ain't dere," he said.

The crew descended on the food like javelinas at a deer corn feeder.

While they ate, Reginald beckoned me into the field office. "The Ranger man you spoke about, he came by here yesterday, after you left. He came in a strange boat with a, how do you say? A *hélice,* like on a airplane. Very loud."

"It was an airboat." O.B. Hadnott hated airboats.

"Okay, yes. He was with two other men, men in green uniforms."

"Probably the Texas Parks and Wildlife boys. What did they want?"

"Charlie, do you know that one of the crew, the young man, Judson Strayhorn, he was found dead?"

"I heard."

"It is hard to believe."

"Yes, it is. Did the Ranger question the men?"

"He question all of us, Charlie. And then he leaves again on the *hélice de bateau.*"

I was curious to know what O.B. had learned from crew, but I would have to wait until I saw him again.

Suddenly Reginald furrowed his brows and stuck his head out the door, eying the camp anxiously. "Where is Antoine? Where is Julien? They came back with you, yes?"

"'Fraid not, Reginald. Antoine quit the job. Probably for good. And nobody seems to know where Julien is. It looks like you're still The Man."

He sat down heavily in the chair, his head dropping to his chest. For a moment I thought he was going to cry. "This cannot be."

"Come on, Reggie, cowboy up. Try to see this as an opportunity— your chance to head up a world-class archeological project, serve your country, maybe even earn a Legion of Honor that you can pin to your chest."

"But the men do not respect me."

"Then *earn* their respect. Lead by example. Let them know how important their work is."

Reginald continued to shake his head, so I continued with my pep talk. "Hell, show 'em the ship manifest and tell 'em exactly what they're looking for. While you're at it, be sure and remind them that there's a big bonus waiting if they find the settlement."

"They will not listen to me, Charlie." He looked at me pleadingly. "I cannot do this." His head sunk again. "I hate this place," he mumbled.

A scene from the movie *Patton* popped into my head, when George C. Scott slapped around the shell-shocked soldier in the MASH tent. *"I won't have cowards in my army!"* For a second I thought about slapping the frightened little Frenchman; instead, I marched out to the mess tent and planted myself in the middle of the men.

"Listen up, guys! Julien Dufay sent me here to tell you that when he's not here, Reggie's in charge. Antoine's not coming back, and Julien says you can do what his new chief archeologist says, or you can find another job and kiss your bonus *adiós*. It's your choice. He also said he doesn't want any more drinking, he doesn't want any more smoking weed, and he doesn't want any more grab-ass. And he by-God better see some progress by the time he gets back!"

Christ, I felt like I was channeling my inner Texas football coach. Well, somebody had to get the project kick-started again.

I repeated the whole spiel in Spanish for the Mexican workers, and they nodded in accordance. They were glad to get back to work. The sooner they finished this job and wired a big share of the money home, the sooner they could move on to roofing or drywall or row-picking or any of the other shithole jobs most "real" Americans passed over.

Clifton, Vinny and Omar never looked up from their barbeque, trying hard to appear tough, self-possessed and indifferent, doing their best to pretend I wasn't even there. But I know they could feel me staring at them. Clifton made a show of dumping his plate of food onto the ground in front of him.

"Now, why you go and waste dem good groceries for, Mr. Sloan?"

"Shut the fuck up, Dodo," said Clifton.

—

As I motored downstream I began wondering about Julien. At first I wondered if his non-appearance was just him being Julien, irresponsibly abandoning his project at the worst possible time, probably to rush off to New York or Milan to bid on an overpriced Rauschenberg Combine for his museum. (I'd seen one once before, in New York. Damn thing looked like a glorified trash pile.) In the last week his jobsite had almost been washed away, his lead archeologist had quit, and his men were slacking off and getting wasted on his dime. So, where was he? On top of all that, there was Judson's murder, the ultimate bad juju of the whole snake-bit operation.

By the time I reached Port Lavaca, my mood was not much improved. I had decided to hunt down Julien, partially because I wanted to channel my negativity toward something specific, and also because I was worried about the son of a bitch. Where had he gone? Someday I was going to have to resolve my conflicting feelings about the guy, but not today.

I headed for the marina and used Crenshaw's phone to call Julien's home number. Marguerite answered on the fifth ring. It was two o'clock in the afternoon, still early in the day for her. She told me her husband was at the work site. He had declined to go back to Houston after the cofferdam tour.

"I've just been to the site, Marguerite, and he hasn't been there. I guess he's probably at the ranch."

"*Quoi?*" There was a sudden urgency in her voice. "Are you sure, Charlie? What has happened?"

"Nothing. It's no big deal. I was in the neighborhood and just wanted to tell him hello, that's all." I didn't want to tell her the real reason I was at the camp.

"Something bad has happened, hasn't it?"

Was I somehow telegraphing my concern? Damned women's intuition.

"No, of course not. I'm sorry to bother you at home. I just didn't want to waste a trip to the ranch if he was with you in Houston."

"You will call me if he is not there, okay Charlie? Promise me you will."

"Sure, okay. I'll call you either way. You can talk to him yourself."

Why was she so jumpy? I thought back to the last time I'd seen Julien, sitting slumped over on the stern of the *Anomaly*, Marguerite trying to comfort him. I had been pretty upset at the way the *Belle* tour went down. My esteemed French guests had embarrassed the hell out me in front of Jim and Holly. Mostly I was pissed off at Antoine, the insufferable prick. For three days I had been brooding about how the whole fiasco had affected me, but now I thought I could guess how it had affected Julien.

The contrast between the projects couldn't have been more obvious. One site was efficient, energetic, pioneering in its methods and hugely productive. The other site looked like a group of strung-out day workers had been rounded up from under the bridge in Corpus and were half-heartedly digging ditches in the woods. Julien couldn't have failed to notice the difference.

I left my boat in the marina, and Crenshaw gave me a ride to my car. "I'll pick up my boat later if that's okay with you, Mr. Crenshaw."

"Like I said. There's an empty slip that's paid up through the month. You're welcome to it."

I arrived at the Kestrel Ranch gate and found it locked. The chain I'd snapped before had been replaced, and I didn't have combinations for any of the locks, so I waited until the next visitor came along, which didn't take long. A nondescript rental car pulled up, and a kid in his late twenties dressed in Dockers and a white button-down shirt got out to spin the combination on the lock.

"You work for DeBergerac?" the kid asked when I rolled down my window.

"Yeah, friend of Mr. Dufay." I didn't say which one. He nodded and opened the gate. "Go ahead and drive through first," I said. "I'll lock it back. Hey, do you remember the combination? I forget it every time."

A long spume of white caliche dust trailed my pickup as I traveled down the unpaved road to the ranch house where I hoped to find Julien. A road crew had added a fresh layer of dirt and gravel after the rain. When I arrived at the big house, there were at least a dozen cars parked outside: pickup trucks with DeBergerac logos on the side and more rental sedans. Inside, the place buzzed with activity. Earnest-looking men were working in groups throughout the house, some of them young and clean-cut, some middle-aged with short-sleeve shirts, neckties and pocket protectors. A few of the men looked up from their conversations and computers and eyed me curiously.

The Hispanic cook walked into the room with a platter of tamales for the guests. I spoke to her in Spanish, and she told me she hadn't seen Julien since we'd last been there together.

The kid I'd met at the gate was heading outside with some rolled-up plans and a folder under his arm, so I walked out behind him.

"You going to the well site, too?" he asked.

"Yeah, which one you going to?" I wanted to learn more about DeBergerac's activities on the ranch. Maybe my newfound buddy would help fill me in.

"Twenty-six."

"Hey, me too. I'll follow you."

I could see the drilling tower on Well 26 rising out of the post oak and mesquite two miles before we got to the site. As we pulled up to the rig I was blown away by the magnitude of the project. The graded caliche pad covered eight to ten acres, and in addition to the five trailers (the toolpusher's office and roughnecks' dog houses, I assumed) there were a dozen silver tanker trucks, a long row of stationary fiberglass storage tanks, and miles of stacked steel pipe crowding the pad. Four industrial generators provided power to the site.

My inadvertent tour guide stopped his car in front of one of the trailers, so I pulled up next to him. I must have been gawking, because he walked over and asked if this was my first visit here.

"Yeah, it is. I wasn't sure what to expect."

"What's your position here?" he asked in a friendly tone. "You with the drilling crew or the seismograph crew?"

"Independent," I answered. "Landman, working with Mr. Dufay."

He nodded. "The company uses a lot of independent landmen. I don't know half of them. But I can see why they hire you guys. If somebody with a DeBergerac business card starts researching a property, every drilling company around tries to get in on the play."

I shook my head knowingly. "Tell me about it. What is it you do?"

"Fracture monitoring."

"Say again?"

"I help monitor and measure the fractures in the shale . . . you know, to determine how much pressure to apply and how often. You know much about hydraulic fracturing?"

"Not a damned thing. I've been around a lot of wells, but I don't remember seeing a site like this before." We had to shout at each other over the roar of the gennys and the rumble of the machinery.

He laughed. "No, you wouldn't have. The basic fracking technology has been around for a while, but mostly experimental, you know? This is our first full-scale rig that uses our new technology. The other twenty-five were just little test wells and prototypes."

"Fracking, huh? Looks like you boys have gone all-in on this one. It's pretty impressive. How's it work?"

"Well, we drill down to the shale layer, which happens to be relatively shallow in this area—first we go vertical and then horizontal—and then we set off explosives to open up fissures in the shale. After that we pump a slurry of water, sand and chemicals into the fissures at very high pressures, which creates larger fissures, which then releases the gas that's trapped inside. The results are pretty exciting."

"I bet they are. What kind of chemicals you use in that slurry?"

"Heck if I know. That's another division. But I know it's proprietary. Gives DeBergerac the edge in the field. I hear it's pretty nasty stuff. After they use it they pump it out of the well, load it in trucks and haul it off."

"Glad I don't have to pay the hauling bills."

"No kidding. Hey, you said you're a landman. Have y'all secured the drilling rights on the ranch bordering this one, yet?"

"You mean the Sutton Ranch?"

"Yeah, that's the one. That's where the seismograph boys say all the gas is located."

"We're still working on it," I lied.

"Well, you must have made *some* progress, because I heard that the lawyers have just about locked it up."

Somebody yelled for my new friend, so he said goodbye and disappeared into one of the trailers. I left the site and swung by the ranch house one more time to ask about Julien. Nobody had seen him or heard from him. I was about to leave when one guy spoke up.

"If you wait around a few minutes you can ask his brother, Jean-Marc. He's on his way here now from Houston."

Sure enough, five minutes later a company helicopter came buzzing in from the east. I stood by my old truck and waited for the chopper to settle onto the concrete pad built to the side of the house. Jean-Marc stepped down from the passenger side of the cockpit wearing a stylish light-grey suit. The air from the rotor blades didn't disturb one hair on his well-gelled head.

I cut him off before he reached the front door of the house. "Hello, Jean-Marc, I'm Charlie Sweetwater, a friend of your brother's. We met in your office in Houston a few months ago."

He shouldered by me impatiently and kept walking. "Whatever it is, take it to your supervisor."

"No, it's nothing like that. I don't work for the company. I'm here about your brother."

Jean-Marc looked at me for the first time. I could tell by his surprised expression that he recognized me. "Go . . . away," he said coldly, attempting to shoo me away with his hand as he walked off. I grabbed his wrist, a gold cufflink biting into my palm.

"Hey, Johnny-Mack. Why don't you just listen to me for *one minute.*" He turned, startled and outraged at the same time. "I just want to ask you if you've seen your brother in the last three days. Nobody seems to know where he is."

He wrenched his hand free and stepped back. "Do not *ever* touch me again, do you understand?"

I laughed. "Jesus, you're a self-important SOB. I'm guessing the answer is no, you haven't seen Julien?"

Jean-Marc stormed into the house, and I could hear him ordering some of the workers to throw me off the ranch immediately. A moment later a couple of the computer geeks peeked around the doorway to get a look at who it was they were supposed to evict. They were unsure about what to do next.

I laughed at the timid faces. This wasn't in their job description. "Don't worry, gentlemen, I was just leaving."

FROM THE JOURNAL OF PÈRE POISSON

It was during the Feast of the Martyrdom of John the Baptist that La Salle was overcome by a great melancholy. He has isolated himself and withdrawn from his duties. Some sort of blackness seems to have settled over him. Almost all of the workmen feel his absence to be a kind of blessing.

Père Poisson
NOVEMBER 1685

CHAPTER 18

The next afternoon I returned to Port Lavaca to pick up my boat. I decided to drop by Miguel's marina for a beer and some helpful advice. I needed an objective, disinterested perspective on what had been going on.

It was disinterested all right.

"Who gives a shit?" Miguel rumbled from his barstool behind the counter. I had just recounted the events of the last few days, and he hadn't looked up once from his wrestling magazine. I saw that *Mil Máscaras* was on the cover of this month's issue.

"I know what you're thinking, Miguel. You're thinking I'm getting what I deserve for not minding my own business. You're thinking I'm in over my head."

He flipped a page and scratched his collarbone with a coarse, tattooed hand.

"You're thinking I'm mixing with people I have no business mixing with, right?" I took a long swig of beer. "Well, maybe you're right, *amigo*. Maybe I ought to wash my hands of the whole mess and focus on doing what I do best: shrimping, fishing, providing local color. Stick to my skill set, you know?"

Miguel continued to scan *Super Luchas,* his dark, pitted face as expressionless as a carved Olmec head.

I set the empty longneck on the counter. "It's decided then. The hell with all of 'em." I rose from my stool and prepared to leave. "I'm glad we had this talk, Miguel. I feel like we shared a moment there."

I'd pushed open the screen door when I heard Miguel clear his throat behind me. It sounded like someone shoveling gravel.

"Hey, *pendejo*," he said in a low voice. "That French *maricón* you're looking for is at the Palacios Hotel. In case you're wondering."

"Julien Dufay? At the Grand Hotel Palacios? Now why in the hell would you know that, Miguel?"

"It's a small town. I know people there."

"Ah, that's right. I forgot you've got a sweetie over there. How's that going, by the way, her being all the way across the bay and everything?"

"You just decided to start minding your own business, remember?"

"Well, yeah, that's true. But because you've been such a great listener today, I feel the need to repay the favor and offer some advice. Have you ever heard the saying, *Amor de lejos es amor de pendejos?*" (*Long distance love is for dumbasses.*)

"Have you ever heard the saying 'fuck off'?"

—

The Grand Hotel Palacios was a rambling, three-story Greek Revival that fronted Tres Palacios Bay. It was an absurdly outsized structure for the small, one-time rice farming community. Back in its day, the hotel had hosted Big Band hit-makers and movie stars. Now the sagging three-story clapboard building, with its small rooms, eccentric décor and water-stained wallpaper, persisted in a state of genial decline.

I climbed the steps to the entrance and greeted a group of old men sitting in ladder-back rocking chairs on the colonnaded front porch, smoking cigarettes. Cash-strapped pensioners or crapped-out snowbirds, I guessed, who had decided to make their last stand at this venerable old dowager of a once-grand hotel on the edge of the Gulf. I wondered for a morbid second if I was glimpsing my own future. However, these three guys seemed pretty cheerful about things.

"Afternoon, mister," said one old duffer wearing light cotton coveralls and a Panama hat.

"Have a beer?" asked his neighbor, nodding to a Styrofoam cooler sitting at his feet. He was holding a tallboy, alternating sips with puffs on a Lucky Strike.

"Thanks, gentlemen. But I'm looking for a fellow who's supposed to be a guest at the hotel. A Frenchman, probably checked in two or three days ago."

"Oh yeah, a short, stringy guy. Remember him, Sam? I believe it was three days ago he showed up."

"Yeah," said Sam. "No suitcase. Never said a word when he checked in. Kind of an odd fella. You say he's a Frenchmen?"

"Yeah," I answered, "A real one."

"Well, that's a hell of a thing. I never seen one, least not that I know of. I guess he's still here, but ain't no one seen hide nor hair of him."

"He's holed up up there," said the skinniest guy, pointing upwards toward the tall portico roof above him, "In the Rita Hayworth Suite."

I thanked the old coot brigade and went inside. Nothing much had changed since the last time I'd wandered through the old hotel. The lobby was dimly lit, and the whole place smelled like my grandmother's house. It was filled with over-stuffed antique furniture and featured a grand piano whose surface was covered with condensation rings from countless highballs. Dark-stained bookshelves lined the room, and dozens of vintage black and white photos hung on the wall.

Despite the stuck-in-time shabbiness of the place, it still whispered of a vibrant and glamorous past. On the staircase wall, an array of autographed photos of famous guests caught my eye—Benny Goodman, Bob Hope, Delores del Rio and, yep, Rita Hayworth. *Zowie.*

I dinged the bell at the front desk, and a middle-aged man in an open hula shirt stretched over an undershirt appeared from a room behind the office, wiping his mouth. Over his shoulder I could see a TV dinner sitting on a tray in front of the television set. *Walker, Texas Ranger* was on. O.B. Hadnott thought that show was a load of shit.

"Welcome to the Grand Hotel Palacios," he said. "How can I help you?"

"I'm here to see a guest by the name of Julien Dufay. He checked in here three days ago."

"Oh, yeah, the French fellow. He's on the third floor, room 313."

"Thanks," I answered, a little surprised he was so forthcoming with the room information. "Is he there now?"

The man looked back at the rack of room key nooks; there was only one compartment without a key, the one with the little brass 313 plaque over the cubbyhole. "Looks like he's still in there, mister," he said. "To be honest, I haven't seen him or heard from him since he checked in. I figured he'd get hungry at least, wouldn't you think?"

"You'd think."

What I in fact thought was that this old hotel would be a great place to hide out, to take yourself off the grid. At least until someone walked up to the front desk and asked for you. And what were the odds of someone looking for someone like Julien at a hotel like this?

As I walked down the creaking long-leaf pine hallway toward Julien's room, I felt a knot of apprehension growing in my chest. This was the kind of place where people came to die: either happily, like my friends on the porch, or unhappily, and perhaps by their own hand. There were ghosts in this place. I knocked on the door of room 313.

"Julien? You in there? It's me, Charlie."

No answer. I knocked again, harder, and then put my ear to the door. I could hear a ceiling fan whirling away, but no other sound or movement. I pulled out my Blockbuster Video card and jimmied the spring bolt until the latch slid back, and the door popped open.

With the shades drawn, the only light in the room came through the hallway and from sunlight seeping in around the edges of dirty venetian blinds. The Rita Hayworth Suite, indeed.

I looked nervously around the sitting room and saw no sign of it being occupied. At some point during the last forty years a rusty fridge and a stained enamel kitchenette had been appended to the room to accommodate long-term guests. No dirty plates or food wrappers were evident, and the only used dish I could see was a chipped ceramic mug sitting in the sink.

"Julien?" I repeated.

A tiny bathroom adjoined the sitting room. I jerked on a long pull-string which lit a bare light bulb on the ceiling. I held my breath and threw back the plastic shower curtain, not knowing what to expect, but found the tub empty except for the silverfish that scurried toward the safety of the drain.

A hand-carved sleigh bed filled the bedroom, and I noticed a crescent-shaped lump under the covers. I approached cautiously and patted the inert figure on the back. "Julien? Is that you, buddy?"

The body rolled over slowly, and Julien turned his face to me, his bleary eyes blank and uncomprehending, his unshaven face slack, like he was coming off a King Kong-sized bender. He smelled nearly as rank as he looked.

"Jesus, man. You look terrible." I raised the blinds in the bedroom, and late afternoon sunshine flooded the room. He flinched at the sudden infusion of light. "We've been worried about you."

"Shut them," he said.

I lowered the blinds to three-quarters and went into the kitchen to wash out the mug and fill it with water. He refused to take it when I held it out. "When's the last time you ate, Julien?"

He blinked dully and closed his eyes. "Go away."

"No can do, *amigo*. Marguerite would have my ass. And you've got people depending on you." Standing over him, I took note of his ringed eyes, his tousled hair and his wrinkled shirt. "But first we need to get some food in your skinny French belly."

The phone in the room didn't work, so I went downstairs and asked the manager to order a quart of *caldo de pollo* from the local Mexican food restaurant.

"I'm not sure they deliver," he said, "but I can call 'em and ask."

I gave him a twenty-dollar bill. "Whatever it takes. Keep the change. By the way, what's your name?"

"Carl."

"Carl, I'm Charlie. I'd be much obliged if you'd bring it upstairs when it arrives." I started to put away my wallet and then opened it back up and pulled out another couple of twenties.

"Hey, while you're at it, I know it's not your job, but do you think you could pick up a quart of milk, along with a fifth of scotch at the liquor store? It's kind of like medicine for the guy upstairs."

"Sure thing, Charlie. Hair of the dog and all that."

"He's not a drunk."

"Oh, sorry. What's wrong with him then? Is he gonna be alright?"

"He will once I get some food in him."

I sat with Julien in the bedroom until Carl arrived with the soup and the bottles.

"Julien," I said, "I'm going to ladle you up some of this here Mexican soup, and I want you to try and eat it. It's not a Marseilles *bouillabaisse* but it doesn't look half-bad." I selected a bowl from the mismatched dish set above the sink and brought him the soup and a handful of saltines. Julien turned away when I held out the tray.

"Okay, here's the deal, Jules. Either you're going to feed yourself or I'm going to spoon feed you like you were a spoiled little toddler— and that's not going to be any fun for either of us."

He sat up against the oak headboard and glared at me through bloodshot eyes. "If I eat will you go away?"

"I don't know yet. Probably not. I might just stay and make you have a drink with me, too. You look like you could use one."

He ate about half the soup and a package of crackers and then held out the tray mutely.

I took the tray and gave him a large glass of water, which he did finish. With some effort, he got up and wandered dispiritedly into the bathroom. He was fully clothed, as if he'd been dumped into bed three days ago like a sack of laundry. Through the door I saw him stare at his unshaven face in the mirror.

I pulled the sheets off the bed and dug around in the closet for some fresh linens, leaving them folded at the end of the sagging mattress lest Julien return to the hole he had dug for himself under the covers. I poured a glass of scotch-and-milk for the invalid and a double shot, neat, for myself, and opened the French doors that gave out onto the suite's small balcony. Across the sloping lawn Tres Palacios Bay shimmered in the fading light.

A few minutes later Julien came outside, drying his face with a hand towel. "How did you find me?"

"Friend of a friend." He took the drink and collapsed into a wrought-iron patio chair on the balcony.

"Is this is your idea of a vacation resort?" I asked. "It's a little down-scale from what you're used to, isn't it?"

He sipped his scotch-milk punch slowly. "What day is it?"

"Friday. You've been here three days, in case you didn't know. I can drive you to Houston if you're ready to go home."

His head drooped between sips, as if he didn't have the energy to hold it up.

"If you're not up to it, I'll call Marguerite and tell her you're here. Should I call your brother, too?"

He looked up quickly. "No. Not him." He closed his eyes tight and began talking, as if to himself. I could barely make out his words. "I am tired of his pressure to hurry up. *Dépêchez-vous! Dépêchez-vous!* Hurry and finish the project!" Then he started speaking softly in French until his voice became inaudible.

"Why the hurry, Julien?" I said after he became quiet. "It is *your* project. Isn't it?"

"He shook his head slowly. "No. My brother set the conditions."

I remembered Marguerite telling me that Jean-Marc had "sponsored" the project. "Conditions?" I asked.

"I have the one chance and then, *pouf,* it is over, and he will . . . ."

"He will what, Julien?"

"My family hates a failure," he said weakly. He went inside, dumped his mug and poured three fingers of Cutty Sark. Straight, this time.

We sipped our scotch in the twilight.

"Hey, I dropped by the site yesterday," I began, "and Reginald said to tell you he's working out a pretty exciting dig strategy he thinks will put you on more artifacts. Things seem to be moving forward." Right now didn't seem a good time to tell Julien that his life's pursuit was floundering, and a kid had been murdered after fleeing his camp.

Julien rearranged himself and looked me in the eye for the first time.

"Listen to me, Charlie. The project is hopeless—a failure. I am a failure. Stop lying to me and acting like you care what happens. I do not want sympathy from you, or my family. I just want . . . to be left . . . alone."

He leaned his head against the building and closed his eyes, his face contorted with tension and pain. He seemed to be in the grip of some terrible emotion or distress. At length his face softened and relaxed. I don't think he was sleeping; it was more as if he had withdrawn into a cocoon. Whatever fit had seized him abated, for the moment.

Clinical depression, maybe? But I wasn't a shrink, and I wasn't any closer to figuring out Julien Dufay than I was the night he swam up to my boat. I walked him inside, eased him onto the couch and covered him with the blanket.

"I'm calling Marguerite," I said. "I'll be back in a minute."

After I made the call, I sat in the dark room with Julien for three more hours, until I heard voices in the hallway. I met Marguerite and Laurent at the door and began describing Julien's bizarre behavior.

"I already know," said Marguerite. "This is not the first time." She caressed my cheek. "*Merci,* Charlie. Thank you so much for being our friend. Now, will you please help me move him to the car so I can take him home?"

———

I sometimes wonder whether La Salle knows where this "great river" is located at all. Suppose it lies hundreds of leagues to the west? Suppose we sailed well past it? Who would know?

Père Poisson

DECEMBER 1685

CHAPTER 19

I carefully wrapped two long slabs of venison backstrap in butcher paper and iced them down in the cooler—a gift from Raul, who'd just returned from a Hill Country deer hunt. Only in Texas would raw meat from a fresh-killed whitetail buck be an appropriate way to show a gal you care. Or at least I hoped it would. I decided I'd better throw in a couple of bottles of Bordeaux claret just in case— it would be a nice pairing for the meat.

I felt I should to apologize to Holly for the bad behavior of my French companions at the cofferdam the week before. I'd already made the appropriate apologies to Jim Brannan. A bottle of 21-year-old single-malt scotch did the trick. I also told him about Julien's search for La Salle's fort, minus the particulars. It seemed silly not to mention the project after Jim had opened his cofferdam doors, so to speak, for the moody Frenchman. I could tell Jim was disappointed he wasn't involved in the project himself, but it wasn't in him to be resentful.

"I wish the man luck," he said. He also offered to share THC resources and expertise with Julien, if he wanted it. I could have told him, but didn't, not to hold his breath.

It was a beautiful December morning, so I decided to leave at the crack of dawn and cruise over to Palacios in the Riva, my new Italian muscle boat. I had to admit, it was kind of fun flying by the lumbering tugboats as they pushed their heavy barges down the Intracoastal Waterway, the boat captains gawking at me and my glamorous play toy. But another part of me felt like a big fat poser. It was a vain and impractical vessel for the blue-collar Texas coast—like having a Maserati on a cotton farm. I knew that eventually, I'd have to get rid of it. But not just yet.

Besides seeing Holly, I had another reason for going to Palacios: the county courthouse. Julien's comment about his brother pushing him for progress on the Lavaca River project got me to thinking. Jean-Marc didn't strike me as the kind of guy who would give a rat's ass about a dead French explorer—unless, as Marguerite had said, it had something to do with *le gaz*. The guy at the Kestrel Ranch said the DeBergerac lawyers had all but "locked up" the mineral rights to Sutton's land. Had Clyde Sutton decided to play ball with DeBergerac? It seemed unlikely, but many's the rough old boy who did an about-face once he saw the size of those royalty checks.

"That's where the gas is located," the kid had said. Jean-Marc's *"pot of gold,"* as Marguerite had described it. Maybe the Texas General Land Office and the Calhoun County Clerk could help me figure out what Julien's brother was up to.

I tied off at an empty slip outside the Texas Historical Commission project headquarters—a converted waterfront warehouse now used by the THC to examine, treat and store the artifacts from the *Belle* excavation. A young woman wearing rubber boots and a Texas A&M sweatshirt was hosing down plastic tubs on the dock.

"Hi, there," I said.

"Hi, yourself," she said cheerfully. The girl was fresh-faced and perky, probably an Aggie grad student from the archeology program.

"Is Holly around?"

"No, Sir. She's at the site, but everyone's coming back early evething. Mr. Brannan gave us the day off tomorrow."

"He's getting soft in his old age."

The girl laughed. "No, he's all happy because the Governor sent us an awesome letter this week thanking us for uncovering a 'real Texas treasure.' Nice huh?"

"Real nice. I guess y'all have earned a break."

"Have you been out to the site?"

"A couple of times. It's remarkable."

"It's *totally* remarkable," she said, twisting the nozzle on the hose sprayer to shut off the water. "I've only been working here for a month. Thirty days straight, no break—but it's been worth every minute."

"Can't get any better field training than this."

"No, Sir. That's for sure."

"Does Holly also have tomorrow off?" I asked.

"I doubt it. She's been on the site every day since the project started. And as soon as she gets back here, she works some more in the lab."

"If she shows up before I get back, tell her Charlie Sweetwater came by looking for her. I don't want to miss her before she goes home."

"Oh, you won't miss her. She never goes *out*, except to the site. You do know that she *lives* here, right? Above the lab?" The girl widened her eyes and nodded emphatically to communicate, I guess, the extremity of Holly's dedication. "I mean, she has a real house in Galveston and everything, but for the past six months . . . ." She cocked a thumb at the warehouse.

"No kidding," I said.

"In fact, all of us stay here—at least we do when we're working on the project. It's sorta like living in an army barracks or something. At first it was kinda cool, but I am *soo* ready for my own bed, my own bathroom. Ready for some, you know, *privacy*. You learn *waay* too much about your roommates when you live together like this."

"I bet you do. If you ever decide you like living in community quarters, you let me know. I'll hire you out to work on my shrimp boat. Two weeks sharing an 8-by-12 cabin with a couple of co-workers and you'll know each other inside and out, I promise you.

"Ha ha, no thanks."

"So, I should come back when? Around five?"

"That would be my guess."

"I'll see if I can talk Holly into getting out of the lab for a little while, maybe treat her to a fancy dinner."

The field student laughed. "In *this* town? Good luck."

"Any recommendations?"

"Just remember the Dairy Queen closes at nine."

—

The Calhoun County courthouse was only a short walk from the harbor, and the road took me through the heart of the small town. Not even a hundred years old, and Palacios' future was already forty years behind it.

It had been a bustling training center for the National Guard and, later, for anti-aircraft gunners in the Second World War. During that time, the population swelled and the nightlife became vibrant enough to attract the likes of Anita O'Day and Glenn Miller, who entertained in a big pavilion out over the water. But things went downhill fast after the war ended, and downright plummeted after two vicious hurricanes ravaged the town. The only people who seemed to be thriving these days were the Holy Rollers—there were fifteen churches and a year-round Baptist camp retreat in the community—and shrimpers, primarily Vietnamese post-war immigrants who settled there in the late seventies. That old maverick Edward Abbey hit the nail on the head: "Any town with more churches than bars has an incipient social problem."

The courthouse was Palacios' most distinctive feature—a monolithic two-story stone structure with arched windows and a squat bulbous dome sitting atop the central tower like a jaunty red party hat. Romanesque Revival architecture had a brief but indelible impact on Texas courthouse design in the first half of the century. Architects, especially architects from the Eastern seaboard, thought a Moorish theme would be an appropriate flourish for their Gulf Coast projects. They said the palm trees and humidity reminded them of northern Africa. But Palacios was no Casablanca. Not even close.

The County Clerk's office was on the second floor of the courthouse, and a woman sitting at a high desk guarded the entrance to the cavernous room behind her. The woman's name was Sylvia; it said so right on her nametag. She looked about what you'd expect a woman working in a county records office to look like. Because I had no idea how to research land titles and lease proposals and such, I decided on the upfront approach.

"Sylvia, I'm new at this. If I wanted to find out who owns the mineral rights on a certain ranch, where would I look and what would I look for?"

Sylvia peered at me over her glasses. "You a landman?"

"No ma'am. Shrimper. Hardly know my way around on dry land."

"I see. Do you know the name of the ranch?"

"It belongs to a man by the name of Clyde Sutton, and I guess it's registered as the Sutton Ranch. The Lavaca River runs right through the middle of it. You heard of it?"

She pursed her lips. "Of course I have. Once again, it seems to be the most popular ranch in Calhoun County, at least in this office."

"Why do you say that?"

"Because every landman and every oil and gas lawyer from Midland to Houston has been through the file on that ranch at one time or another." She narrowed her eyes. "Why are *you* here, if you're a shrimper?"

"The old man's sort of a friend of mine."

"Sort of a drunk, if you ask me."

"He's had a rough time."

"Rough's no excuse, mister."

I guessed that she was a stalwart member of one of the community's many churches—one of the non-drinking denominations.

"Why all the interest in his ranch?" I asked.

"At first it was because of the lawsuits with the refinery—that was quite a while ago—but lately everybody's interested in the mineral rights."

"So, what have all these lawyers and landmen found?" I asked.

"I'm not doing your work for you, mister."

"Okay, Sylvia. You win. Can you at least point me in the right direction?"

She sighed, as if the effort was almost too much for her to bear. "There's an index book, over there, third aisle. Under 'S.' Do you think you can find it on your own?" she asked with a frown.

"Sure I can," I answered. "Under 'S' . . . for surly."

Sylvia looked at me sharply and decided to throw one last jab. "If Clyde doesn't settle up his property taxes soon, his name's not going to be the last name on that ranch."

"Sutton owes back taxes?"

"Like I said, do your own homework."

I thumbed through some of Sutton's well-thumbed-through documents, but I didn't understand enough about deeds and contracts and clauses to make any sense of it. I saw some official looking correspondence from the County Tax-Assessor in the folder and remembered seeing a sign in the foyer of the courthouse saying that their office was on the first floor. Maybe they could help.

The tax clerk's name was Maureen, and she must have been Sylvia's good twin. When I asked her about Sutton's problem with the back taxes, she patted me on the hand.

"Well, hon, Sylvia's right. Clyde sort of neglected to pay his property taxes for the past five years."

"Don't y'all send out notices?"

"Of course we do, sweetie. Like clockwork. But we never got a response. We've been in what they call the 'redemptive phase' for two years, but . . . not even a phone call."

"Where do you send the notices?"

"I don't generally remember every landowner's address, but I think Mr. Sutton's tax notices went to an estate lawyer in Victoria."

I couldn't believe Clyde would risk losing the family ranch over a tax problem with the county, not without putting up a fight. I wondered if he even knew he had a problem. Maybe his lawyer in Victoria assumed his client had taken care of the property taxes, or maybe Clyde assumed his lawyer had. Maybe the lawyer had moved offices and wasn't receiving his mail. Or maybe Clyde just had a sorry lawyer.

"Maureen, what happens if the taxes aren't paid?"

"The county puts a lien on the property."

"And if that's not paid?"

"Liens have to be settled within sixty days or the county auctions off the property to satisfy the tax liability. But now that the tax bill's paid, the lien's been lifted, and it's no longer our problem."

I looked up quickly. "Sylvia told me Sutton hadn't paid the taxes."

Maureen was evidently a girl who liked her drama. "Sylvia doesn't know squat," and then she added in a low voice, "even though she *thinks* she knows everything. And I never said *Mr. Sutton* paid the taxes."

"Who did?" I had a sinking feeling in my stomach.

"The DeBergerac Corporation paid his bill. We only posted the lien last week, and their representatives were over here right quick to pay it. They said they'd get with Mr. Sutton's attorney to work out the details."

"Oh, I'm sure they will. You say Sutton's lawyer worked this out with DeBergerac? Do you happen to know how I can get in touch?"

She tapped her pen on the desk and then held up a finger. "Just a sec, hon."

She returned and handed me a slip of paper with a name, phone number and Victoria address.

"Thanks, Maureen. You're a fine public servant."

"Don't mention it," she said with a wink.

I found a pay phone outside the courthouse and wasn't a bit surprised to hear that Sutton's lawyer had gone on a month-long cruise to South America—courtesy of DeBergerac, I'd bet. I hung up the phone and pushed open the bifold door, brushing past the man waiting outside.

"It's all yours, mister," I said to his back.

I hadn't taken two steps when a searing pain shot through my upper arm. I tried to twist around, but it was like a hydraulic clamp had seized my limb.

I heard Monroe's voice next to my ear, calm and casual, "Howdy do, friend." My right arm was immobilized by his grip as he led me down the brick path along the secluded side of the courthouse.

"Let go of my arm, Monroe." I was starting to lose feeling in my right hand.

"Sure, Charlie—as soon as we've had a little heart-to-heart." He propelled me forward along the courthouse walk.

"What the hell do you want?" I asked through gritted teeth.

"Not much, really," he answered, nodding politely to two women who walked by. "Morning, ladies," he said. They acknowledged his greeting and returned to their own conversation. We stopped in a small arbor covered in primrose vines. It was out of sight of the street, a fact I found more than a little disconcerting.

"You have business here at the courthouse, Charlie?"

I thought not saying anything was a good strategy at the moment, and I kept on not saying it. When I didn't answer, Monroe sighed, as though confronted by a slightly backward child.

"Why don't you make this easy for all of us and just stick to your shrimping?" He wore the same bland smile I'd seen during the rainstorm, and the same black, unblinking eyes bore into mine. I did my level best to stare back at him with the same cool surmise, but it was like looking into the eyes of a basilisk. "I've got enough on my plate right now," he continued, "but I'll make room for you if I have to."

He released my arm and ambled away. "I'll see ya around, friend." he said over his shoulder. I sat down on a bench and tried to massage the feeling back into my arm, listening to him whistle an unrecognizable tune until he rounded the corner.

—

I spent the rest of the afternoon on my boat, waiting for Holly, worrying about Monroe, and thinking about the raw deal Clyde Sutton was getting. The old rancher was getting bushwhacked by Jean-Marc and his lawyers, and DeBergerac was going to carve up his ranch to get at the gas. Drillers generally have no interest in owning property, so they would most likely force Clyde to give them *very* favorable terms on the mineral access before they gave him back his ranch. And even though the royalties could be sizable, I had the sense that Clyde just wanted to be left alone.

But he was about to have more company than he knew. I imagined him a year from now, sitting alone on his front porch, drinking too much whiskey and cursing the endless parade of tanker trucks that rolled across his ranch—driving right over the memory of his wife and the longhorns they watched together in better times.

Holly returned from the cofferdam about an hour before sunset. I waved at her, and she responded with a wry smile and a shake of her head. After she secured the crew boat, the workers disappeared into the Texas Historical Commission warehouse. Holly walked over and looked down at the Riva from the pier.

"That's the most preposterous thing I've ever seen."

"It's a boating classic," I protested. At least she was smiling.

"Not in these parts."

"Think of it as—as an anomaly."

"Well, I hope you didn't bring it here to impress me."

"You know, I have to admit it crossed my mind. A long time ago, a car dealership in Aransas Pass loaned my high school a Corvette convertible to drive the Homecoming Queen down Main Street for the big parade. Guess who got to drive that car?"

"Young Charlie Sweetwater."

"For one day I was the coolest kid in town. Girls couldn't resist me."

"This boat's supposed to make you irresistible?"

"Of course. And tonight I want you to be my Homecoming Queen. I thought maybe we could go out to dinner."

For a second Holly looked surprised, as if the question was unexpected. "What's the occasion?" she asked.

"It's my way of saying I'm sorry for bringing Antoine, the world's biggest asshole, to your archeology site. I had no idea he was going to behave that way. Or that Julien would act the way he did, either."

She straightened up and looked toward the THC building. The girl with the Aggie sweatshirt and some of the other team members were watching us with interest. "I don't know, Charlie. There's so much work, and I was going to—"

"You deserve a night off," I interrupted. "Your crew's going to take the night off—your intern told me so—and all day tomorrow, too. Even Jim's taking a breather from the project. I happen to know he's going fishing tomorrow."

While Holly contemplated my offer, the THC crew carried bins of newfound artifacts into the tin-sided building. One of the crew members smiled and waved at Holly before sliding the cargo door closed.

Holly responded with a tentative wave. "I don't want to go anywhere local," she said. "I mean, if that's okay with you—too many inquisitive eyes."

"That's too bad. The Dairy Queen came highly recommended, but I know just the place."

———

CHAPTER 20

Cruising across Matagorda Bay in the Riva couldn't have been more pleasant: calm water, a gorgeous sunset and endless flocks of ducks, cormorants and pelicans on the bay. The birds took flight ahead of the sleek runabout, scattering and then converging again, forming intricate flight patterns in the pink and violet sky. Holly sat next to me, relaxed and happy, her thick mane of hair trailing behind her as we skipped across the surface of the bay.

"That was more fun than I expected," she said as we nosed into a slip at Miguel's marina.

The marina was almost empty, just like I'd hoped. I took Miguel aside and explained my dining plan to him—smoked venison with an espresso rub and lump crab butter sauce, a candlelit table on the deck. But he gracefully declined to participate.

"Screw you. Cook it yourself. I'm going fishing."

He snapped closed his bait box and threw a twelve-pack of Miller Lite into a portable cooler. I noticed his rods were already in his truck. But before he departed, he left me with a valuable safety tip, congratulated me on my fine sense of style, and wished me a pleasant evening: "You burn down my place and I'll shove that pimped-out clown-boat up your ass. And you better goddamn lock up when you leave."

I walked into the kitchen and stuck my head out the serving window. "Uh, Holly? Slight change of plan. Miguel has a prior engagement, so *I'm* going to cook for you tonight."

"Gone fishing?"

"How'd you know?"

"He has a girlfriend in Palacios. They like to night fish on the jetties near our warehouse. Her name's Rosie. Nice girl."

I struggled to imagine Miguel with a girlfriend, much less a nice one.

The kitchen was very small, so Holly sipped red wine and watched me cook from Hinkies' pass-through window. As I worked on dinner, making the crab topping, tossing the salad and prepping the venison for the stovetop smoker, Hinkie took care of the last table of marina customers and then called it a night. Holly and I spread some newly laundered aprons over a wooden picnic table and fired up an ancient Coleman lantern, trimming the wick down low for ambiance. It wasn't Galatoire's in New Orleans, but with present company it wasn't bad.

We stood at the rail and watched a full moon rise over Matagorda Bay. I hoped that for one night at least, Holly and I could forget about temperamental Frenchmen, both living and dead, and concentrate on each other.

No such luck.

"So tell me about your friend's excavation project," she asked before I'd even finished twisting a corkscrew into the bottle of wine I'd selected for dinner.

I sighed. "I guess Jim told you."

"He did. Have they found the settlement yet?"

"Do you really want to talk about that? You're off the clock, in a classy seaside restaurant, having a romantic dinner." The whiteboard nailed to the wall read DEAD SQUID—$4 BAG, CHICKEN NECKS—$1.40 BAG.

Classy.

Holly laughed. "What do you think? Besides, what else are we going to talk about? Your fancy boats? Fishing? Turtle excretion devices?"

"Turtle excluder devices. Very funny."

"We can talk about that stuff, or we can talk about a subject where we have overlapping interests."

"La Salle?"

"Of course, La Salle."

"I kinda wanted to talk about you. Get to know you better—how a nice girl like you, etcetera."

"Talk about me? Well, okay. Let's see . . . . I'm a professional marine archeologist—one that's married, if you were wondering, but only to my work. I'm doing something I've wanted to do since I was a little girl, and for the past fifteen years I've been living and breathing the job. How's that? Too fluffy?"

I wondered if Holly was fucking with me, or if she was being serious. "Did your folks give you Marine Archeologist Barbie as a kid?"

"No," she smiled. "Flipper was my hero,"

"The TV-show Flipper?"

"Yeah. At first I just wanted to be under the sea, like that plucky dolphin and his two human friends. I liked being underwater." She rested her forearms on the rail. "The otherness of it, you know? Every sensation is so *different* when you're diving. So I figured out a way to make a living at it." She paused and took a drink of wine. "And also, my dad drowned at sea when I was five."

It took a second for my mind to register that last part. "Damn, Holly. I'm sorry. I didn't know that."

"We're getting to know each other, right?"

"How did it happen, if you don't mind me asking?"

"He was a boat captain in the Merchant Marine. Operated freighters, container ships and tankers all over the world. He was sailing a Ready Reserve Fleet tanker from San Francisco to Saigon when a typhoon blew the vessel into an atoll near the Marshall Islands. It broke in half, and Dad went down with the ship. Captains aren't really supposed to do that."

"Do you remember him?"

"Barely. He was gone so much of the time." She captured a strand of hair that had blown across her face and twirled it absently, gazing out at the bay. "But after he died, I always imagined him resting down there on the bottom of the sea in that warm, quiet water, surrounded by bright colored fish and filtered blue light. I even traveled there once to dive the wreck. It was almost exactly as I had imagined it."

She took a deep breath and stood up straight. "Anyway, that's what put me underwater, so to speak."

By that time, supper was ready. The smoked venison had rested, so I sliced it on the bias, took thick plates out of the warming drawer of the oven, and plated the meat on pools of compound butter. The sauce was added and, to complete the spread, a rice pilaf and a field green salad with homemade vinaigrette dressing. We carried our plates outside and sat down to a fine meal on a white tablecloth with soft light.

"To Flipper," I said, raising my glass.

Holly smiled. "*Chin chin.*"

We touched glasses and then dug in. It gave me pleasure to see her eat with such gusto. Most dates I'd had just picked at their food and left half of it on the plate. Holly finished her plate and went back for more. After we'd cleared the table, I refilled the wine glasses.

"So about me," I began.

"Jim's already told me all about you," she said, cheerfully. "And although your colorful history is quite entertaining, what I'm really interested in is your more recent past."

"You mean like my epic sailing trip from Hong Kong to Fulton on the *Li Shishi?*"

"I mean like La Salle. Specifically, that project you're working on with Julien Dufay on Garcitas Creek."

I didn't know whether to be flattered that she'd bothered to ask Jim about me, or miffed that she didn't want to hear my own version of the Charlie Sweetwater story. Jim wouldn't be able to exaggerate or embellish my exploits nearly as well as I could.

"Okay, but James Brannan's a big fat liar," I said. "And he doesn't know about my secret crime-fighter alter-ego. I've saved the world, jeez, I don't know, at least five times already."

She drummed her fingers on the table and assumed a bored expression.

"Okay, I guess you'll never know my life story. My tell-all autobiography isn't to be opened until one hundred years after my death . . . . Anyway, the excavation isn't on Garcitas Creek. It's on the Lavaca River."

Holly sat up straight and looked surprised. "You're kidding, right?"

The abrupt change in her demeanor quickened my pulse and dredged up a doubt I had been harboring for some time. "No, I'm not kidding. We . . . *they,* have been digging on the west side of the Lavaca River for over four months now. I've only been on the scene for about eight weeks."

"But that's not where the settlement is located. The site is on Garcitas Creek," she said authoritatively.

"How do you know that? They've found lots of artifacts where they're digging. I've seen 'em. I've seen a map, too," I protested. I wasn't exactly sure why I was trying to defend Julien's project.

"What maps? What kind of artifacts? Does Julien even know what he's looking for?" Seeing the stricken look on my face, Holly backed off a little. "I'm sorry, Charlie. I don't mean to be so . . . harsh. It's just that it's a subject I've researched a lot."

I took a deep breath. I wanted to know. I wanted to know whether Julien was boldly defying convention and playing a daring hunch that would spawn a fabulous museum and fulfill his dream. I wanted to know whether he was in possession of historic documents so rare that even experts like Holly and Jim were unaware they existed. Or whether he was on a futile, ill-informed snipe hunt that would embarrass everyone associated with the project including, it seemed, me.

"I saw a journal, written by La Salle's brother."

"Jean Cavelier? Yes, he was a priest. And for political and self-serving reasons his journal was reshaped so many times by the superiors in his order back in France that it's considered completely unreliable as a historical source."

"Oh. Anyway, in this journal there was a map showing where the settlement was located."

Holly looked doubtful. "Showing *exactly* where?"

"Well, showing more or less where. The X looked closer to the Lavaca River than to Garcitas Creek, but Reginald, Antoine's assistant, showed me other documents, too. Like a journal from a Franciscan priest named Pierre Poisson, which contained more precise information. I saw a pretty detailed map showing the location of the settlement, and even a sketch of the fort they built: a big compound with a ring of barracks and a two-story main building, all surrounded by a tall timber palisade."

"You say you saw these documents?"

"Well, most were copies of the documents, except for the journal I just told you about."

Holly sat back and shook her head. "Charlie, it's all wrong. No La Salle scholar that I know of has mentioned these journals of Pierre Poisson. And there was no fort, not like the one you describe anyway. The Spanish searched for the French outpost for several years, and when they found it, they described it as a single two-story building made from salvaged ships timbers, and a collection of small shelters, daub and wattle huts really, inside a rustic fence. It was located about five miles—two leagues—up the Garcitas River."

"It was the River of the Beef, Reginald said."

"Yes, the *Rivière aux Bœufs,* meaning the bison, but it's the *Garcitas,* Charlie. And the fort you described didn't really come until later, when the Spanish built their presidio directly on top of the ruins of the failed French settlement. That's the theory anyway."

"How do you know all this?" I asked. I felt like I'd been stuck on the Quick-Start page of a technical manual, and somebody had suddenly come along and opened the page that showed the exploded view of all the parts and how they fit together.

"A lot of it is in Joutel's journal."

"Who?"

"Henri Joutel, La Salle's friend and loyal aide. He wrote down the story of the last expedition. It's an extraordinary resource. And further confirmation comes from maps, notes and correspondence from Spanish soldiers who journeyed to this area later to find out what La Salle and his king were up to. The Gulf of Mexico and its surrounds were highly contested geography in the 17th century. There were silver mines, navigable rivers, rich land—all claimed by the Spanish, and they didn't want the French anywhere near them. Surely your friends are aware of these documents?"

"I don't know, Holly." It was easy for me to see how Julien, French to the core, would disregard non-French sources as unimportant. I tried to remember which documents Reginald said were given to them by Julien's brother.

"And what does he make of the studies by Bolton and Gilmore?"

I raised my palms and shrugged. I was out of my depth. The evening wasn't going as I'd hoped.

"A historian named Herbert Bolton found what he thought to be the settlement site in 1914, but some of the ceramic pottery shards and other artifacts weren't identified as 17th century *French* artifacts until 1950 by archeologist Kathleen Gilmore—a person I admire very much, by the way—when archeological methods had become more sophisticated."

"But they didn't find the fort?"

"Ran out of funding. Jim's been aching to take on the project for years. Once the *Belle* excavation is completed, it was next on his list."

"But Julien beat him to it."

Holly laughed. "This isn't some macho competition. It's about scholarship, responsible archeology and correct methods, all that boring stuff. Jim would be happy for someone else to excavate the La Salle settlement if it were done properly. You know him better than that."

"You're right," I admitted. "But I think Julien sees it differently. More like a race, as you say."

"Is that why he's been so secretive about it?"

"I think that's part of it. It's also his nature to be that way. I think he and his brother planned to keep the whole thing under wraps from the beginning. Early on they encountered a wrinkle that they thought might delay or shut down the project."

"What was that?"

"They discovered some human bones on the site that they were afraid would attract too much interest."

"Recent bones?"

"I didn't see them, and of course I'm no expert, but someone who did see them said he thought they were very old."

Holly raised her eyebrows. "Well, you're right that the bones would have attracted interest. They would need to be verified by the proper authorities—local law enforcement and a forensic specialist at least."

"Like I said, I never saw them. They just covered them back up."

Holly was silent, and I wondered if I was being implicated in an unforgivable archeological *faux pas*. "This all happened before I got involved," I added hastily. "Anyway, I think Julien's been getting pressure from his brother to keep the project quiet, and to wind it up quickly for reasons that have nothing to do with archeology."

Holly leaned forward, interested. "What do you mean?"

I told her about the gas, and about my encounters with Jean-Marc and Clyde Sutton. And I told her what I had learned from the Calhoun County Courthouse.

"Is Julien in on this? Surely he knows what his brother is after?" she said.

"I think he probably does. But Julien has no interest in gas or oil or the business of getting it out of the ground. I don't think it even figures into his thinking."

"If DeBergerac settled the lien on Sutton's ranch, then why does Jean-Marc care about the Lavaca excavation?"

I pulled on my earlobe, trying to puzzle that one out. "I don't know. Maybe Jean-Marc was working the land grab from two different angles." I thought about the archeology contract. "Holly, when you guys, I mean you archeologists, get the rights to dig on someone's land, does the contract generally mention the mineral rights?"

"Not any contract that I've ever seen. Since we're only interested in past human life and culture, we generally don't find anything of interest deeper than ten feet or so. So a clause specifically granting or *excluding* mineral rights would be absurd."

"Unless you were interested in digging, or *drilling,* a lot deeper."

"Is Jean-Marc that devious?"

"I wouldn't be surprised if he carried pictures of Machiavelli and the Borgias in his billfold."

Holly bit her lip and shook her head sadly. "Sounds like the brother is the only one who's going to get what he wants, doesn't it? He and his company get their gas, but Julien will never find the fort. And Sutton will be forced to play unwilling host to an army of unwanted guests for the next decade."

I sat back in my chair, defeated. What a mess. DeBergerac had Sutton over a barrel, and if for some reason the tax lien couldn't force Sutton to open up his land for drilling, they also had an excavation site (and road access!) that was large enough to put down a fracking pad so they could begin probing and penetrating the ranch with their drills.

And I had inadvertently done my part to keep the excavation project alive when I convinced Clyde Sutton to let Julien stay on his land. If the project had died, then maybe Judson Strayhorn would have lived, and he and Hoyt could laugh about the long miserable summer they spent on Julien's boondoggle. I grabbed the bottle of wine and filled my glass to the brim.

"Don't beat yourself up, Charlie. You didn't know."

"But I should have. There was something whomper-jawed about the whole thing from the beginning. I chalked most of it up to the eccentricities of a volatile Frenchman with too much money and no common sense. He had a way of getting inside your head, though."

We sat quietly, watching the moon, listening to the slap of mullet as they launched themselves from the water and then fell back in the channel. A moment later we heard several whooshes of air as a pod of dolphins swam through, no doubt pursuing the school of fish. The dolphins were faster than the mullet, and they worked in concert to corral and block the hapless fish, taking turns gobbling them up in a remorseless bloody ballet until each dolphin had its fill. The problem with people like Jean-Marc is that they never had their fill. They were never sated.

"Charlie," said Holly gently, stirring me from my dark reflections. "I think I'm ready to go back now. It was a lovely dinner. I really mean that." She rested her hand on top of mine and smiled at me from across the table. I did my best to smile back.

I locked up the marina, and we cruised back to Palacios in silence, dodging crab trap buoys in the cold moonlight, our jackets zipped tight against the brisk night air.

——

CHAPTER 21

Raul and I spent Christmas Day on Ransom Island with my Uncle Rupert and his wife Vita, together with family, friends and a small band of colorful hangers-on that, after more than thirty years, had taken possession of their own personal barstools as intractably as barnacles cling to a rock. For them, The Shady Boat & Leisure Club, as Rupert's beer joint and bait palace was called, was a cross between a retirement home and Shangri La. Reality intruded only reluctantly, which was just the way the Shady's regulars liked it.

For the feast, Rupert attempted to deep-fry a turkey the size of a shoat and almost incinerated the deck when the hot peanut oil boiled over and caught fire. The decrepit old bar had withstood much worse in its sixty-year history: hurricanes, fistfights, an attempted takeover by the Galveston Mafia, and parties that lasted for days on end. A little grease fire barely raised an eyebrow. Luckily, Vita had a back-up turkey baking in the oven, and tradition was preserved.

Rupert said a prayer over a long table that was crowded with platters of sliced turkey, heaping bowls of mashed yams, green beans and stuffing, as well as assorted contributions from our Vietnamese friends: pan-seared garlic prawns, sticky rice and platters of *banh chung*. Place settings included sweating cans of beer and tall glasses of Crown and Coke (a Vietnamese favorite). It wasn't exactly a Norman Rockwell tableau, but it was festive and warm and full of good cheer.

This year, O.B. Hadnott drove over from Corpus to join the celebration, bringing his wife Trinny and their two kids. They seemed to be having a ball. O.B. dutifully passed bowls of food across the table with his long arms, stifling a grin every time Rupert told an off-color story, which was often. Aunt Vita just shook her head in resignation.

After the table was cleared and the dishes put away, most of the guests moved to another part of the great room for that other sacred American holiday tradition, watching the ballgame on television. Even the Vietnamese had become football fans after one of their own, a local boy from Fulton, became a star linebacker at Texas A&M. Today the fighting Aggies were battling Michigan in the Alamo Bowl. Jesus loved football (it's a well-known fact), and so did we.

O.B Hadnott and I wandered out to the deck to stretch our legs and let our dinner settle so we could make room for dessert. The bay was calm and empty; the only boats in sight were tied up securely in Rupert's boat slips.

"Any progress on the Judson Strayhorn case, Captain?" I asked.

"Very damn little. We can't find a gun to match the bullet."

"We missed each other at the Lavaca site last week. Did you learn anything after questioning the crew? I'm curious to know what Clifton, Vinny and Omar told you."

"Their story checked out. The rifle they were hiding in their tent was the right caliber, but ballistics said the bullet that killed the Strayhorn boy came from a different .30–06. Several witnesses verified that the three troublemakers had been passed out drunk the night the coroner says the boy was shot. Too bad. I liked 'em for it."

"Those three are model citizens, aren't they?"

"Can't arrest 'em for being worthless. I also talked to the archeology guy, Reginald. No help there, either. Still haven't been able to locate his associate."

"Antoine Gillette?"

"Yeah, Gillette. I know he quit the project, but . . . ."

"He didn't go back to France?"

"If he did, that's it. My jurisdiction stops at the state line."

I wondered if Antoine was hiding out in some dumpy hotel feeling sorry for himself. It didn't seem likely.

"What about those Sutton boys?" I asked. "You have a chance to meet them?"

O.B. scratched his close-cropped scalp. It was rare to see him outside without his Stetson, as evidenced by the distinct tan line that ran horizontally across his forehead. "Yeah. I visited with Clyde Sutton *and* his three sons."

"Could you get 'em to talk?"

"Oh yeah, especially the twins. Those two . . . ." he shook his head, "One of 'em will lie, and the other one will swear to it. The big one just sat there and nodded. They said they knew nothing about the shooting. It felt a little rehearsed if you ask me. Nice family."

"Can't arrest 'em for being dysfunctional. I think Old Man Sutton's bitterness has soured just about everything on that ranch, including his sons. And it's fixin' to get worse."

"What do you mean?"

I told Hadnott about the politics and maneuvering going on with the Dufay brothers, DeBergerac and the Suttons. O.B. listened carefully. While I was at it, I told him about the bones Hoyt said they'd found and then covered up early on in the project. "I guess all that doesn't necessarily relate to your case," I concluded.

"Old bones, probably not. But that other . . . ." he mused, "When there's enough money involved, people are like to do some damned fool things."

Trinny stuck her head out the door and rattled a phrase in singsong Vietnamese. "Yeah, honey," said the Ranger, "I'm just wrappin' up here. I'll be there in a sec."

"You understood that?" I asked, astonished.

"I'm adaptable," he answered. "Hell, I moved down here from the Panhandle, didn't I?"

O.B. paused, as though weighing whether to say anything else.

"Listen, Charlie. That guy Monroe Chambers that you told me about? I did some checking on him. He's a pretty bad *hombre*, it turns out. He's ex-Houston PD, and they didn't exactly give him a gold watch when he left."

Hadnott picked up his neglected Dr Pepper and took a small swig. "Seems about five years ago, Officer Chambers and two of his buddies rousted a Hispanic kid from one of those Tex-Mex icehouses out by Navigation Boulevard. Kid's name was Tomás Pacheco. Young Tomás may have had a chip on his shoulder, or he may have gotten on the outside of too much tequila. Or those cops may have just decided it was a good night to chouse a Mexican.

"Whatever, he shows up at the city jail in the company of our three HPD friends, and he is in a world of hurt. Chambers and his pals said he slipped off a levee and rolled down into a bayou trying to flee arrest. Said he came up swingin'.

"But the jailer testified at an inquest that it was clear the kid had had the shit beat out of him. Someone had laid the side of the kid's face open with a sap, and his torso had been worked over with something, probably a nightstick, but it could've been fists. Monroe—well, his buddies said Monroe always liked to use his hands.

"The jailer said he'd be damned if he'd book a guy in that kind of shape and told the officers to take him to the hospital. Chambers and the others said sure, and that's the last anyone heard of the kid. At least until they fished his body out of Buffalo Bayou two days later."

"Monroe and his pals finished the job," I added.

O.B. nodded. "Or Pacheco died on the way to the hospital and they ditched him. Autopsy report said his insides were beat to pieces. Anyway, Monroe rolled over on his two buddies at the inquest. Didn't blink an eye. The other two cops went up for manslaughter, but Monroe was able to skate with a dishonorable discharge from HPD. But that ain't what bothers me."

"What is it, O.B.?"

"That Mexican kid? Had a clean sheet. He'd mustered out as top kick sergeant from the Army. He'd just gotten home from Desert Storm three days before. Had a wife and a little girl waiting for him."

"Some homecoming."

O.B. placed his hat on his head, stood up and brushed off the seat of his khakis. "You watch out for this Monroe; he likes to hurt 'em."

"Yep. And Merry Christmas to you too, Captain."

▬

Three days after Christmas me and my two associates were in our corporate office, winding up a high-level directors' meeting over a bucket of Popeye's Fried Chicken and a jug of HEB sweet tea. The last person I expected to see waltzing through the warehouse door was Julien Dufay. But there he was, with Laurent trailing a few feet behind. The two of them looked like they'd just left the rowing regatta at Henley-on-Thames. Today's fetching ensemble featured striped Breton sweaters and wool scarves. It was chilly outside, after all.

Julien lit up when he saw me and marched straight into my office, ignoring Raul and Sammy, but doing a quick double take at the six-foot Modigliani hanging on the wall behind me. He probably owned the real one.

"Give me your hand, Charlie," he said eagerly.

"Do what?"

"Your hand—hold it out."

I extended my hand as if we were going to shake on something. Julien grabbed it, pressed a coin into my palm and then closed my fingers.

"We have struck gold, my friend!" he said.

I opened my hand and examined a bright gold coin, slightly bigger and heavier than a U.S. quarter. On one side there was a king's crown sitting atop a royal monogram decorated with a *fleur de lis,* and on the other side, the profile of an old man with a big nose, wearing a wig.

"Nice. Is there chocolate inside?"

Julien laughed. "Ha! *Regardez!*" With his finger he traced out some Latin writing on the face of the coin. "The motto under the portrait says, 'Louis XIV by the grace of God king of France,' and on the other side, under the royal monogram, 'Christ reigns, defeats and commands.'"

"That's heavy shit, Julien. Where did you get this?"

He stepped back and crossed his arms smugly. "Where do you think? Eh? This coin belonged to the Sieur de La Salle. We found a great mass of them at the site, eh? *Une tas!* More than three hundred. Tell him, Laurent."

Laurent nodded obediently. "It is true."

"*Oui,* it is true. Reginald was digging a new trench on the site and then, *voilà!* The *Louis d'ors* appear like magic from the soil! We have struck gold, Charlie!" he repeated.

Julien bowed at the waist and then turned left and right as if to accept applause, acknowledging the imaginary crowd with a nod of his head and a wave of his hand. Raul and Sammy stared at him like he was an animatronic buccaneer from Disney's Pirates of the Caribbean ride that had escaped and wandered into our office, plunder and all.

"Well, that's great news, Julien. Congratulations, I guess." He looked ten years younger than when I last saw him at the Grand Hotel Palacios. His sense of Gallic infallibility had been restored, and the roller-coaster ride that was Julien Dufay's life looked like it was on the upswing for the moment.

"Yes, it is very good news. It is so good that I call the representative from the *Musée de l'Histoire de France* to come to see our progress. He is coming from Paris tonight—his first time to Texas. Marguerite and Laurent will capture it for their film, *oui,* Laurent?"

"*Oui,*" said Laurent.

"That's fabulous, Julien," I said, although I still had serious doubts about the authenticity of the site, especially after what Holly had told me. I would be curious to hear the opinion of another expert, namely the big dawg from the French history museum.

"Come to the site tomorrow, Charlie. You are part of my project. We share in the good and the bad, *pas vrai?*"

I looked over at Sammy and Raul. "Do you guys think you can live without me for a day or two?"

The two pretended to deliberate. "Gee, I don't know, Charlie," said Raul. "The icebox needs to be defrosted."

"And who is going to shoo away the seagulls from the dog food bowl?" Sammy asked.

"There you have it," I said. "I'll be there."

"*Excellent.* It will be a fantastic day. *Fantastique!*"

I introduced my two partners, and Julien shook their hands, said goodbye and then left the office. I followed him outside.

"I'm glad to see you're doing better, friend. I was worried about you the last time I saw you."

"What . . . ? Oh, that. I was tired. I only needed to rest. There is no need to worry about me."

He walked away with a bounce in his step. "Oh, Julien," I called after him. "Your coin."

"It's a gift, Charlie," he said, looking back. "A keepsake. It will bring good luck."

———

To date, almost half of our original colonists have deserted or perished, yet La Salle listens to no voice other than his own, neither seeking nor accepting any deliberation or caution. I remain certain of two propositions. We are God's children, and God loves his children. If these are true, He will find a way to preserve us. He cannot desire that we perish in this meager, plague-ridden place without some purpose. Were there an insufficient number of graves in France, requiring this foolish voyage?

Père Poisson
DECEMBER 1685

CHAPTER 22

The next morning, the representative from the French museum arrived in a DeBergerac helicopter, along with Julien, Marguerite and her two-man film crew. Even though the camp looked better than I'd seen it in months, Reginald was still sweating bullets in anticipation of the Big Croissant's arrival.

I stood near the cook tent with Dodo, watching the show.

"*Mais,* he come wid more fuss den da Ringlin' Bruddahs Circus, him," the little Cajun said with a grin. "Dem boys been runnin' around like a buncha red ants fo' three days fixin' dis place up. I hope da King o' Mardi Gras appreciates it."

He turned back and began to tend to his Dutch ovens and camp stove griddles. Julien had insisted that Dodo lay on the Cordon Bleu cuisine out here in the boonies, and the cook had obliged with a roast of beef and Roquefort baguettes, plus a *Gallette des Rois,* the traditional French dessert cake that celebrated the Epiphany.

I was impressed. Julien had brought in cases of red and white wine and a chilled magnum of Taittinger that must have cost a grand. Good thing. Port Lavaca's wine cellar didn't extend much beyond screw-top Boone's Farm and Mad Dog 20–20.

Julien helped his guest climb down the ladder and then took him by the arm and ushered him toward the field office. The middle-aged museum guy wore a khaki-colored safari suit and an enormous bush hat with one flap pinned to the crown.

I wondered what Jungle Jacques expected to see out here on the South Texas savannah. Bistro-size buffalo? Rattlesnakes longer than a Citroen? Naked Kronks with six-foot longbows? If La Salle's story was his only point of reference for the area, I guess I couldn't blame him. I was surprised he wasn't carrying an elephant gun.

The tour started off well enough. Reginald, Julien and the expert sorted through and examined the artifacts discovered at the site. Afterwards, they wandered around the dig site, which had once again been divided into grids with plastic ribbon, each grid marked with a numbered flag. Marguerite and her cinematographers followed them, often zooming in on their faces as they spoke, like a Cousteau documentary.

The workers were nowhere to be seen. Dodo told me they had been asked to stay in their tent, sequestered, it sounded like.

"Dodo, is Hoyt Archer in there? Please tell me he didn't decide to come back here after the funeral."

"He come back alright, don' ast me why. Dis outfit ain't no place for him, no."

I agreed with Dodo, but I guess I wasn't that surprised the kid had returned—and it wasn't just the money, either. He'd signed on for a job and he was going to see it through; there wasn't any quit in the boy. But I still worried about him.

After the muckety-mucks walked the site, they returned to the office, passing by Dodo and me without acknowledgement.

Through the open window I could see them huddled over the maps and documents—the same ones, I supposed, that Reginald had showed me before. Laurent and the cameraman crowded around the door, pointing the camera, mic and light into the cramped office.

Before long, the voices became louder and I noticed a change in tone. It sounded like Julien and his esteemed guest were arguing.

"What's going on in there, Dodo? What are they saying? I can't speak a lick of French."

Dodo listened for a bit and then chuckled. "Julien, him say da documents he have came from da man's own museum, so how can dere be anything wrong wit' 'em? And the museum man, him say dey may be authentic but dat don' make 'em accurate.

"Julien ask him why he find so many French thing in this ground here, him? Da big shot say it prob'bly stole by da Indians. Dis was prob'bly an Indian site.

"Julien tell him he wrong. Dat dis be Fort St. Louis itself.

"The man ax, where da fort, den?"

Dodo shook his head. "Now Julien say he still not find the fort because he have bad help."

He looked at me. "That boy Reginald, he don' have a prayer, him. Somebody got to be blamed. Dat Reginald, him gonna get cook, den him gonna get eat.

"Now Julien's telling da man to look at da map from dat priest journal what he got."

It was quiet again as the expert examined the document. I heard him ask Julien a question, so I looked at Dodo.

"Him ax where da journal come from? Da man say he never hear of dis Poisson before, or da journal. Wonder if it authentic."

As the voices rose, the back-and-forth got faster and more vehement, and then something set Julien off. He stormed out the door, shoving the camera crew aside, and began berating the expert from outside the trailer. Jungle Jacques stomped out next, red-faced and furious, marching right by Julien toward the helicopter. Julien walked behind the man, bellowing and fuming, waving his arms, and, in general, throwing a perfect Gallic hissy fit.

"It looks like the evaluation is over, Dodo."

"Ya tink? Dey won't be wantin' dey fancy groceries, I reckon." He kicked at the dirt in disappointment.

After Julien had said what he had to say, he left his esteemed guest sitting alone in the chopper with the pilot. As he walked by me, I offered some words of encouragement. I've never been particularly good at timing.

"You'll find your fort, Julien."

"You are damn right I will. What does he know? He is an *idiot*."

"You just may not find it here."

Julien stopped and looked at me, still red-faced with anger and frustration. "What did you say?"

"I'm just saying you might consider looking for the fort in another location."

It looked like Julien's eyes were going to explode out of his head.

"I know people who can show us where the La Salle settlement is located," I continued. "It's on Garcitas Creek, four or five miles west of here. A previous excavation pretty much confirmed the location, but they ran out of funding, which opens the door for you to go in and complete the project."

Dodo took a couple of steps back, as if he suspected Julien was going to spontaneously combust.

"Who in the hell do you think you are?" Julien walked toward me threateningly. "You think you are the expert now, *eh? Non monsieur!* I will tell you what you are. You're an ignorant *inculte* shrimper, that's what you are. I keep you around to run errands and to entertain me—and also to *entertain* my wife."

He saw me look away for an instant when he mentioned Marguerite.

"*Hein?* You think I don't know about you two? About you fucking my wife?"

"Julien—"

"Now you try to trick me into leaving, so you and your friends who are digging up *my* ship can claim *my* fort, too. No!" The veins stood out on his neck and he gritted his teeth as he spoke. He wagged his finger in my face. "No. I will not fall for it. You just use me so you can steal my idea, *my grande vision.*"

"Use you?" I laughed. "Like your brother is using you to steal Sutton's gas? Like that, Julien? Like you used me to convince Sutton to let you stay on his land? Get off your high horse and listen to yourself. You can either admit you're drilling a dry hole and move on, or you can march around like Napoleon bitching about how the sun got in his eyes at Waterloo."

Julien moved so close I could feel his breath. If he touched me I was afraid I'd break his big French nose.

"Get off of my project," he hissed. "You are finished, *fini!*"

"Gladly. You're not only a fool, you don't know who your goddamn friends are."

I climbed into my truck and tore down the dirt road, throwing dust and gravel in all directions. For the first time, I *hoped* Julien would fail. It appeared he would damn well make sure of it himself.

I was furious at myself for wasting so much time on this whacked-out Frenchman. I wished I'd have slugged him back at the camp. I wished I could take back the things I had done for him. I made a mental note to return that fancy speedboat, if I didn't torch it first.

Speeding down the country road towards Port Lavaca, I passed the battered wooden sign for Sutton's Ranch. I slammed on my brakes and turned around in a ditch. Maybe I *could* undo some of the things I'd done.

CHAPTER 23

Clyde Sutton's hellhounds charged up to my truck when I reached the ranch house, but I was in no mood to wait in the cab this time. I stepped out and faced the animals head on.

"Back off!" I yelled. *"Vayase!"*

The dogs skidded to a stop in the dirt driveway and looked at each other as if confused about what to do next. One mutt abruptly flopped down in the dust and began biting at a flea on his belly.

I banged on the front door. "Clyde? It's Charlie Sweetwater. I've got something to tell you."

I heard heavy footsteps and then the door flew open to reveal Clyde Sutton's bulky figure planted unsteadily in the doorway, holding a shotgun. It was pointed at my belt buckle.

"You must be the stupidest sonofabitch that ever shit between two boots, showing up at my house like this," he said. "I could blow a hole in you just for steppin' on my porch." Clyde's breath smelled like he'd been making out with Jim Beam.

"Easy, Clyde, I'm not here for a confrontation. I just want to talk." Over the man's shoulder I saw a fifth of bourbon sitting on the coffee table. It looked like the seal had been cracked before breakfast, judging by the little bit remaining in the bottle. Whiskey and shotguns—boy, could I pick 'em.

"Last time you were here I got talked into letting those French fuckers stay on my land. I shoulda known you were on their side."

"I'm not on their side."

"You said all they wanted was to dig up bones. You were lying."

"Clyde, can I come in?"

"Hell no, you can't come in. You here to help me work out another *deal?* Now that they got me clamped down like a steer in a squeeze chute?"

"You heard about the tax lien?"

Clyde pumped a shell into the chamber of the shotgun. "What the fuck do you think? You've got ten seconds to get off my ranch."

There was nothing else to say. I don't know what I could've hoped to accomplish by apologizing to Clyde about something that couldn't be undone. Except to ease my conscience a little. I'd had a fleeting hope that maybe we could figure out a way to fight back together. At the very least, I wanted to let him know that I was against what DeBergerac did, and I would have warned him if I'd seen it coming. I wanted to tell him that I was on his side. But seeing Clyde's crazed eyes, I realized he wouldn't have believed me anyway.

"I'm sorry, Mr. Sutton," I said, and walked to my truck. But before my wheels rolled over the cattle guard a shotgun blast shattered my back window on the passenger side. I floored the gas pedal and moved out of range as fast as my Ford would go. I didn't slow down until I pulled up in front of Miguel's marina.

When I walked inside, Miguel was leaned over the bait well dipping live shrimp into a plastic pint container for a customer.

"Miguel, be a good man and bring me a pitcher of cold beer and a cheeseburger. It's been a hell of a day."

When it became clear that Miguel wasn't going to acknowledge me or my order, Hinkie spoke up. "I'll get a pitcher of beer for you, Charlie," he volunteered. "Light beer or reg'lar?"

"Gimme the hard stuff, Hinkie. Make it Schlitz."

"You got it, Cap'n." Hinkie grabbed a pitcher and hopped over to the beer spouts. Miguel never looked up from the live-bait well.

It was warm out on the deck and I closed my eyes to the glare of the sun reflecting off Powderhorn Lake, trying to let the adrenaline drain from my body. I could still feel glass from the shattered wind-shield in my scalp. Was Sutton trying to hit me? Or just scare me? I guess I couldn't blame him for twisting off like he did. I guess I had it coming.

Hinkie came out and delivered my beer. "You're a life saver, Hinkie. I was in danger of becoming a bitter and cynical man." I took a long pull from my mug.

"Your burger will be ready in a few. Miguel told me to tell you that he didn't drop your meat patty on the floor."

I shot a disapproving glance at Miguel, who glowered at me from the pass-through window. Ten minutes later he dinged the bell, and I watched him grab a fat dill pickle out of a gallon jar and toss it into my basket. "Order up," he said dourly.

"Thanks, brotherman," I yelled.

I had squirted the mustard and mayo onto my cheeseburger and was getting ready to take the first bite when a massive body put my table in shadow. I looked up and saw Junior Sutton standing in front of me, big as a billboard. His two little brothers stood off to one side.

"Looky here, Ricky," said one of the twins, Randy I guess it was. "Our frog-loving friend was dumb enough to show up in our county again."

"Maybe he's looking for another rancher to fuck over," Ricky replied.

"Or maybe he comes here to find new boyfriends—to fuck over." Ricky and Randy snickered at their joke.

"Hey, it's the Sutton Gang. Hello, boys," I said, swinging my legs out from under the table. "What's up?"

"I'll tell you what's up, asshole. If our daddy ever sees you again, he'll take your head off."

"He just gave it a pretty good try."

They looked puzzled. I guess they didn't know that I'd just left their ranch.

"So, tell me," I continued. "Is this a social call? Maybe y'all came by to solicit my advice about college? You know, I'd give you a referral for my old fraternity at UT, but the Fijis have a minimum height requirement." I looked over at Junior. "And a weight limit. Sorry. I didn't make the rules."

"Can you believe the mouth on this shithead?" said one of the twins.

"Think how funny it's going to look with no teeth," said the other.

I put my burger down.

"Look, boys. I tried to apologize to your father a little earlier and got a load of buckshot for my trouble. I just want to sit here and eat my cheeseburger in peace. My friend, Miguel . . . ." I looked toward the building but Miguel was nowhere to be seen. *Damn, there's never a convicted felon around when you need one.* "My friend, Miguel, made it just the way I like it."

"Just the way he likes it," said a twin.

The other twin slowly scooted the cheeseburger basket toward the edge of the table until it toppled onto the deck.

"Is that the way you like it?" he asked.

While they guffawed at their cleverness, Junior reached down and grabbed my pitcher of Schlitz. He planted his gigantic ass on the edge of the guardrail and started chugging the beer directly from the pitcher.

I could see where this was going. There was no talking my way out of it. I bent down as if to retrieve my burger basket and swept my arm behind Junior's fat ankles, lifting them up with all my strength and sending him ass over teakettle into the channel. The splash rocketed ten feet above the deck, soaking a pair of panicked customers two tables down.

Before the runty twins could react, I grabbed the closest one by the collar of his jacket with one hand, and took a hold of the back of his Wranglers with the other, and tossed him into the bay behind his brother.

His twin—Randy I think it was—was hopping around with his fists up in a pugilist's position. I swear to God he looked like that mean little Irish drunk that Notre Dame picked for their mascot.

"Come on, motherfucker," he crowed. "Come on!"

Loudmouths always talk when they should be fighting. I walked calmly toward him, and when he threw his first punch, I grabbed his arm and used it to swing him around and over the rail to join his siblings. Chuck Norris it wasn't, but it got the job done.

I leaned out and watched the boys thrash around in the water. The winter bay looked cold as hell. Randy's beat-up cowboy hat had fallen to the floor so I tossed it down to him. "You boys owe me a cheeseburger!" I yelled. "And a pitcher of beer."

It would take them a couple of minutes to swim around to the boat ramp and climb out, so I reluctantly walked away, apologizing to customers as I left. "Sorry folks. But I can't abide intemperate conversation while I'm eating lunch. Plays hell with my digestion."

Inside the marina, Miguel was leaning against the doorframe with his arms crossed. His lip curled up slightly in either a sneer or a grin; it was always hard to tell which with him.

"They asked for it, Miguel. What else could I do?"

He shook his head and cocked his thumb toward the door. "You got about ninety seconds before they come after you," he said.

"I'm on my way. Put the meal on my tab."

"You ain't got no tab."

I threw a twenty on the counter and loped outside, wondering how far I'd get before I'd see the Sutton brothers' truck in my rear-view mirror. No doubt there would be a rifle hanging in the gun rack behind their seat.

I pulled out my pocketknife as I searched the lot for their truck, but when I found it, I saw that the oversized tires had already been slashed. Their fancy supercab rested on the oyster shell parking lot like a chrome-plated chunk of cement.

I smiled. When it came to violence, Miguel always knew what was going to happen before I did. While I was out on the deck doesy-doeing with the Sutton brothers, he had thought to give me a bit of a head start once it was time to scram. Sometimes it pays to hang out with the criminal element.

The bulk of the provisions for our permanent settlement had been

placed aboard La Belle for safekeeping. In January, La Salle left with

a party to seek the great river. In his absence, a terrible storm arose.

La Belle has run aground and all are concerned that she may be lost.

Père Poisson

JANUARY 1686

CHAPTER 24

People think the south coast of Texas is a tropical playground, and that it can be. But spend a few winters down here and you come to realize that the same frigid mass of Canadian air that turns Amarillo and Wichita Falls into dusty ice skating rinks is separated from Fulton and Rockport by nothing more than a few barbed wire fences. When the northwestern horizon turns the color of dull lead and the wind begins to box the compass, we coastal lifers know it's time to get below and hunker down.

On Friday night the arctic front struck us like a body blow, shoving a warm January aside and sending the temperature plunging by fifty degrees. I responded sensibly by laying in a big supply of Irish whiskey, cooking up a pot of chile-spiked Holy Posole stew and spending the night at Rattlesnake Point finishing Joseph Conrad's *Lord Jim*.

By Saturday the wind had stopped, but the thermometer continued to fall. I went to town to get the back window of my truck fixed, and by the time I drove home that evening, a kind of frozen swash line was building up along the shore of Aransas Bay. Frosty rings had formed on the pilings, leaving an icy girdle from the high-tide line down to the water. The live-aboard shrimp boats in the harbor were buttoned up tight, smoke from the Vietnamese cooking fires spiraling into the grey sky.

It was dark when I arrived home, but I wrapped any exposed pipes I could locate by flashlight and went to bed hoping like hell there was enough propane in the tank to heat the house through the weekend. Conrad gave way to Graham Greene. I was determined to read my way back to the tropics.

The next morning I cloaked myself in a blanket and wandered around the house sipping hot coffee while I listened to the news on the radio. The weatherman said that the huge mass of Canadian air, an "Alberta Clipper," he called it, had wreaked havoc as it passed through America's heartland, and then it had stalled and was sitting on the Gulf Coast like a block of ice. He said the temperature had dropped to eight degrees Fahrenheit—the coldest day on record since 1920.

That meant this storm eclipsed the Big Freeze of 1982. I remembered that event as a ball-freezing nightmare. Fishermen had caught hypothermia and nearly died trying to cross the bays in open boats. Boats burned to the waterline when butane stoves blew up. Plumbers from Brownsville to Houston worked until Easter fixing busted pipes. And today was colder by at least five degrees.

I rubbed out a peephole in the condensation on the window and peered outside at the frigid day. Something about the bay was odd; the color was wrong. Instead of its customary grey-green color, the bay was clouded over, opaque. I dressed in multiple layers— a Pendleton wool shirt, a Texas Tech hoodie and a moth-eaten Navy peacoat that my uncle Noble had mustered out of the service with—and then wandered down to the shore for a closer look.

Incredibly, the bay seemed to be frozen solid, at least as far as Lap Reef. I tentatively stepped onto the ice to test its strength, but it wasn't solid. Not exactly, anyway. It was a viscous, gelatinous mass, like something out of a science-fiction movie; I could pick up a handful but couldn't form it into a ball.

In the distance, I saw pockets of open water where currents had carved winding rivers through the icy mush. It was thrilling, but oddly disconcerting to see my familiar bay transformed into a giant Slurpee.

The surface undulated almost imperceptibly, as if it were alive— like the membrane of a gargantuan sea monster slumbering in the bay. I tossed out an oyster shell and it disappeared into the mush without making a sound. Damn. I shoved my frozen hands into my coat pockets and headed for the house. The low temperature had not suppressed the humidity and I exhaled dense plumes of vapor with every breath. Only ten minutes out of doors, and already I could feel the cold clear down to my bones.

Inside I found a message from Holly on my answering machine, inviting me to join her for lunch in Palacios. "It's going to be too cold to work at the site this weekend," she said, "so I thought I'd see if you'd join me for some fried shrimp or something."

It wasn't the most romantic proposition I'd ever received, but it quickened my pulse and inspired me to dig around in the steamer trunk for my Greek fisherman's cap to go with the peacoat—the Old Spice guy look, basically. I wished I had a seamen's duffle to throw over my shoulder to complete the ensemble. Driving to Palacios, icy air clawed to get in my truck, but I blasted the heater and cheerfully whistled the cologne's theme song all the way there.

Standing in front of the dented metal door of the THC building (formerly a well-service business according to a faded sign), I felt like a college kid ringing the doorbell at a girl's dorm to pick up my date. That image vanished when a skinny guy with a wispy beard and a stud earring answered the door.

"Um, is Holly here?" I asked. "I'm Charlie."

"Yeah, come on in. I'm Steve. I remember you from the cofferdam. You've been there a couple of times."

"I'm a *La Belle* groupie. I can't help myself."

I followed him into the cavernous warehouse and was met by a strong odor of saltwater, chemicals and something else. Popcorn? Several cats watched me from the shadows. An upright burner attached to a 50-gallon drum of propane roared in the corner, bravely trying to heat the air. Holly appeared at the top of the second story landing that led, I assumed, to their living quarters.

"I'll be down in a sec," she yelled.

Besides Holly, Steve and a guy leaning over a huge vat of water checking a thermometer, no one else seemed to be in the building.

"Where is everybody?"

"Jim and Holly sent them home for the weekend," said Steve. "It's not supposed to thaw out until Monday. Weird weather, huh? Have you ever seen it this cold here?"

"Just once. But not *this* cold. We can ice skate out to the cofferdam if it keeps up." I looked around and noticed dozens of liquid-filled vats and rows of stacked plastic tubs for storing artifacts, labels attached to each container. The industrial gas heaters kept the inside of the warehouse surprisingly warm. "So this is where you examine all your treasures, huh?"

"The initial evaluation, yes. Mostly we're just stabilizing and cataloging the artifacts before we ship them off to A&M for a more detailed analysis. Sorry about the smell. We use a lot of PVA in the emulsions, also PEG."

"Beg your pardon?"

"Polyvinyl acetate, and polyethylene glycol—to help stabilize and preserve the 'treasures.'"

"Right. Smells like popcorn."

Steve laughed. "We use a lot of that, too. We must eat about fifty boxes of popcorn a week in this place. Archeologists are lousy cooks. If we can't eat our meals out of a can or cook it in a microwave in less than five minutes, forget about it."

"Never met a fat archeologist, now that I think of it."

The other guy was standing over a table now, examining an object that resembled an elongated tar ball. He looked up briefly. "A shoe," he said portentously.

On closer inspection, I could see it—a waterlogged boot with the top folded down, the toe curled upwards at a ninety-degree angle. "Does it belong to the guy you found on the ship?" I asked.

"Dead Bob? Who knows? Maybe."

"His name was Bob?"

"That's what we named him, at least for now."

As Holly descended the stairs she gave instructions to her assistants regarding electrolysis baths and other arcane tasks. "I'll be back later," she said. "Try to keep warm."

"Nice digs," I said, opening the truck door for her.

"I guess the place does look pretty grim from a layman's perspective. To me it's like camping out in a toy store."

"A toy store featuring happy little playthings like Dead Bob's shoe."

Holly laughed. "Don't forget the roach eggs and the rat bones."

"You're saving that kind of stuff too?"

"Sure. Every object found on the boat's a clue. Apparently the *Belle* was infested with the nasty little buggers."

Holly directed me to a Vietnamese restaurant located near the harbor that turned out to be a culinary sensation. Inside was warm and smelled of lemongrass, coriander, and sesame oil. It was packed with locals. Instead of the fried shrimp that Holly had suggested on the phone, we asked the owner to prepare a selection of his signature dishes—cook's choice.

If nothing else, Vietnamese immigrants had advanced Texas coastal cooking by light years since they'd started arriving twenty years ago. Until recently, the only way to order seafood in most Gulf Coast towns was battered and fried—with a side of coleslaw and fries. Hush puppies if it was a class joint.

"Good call, Holly."

"Thanks. Whenever we can't possibly stomach another Top Ramen or Chef Boy-ar-dee, we'll sneak over here for a treat."

We talked about the *Belle* excavation for a while and about the freaky weather, and then the conversation shifted to the Lavaca River project. I told Holly about the VIP visit from the French museum guy and about Julien's meltdown.

"I almost feel sorry for Julien," she said. "Having invested so much into a project, only to find he's been wrong from the start."

"He's still not convinced he's wrong. I assume his crew is still digging."

"Not now, of course," she stated for clarification. "Those boys are surely watching a ballgame in a warm bar. Aren't they?"

We looked at one another with dawning apprehension.

"Charlie," she said with some urgency. "Would that lunatic really make them stay at the jobsite on the coldest weekend of the century? Do you know that three duck hunters died yesterday from exposure? Right here in Matagorda Bay? Does the camp even have heat?"

"They have some propane for the cook stove, but no heaters as far as I know. I doubt Julien would even think to provide them. To be honest, I doubt Julien's there at all."

"But you think his crew might be? We've got to go out there, Charlie. This is crazy. There's no good reason to work at these temperatures, anyway. The soil would be too hard. The workers would damage the artifacts trying to extract them." She signaled for the check and started digging in her bag for some money. "I'm buying, you go heat up the truck."

I groaned as I pushed back my chair. This was not how I envisioned my afternoon with Holly, taking another trip to that wretched project site.

When we arrived at the camp, it seemed empty. Thank God. Maybe Julien had come to his senses, shown compassion and sent the crew to a La Quinta for the weekend. Holly was scanning the excavation with knitted brows.

"I don't understand the methodology here," she said. "There's no rhyme or reason to the grid."

The site looked significantly different since I'd last seen it, spiffed up for the arrival of Monsieur Big Shot. Many of the flags and ribbons had been trampled or pulled up, and I noticed new excavations in one particular area. Fresh dirt from a bunch of foxholes had been tossed haphazardly into the previously-dug trenches. Across the field I saw a face appear then disappear in the camp trailer window.

The door to the crew tent opened tentatively and Hoyt stepped out, wrapped in his bedroll, a surprised look on his face when he saw us.

"Hey, Charlie," he hollered, giving us a wave.

We walked over and I introduced Holly. "So, what's going on here, Hoyt?" I asked. "Where's Julien? Where is the rest of the crew?"

"We haven't seen Julien for over a week. And the rest of us . . . ." He looked nervously at the trailer. "Why don't you come inside?"

Inside the tent a small group of men sat huddled around a campfire, wrapped in blankets. A section of corrugated siding had been placed under the coals to keep the fire from burning through the plywood floor.

Despite the improvised tepee opening that had been fashioned above the fire, the tent was hazy with smoke and smelled like the inside of a barbecue pit. Holly said nothing, but I could tell she was appalled at the sight.

"I hope you an' dat pretty lady is thinkin' warm thoughts," said Dodo, looking up from the fire where he rotated some sort of varmint on a spit. "Cause dis place is colder den a banker's black heart. We done run outta groceries yesterday. You want some nutria, you?"

"No thanks, Dodo. It sure smells good, though." I turned to Hoyt, trying not to look shocked. "Have y'all been holed up here since the weather turned?"

"We spent Friday night knocking sleet off the tent so it wouldn't collapse. Since then, we've only gone out to get more wood for the fire and to, you know, use the latrine."

"Why don't you just walk out of here?" asked Holly. "Lolita is less than ten miles from here as the crow flies."

Hoyt shifted his feet and looked down. "We can't leave the site. It's in our contract."

Holly looked at me, confused.

"Their bonus is dependent on them remaining at the camp until the project is finished."

"That's ludicrous," she snapped. "It's not even legal." No one would meet her eyes.

"Besides," said Hoyt. "It's not safe to cross the ranch on foot."

Holly looked at me again, demanding clarification.

"I'll explain later," I said.

I glanced at the empty cots where Clifton, Omar and Vinny usually slept. "I see the three horsemen of the apocalypse finally had enough. Good riddance, I say. Is Reginald in the office trailer?"

"I am here," said a timorous voice near the fire.

"Reggie?" I saw his head appear from beneath a blanket. "Is the power out in the trailer? When I walked up, I thought I saw someone in there."

"They are in there," said Hoyt.

"Who?" I demanded.

"Them," said Hoyt. "They kind of run the camp now."

"That true, Reggie?" I asked. I could feel heat rising to my face.

"It is true," he said. "Since Julien left the camp the *priorité* has changed. I read the ship's manifest to the men, just as you suggest, Charlie. And when I read the part about the two thousand *livres*— the two thousand *Louis d'ors*—*ma foi!* Now we dig only for gold. They tell us where."

"Where is that gold you already found?" I asked. "Those three hundred French coins?"

Reginald poked at the fire. "In *le coffre-fort,*" he mumbled. "The strong-box. But I do not tell them the combination, *non, monsieur.*" He looked up at me. "No matter what they do to me."

I noticed he had a black eye and a split lip. The bastards had tried to beat it out of him.

My heart began pumping like a piston. "This is bullshit." I stormed out of the tent toward the trailer. When I got there, I pounded twice on the door and charged in. It was hot and stale inside, full of cigarette smoke. I noticed a small electric heater glowing red from the corner. Scratch marks and dents covered the safe—*le coffre-fort*— still locked, and lying on its side under the drafting table.

The three men looked up at me with amusement, their eyes red and malicious. Vinny sat cross-legged on the floor, Clifton stretched out in a folding chair, and Omar had his legs draped over the side of the armchair and was smoking a joint. Beer cans, tequila bottles and over-filled ashtrays rested on the table—right on top of Julien's historical maps and documents.

"Glad you stopped by, dickweed," said Clifton. "Did you bring that pretty split-tail out here just for us? That's mighty nice of you."

"Let's you and me talk, Cliffy," I said. "Outside."

Clifton smiled. "I was hoping you'd say that."

I walked out first. When I heard Clifton close the door behind him, I spun around and buried my fist in his diaphragm. A right jab to the nose sent him crashing back against the trailer. Before he could recover I pinned him against the thin metal door with my body, my hand clasping his throat, my thumb digging viciously into his voicebox. I heard someone pounding on the blocked door from inside.

"You crossed the line," I hissed into his ear. "And now it's time for you to seek other employment." I could feel the door shoving outward. Vinny was yelling for me to open up.

Clifton looked at me though wild, murderous eyes, sputtering and gasping for breath. I wasn't exactly sure what the next move should be. I hadn't intended to play it this way; I guess I just wanted to run their asses off the job. The truth was, I wasn't thinking at all, and my temper had put me in a precarious spot once again. Clifton was off balance against the steps and couldn't get any leverage against my chokehold and Vinny was stuck inside the trailer, but that status quo wouldn't last long. Time to move.

I slammed Clifton's head against the door repeatedly until I felt his body grow slack, then I backed off the steps and set my feet to defend myself against Clifton's buddies. The door flew open and Vinny rushed out first. I knocked him down to the ground with a roundhouse to the jaw and then kicked him in the head. He tried to raise himself but fell back to the frozen ground, unconscious. Omar appeared next, leaning calmly against the doorframe with his arms crossed. I caught the bright glint of a knife blade palmed in his rough hand.

"Hey, podjos," I heard Dodo say from behind me. "I think we all take a break now." I heard a bolt-action rifle shunt a bullet into the firing chamber.

I turned around and saw that Dodo had a .22—his squirrel gun—cradled in his hands. He was pointing it toward the ground but he jerked the barrel up suddenly and aimed it just to the right of my head. I flinched involuntarily.

"Nuh-uh, young fella," he said, looking over my shoulder at Omar.

When I turned around, Omar had taken one step down, but he halted abruptly on the second step when Dodo pointed the gun at him. I noticed that one of Omar's hands was concealed behind the door, probably holding the knife. The empty scabbard dangled from his neck.

"Some *fais-do-do* dis is. But we gonna chill out now for true, 'fore somebody gets bad hurt," Dodo continued in a firm tone.

Omar backed into the office, a sardonic grin on his scarred face. Clifton and Vinny started to moan and move around.

I rubbed my knuckles gingerly. Hitting someone in the jaw in ten-degree weather hurts like hell.

"Didn't know you had a gun out here, Dodo," I said as I walked by him.

"Julien, him forget to make da groceries all da time. Somebody got to put meat in da pot, huh?"

Holly stood nearby, watching me apprehensively, like I had begun sprouting werewolf fur. I didn't know what to say to her, so I marched into the crew tent.

"Hoyt, grab your duffle bag. I'm driving you and the rest of these Eskimos to a motel in town, until this place thaws out."

"All of us?" Hoyt asked, looking out the door.

"Fuck those three. They can freeze to death or burn the whole place down for all I care."

I repeated the command in Spanish to the Mexicans to grab their personal belongings and climb in the truck. *"Ándale!"* I yelled to get them moving. "The company is paying for the rooms." *Even though Julien doesn't know it yet,* I said to myself.

Dodo and Holly sat with me in the cab, and Hoyt and the Mexicans crammed into the back seat. Nobody said a word on the drive back to Port Lavaca, and I had no clue what was going on in Holly's mind. After I'd checked the crew into the hotel, using my credit card to pay for the rooms, I dropped Holly off at the laboratory in Palacios. Before she closed the passenger door she turned around and looked at me long and hard.

"I haven't made up my mind about you yet," she said.

CHAPTER 25

I had been moping around the office all week, and both Raul and Sammy were damned well sick of it. Since the big freeze, dead fish had been floating up by the tens of thousands in the bays and bayous around Fulton: the selfsame bays and bayous that I liked to fish when I needed an attitude adjustment. It would take years for the stocks to recover.

Even the thought of getting on the water was problematic. Every time I saw the tarp-covered shape of the Riva speedboat bobbing in her slip, my stomach started grinding, reminding me of Julien and his ruin of a project.

On top of that, the phone had been ringing off the hook, almost all of the calls originating from the same Houston telephone number. Sammy picked up the first call of the day, and a DeBergerac secretary told him she was calling from the office of Julien Dufay and would he please put Charlie Sweetwater on the line right away. I refused to take the call, and for two days the determined bitch had been calling the office *every single hour*.

The phone rang again and Raul and Sammy groaned in unison. *"Dios mio,"* Raul moaned. "Please, for God's sake, *please* answer the phone, Charlie."

"We would be very grateful if you talk to him," Sammy added.

"I don't wanna talk to the son of a bitch. Just take the phone off the hook if you don't wanna hear it." I said this even though I knew they couldn't, since it was our only business line.

Raul threw down the new TED grill design he was working on and walked outside in a huff.

"What happened between you and Mr. Dufay?" Sammy asked.

"Nothing. The guy's an asshole, what can I say?"

What I *could* have said was that, from my perspective, Julien and his bogus project had made me look like a liar and a thief to a hard-luck rancher, a fool to my friend, Jim Brannan, and a loutish thug to a woman I badly wanted to win over. Not to mention a petulant pain in the ass to my two closest *compadres*. The fact that I had brought most of it on myself put me in an even blacker mood.

"Usually you don't let people like that bother you, Charlie," said Sammy, as he tapped away at the computer terminal.

I ignored him.

"What is it you always say? 'We are all formed of frailty and error; let us pardon each other's folly.' Voltaire, right?"

"Don't lecture me, Sammy, especially with my own lectures."

"Well, as my uncle Nu Dang likes to say—"

"And no Vietnamese aphorisms either!"

Raul came back into the warehouse with fresh resolve. "Listen, *Tío*, I just had an idea. The weather dude said that the next few days are going to be terrific. Hardly any wind, high in the mid-sixties. Why don't you take the *Li Shishi* out in the Gulf and put some hours on those new cylinders—make sure they're not missing anymore. And since you'll be out there anyway, you might as well take a rod or two. The freeze sure didn't affect the fishing around the offshore rigs."

Sammy looked up hopefully. "That's a great idea, Raul. We can handle the office while the boss is evaluating the diesels."

"Sure we can," said Raul.

I narrowed my eyes at the two conspirators. "Y'all are about as subtle as a race riot." But of course, they were right. I needed a change of venue. I needed to shove off before my own partners gave me swimming lessons with an anchor chain wrapped around my neck.

Two hours later I was underway, waving at Nu Dang, who glared at me from his shrimp boat. Our office phone reverberated across the harbor, but somebody picked up before it completed the first full ring.

I tethered the *Li Shishi* to an offshore platform fifteen miles southeast of Cedar Bayou. In no time at all I'd rigged up a red cedar plug, lobbed it into the water and propped my feet up on the transom with my face to the bright afternoon sun and a cooler of beer at my side. My partners were geniuses.

After two hours of catch and release, I selected a nice red snapper for supper—a twenty pounder, perfect for the grill—and had it gutted, skinned and filleted into steaks within minutes. I moved the boat further away from the bright lights and noise of the offshore rig and set my anchor about the time the sun torched the horizon. The salad had been tossed, and the coals in my trusty hibachi were almost ready for the meat when I heard the distant roar of a crew boat approaching.

It seemed odd they were heading toward me instead of the rig. Maybe they were planning to clear a pipe casing with perforation explosives and wanted to tell me to turn off my radio so it wouldn't interfere with the VHF detonation signal. After all, it was an active rig.

When the crew boat was within thirty yards, the last voice in the world I wanted to hear shouted at me across the water.

"Charlie. It is I, Julien! Permission to come aboard your vessel?"

God *damn* it.

Sammy or Raul must have told that secretary I had gone fishing, and they must have guessed correctly where. Geniuses? My partners were heartless traitors.

"What do you want, Julien?" I yelled back.

"I want to come onto your boat."

"I've got company," I lied.

"I do not think so. Your nephew said you went out alone."

The bastard!

"I just want to talk with you. I will not take no for an answer."

"Not only no, Julien, but *hell no!*"

Julien said something to the boat skipper and then, without warning, dove headfirst into the ocean. The crew boat continued to idle for a moment and then sped off toward the rig, leaving Julien in the water swimming resolutely toward the *Li Shishi*.

I closed my eyes in frustration, hoping that when I opened them he would be gone—an *hors d'oeurve* for the Kraken, or flushed down the watery maw of Charybdis. Where are our mythological monsters when we need them?

When Julien reached the *Li Shishi,* he patiently tread water by the side of the boat, bobbing up and down in the cold swells, expecting me to throw down the ladder.

He was shivering, but wearing the same silly grin I'd seen when I pulled him from the Gulf the first time, almost a year and a half ago.

"What is so goddamn important, Julien, that you had to come all the way out here to see me?"

"We are still partners, no? We need to talk about our project."

It might have been my imagination, but he looked like he was turning a little blue in the water—make that *bleu.*

"You fired me, remember? *Fini?* I've retired from archeology." I went to check the coals in the hibachi.

"I can stay afloat a very long time, Charlie," I heard him say.

I doubted it. I recalled the weird slush-rimed bays a few days before. The Gulf water had to be colder than hell. Hypothermia would set in after an hour, if not sooner. I wondered what kind of shitstorm the DeBergerac Corporation would strap on me if I stood by and watched the Prodigal Son drown right before my eyes.

I retrieved the rope ladder from the lazaret, hooked it over the gunwale and tossed it over the side, leaving Julien to struggle onto the boat by himself.

When I came out of the galley with *two* snapper steaks, Julien was standing on deck, dripping wet, shivering and indeed slightly blue, but still wearing his stupid grin.

"You know where my clothes are," I said as I walked by him with the platter of meat. "We eat in twenty minutes."

—

"That was delicious, *camarade,*" said Julien contentedly from across the mess table. "I love the *vivaneau,* fresh from the ocean."

"You want another *Old Meel-wau-kee?*" I asked in my best fake French accent. I had intentionally and, I admit it, spitefully, offered only beer with dinner, and cheap beer at that, even though I knew Julien would have preferred one of the nice rosés I had in the ice chest. Me too, for that matter, but I was still feeling obstinate. He graciously accepted the beer and drank it without complaint. Equanimity seemed to be his latest emotional coloration, subject to change, of course.

"How is Marguerite?" I asked, making small talk.

"She is good. But I am afraid she has lost her passion for film—not a surprise, eh? Her new *raison d'être* is *haute couture* . . . runway shows. This week she is in Paris directing her first event."

"Will she finish her documentary of the La Salle project?"

"Ha! What is there to document? My failure to find Fort St. Louis? My fight with *le Directeur du Musée de l'Histoire*? He flicked his hand, *"J'ai vraiment coupé les ponts avec lui!"* Julien laughed and then translated: "I really burn the bridge with the museum director. On the way back to Houston, I think he was afraid I would push him out of the helicopter, and I confess that I thought about it. So, after we return, I ask Marguerite to burn all the recordings—every minute of tape, *de bout en bout*—from the start to the finish."

Besides his dark musings at the old hotel in Palacios, which were more like the mutterings of a manic-depressive sleepwalker, this was the first time I had ever heard Julien acknowledge that he had been wrong about anything, and I told him so.

"I am not so un-self-aware as you might think," he said. "I realize the project has been a disaster from the beginning—*malchance*, bad luck all the way." He looked at me and shrugged. *"C'est la vie."*

Strangely, it saddened me to hear him admit defeat. His enormous enthusiasm for the project and his dogged persistence, as misguided and imperious as they might have been, were still energizing in a way. It's hard not to admire, or at least respect, someone who chases his passion so relentlessly, so heedlessly. I popped up and grabbed a bottle of Haitian rum from the cabinet.

"Do you remember this?" I asked him.

"Ah, God bless you, Charlie! Of course I remember. I believe it unfroze my blood after you rescue me from the water before."

I poured two snifters of rum. "To pipe dreams," I said. We touched glasses and downed our drinks.

Julien cleared his throat. "Charlie, there is a reason I came out here in the ocean to see you," he said. "I want to apologize for what I said to you at the camp. I lose my temper. I do not want our *amitié*, our friendship, to end like that. I know it is hard to believe, but I do not have so many friends that I can lose."

I did not find it hard to believe in the least, but for a change, I kept my mouth closed. Never miss a good opportunity to shut up, Will Rogers said. I poured another two fingers of Barbencourt into our glasses. "I accept your apology," I said.

For a few moments we sipped the rum, enjoying the peaceful evening. "Julien," I said, breaking the silence, "Since we're coming clean here, I should tell you that I visited the camp last week, during the cold weather. I made some decisions without your permission."

"Yes, I was told. You put the crew in a hotel to keep them warm. Thank you."

"I also fired some men that were taking advantage of your absence. They were no good, Julien, and they were not working in your best interest."

"But you acted for my best interest, Charlie."

"Well, those three guys were *way* outta line. But even so, I definitely lost my temper."

Julien shrugged. "Losing the temper is something I understand very well."

I removed the dishes from the table and began washing them in the sink. "At the site, they told me they hadn't seen you in a week. I was afraid that you were ill again."

He sighed and sipped from his rum glass. "Yes, I was ill, if that is what you call it. In La Salle's time they call it the *mélancolie*, and that is an appropriate term for it. Personally, I like the term from a French doctor in a later century. He called it *folie circulaire*, circular insanity—a better description, because it comes, and then it passes, and it comes back again. Always when I do not expect it."

"They have medication for that, you know."

"I do not want the medication. *Sacrebleu!* You sound like Marguerite," he said edgily, and for a moment I was afraid that I'd set him off. But he took a deep breath and smiled. "The medication—it interferes too much with my work."

I decided to let it go. "To your work," I said, picking up my glass and leaning across the table to tap his glass with mine.

We talked and drank until well past midnight, and then I went outside to check the anchorage and make sure the mast light was on. It was a cold, clear night, and the immediacy of the stars was almost shocking. They were sprayed across the canvas of the sky like a Jackson Pollock abstract. When the eccentric artist worked, he said he wanted to be *in* the painting, and I think I understood what he meant. Julien followed me out and I watched him gaze up at the mast light.

"Allô vieil ami," he said softly. "Your light kept me alive, Charlie. Do you remember? When I was in the water, I did not lose hope as long as I could see this light." He put his hand on my shoulder. "Thank you for letting me on your boat again."

"I don't regret it," I said. And at that particular moment, at the end of a fine day, semi-drunk on fine rum, I meant exactly what I said.

—

The next morning, a steady ten-knot breeze blew from the west, and Julien convinced me to raise the sails on the *Li Shishi*. When we hoisted the red cambered canvas, the stiff horizontal battens unfolding the sailcloth like an accordion, Julien cheered. He was nimble on deck and surprisingly knowledgeable about basic sailing techniques. I suppose yacht sailing is a mandatory skill taught to all offspring of the super-rich.

On one broad reach, he balanced himself on the prow and opened his arms to embrace the wind. He was clearly enjoying himself out here on the salt. We sailed through the day, drinking mojitos and moving in the general direction of the mainland, in no real hurry to get there. By late afternoon we were within sight of Matagorda Island.

"Charlie," Julien began, as we lounged on the back deck sipping our drinks (my foot resting on the tiller to make course corrections). "The other day, at the site, did I hear you say that you know where Fort St. Louis is located? Or is this just my imagination?"

"No, I said it. I haven't been there, but I know where it is, generally." The mention of Fort St. Louis immediately put me on my guard. I was hoping we'd closed the book on that subject.

"What do you think will happen?"

"To what? To Sutton? To the buried settlement?"

"Yes, to all . . . generally."

"I guess that depends on you and your brother, doesn't it? Since y'all wrangled control of Sutton's ranch, I'm sure you'll get whatever you want, and Clyde will get whatever he's forced to take when it comes time to settle up the lien DeBergerac paid."

"I did not know about this tax business until later. It was all my brother." Julien sighed. "Jean-Marc will get what he wants—he always does. And now that he knows he will have his mineral rights, he will shut down the La Salle project and force me to leave."

"Can he do that? Can he force you to leave?"

"It was one of the conditions I had to agree to when he led me to the Fort St. Louis site."

"The wrong site."

Julien looked away sadly. "Yes."

"So, what was the angle? Was he going to drop a drilling pad right on top of your dig location?"

He nodded. "He gave me nine months to complete the excavation, and then, yes, the company was going to drill, using their new technology—slant drilling and whatever. Unfortunately for Mr. Sutton, the contract did not specifically exclude the mineral rights on the land we lease. I hoped that maybe in a year or two, after the company finish its business and has taken all of the gas, I could negotiate a long-term lease with Mr. Sutton—to continue my work."

"For your museum."

"Yes, for my museum. But then Jean-Marc found out about the tax problem . . . " Julien shrugged, "and the plan changed."

We sat quietly and listened to the junk slashing through the water towards Matagorda Island. I excused myself and went below to mix another round of drinks. It was a raw deal for everyone except Jean-Marc and the stockholders of DeBergerac Corporation. As usual, there was no besting a corporation of that size, especially an energy corporation, especially in Texas. It seemed pointless to try.

Through the galley porthole I saw the dim outline of the shore. I could just see the top of a solitary tower rising up from a green strip of land on the horizon—most likely the observation tower at the Aransas Wildlife Refuge. I still got a chill every time I saw that tower. It had served as a refuge of last resort for Raul and me during Hurricane Lana some years before.

But somehow we had survived, just as the whooping cranes, bobcats and alligators had survived, and even thrived, since that brutal storm. The refuge was a redoubt protected from the tender mercies of what Mark Twain called "the damned human race." Protected from careless ranchers and farmers who overgrazed and overcleared their land, from petroleum companies who poisoned the lakes and dredged canals that destroyed the wetlands, and from avaricious real-estate developers who scarred the land with roads and sprawl. Protected even from the likes of Jean-Marc Dufay and his clever scientists, lawyers and landmen.

I tapped my forehead with my fist. I could feel a plan trying to work itself out in my mojito-muddled brain. *Just maybe.*

I went on deck and handed Julien his drink. "Julien, if I were to put you right on top of La Salle's little colony, and in return I asked you to let someone else direct the excavation, would you be interested?"

Julien's eyes cut to mine and I saw them widen with interest. "*Assurément* I would be interested. And of course I will fund the project, too"

"I thought the company had cut you off."

Julien laughed. "I have my own money, remember? I am heir to one of the richest families in the world."

"Jean-Marc might not like how this plays out."

"*Tant pis,* he will get over it. There is always another hole to drill. What is your plan?"

"I'm still sorting it out, Julien. You'll have to trust me on this one."

Julien sat back with a grin on his face. "*Bien,* I have always trusted you, Charlie."

I hoisted my drink. "To lost causes then."

_____

CHAPTER 26

I found Jim Brannan having breakfast at his customary booth at Klein's Cafe in Rockport. For all his *joie de vivre*, Jim was a slave to habit—as predictable as the diurnal tide. Each of the items on his breakfast menu were laid out in front of him on separate plates, arranged just so: two eggs, over medium; two slices of bacon, extra crispy; one biscuit, dry; whole milk; one half of a cling peach, canned. Coffee with skim milk, cupped.

"Jim, what do you think would happen if one morning Leticia brought you a scrambled egg? On the same plate as your biscuit? End of the world?"

"As I know it," he smiled. "Sit down, Charlie. And don't touch my plates." I'd been known to move them around when he wasn't looking.

"How's the project going?" I asked.

"Beautiful, Charlie, just outstanding. Ol' La Salle couldn't have crammed more goods onto that vessel. We've damned near filled up our warehouse in Palacios with artifacts. It's like we found a textbook starter kit for a 17th century New World colony."

"A starter kit for Fort St. Louis?"

"Exactly. Apart from the guns and cannons they carried to defend themselves, and the crates of items they packed to trade with the

Indians, they also brought specialized trade tools and supplies. They were planning on staying. Think of Jamestown, but on the Texas coast. And French, of course."

Jim plunged ahead. "And think of how *different* Texas would have been if they had succeeded in establishing a settlement here." Jim crosscut his eggs into little pieces with his knife and fork. He would finish each plate completely before moving on to the next one. The eggs were always the first to go.

"It means that a croissant would be sitting on your plate instead of one of Leticia's biscuits. Spooky, huh?"

"Exactly." As he moved on to the bacon, Leticia brought him a fresh cup of coffee. No refills for him . . . always a new cup, always three total.

"How's the project going with your French friend?" he asked.

"He's just come around to the notion that he's not going to find a French settlement on the Lavaca River."

"I could have told him that."

"In a way, you did. Holly gave me the straight skinny on the real location. Julien had received bad information. I assume she told you about the whole mess?"

"Yep. His information was bad all right, from the beginning it seems. So he's calling it quits?"

"He was going to, until I told him you'd show him where the real site is located, the one on Garcitas Creek."

Jim suspended his coffee cup halfway to his mouth. "You told him *I* was going to show him the site?" He set down the cup and shook his head. "Why in blazes would I do that?"

"Archeological courtesy?"

"Jeez, I don't know, Charlie. Holly told me what kind of half-assed operation he was running over there on the Lavaca. As a professional dig, it made a pretty good mud puddle, sounds like. And this guy, Julien, he seems, I don't know, a little odd."

"Odd doesn't even begin to describe Julien Dufay. But you do think the project would be important, right?"

"Oh, hell yeah I do. It would complete the La Salle story. I'd be all over it right now if I had the financing lined up. In fact, that's what I plan, or what I *planned* to concentrate on as soon as the *Belle* project was finished."

"What if I told you you would have the financing? And that you would be directing the project?"

Jim's eyes widened and a wary smile appeared on his face. "I'd say you were out of your mind."

"Julien is willing to finance this thing and put you in charge of it—*if* we can get permission from Mr. Sutton to dig at the new site. But that could be tricky."

"Why would it be tricky? Sutton's already allowed Mr. Dufay access to the Lavaca River site. Why wouldn't he do the same for the Garcitas Creek site? They're both on his ranch."

"DeBergerac Corporation, that's why."

Jim put down the knife he'd been using to slice his biscuit. The canned peach, the lone survivor, sat mutely awaiting its fate, like Custer's last cavalryman.

"I don't get it. Julien Dufay *is* DeBergerac Corporation . . . isn't he?"

I explained to Jim about the company's strong interest in the gas deposits hiding inside the shale under Sutton's ranch, and about Jean-Marc's schemes to gain access to the drilling rights so he and his division could capture the gas using their new fracturing technology.

"I still don't get it," said Jim. "Julien Dufay is a director and major stockholder in DeBergerac, and they paid the lien on the ranch, which gives them a hell of a lot of leverage. It wouldn't seem like he'd have any problem getting access to the Garcitas site. Sutton won't have much choice in the matter."

"Julien's not orchestrating that deal. It's his brother, Jean-Marc—he brought Julien onto the project with the understanding that Jean-Marc would call the shots. But now the brother has the upper hand on the mineral rights, so Julien is pretty sure the Fort St. Louis project is dead. His brother doesn't give a shit about archeology. He was only interested in the Lavaca site to gain a foothold on the ranch so he could put a pad there and slant drill for as much gas as he could suck out. But now that he's got the leverage . . . ."

"He can sink his wells anywhere on Sutton's ranch he wants."

"Precisely."

"And he'll shut down the Fort St. Louis project."

"Right. But Julien's willing to fund the project himself—out of his own pocket, and let you and your team run it."

"But why does he need us? He can find the site and do the excavation himself. All he has to do is read the Bolton/Gilmore studies. It's not like they're a big secret."

"He's not an archeologist, Jim. He doesn't read obscure research journals for fun like you do. Besides, he wants to do it right this time. The Lavaca camp was like something out of *Heart of Darkness*. He knows it was a cluster-fuck. A kid even got killed out there."

Jim nodded. "I heard about that."

I continued. "Julien's seen the *Belle* project and how successful it is. Unlike his brother, he *is* interested in archeology, and doesn't give a shit about oil and gas, or about the company share price. He wants to make his mark with cultural contributions—art and museums and whatnot. He fancies himself a Renaissance Man. A Patron of the Arts."

"I see." Jim patiently finished his peach, cutting it into equal quarters and forking them into his mouth, chewing quietly. After he finished, he motioned for Leticia to clear away his dishes.

"Actually, I don't see," he said. "There's still the problem of convincing the brother—what's his name, Jean-Marc?—to negotiate access to the site. What if it's located right over a gas deposit?"

"Jean-Marc would never do it. He'd probably try to keep us off the ranch so we didn't get in his way. No, Jim, we've gotta figure out a way to get DeBergerac off that ranch, and then to convince Clyde Sutton to sell the ranch, to us."

"Huh? What are you talking about, Charlie? I don't want a ranch. And I doubt DeBergerac will leave until they get what they came for."

"Didn't you tell me you got a personal letter of commendation from the governor for your 'momentous' discovery of *La Belle*? 'A priceless gift to the people and history of Texas,' blah, blah, blah?"

"I did. Or rather the Texas Historical Commission did."

"And aren't you big fishing buddies with the guv's chief of staff, *and* the land commissioner?"

"You know I am. You took us fly-fishing on your boat four years ago, to the Graveyard hole on the Upper Laguna Madre."

"Yeah, I remember. We slayed 'em that day, didn't we? Your pals had a ball, and I think now's a good time to give them an opportunity to repay the favor."

"What are you getting at, Charlie?"

"I'm willing to bet that Clyde Sutton will do just about anything to keep DeBergerac from turning his ranch into a giant pincushion. He might even consider selling a chunk of it to the State of Texas."

"Sell his land to Texas? What on earth for?"

"Why, for the La Salle State Park and Historical Museum, that's what for."

For a moment Jim looked confused, and then a wide grin appeared on his face. "The La Salle State Park," he said in wonder. "I like it, Charlie. You can't drill in a state park—can you?"

"Not if Sutton makes it a condition in the deal."

"You think he'd go for something like that?"

"I might not be the guy to ask him. He put a load of birdshot through my truck window the last time I talked to the old bastard. But he's got 50,000 acres of land. Enough to where he could hold on to the original Sutton homestead—I think he told me it was a couple of sections—and sell the rest to the great State of Texas. I have a hunch he might be happy to see his land returned to its original state, with waist-high bluestem grass, gallery forests along the rivers and draws, maybe a small herd of buffalo wandering around—like when La Salle first laid eyes on the area three hundred and ten years ago."

"It sure can't hurt to talk to him, can it?" said Jim.

"No, it can't hurt. If we catch him sober and in a decent mood. But before we do that, do you think you could call your politico friends in Austin and test the water? See if your brilliant idea is even possible?"

Jim snorted. "My idea. You're a born hustler, you know that?"

"No, a poker player. And we have to have something to buy into the game before we sit down at the table with Mr. Sutton." *Otherwise he might shoot out my window again, and me along with it*, I thought.

Jim motioned to Leticia for the check. "Charlie, you never cease to amaze me. I don't care what everybody else says."

Leticia walked by to leave Jim's check, but I snatched it from her hand. "I'll get this, Letty. And by the way, would you scramble me up a couple of eggs, with sausage and hash browns?"

"Sure thing, Charlie. All mixed up together, as usual?"

"Oh, hell yes. Dump it all on one plate, cover it with salsa and throw a flour tortilla on top."

"Degenerate," Jim muttered.

FROM THE JOURNAL OF PÈRE POISSON

For three days, we have searched for my friend, the Marquis de la Sablonniére. Early in the morning, he left the encampment, either hunting for game or making his escape. Yesterday, late in the afternoon, one of the children stumbled upon his shoe. This land is so coarse that no one would travel very far without his shoes, and so I am concerned that some terrible misfortune has come upon him. I cannot yet say a funeral Mass for his soul without more evidence, but tonight my fears have overcome my hope for his safe return.

Père Poisson
JANUARY 1685

CHAPTER 27

The phone connection from Nicaragua was lousy.

I managed to gather from Raul that he was having some degree of success touting our TED units to the local shrimping consortium in Puerto Cabezas, but the state-run telephone system sounded like someone was crunching up a box of saltine crackers next to my ear. I thought the staccato knocking was part of the sonic clutter, but then I looked up and saw O.B. Hadnott rapping his big knuckles on my office window.

"Okay, *sobrino*," I said into the phone, "Just make sure you coordinate the details with our distributor in Panama before you fly out in the morning." I motioned for Captain Hadnott to come in and take a chair, but Quay appeared to be sewn to the seat cushion. The Ranger glanced at the dog and continued standing in the doorway, rotating the brim of his hat in his hands.

"Listen, Raul. I gotta go. I've got company. It sounds like everything is copacetic, so I'll pick you up at the airport tomorrow afternoon. Oh, and don't forget to sneak in that box of Montecristos I asked you for. *Buen viaje.*"

Hadnott walked in and put his silverbelly Stetson on top of a filing cabinet, crown side down. "Were you conspiring to smuggle illegal cigars past Customs in contravention of federal statutes?" the Ranger asked.

"Damn skippy."

"Save me a couple."

I shook O.B Hadnott's hand and then kicked the guest chair until the dog grudgingly climbed down.

"That's one ugly dog," said Hadnott.

"Yeah, he's really self-conscious about it, too." We watched Quay wander out the office door and lift his leg to pee on a pallet of turtle shooters in the warehouse. "What can I do for you, Captain Hadnott?"

He sat down heavily in the chair and exhaled. "I need an expert's help regarding an area I think you've fished before."

I feigned surprise. "This is big. Have you finally decided to graduate from bottom fishing with cane poles and chicken gizzards to something more respectable? Like spin casting or even fly-fishing? Progress from hardheads to trout?"

"Ain't nothing wrong with bottom fishing," he replied defensively. "And I like hardheads. They remind me of West Texas bullhead catfish. No, I'm here because I remember you telling me you've done some angling around the mouths of the Lavaca and Garcitas rivers—that you know the waters in that area pretty good."

"Yeah, I have and I do, although there are a couple of guides in Port O'Conner or Palacios that know the area a whole lot better than me, like Captain Joe, for example."

"Yeah, but you're handy. Are you familiar with Venado Creek?"

"Sure. It's close to the bay. O.B., are you planning a fishing trip, or does this have something to do with Judson Strayhorn?"

The Ranger looked up quickly. "Okay, I'll get right to it. I'm having trouble understanding how that boy ended up snagged in a tree root on Venado Creek. If he wanted to walk away from that jobsite, it seems like he would've headed north toward the road instead of south toward the bay. Seems like he'd have followed the river straight up to the paved road, especially since he was traveling at night. But Venado Creek . . . ?" O.B. scratched the back of his head. "It's south-west of the camp."

I'd seldom seen the Ranger be anything less than decisive. He was clearly stumped.

"Flood water finds its own way to the sea, Captain, and believe me, after that rain there were river tributaries spilling out all over the place. It was God's own rinse cycle out there. I suppose his body could've washed down river a hundred different ways in one of a hundred different tributaries. Or young Strayhorn could've gotten lost and ended up turned around."

"You got a map we can look at?" he asked.

I dug through my file cabinet and pulled out the Hook 'N' Line Fish Finder map for Lavaca Bay/Espiritu Santo Bay/West Matagorda Bay.

Officer Hadnott pulled some reading glasses out of his pocket and studied the map, finally pointing to a spot on Venado Creek about a quarter mile up from the mouth of Lavaca Bay.

"Here," he said. "A fisherman found Strayhorn's body right here." He pushed the open map across the desk.

I noted the location—approximately halfway between the Lavaca River and Garcitas Creek—and then I followed the Venado upstream with my finger. "I've been there before," I said, tapping the map twice on a thin blue vein that branched off from the creek. "That's Smuggler's Bayou. It's really narrow, but I've taken a jon boat through there before."

O.B. nodded. "So you know the area then . . . but here's the thing, Charlie. A bunch of illegals were picked up in a raid on the cement plant in Port Lavaca a couple of days ago. The Border Patrol hauled the group down to the detention center over in Corpus, and when they were checking in the illegals' personal effects, the property officer noticed a real nice REI backpack with a non-Hispanic name written on the inside tag."

"Judson Strayhorn?"

"Yep. So he makes a call to the sheriff, who runs the name through the database, which ultimately leads them to contact me.

"I *habla* just enough to question the fella that was carrying the backpack, a kid in his twenties. First time over. It turns out he and two others decided to take a shortcut across the Sutton ranch to avoid highway traffic on the way into Port Lavaca. The kid ran across the backpack on the ground when they were cutting through the ranch."

"You think the kid had anything to do with the bullet in Judson's back?"

"Nah. This kid was fresh off the *hacienda*, green as they come. Scared to death. The two fellas he was traveling with were from the same little village, in some state that started with a Q—had a shit-load of vowels."

"Querétaro."

"Right, a real mouthful. Anyway, I had the kid remanded to my custody so he could show me exactly where he picked up that bag."

I turned the map around to face Hadnott. "Sounds sensible. Can you show me the spot on the map?"

"Not yet. But that's what we're about to find out. That is, if you're not busy."

I sat back in my chair. "Right now? Is the kid with you right now?"

"He's out in the car. The detention center couldn't spare any personnel, and none of the DPS officers on duty speak Spanish. Not as good as you anyways. Also, you already know something about the ranch. Will you help me pinpoint where that kid found the backpack?"

I folded up the fishing map and grabbed my coat. "Captain Hadnott, you ought to know that there's nothing I enjoy more than fighting crime with you. But one of these days you're going to have to give me my very own cinco-peso Ranger badge, honorary, of course. That and an Oscar-Meyer Weiner whistle are the only two things I've really ever wanted to possess in my life."

O.B. Hadnott's mouth twitched, as close as he usually came to a smile. "Son, you're a self-confessed cigar smuggler. You're lucky I don't slap the bracelets on you right now."

———

As we drove to Clyde Sutton's ranch, I tried to put the Mexican kid—his name was Carlos—at ease. He sat timidly in the back seat of Captain Hadnott's patrol car, wondering what new calamity awaited him.

So far, Carlos' quest for wealth and adventure in *El Norte* had been a profound disappointment, starting with the expensive *coyote* who had merely led Carlos and his buddies to a shallow spot on the Rio Grande and told them to run like hell to the other side. Next, they met their risk-averse driver, who took them only as far as Falfurrias before he dumped them by the side of the road and pointed in the general direction of Port Lavaca (*adios, pendejos*). It took them five arduous days of covert cross-country trekking through South Texas brush country to arrive at the cement plant.

The work at the plant was hard, but it paid well, at least compared to the handful of pesos the family *ranchito* brought in back home.

But before Carlos could collect his first paycheck, *La Migra* raided the factory and a beefy border patrolman shoved him into the back of a green-and-white panel van. Now he found himself sitting in the back seat of a patrol car with a tough-looking *Rinche* who scared the living shit out of him.

I told Carlos to look on the bright side—Querétaro's *Gallos Blancos* soccer team had finally won a division title. He managed a shy laugh and asked me where we were going and if the lawman was going to shoot him. I assured him that he was safe, and that within a few days he could go back to his peaceful *pueblito* in Mexico to help his dad prepare for spring planting.

We entered Sutton's ranch at the north gate and took the partially-improved road to the soon-to-be-abandoned excavation site. Carlos said he remembered crossing the Lavaca River and walking between two big lakes just on the other side of the river—Redfish and Swan Lakes according to our map, a spot about one mile south of Julien's crew camp.

O.B. didn't want to drive up on the jobsite, so we stopped a couple of hundred yards short of the bluff where the camp was located.

"From here, we walk," said the Captain.

——

CHAPTER 28

We followed Carlos across an open field of thorny scrub, prickly pear and mesquite until we reached a faint road that moved off to the west. The road passed through or around thickets of cedar elm and live oak and crossed numerous game trails and washouts. Occasionally, Carlos would pause and look around to get his bearings.

Before long we came to a shallow creek, narrow enough to step over.

"*Aquí*," said Carlos, walking up to a large mesquite near the creek. He pointed to a grassy spot under the tree that looked like it had been a bedding spot for deer.

"Tread lightly around here, boys," said Hadnott.

I followed his meaning. If Judson had been here he also might have died here, and the Ranger didn't want to contaminate a potential crime site with our boot prints. He asked Carlos for more details: what path did he and his friends take to get here? (west to east, parallel to the bay); what time of day? (early morning); did they see or hear anything unusual? (no); did they find anything else besides the backpack? (no); what kind of shoes were the three of them wearing? (Adidas). I translated the information for Hadnott.

The Captain scribbled notes on his pad and then we began examining the area. Carlos waited patiently, squatting on his haunches in traditional *campesino* fashion. Not far from the mesquite tree, O.B. knelt next to a game trail. He beckoned me over with a wave of his hand.

I took a knee beside him and saw a boot print that could have belonged to Sasquatch. "Know anyone who might wear a size-15 boot like that?" he asked.

"Sure do." Junior Sutton, the beer keg that walked like a man.

"Yep," he said. "Me, too. This print looks pretty recent. It was after the rainstorm, that's for sure." He rose and scanned the horizon. "Have you noticed any deer blinds since we passed that one near the gate on the highway? Or cattle, even?"

"No, I haven't. No cattle, but lots of deer. I've seen tracks and piles of scat all over the place. I don't think Clyde Sutton has leased out his ranch to hunters in a long time, if ever at all. I doubt if he'd put up with the aggravation."

"Doesn't appear the family does much hunting, either. Not on this part of the ranch, anyway."

"Not for deer, anyway," I added.

"If Strayhorn was here, do you have any idea why he would have been heading west from the camp, instead of north toward the road?"

"A precaution maybe? If he kept going west he would hit Garcitas Creek, and then he could follow it upstream until he hit the highway."

"Precaution from what?" asked O.B.

"Maybe he was scared of the Sutton brothers. Like I said, they harassed the camp pretty regularly. Maybe Judson kept off the dirt road leading to the camp to make sure he didn't run into the brothers."

Carlos asked me what had happened to the guy that owned the backpack. When I told him the guy had been shot in the back, his eyes widened in fear. I told him not to worry; he was not a suspect.

O.B. walked slowly along the game trail. Twenty yards down the trail he waved me over to a patch of purple sand verbena flowers that had been fouled by a prodigious pile of shit.

"Gawd Almighty!" I said, jumping back. "What's that from? A Black Bear?"

"Not unless this bear uses toilet paper." He nodded toward a wad of paper lying in the grass.

O.B. backtracked and found more tracks from the oversized boots, leading down the sandy path and into another thicket of mesquite not far away. "Charlie, tell our undocumented friend over there we're going to do some more hiking."

We walked parallel to the path for about a quarter-mile before it split into multiple trails that all stopped at the edge of a small natural lake surrounded by live oaks, pecans and hackberry trees. The murky lake appeared to encircle a densely overgrown island, forming a sort of moat around it. Probably a long-ago oxbow formed by the creek.

Near the road a wooden skiff rested in the pond, its bow tied to a tree trunk. The tire tracks in the muddy road were very recent.

"Fishing hole?" O.B. asked. Across the water on the island we could see a sloping beach where the skiff probably landed when taken across.

"Maybe. Maybe not."

"Maybe we oughta take a closer look at that island," said O.B., approaching the skiff. "And I think this little boat has our name on it, what do you say?"

"I say that without paddles, we'd be better off swimming." But the Ranger had already placed his big-booted foot in the bow of the skiff. I motioned for Carlos, and the three of us climbed into the boat.

After two or three minutes of fruitless hand paddling, I cursed, slipped over the stern, and paddle-kicked us to the other shore. We landed the skiff and climbed onto the isle, slipping several times on the muddy slope. Captain Hadnott commented that the slopes of the bank had been used frequently and recently for dragging something on or off the island. But what, we both wondered?

"Jesus, what's that stink?" I asked, as a random breeze wafted an acrid chemical odor out of the brush ahead of us.

Hadnott took a whiff and frowned. His hand hovered above the Glock in the Kydex holster on his right hip. He looked like a bird dog on point as we followed him into the woods. We made our way through the trees and were surprised to come upon a small clearing, hidden by the ring of big hardwoods. Might have been a nice picnic spot once. Now it looked like a cross between a hobo jungle and the city dump.

An enormous camo tarp was strung between the trees, covering half a dozen portable tables laden with propane camping stoves, beakers connected to a rat's nest of glass and rubber laboratory tubing, Bunsen burners, cases of Red Devil Lye, and industrial containers stamped with hazardous chemical logos. A couple of fold-out Army cots with dirty sleeping bags competed for space. The ground inside and out was churned and muddy and the entire clearing seemed lifeless, stripped of any growing thing. A couple of the chemical barrels had overturned, and something toxic and corrosive had cut a path of destruction down toward the lake; that's probably what we had smelled.

But what was genuinely mind-boggling was the trash, and the random nature of it: scores of boxes of cold-and-allergy medicine, their discarded blister packs empty of pills; hundreds of paper matchbooks, all missing their strikers; discarded propane tanks—far more than the camp stove would require. And there was an ankle-deep proliferation of the usual white-trash campout garbage—empty Dinty Moore beef stew and pinto bean cans, dozens of beer and whiskey bottles, used toilet paper, plastic grocery sacks.

"What the hell, O.B.?" I asked. Carlos hadn't said a word. He'd picked up the menacing vibe from the tableau in front of us.

"Meth lab," said Hadnott. "Let's back away. These things can blow up if you look at 'em sideways."

"Looks like Clyde's sons have discovered a new vocation in chemistry. You ever seen one of these setups before?"

"Yep," said the Ranger.

Hadnott elaborated, in short, economical sentences. Home-brew meth was the new thing. Methamphetamine was easy to cook and transport. You could buy the fixings at any drugstore or industrial wholesaler. Plus, the finished product made the customer (which was often as not the cook as well) feel ten feet tall and bulletproof. Trouble was, anybody who used it for very long also became as crazy as a shithouse rat.

"Paranoid, violent, strung-out, even murderous," Hadnott concluded. "Pretty much sums up Junior and his two peckerwood brothers. Probably why they're so prickly about a bunch of strangers setting up camp a mile from their little dope operation." O.B. shook his head in disgust. "Let's get back to town so I can make some calls. I think I'll organize a stakeout."

We retraced our steps back to the skiff, each of us carefully hopping over the noxious chemical rivulet that drained to Venado Creek and eventually, the bay. I pictured old man Sutton, the care he'd lavished on his pet longhorns, the afternoons he'd spent with his wife among the spring wildflowers in his own little corner of paradise. He'd be sick if he could see what his boys had wrought. *Some legacy,* I thought.

When we reached the shore we stopped to consider the slick muddy slope that led down to the boat.

"I don't really fancy sliding down that bank on my butt," I said.

"Me neither." O.B. paced up and down the bank looking for a step-down of some kind. He spotted a big log jutting out into water. "This'll do."

"Uh . . . " I started to say.

He stepped carefully onto the "log" and it exploded under the weight of his Lucchese boot. The eight-foot long alligator whipped its head and massive tail in a convulsive arc, hurling Ranger Hadnott into a clump of bulrushes on the bank. It'd be hard to say which of the four of us—three humans plus one gator—was more startled. I voted for me.

The alligator spun around, opening its maw to expose pinkish white flesh and what seemed like a thousand sharp teeth. O.B. crab-walked backwards from the creature, cursing and shouting.

The gator hissed and advanced up the bank with surprising speed, as O.B. scooted further up the slope, grabbing frantically for his pistol. He fired four shots down the throat of the giant reptile and then, after it stopped, fired four more into the top of its head. The gator slid backwards down the bank until it submerged into the muddy water and drifted slowly away. O.B. jammed another clip into his pistol and fired one more shot at the monstrous creature for good measure. It wasn't clear to any of us if the damn thing was dead.

O.B. stood up and with great deliberation, reloaded and holstered his gun. Carlos and I stood by, astonished.

"Holy shit, Hadnott! That was . . . spectacular!"

"First time I've ever seen one of those prehistoric sonsofbitches up close," he replied, trying his best to look unperturbed. "Can't say I care for 'em much." He picked up his Stetson and tried to brush off some of the mud. "Let's get back to the car."

With some apprehension, I kick-paddled the skiff back to the shore while the Ranger sat on the stern with his pistol in hand, scrutinizing the surface of the lake for any disturbance. We arrived safely and without incident.

"You boys go on ahead," said the Ranger, walking toward the woods and fumbling with his fly. "I'll catch up. That little episode liked to scare the piss outta me."

Carlos and I walked on. He asked me numerous questions about alligators, which I answered as best I could.

"*Pues, no hay cocodrilos en Querétaro,*" he said in conclusion. "*Gracias a Dios.*" (There are no alligators in Querétaro, thank God).

I was tempted to tell him that the section of the Rio Grande where he'd crossed was swarming with them, but I had a hunch not even that would have kept him and his *compañeros* from crossing back over to *El Norte* the first chance they got.

We cleared the trees and walked up on something far worse than *cocodrilos*.

The Sutton brothers emerged from behind some catclaw bushes and formed a loose semicircle around us. One of the twins pointed a .30–.30 at me, and I saw that their brutish brother had a pistol holstered on his belt. It was a bad scene made worse by the picture the Ranger had painted of homicidal speed freaks with a headful of black snakes and a big, felonious investment to protect.

"Goddamn, it's Christmas in January, Ricky."

"It's a gift, alright. I purely hate trespassers."

"Big brother?" said Randy. "Would you mind pulling that pistol outta his jacket?"

"I don't have a gun," I said.

"Uh-huh. I guess them was firecrackers we heard a little while ago."

Junior clomped over and pawed around inside my jacket with his beefy mitts.

"Told ya," I said. Out of the corner of my eye I glimpsed his open right hand fly up unexpectedly. It caught me on the side of the head and sent me to the ground like a poleaxed steer. I'd never been hit that hard in my life.

The twins laughed uproariously while I struggled to stay conscious. "Junior's a little sore about you shoving him into the bay," I heard through ringing ears.

I pushed myself up and rested on an elbow. Junior towered above me, and Carlos was frozen in place a few paces behind.

"Ya think we should let Junior have his fun, Randy?"

"I think he's going to do whatever he wants to do, Ricky."

"Hold on, boys," I said, struggling to form my words. "Let's talk about this."

"I don't think Junior wants to talk."

Junior reached down and lifted me up in one fluid motion, pinning my arms to my side. He held me up, eye level, and I wondered if he meant to break me over his knee.

"Y'all don't want to do anything crazy here," I said quickly, my feet dangling six inches above the ground. "I might be able to help you out later on."

"I doubt it," said Randy, "Not after the gators in yonder pond tuck your body down in their hidey-hole 'til you're ripe."

If he meant to scare me, it worked. A beating was one thing, but these boys were upping the ante.

There wasn't much time. I slammed my forehead into Junior's nose and then kicked at his groin with my boot. He grunted and dropped me to the ground. I scuttled backwards and was about to leap to my feet and run when I realized that Ricky was practically on top of me, his rifle pointing at my chest.

"Don't move, motherfucker," he said. "You either, wetback."

I lay back heavily. "You going to shoot me, Sutton? Like you did that boy from the camp?"

Ricky laughed. "That was different," he said.

"Yeah," Randy added. "Ricky give 'im a three-second head-start before he shot him." They both laughed. "We left him for the gators, but that flood washed him downstream. Bad luck. You, on the other hand . . . ."

The brothers froze when O.B. Hadnott's voice boomed out from the woods. "Any of you cowardly bastards so much as twitch funny and *I will shoot.*"

Ricky and Randy looked at each other and then turned their heads slowly toward the voice. The Ranger was striding toward them with his gun in firing position, his eye sighting down the barrel at Ricky.

"Turn back around!" yelled O.B. "Sutton, you've got about one second to lay down that rifle."

Ricky leaned over slowly and dropped the gun on the ground. Junior was sideways to Hadnott, and I saw his hand creeping over the grip of his holstered pistol, out of the Ranger's line of vision. I struck out with my leg and my heel landed on the side of his knee; the ligaments made an audible pop as the knee bent sideways. Junior groaned and bent over, balancing his great weight on one leg.

"He's got a gun, Captain," I said.

O.B. picked up the rifle and handed it to me, then he walked over to Junior and carefully moved his hand toward the pistol in the other man's holster. "I'll take this, big boy."

Junior continued gripping his knee, watching the Ranger with predatory eyes. Suddenly his hand shot upwards toward the Captain's chin, but O.B. was faster. He slipped the punch and then pistol-whipped the barrel of his Glock against the side of Junior's head. The big man toppled to the ground like he'd been dropped off a roof.

"You can't fix stupid," Hadnott observed with a shake of his head.

I stood up and rubbed my own head, which still throbbed from Junior's slap-down. "I'll take that honorary Ranger badge now, O.B.," I said weakly.

"Right. That and the weenie whistle. Help me truss 'em up and then bring their pickup over. I reckon we can take the Strayhorn boy's murder off the books, thanks to the Doublemint twins here."

"We didn't kill nobody," said Ricky. "And you're trespassing on our land. We got our rights."

"That's true, dipshit," answered the Captain. "You're under arrest for felonious assault and resisting arrest, and you do have the right to remain silent . . . but when we get back to the station, y'all can tell me all about your little science experiment, and about the plans you had for my *amigos* here. And *then* we'll talk about the Strayhorn boy. But until then, I'd advise you to keep your mouths shut."

On the drive back to Port Lavaca, Carlos seemed apprehensive, wondering if the fun was over yet. They'd never believe this shit back in Querétaro.

While the powers-that-be booked the Sutton boys for assault, threatening a law officer and murder—and they threw in a felony narcotics charge for good measure—Carlos and I grabbed a hamburger at the local Whataburger. Late in the afternoon, O.B. wandered outside, stretching his back wearily.

"How'd it go," I asked.

"We got a confession for the Strayhorn murder. Seems the kid stumbled on the Sutton brothers' set-up just as they were unloading a truckload of supplies. They'd been up a couple of days by then, sampling their own product. Ricky pulled the trigger, but they drew straws to see who got to shoot him."

I shook my head in dismay. "Damn."

"Thanks for your help, Charlie. In return, I'm letting the cigar thing slide."

I acknowledged his comment with a short laugh and asked if he wanted to grab some dinner.

"I appreciate the offer, Charlie, but I think I'd like to wrap this up and get home. Mrs. Hadnott said she's preparing something special for supper tonight. I won't be able to pronounce it, but it'll be awfully good."

"Okay, Captain. Can't say I blame you." It had been a little over fourteen years since he and Trinh An Phu had tied the knot, and he still acted like he was on his honeymoon.

"What do we do about Carlos here?"

The Ranger eyed the young Mexican sympathetically. "Oh yeah. What does he want to do?"

"You want me to ask him?"

O.B. nodded. "Your Spanish is better than mine."

It was probably against ten different regulations for a Ranger to cut an illegal loose, but I think O.B. had decided the kid had earned the right to have a say in the matter.

I spoke briefly with Carlos, presenting him with his choices. I smiled at his response.

"What'd he say?" asked O.B.

"He asked if we would please take him back to the detention center in Corpus so they can take him across the border as soon as possible. He says life in this country is much too complicated. He wants to go home."

"Well, after today I can appreciate his point of view."

CHAPTER 29

Jim Brannan called me the next morning to tell me that the governor was *very* interested in the state park idea. Her chief of staff said that she'd been looking for a signature action to close out her term, and she thought this one was a dandy.

"Did you tell the guv's guy I was a genius?"

"Your name didn't come up. Listen, time is short. The next step is for you to convince Clyde Sutton that it's a good idea to sell most of his ranch to the State of Texas. You think you can get on that right away?"

"I guess you didn't read the paper today."

"Not yet. Why?"

"Clyde Sutton's three sons were arrested yesterday for the murder of Judson Strayhorn."

I heard Jim whistle on the other end of the line. "Murder, huh? Well, I guess that puts a wrench in the works, doesn't it?"

"It gets worse. I helped bring 'em in."

There was a long pause on the telephone before Jim spoke. "I don't guess Clyde Sutton would have much to say to you right now."

"No, I don't expect he would. Nothing Christian, anyway. But he might talk to you."

"I don't know, Charlie. Didn't you tell me he shot out your truck window last time you went out there?"

"He was about two-thirds drunk when I showed up. But I wouldn't advise you to drive up to his house, either."

"I guess I could call him, but it seems like this deal should be explained face-to-face."

"Yeah, I agree." I picked up the Corpus newspaper and looked closer at the murder story I'd been reading. The article said the arraignment for the Sutton brothers was scheduled for 9 A.M. tomorrow.

"You know what, Jim? I think you might be able to catch him at the Calhoun County Courthouse. His boys' arraignment is *mañana*. He's not apt to have his shotgun or a whiskey bottle there."

"You think he'll talk to me? On the courthouse steps? I wonder."

I wondered, too. He would have his guard up at a public gathering like that, especially with the media there; they would be eager to capture a father's shame at seeing his sons marched out of the courthouse in handcuffs. I doubted Clyde Sutton harbored much affection for his boys anymore—he'd given up on them years ago—but he wouldn't cotton to the public humiliation of a perp walk, either.

Then I recalled my first visit to his house, and how tenderly he'd talked about his late wife, how his countenance changed when he reminisced about their time together on the ranch. I had a sudden hunch he'd be more accessible if a woman made the presentation.

"You're right, Jim. He probably wouldn't talk to you . . . but he might talk to your co-director."

"To Holly? Why her?"

I explained my theory to him. "Clyde might decide he can trust Holly. This project is important to her, and she doesn't want to see Clyde Sutton steamrolled by DeBergerac either. She thinks the guy's had enough bad luck."

"He's had plenty, that's for sure. And now his three boys could potentially spend the rest of their lives in prison, that is, if they don't wind up on death row. Can you imagine how low the old man must feel?"

"Clyde won't want sympathy from us," I said. "But he might surprise us concerning the governor's proposal. The only things about that ranch he seems to value anymore are the good memories he had there before his wife died—before the big corporations started fucking him over, and before his kids turned into animals."

"Doesn't he realize how much money he stands to make if DeBergerac's wells hit? He'd become a rich man. He could buy a nice beach house in Belize and drink piña coladas all day and for the rest of his life. Most landowners would love to have that kind of break."

"I don't think that's what Clyde wants. His life is a train wreck, and he has nothing to show for it except his ranch. At the end of the day, I think he wants to die in his own bed, looking out at his land. The state'll offer him enough to see him through."

"His sons certainly won't be able to spend the money."

"I expect they'll earn their fortune in the license plate-making and cotton-chopping rackets."

Jim sighed. "I'll call Holly and run it by her."

—

Later that afternoon, Sammy and I picked up Raul from the Corpus Christi airport. Before we left, I'd bought a half-bushel of oysters from Nu Dang and laid them out in a big tub of ice in the middle of the warehouse. Since Sammy and Raul did most of the traveling for the company, I always liked to treat them to a little Third Coast lagniappe after their long trips. Cocktail sauce, Tabasco and lemons were sitting on the table next to the tub, although I preferred my oysters garnished with nothing more than their own briny juice. Bottles of beer were cooling in the Igloo.

"Well done, *Tío*," said Raul when we returned from the airport. "Once again you have outsmarted the wily oyster."

"Thank Sammy's uncle," I said. "He raked these babies off of Long Reef just this morning."

Sammy rummaged around in the cabinet and came back with a package of saltines, frowning when he opened the sack. "How long have you had these, Charlie?" He held up a soggy cracker, streaked with mold.

"Dang it! I knew I forgot something. Lemme run over to the Sav-Mor and grab a box. Meanwhile, the oyster knives are on the table. Dig in, boys."

I couldn't have been gone more than fifteen minutes, twenty tops, and when I returned, Raul and Sammy were standing awkwardly around the table, looking like they'd just seen a ghost.

"What's up, guys?"

Raul looked at me with a bemused, faraway expression. "We had a visitor, Charlie." I noticed Quay had roused himself from his customary spot in the office and was sniffing around the table in an agitated manner, as though another animal had recently marked his territory.

"What happened?" I asked with alarm. "What visitor?"

"A man," Sammy answered. "He seemed to know you."

I looked around warily. I'd never seen my partners so unnerved. "What did this man look like?"

Sammy turned to me. "Dark hair, slicked back and shiny, like it was wet. Dark eyes, too. And his face was . . . ." He brought his fingers up to his cheeks.

"*Una cara de piña*," said Raul. "Like a pineapple."

I took a deep breath. Monroe Chambers. Shit. "What did he say?"

Sammy shook his head. "Not much of anything. He talked about oysters."

"Oysters?"

Sammy nodded. "The warehouse door was open and he just walked up from nowhere, and started talking about oysters—like he was giving us a lesson."

Sammy and Raul were staring at the tub of oysters. I noticed a jumble of shell fragments scattered about. "Go on, Sammy," I said.

"He told us that oysters have shells as hard as rocks . . . so the oysters, they believe they are protected when they are inside their shells." The boys stood quietly dazed.

"Go on." I tried to keep my voice calm. "What else did he say?"

Raul picked up one of the oysters, and I noticed with a shock that a nail had been driven completely through its shell. "The man walked over to one of those pallets there," said Raul, "and he pulled a nail out of the wood, with his fingers . . . and then he *pushed* the nail right through the oyster. He said there are snails that can do that—that can drill holes into an oyster to get inside."

He carefully set down the impaled oyster and next picked up a broken half shell. "This one," he continued, "he smashed into the corner of the table." Raul held the piece of shell and demonstrated by feigning a slow-motion blow to the metal table, as if he were trying to convince himself it really happened. "He said a stingray can crush an oyster just like that . . . using its teeth."

"Christ almighty, boys, I'm sorry."

Raul seemed not to hear, staring at the oyster fragments left on the table. Sammy stood beside him, mutely watching the table along with Raul.

"And last, he picked up this one . . . " Raul picked up a halved shell, empty of its oyster, "and he twisted it open with his hands . . . like he was opening a jar of pickles." He shook his head. "*With his hands*, Charlie. I didn't know that was even possible."

Raul dropped the shell as though it were red-hot. "And the whole time, he never raised his voice. Like he was just making conversation."

Sammy looked at me. "How do you know this man, Charlie?"

I assured them it was a long story and had nothing to do with them, and that the situation was being handled. They were polite enough not to call me on my bullshit, for that's what it truly was, but they weren't by a long shot comforted. In the meantime, the coming home party was definitely over.

My two partners decided they wanted to go home, and who could blame 'em? If Monroe wanted to put the fear in us, the son of a bitch had succeeded. After Sammy and Raul left, I called Hadnott on the office phone and told him what had happened. I already knew there was nothing he could do to Monroe. Technically, the man had simply dropped by our warehouse and opened a few oysters. But the demonstration had been more effective than a severed horse head.

"I guess I don't have to tell you to lock your door, Charlie," he said.

"No, Captain, you don't," I answered.

I closed up the office and took Quay with me to the casa. That night I slept with a loaded shotgun by my bedside.

—

The next day the six o'clock news showed the Sutton boys leaving the courthouse in Palacios after being formally charged with murder. Ricky and Randy tried to look tough as they were marched into a police van after the arraignment, but it was easy to see they were scared shitless. Their big brother clumsily maneuvered a wheelchair, his busted knee wrapped in a cast, his moon-shaped face blank and emotionless. I caught a quick glimpse of Clyde Sutton leaving the courthouse as well. Jim and Holly were close behind. I turned off the television and waited.

Jim called me later that evening to tell me that Sutton was willing to play ball.

"Holly was masterful, Charlie. I mean, she knew just how to talk to the guy."

"How did she talk to him?" I asked.

"Straight to the point. No bullshit. She caught up to him when he was getting in his truck, and in two minutes she laid out the whole deal: Sutton's options and the pros and cons of each one."

"What did Clyde say?"

"He asked us to follow him to his house so we could talk in private."

"Yeah?"

"We were there a couple of hours, and before we'd left, we'd already marked up a map of the ranch, worked out a rough outline of where we thought the state park should be, and identified which area he wanted to keep for himself. And you were right about Sutton being sentimental about his land. He got misty-eyed when he told us about the long drives he and his missus—her name was Lilian, did you know that?—would take around the ranch.

"But he was adamant that the only way he'd agree to this deal was if there was no way that DeBergerac or any other oil company could ever get their hands on the mineral rights."

"Don't forget that DeBergerac fixed that county property lien."

"I asked the governor's chief-of-staff about that, and he said it was nothing to worry about. They'd already figured out a way around it."

"Why do you think Clyde was so cooperative, Jim?"

"Who can say for sure? It's like he's written off the future and is only interested in preserving the past, at least the good parts of it. His boys had just been booked for murder and he never mentioned them once during our discussion. It sure seemed like he'd written them off. And regarding his ranch, he told us he'd rather see the land returned to the way it was before his family settled there than be forced to watch the oilmen have their way with it."

"Have you called the governor's office yet?"

"Yep. They're already drafting the resolution to fast-track it through the Legislature to authorize and finance the purchase. The Land Commissioner and the Parks Department guys are happy as clams. Holly and I are meeting an Austin survey team at the ranch in the morning to stake out the rough boundaries of the park and assess some kind of fair market value to benchmark against the price Sutton threw out, which, by the way, was so low it's more like a gift."

"Outstanding, Jim. It sounds like this might actually happen. I wish I could join you at the ranch, but since Sutton's gonna be there . . . . I don't want to queer the deal."

"I already asked Mr. Sutton if it'd be alright if you came along."

"What'd he say?"

"At first he called you a name I won't repeat, but then Holly told him that it was you who'd cooked up this whole idea, and that if it wasn't for you it never would've happened."

"Did he believe her?"

"I guess so. He thought about it a minute and said okay."

"I'll be there in the morning."

Jim cleared his throat. "Charlie, you mentioned that your friend, Mr. Dufay, was going to finance the excavation. That hasn't changed has it? He's still in?"

"I haven't spoken with him but, yeah, as far as I know he's still in. I'll call him right away and let him know what's going on."

"Invite him along for the survey, too. As fast as this thing is moving, it would be good to get him involved from the get-go."

"I think he'll be happy as hell." *He better be*, I thought to myself, hoping that he hadn't been overcome by another bout of the *melancholia*.

Later, when I reached him by phone, Julien was overjoyed about the news. He even committed to financing the construction of the museum, too.

"*C'est un miracle*, Charlie!" he exclaimed. "I am ordering the plane prepared as we speak. We can lay La Salle's ghost to rest at last."

I had no way of knowing that the explorer's ghost was more restless than anyone knew.

While leading a hunting party, the Sieur Barbier encountered a group of Indians in possession of some goods from the wreck of La Belle. These savages, less hostile and insulting than those who daily harassed our encampment, had recovered some cloth and a few of our priestly vestments. After difficult negotiations, we recovered our property and agreed to give them three pigs.

Père Poisson
JANUARY 1686

CHAPTER 30

Jim stood atop the bluff overlooking Garcitas Creek and opened his arms to the majestic landscape below, looking for all the world like Moses parting the Red Sea, that is, if Moses wore a gimme cap.

"From this height, La Salle would have beheld enormous herds of buffalo grazing on native grass. He would have seen smoke rising from Indian campfires along the Lavaca River. His faithful lieutenant and friend, Henri Joutel, wrote in his journal that great fields of wildflowers graced their view, and abundant groves of pecan trees and live oaks punctuated a vast prairie. He described the bountiful wildlife, fresh water and plentiful fish."

Jim turned around and made eye contact with the small group of dignitaries that had flown in from Austin. "Despite their incredible hardships, I think La Salle and his colonists surely harbored some appreciation for this natural beauty that surrounded them. If we are careful stewards, we will be able to return this land to its pristine condition. Visitors will be able to stand here and see Texas as it was when its first settlers arrived . . . when La Salle stood on this very spot."

Jim was good at this kind of thing, and today he needed to be superb.

The governor had surprised everybody by insisting that she tour the prospective state park personally. She was joined by Holly, Clyde

Sutton, Julien Dufay, the governor's chief of staff and DPS escorts, three surveyors, four local legislators, and me.

After Jim's recounting of the La Salle saga, and of the Texas Historical Commission's vision for a museum and natural area commemorating the first European settlement on Texas soil, it appeared that the governor and the other politicos were thoroughly sold on the idea. The mild weather served to make this critical visit all the more successful.

"Thank you, Jim," said the governor, after the presentation was over.

She wore a stylish Chanel pantsuit that was as white as her sculpted coif of hair. ("The bigger the hair, the closer to God" she always said.) She had an easy, confident authority that won over everyone in the group. I think that Holly was enthralled by the charismatic governor most of all. "It's an ambitious project," the governor continued, "And I agree that it's a story that needs to be told."

She turned to Clyde Sutton, who stood apart from the group, his arms folded across his chest. "Mr. Sutton, you are the fourth generation owner of one of this state's most storied ranches, and you're telling me you're ready to let go of the better part of it so we can turn it into a tourist attraction. Why?"

"I'm doing it for somebody else."

"Your deceased wife?" asked the governor. Jim and Holly had given her the back-story on Clyde and his ranch as they drove around the property together.

"Yep," he answered.

"Well, it will be a wonderful gift. One that will honor her memory." She turned to Julien "Mr. Dufay . . . ." The governor's Texas accent somehow stretched Julien's last name to three syllables. "Are we going to be able to count on your commitment to finance the construction of this wonderful museum and park facility that Jim so eloquently described? Like I said before, the people of Texas will spring for the land, but the rest of it is not going to come cheap."

Julien nodded slowly, his eyes sparkling. "I will be depositing twenty million dollars into a charitable trust that I have assigned to the project. I am asking my friend, Charlie Sweetwater, to be the trustee of the funds."

The governor glanced at me and raised an eyebrow. I'm sure I looked more surprised than she did. Julien had not mentioned any of this to me. I was completely taken aback.

"You're shittin' me!" I blurted. "Uh, sorry, Governor."

Her eyes crinkled with laughter. "Don't worry, honey, I'm the only child of a very rough-talking daddy. When it comes to swearing, I've either heard it or can top it."

She turned back to Julien. "Twenty million. That's a heck of a gift, especially considering that once this deal is done your corporation stands to be locked out of one of the richest gas deposits in South Texas."

"There are other gas deposits," Julien said with polished nonchalance. "My contribution is independent of DeBergerac Corporation. It is a *personal* commitment, not a corporate one."

"It all sounds too good to be true, doesn't it?" she mused. "But never look a gift horse in the mouth. Right, Jim?"

"No, ma'am. Not this horse."

She grabbed Jim's hand and shook it vigorously. "It was a lovely tour, Jim. And as much as I'd like to stay, I've got to get back to Austin. I'm still governor for a few more days."

She walked over to Clyde and held his hand warmly. "Mr. Sutton, I can't tell you how happy I am that you have chosen to share your legacy with us. It is such a beautiful ranch. I can see why your wife loved it so much. I thank you, and Texas thanks you."

Clyde nodded perfunctorily and pursed his lips, trying to mask the emotion he must have been feeling. The governor next turned to Julien.

"Mr. Dufay," she continued. "This project will be something that both France and Texas will be proud of. I have to say, I am inspired by your grand vision."

Julien shook her hand and smiled. "*C'est beaucoup d'honneur que vous me faites, Madame le Gouverneur.*"

"*Non, monsieur.*" The governor drawled. "*Tout l'honneur est pour moi.*" She winked at Julien and laughed at her atrocious accent. "Now you know why President Clinton didn't invite me into the Foreign Service after the election."

"I think you would be a stellar diplomat," Julien replied.

I happened to be standing next to Julien so, perhaps to be polite, she shook my hand as well. "What is your line of work Mr . . . . Sweetwater, is it?"

"Yes ma'am. Charlie Sweetwater."

"Are you a banker?"

"Shrimper," I replied. "And foundation trustee."

She nodded her head, trying to make sense of my part in this project. "Well, you've got an important job to do."

"Yes, ma'am. Shrimp has replaced tuna as the nation's number one seafood."

The governor looked at me with keen eyes, uncertain, trying to decide if I was being a wiseass. She smiled. "That's right, Mr. Sweetwater. What would we do without shrimp?"

I heard Jim chuckling behind me.

The governor climbed into her white Suburban with her chief of staff and DPS escort and bounced across the mesa toward the highway, followed by the other politicians.

After they disappeared into the trees, I looked at Julien. "How do you know I won't skip town with your twenty million and buy me a couple of thousand hectares on the French Riviera?"

Julien laughed. "Wealth is complicated, Charlie. You do not have the patience for it."

I sighed. "You're probably right, but it might be fun to dock my shrimp boat next to those fifty million dollar yachts in front of the Hotel Hermitage in Monte Carlo. At least for a day or two."

Julien put his arm around my shoulders. "If you decide to sail there in the *Li Shishi*, instead of that smelly old shrimping boat, I promise I will join you there."

I noticed Holly talking to Clyde Sutton, so I went over to them. I wanted to let him know I was ready to bury the hatchet. They both stopped talking when I walked up.

"Mr. Sutton," I said, by way of a greeting.

He dipped his head slightly in response. Earlier, he had shown the state surveyor the boundaries of the homestead section he'd carved out for himself. It was not to be touched during the project or after. On his death, he said he wanted his house razed and his square mile of land folded into the main park. He made no mention of his sons or any other living relative. I had the feeling a big part of him just looked forward to rejoining his wife. He was only marking time until then.

"So," said Holly, sensing the tension, "Mr. Sutton was just telling me that he'd picnicked on this bluff with his wife every year on her birthday."

"It's a fine spot. I can see why you chose it," I said.

"She chose it, not me," he said flatly.

I turned my head and surveyed the flat coastal prairie that spread below. "Well, this view sure beats lookin' out at a patchwork of well sites, caliche roads and aluminum trailers."

When I looked back at him his eyes were fixed on me with an intensity of emotion that I couldn't quite identify. Rage? Defiance? Scrutiny? Or maybe some kind of acknowledgement that although I'd played a part in blowing up his life, I had also tried to set it right. That he acknowledged me at all was probably the most I could hope for.

"Yep." And with that he walked away and climbed into his pickup.

Holly and I watched him drive away. "Well, he didn't take a swing at you," she said. "You think y'all are square?"

"Yeah, I think we're as square as we're gonna get."

"I wonder if Clyde knew that this was the Fort St. Louis site all along?" asked Holly. "It seems like he and his wife would've had to know about the previous excavation in order to grant access to the archeologists. Yet he let Mr. Dufay pay him for access to the Lavaca River site."

"He's a pretty good horse trader. I wouldn't begrudge him the money he took from DeBergerac. Everybody involved in that deal had their own agenda."

"Except maybe you. I still don't understand why you got involved in this, Charlie."

"A pretty girl dragged me into it about eighteen months ago. I couldn't say no."

A faint smile appeared on her face. "Are you ever serious?"

"I am being serious. From day one, I was just angling for a date with the eminent marine archeologist for the Texas Historical Commission."

"Seems like a lot of trouble to go to for a date."

"She seemed worth it."

"You're the gatekeeper for our twenty million dollar fund. I'm supposed to be sucking up to you, not the other way around."

"So is that a yes?" I asked.

"For a date?" Holly laughed. "Sure. Why don't you meet me at the cofferdam on Monday? We're beginning the piece-by-piece disassembly of the *Belle* hull, and you can watch your archeologist girlfriend do her magic. I'll wear my finest coveralls and cleanest rubber boots for the occasion."

"We can share a sack lunch inside the pit?"

"Sure, a tuna fish sandwich and some Fritos. Throw in a Dr Pepper, and you're on."

"Be still my heart. Except that I'll bring a couple of shrimp po'boys instead of tuna—shrimp being the more popular seafood and all."

"Yeah, I heard you tell the governor. You sure know how to impress a girl."

Jim walked up and asked if Holly would help them begin marking the boundaries of the excavation site; they hoped to start digging next month, as soon as the *Belle* project was completed.

"Once the governor gives us the go-ahead," he said, "which she'll have to do before she leaves office, we can begin clearing the site. Mr. Dufay has agreed to transfer his crew tent, office trailer and chuck wagon from the Lavaca site over to here. Can you believe how fast this is progressing?" he said as he walked away.

Jim wisely included Julien in the decision-making right away. Holly and I watched with amusement as the two of them purposefully reconnoitered the site, planting survey flags, pointing out potential locations for the camp tents and trailer. The dark side of Julien's bipolar nature had been absent lately. I wondered if someone had talked him into taking meds for his illness, or if perhaps he had finally found someone down here whose skill set he respected. Which made it all the more mystifying why he seemed to get on with me.

They began unrolling the site maps that Jim had obtained from the previous Fort St. Louis excavation (the correct site maps), and Holly sighed. "Look at them—like a couple of over-excited kids on a scavenger hunt. I guess I better join them before they get out the shovels and start digging."

The party broke up early that afternoon and the state surveyors flew back to Austin. Julien had told Jim and Holly that any and all artifacts his Lavaca River project had produced, including the gold coins, would be donated to the future La Salle museum collection. Jim said he would bring some of his staff to the site the following morning to help transfer the treasures back to the THC warehouse in Palacios for safekeeping.

I offered to take Julien to the Kestrel ranch house for the evening. He declined.

"Perhaps tonight you will allow me to stay on the *Li Shishi* instead?"

"I'll do you one better, Julien. We'll have the butcher cut us some thick steaks and I'll grill 'em out on the deck. It should be a beautiful evening. We'll invite Jim and Holly, too."

"Only if you allow me to select the wine," Julien answered happily.

CHAPTER 31

It was a cool, clear night on the harbor, so Julien and I bundled up in blankets as we lounged on the quarterdeck of the junk. Jim and Holly had already returned to Palacios, citing THC business, but not before they helped us finish a platter of grilled tournedos that were perfectly complemented by the 1987 Silver Oak Cabernet that I knew for a fact had been sitting in the wine cellar at Fin's Liquor Store for at least seven years. Julien bought a case of the stuff. Fin, whose own tastes ran more to busthead Iron Curtain vodka, smiled and took the Frenchman's money.

During dinner, we toasted our good fortune and the success of the *Belle* excavation. We toasted the future of the La Salle Museum/ State Park/and Natural Area. And last but not least, we raised our glasses to the French explorer, whose brilliant, tragic, misguided quest was the catalyst for our own adventure.

"To René-Robert Cavelier, Sieur de La Salle," Jim proclaimed. "Without whom, none of this."

A third bottle was opened after Julien announced that he had spoken with his lawyer and that the La Salle Foundation was now officially established; the funds had been transferred into the account three hours ago. The documents were on their way to the foundation executor and trustee—me—to be reviewed and signed. That explained why Julien had been holed up in my office all afternoon.

In the calm aftermath of the celebratory party, Julien and I sat quietly and listened to the sounds of the harbor: the lapping of the water, the creaking of the wooden hull boats, the quiet voices of the Vietnamese fishermen as they prepared for bed. Occasionally a mullet slapped the water or a blue heron squawked as it lifted into flight. The stars above were big and bright, just like in the song.

"Have you decided who will design your museum, Julien?" I asked.

"I have not. I prefer the modern architecture, but I think a more traditional design is best. Not classical, but more *rustique, eh?* More in harmony with the surroundings. Something that La Salle might have constructed had he succeeded."

I tried to imagine Texas if La Salle indeed had succeeded. Spanish and Mexican culture was so interwoven into the fabric of the state that it was difficult for me to envision French themes running through our arts, architecture, customs, even our language.

"I think that would be an appropriate choice," I answered. Julien filled our glasses yet again and then reached over and grabbed my shoulder.

"Charlie, we have this discussion because of you, because of what you did."

"I didn't pledge twenty million dollars to the project, Julien. *You* did that."

"But the idea for the park, putting the right people together—it was brilliant. You could make a fortune in the oil and gas industry with your head for business and your talent with people. The successful Texans I have seen in that trade—many of them are patrons of my museum in Houston—they are constantly making deals and 'horse trading,' as they call it."

"I'm happy where I am. Savior of turtles, reaper of shrimp, sophisticated layabout."

"Yes," he said, smiling. "And I envy you for that. But we are not so different, you and I. How did your philosopher, Thoreau, say it? 'We hear a different drummer?'"

I quoted the source: *"If a man loses pace with his companions, perhaps it is because he hears a different drummer. Let him step to the music which he hears."* One of a handful of phrases I had committed to memory.

Julien laughed. "Yes! That is it. We are both a bit *out of step* with society. And you know the amazing thing, Charlie?"

"What, Jules?"

"Through all of this, you somehow overlook my . . . idiosyncrasies. You stick with me. Very few people have the patience to do that."

"Marguerite?"

"Yes, she is one. She is a saint." Julien paused and cast a knowing, and what I hoped was a forgiving, glance at me, "In her own way, of course." He hadn't mentioned my dalliances with his wife since he'd lost his temper at the Lavaca River work site. I hoped it would stay that way.

"She's on board with all this? The money and everything?"

Julien flicked his hand. "Of course, she supports me one hundred percent. Or she will. She always has. I haven't even told her about the foundation yet—she is in France this week—but I think she will be very proud."

We finished our wine and opened another bottle. The Silver Oak was doing wonders to keep the chill away. Perhaps it was the wine that prompted me to ask Julien why his mood had been so consistently stable the last few times I'd seen him.

"*Ouf*, Marguerite finally convince me to take some of the *medicament*—the uh, medications."

"Well, the *médicament* seems to be working."

"I suppose so. I do not care for it so much, but . . . she insists."

"Well, for what it's worth, I think Marguerite is right."

"Of course I forget the pills for this trip. But I will start again when I return."

As we sat in the deck chairs gazing up at the stars and a waning crescent moon, a cormorant landed on the rail near Julien. The black bird inclined its snake-like neck toward Julien and fixed its eyes on him.

"What does he want?" Julien asked, staring back at it.

"I don't know." A cormorant had never landed on my boat before.

The bird balanced on the gunwale, its wings extended and slightly drooped, watching Julien with green eyes.

"Let's go below, Charlie."

We moved to the galley below deck and drank one more glass of wine. By the time we finished, our teeth were aubergine.

Tired and pleasantly drunk, we retired to our beds. Julien insisted I take the master bunk while he fixed a pallet on the bench seat behind the mess table. The only light that intruded on the darkness came from the streetlamp in the Fulton Harbor parking lot.

—

I must have fallen asleep as soon as I closed my eyes, because I don't remember anything from then up until the moment some son of a bitch tried to kill me.

I vaguely recall a pillow being pressed into my face with tremendous force; what else could it have been? But mostly I felt the terrible sensations associated with suffocation: the initial panic when oxygen is cut off from the lungs, the reflexive adrenal response—increased heartbeat, the rerouting of my body's metabolic resources to the fight or flight organs. The problem was, I was unable to do either. My legs and arms were stuck under the covers, pinned there by the heavy body kneeling on top of me. I remember the feeling of being underwater, and envisioning a crustaceous old oyster out in the bay, being attacked by one of those carnivorous snails—the oyster helpless as the snail slides on top and begins boring through the oyster's protective shell to get at the living tissue inside, consuming the oyster . . . killing the oyster.

And then the oxygen returned, the weight that pinned me dropped away. I gasped for air as consciousness slowly returned, dimly aware of the pandemonium occurring outside my quarters. When I caught my breath, I realized that two men were fighting in the galley.

"Julien?" I yelled, my voice strangled, my chest heaving.

Two figures scrambled up the companionway stairs, one in flight, one in pursuit. I leapt out of bed and ran topside. Julien and a man wearing a dark ski mask were fighting on the stern deck—Julien shirtless, the other man in a black leather jacket and gloves.

The man in the ski mask was crouched low, advancing steadily toward Julien, holding his arms out in a wrestler's stance, trying to grab a piece of his opponent—any piece. And also to deflect the barrage of blows and kicks Julien was delivering with startling speed and accuracy. Where the hell did he learn to fight like that?

The assailant picked up a deck chair and swung it at Julien, who stepped out of range. When the man swung the chair again, Julien bumped into the mast and couldn't evade the blow. The wooden chair caught the left side of his body, slamming him to the deck. The bigger man was on him in an instant, kneeling over him, his hands wrapped around his neck.

I bolted toward them and slapped the masked figure hard across the ear with an open palm, knocking him away from Julien. The blow also knocked the mask askew, pushing it over the man's eyes. He ripped off the mask and scrambled to his feet, looking around him like a wounded predator. In the dim light, I could see the face of the man who had almost killed me. Monroe Chambers.

Monroe was on me before I knew it. I punched him once and tried to punch him again, but he caught my wrist with his big hand and began twisting it. I rolled my body to keep him from breaking my arm. But then his other hand found my neck. Those fucking hands. Monster's hands. I felt them clutching my throat. He was going to finish what he'd started below.

Out of the corner of my eye I saw Julien appear, delivering two rapid blows to Monroe's kidneys. He grunted and then released me.

"You go too far, Monroe," said Julien, burying his fist into the man's diaphragm. Monroe doubled over as the air was forced out of his lungs, and then Julien delivered a forceful Muay Thai elbow strike to the side of his head. That blow probably knocked him out, but to be sure, Julien brought his elbow back up under his chin and sent the man crashing to the deck.

The two of us stood over Monroe's body, our chests heaving, a panting mist of breath clouding the air between us.

I hurried into the cabin and grabbed my shoes and a jacket. I tossed the jacket to Julien. "You watch him, I'll go call the cops."

Julien nodded and sat down on the bench to catch his breath, his forearms resting on his thighs, just as I'd seen him the night I'd pulled him out of the sea. A troubled expression clouded his face.

I placed the jacket around his shoulders. "Be careful, Julien. Holler if he comes to. The guy's dangerous."

"I know he is, Charlie. He tried to kill me once, too."

I looked at him, not understanding.

"The day before you rescued me. Monroe was on that crew boat. It was he who pushed me into the water."

I could tell that Julien was upset. Not about the fight, and certainly not about the outcome, but because the man who worked exclusively for his brother—the man who once tried to drown him—had been sent to kill me. Julien had to be wondering if Jean-Marc ordered them both.

I had no trouble believing it. Monroe was a killer, but he was also a mercenary. He'd been paid to scare me off. When that didn't work, and when Jean-Marc found out I was behind the maneuverings with the governor, he must have sent Monroe to finish me, hoping the deal would stop or run out of time with me out of the way.

I left Julien alone with his anger and shame and ran to my office to phone the police.

FROM THE JOURNAL OF PÈRE POISSON

Soon La Salle will depart to find the elusive, and now much scorned great river, and if successful will proceed to the French settlements in Canada and thence France to return with a ship. Almost everyone wanted to leave on this expedition, although La Salle could take only provisions enough for himself and a handful of men. Those who will remain number twenty-four: mostly women, clergy, children and cripples. I offered to stay at the settlement, feeling compelled to do so. I cannot leave this frayed and shoddy band alone here. I will pray for La Salle's safe return.

Père Poisson
JANUARY 1687

CHAPTER 32

The next day at the Lavaca River dig site, Julien addressed his crew and I watched the men's expressions when they realized that their six-month undertaking had been in vain. Their contract had come to an end, and they were being replaced by "professionals" hired by the Texas Historical Commission. Half a year of backbreaking labor in a mosquito-infested backwater, with no R&R, and most importantly, no big bonus at the end. Even though they were told they would be paid for work done to date, it was small consolation.

The Mexicans who remained on the job accepted the news passively. I think they had decided the project was lunacy from day one. No doubt they were hoping that this employer would actually pay them for work completed. They'd been stiffed before. As soon as they had their money they would move on to the next menial, yet indispensable, job. For them, it was all about the paycheck.

For Clifton, Omar and Vinny, however, it was about something else. They were seriously pissed off. They started sputtering and snorting and kicking the ground as soon as Julien mentioned that their services were no longer required. When he got to the part about them not getting a bonus, they starting cursing. Unquestionably,

Julien could have handled the announcement better—he was blunt, unsympathetic and unapologetic—but Clifton's group evidently felt they were owed something more.

I was surprised and disappointed to find the trouble-making trio at the job site when I arrived, considering that I had run Clifton and his buddies off less than a week ago. Julien obviously hadn't backed me up on that one. When I reminded him about it, he just said he'd forgotten. In fact, he'd hardly spoken since the police took Monroe into custody the night before. I didn't know if Julien and Jean-Marc had talked about the incident yet, but I did know that Julien spent a good deal of time that night speaking with O.B. Hadnott at the jail. Whatever Julien's state of mind, he seemed to be back to his single-minded quest to unearth the French settlement.

"How do you know this isn't Fort St. Louis?" Clifton demanded to know.

"This is not the site," Julien answered.

"We found a French rifle and lots of other stuff that got y'all real excited. I think the fort is here and you just don't want to pay us our bonus."

"You are not qualified to know if it is here or not. You have been paid well; the bonus was for uncovering the fort, which did not happen."

"What about them gold coins, then? Clifton continued. "The ones you got locked up inside that trailer?"

"I told you, this is not the site."

"If that's so, it sure as hell isn't our fault that you've had us digging in the wrong spot all this time. It's yours."

Julien turned to Reginald. "*Vous expliquer.* I have no patience for this." He waved his hand dismissively and began walking toward the office trailer. Ever the diplomat.

Reginald cleared his throat and went into an academic explanation about the pottery shards that had been discovered at the Garcitas site, and the differences between Spanish and French ceramics, and then he began a discourse about the trading relationship between the aboriginal Indians of the 17th century and the French and Spanish explorers, and how European artifacts might have ended up in the Lavaca River site. He was about as persuasive as a carpetbagger.

Finally, Clifton cut him off. "Reggie, shut the fuck up."

"Yeah, *Regi-nald*," Vinny said mockingly. "Why don't you go hide in your trailer?"

Julien had been fiddling with the satellite phone but he over-heard the tail end of the conversation behind him. He turned around, furious, and walked up to the rabble-rousers. "*Écoutez-moi, vous les ingrats.* You have two choices." Julien jabbed his finger at the three men. "You can leave the jobsite immediately, or you can shut the hell up and do what I say. *Your* job is to disassemble the camp. *Dès maintenant!* Right now!"

I couldn't help but remember Julien saying he'd left his pills back in Houston. And I did not like the way things were shaping up. I noticed Hoyt was looking at me with concern, wondering if the situation was going to turn violent again. Clifton took a step toward Julien, and I took a step toward them both, ready to intervene, or more, if necessary. Omar stood by silently, watching.

From below, we heard a truck engine shift into low gear as it climbed the bluff. Everyone stopped to listen. A moment later, a pickup truck and a station wagon appeared. Jim Brannan was driving the pickup, with Holly in the passenger seat. A couple of THC workers occupied the station wagon.

When Julien saw Jim, his face lit up. He strode toward the truck, seeming to have forgotten about the dispute with his workers. Then he stopped suddenly and turned around. "I offer you this," he said, addressing the crew in a flat, unemotional tone. "You men help us transfer the camp to the new site, and I will pay you . . . " he paused a moment to think, "twenty percent of the bonus I offered you in the contract, eh? That is over one month pay. It is a fair offer."

I wasn't sure what prompted Julien to make this offer—it was such an abrupt change of mind and attitude—but I was glad to see it defused the situation.

The group dispersed and grudgingly went to work.

I turned to Dodo. "I'm glad they're shutting down this site."

Dodo shook his head. "Like dat man sing, if it wadn't fo' bad luck, we wouldn't a had no luck at all, *cher.*"

It was the first time Jim had visited the Lavaca River site, so Julien and Reginald gave him a quick tour and showed them their inventory of artifacts. Jim inspected the articles with enthusiasm, frequently complimenting the two men on their excellent work. Holly was less demonstrative. She had already told me that although the artifacts from the site were numerous—it had been a very popular Indian camp-site for hundreds of years—they were by no means unique. The musket, the verso gun and the three hundred *Louis d'ors* were the notable exceptions. She said the Indians had probably traded for the goods or stole them when they ransacked the French fort.

Work began and Jim's team began packing up the artifacts for transport to the THC warehouse. Soon after, the crew began loading the boxes, tubs and crates into the truck and station wagon. Before we knew it, both vehicles were full.

"I suppose we'll have to make two trips," said Jim.

I offered to haul some of the relics in my old truck. "It's almost a relic itself," I added.

"Excellent idea, Charlie," Julien agreed. "I would like to get as much accomplished today as possible. If we complete the transfer of the artifacts in one trip, this will save us time." Julien's high-handedness with the men had given way to high spirits where the new dig was concerned.

After the camp trailer was emptied and all three vehicles filled, Julien summoned Jim and his staff to the center of the camp. When everyone was gathered, he pulled a small felt bag from his vest pocket and removed a gold coin, and then made a big show of presenting Jim with the shiny *Louis d'or.*

"To bring you success and good fortune," he said. "In the upcoming project and in life."

Jim held up the old coin for all to see and ceremoniously thanked Julien for the gift. The THC volunteers observed the coin with professional appreciation. But I noticed Clifton eyeing the coin in a different way—with an avaricious look that I had seen before. In Julien's absence, Clifton and his group had commandeered the camp when they learned about the two thousand *livres* mentioned in the ship's manifest, forcing the crew to dig for the gold coins when and where they wanted. And now Julien was practically flaunting the treasure in front of them.

Clifton saw me watching him, and he glared back defiantly, like I'd caught him out and he couldn't have cared less. Conrad got it right in *Nostromo*: "There is no getting away from a treasure that once fastens upon your mind."

I felt a nudge in my ribs and found Holly by my side. "Jim put the verso in the front seat of his truck. He wanted it to have its own seatbelt."

"Safety first."

"Since I've been unseated by an old cannon, do you think I can ride with you?"

"Sure. Julien's riding with me too, so if you don't mind sitting between us . . . ."

"Lucky me."

"Well, this has certainly been Jim's lucky day," I said. "He's got a shiny gold coin in his pocket and a smokin' hot cannon riding by his side."

"Too bad he'll have to give up that *Louis d'or* once he gets to the warehouse."

"Give it up? How come?"

"It goes into the collection, bub. Part of the archeologist code— we never keep artifacts. Which reminds me, I'll be needing that *Louis d'or* back from you, too."

"The one that Julien *gave* me?"

"They are priceless archeological treasures . . . and now they belong to the Texas Historical Commission." She smiled after she said it, but she was also holding out her hand.

"You're not kidding, are you?" I laughed. "You've got 298 more of 'em in the station wagon. What's one small trinket for a poor shrimper?"

"Hand it over, Captain. I won't associate with a looter."

"You're a hard man, Miss Hardin." I pulled the coin out of my watch pocket, gave it one last look, and placed it in her palm. "It's supposed to bring good luck, you know. You're tempting fate by taking it from me."

"I'm an archeologist. We don't believe in fate."

I started the truck and called to Julien, telling him it was time to climb in.

Julien walked over, smiling. "I will stay behind, Charlie."

"Stay behind? Why?"

"I used the satellite phone to call my pilot. He will pick me up at the site this afternoon and fly me back to Houston. *Hélas*, I have a board meeting on Monday morning."

"Suit yourself. " I said.

"I will go to the new site and mark the location of the camp tent and office."

"To the new site? Okay, sure. I should be back in a few hours and we can take my truck."

"I won't need your truck, Charlie. I will walk to the Fort St. Louis location."

"Why the heck would you want to walk?"

"It is only four or five miles. Not so difficult. I can swim much further than that, *vous savez?*" He smiled and punched me in the shoulder affably. "*Eh?*"

"I know you are capable, Julien, but is it that important that you go to the new camp right now? If you wait a few hours—"

"Yes, but Charlie," he leaned closer and lowered his voice. "I want to walk up to the site as La Salle once did, and feel like I discover the place for the first time—I want to imagine seeing it through his eyes, you know? I realize it is foolish, but . . . ."

"No, I get it, Julien. That's actually a pretty cool idea. In fact, I'd like to go with you. I bet Holly can deliver this stuff to the warehouse, and you and I'll go to the site together. Right, Holly?"

She nodded. "Sure, I can drive myself."

Julien looked at Holly and me with a twinkle in his eye. "No, you two should be together."

"You sure I can't pick you up at the site?"

"*Non, non.* It is already arranged. Besides, you will have more work to do here when you get back."

"Okay, Jules. You're the boss."

"Don't forget to look for the foundation documents in the mail, Charlie," he reminded me cheerfully. "Sign them and then *you* will be the boss." He stepped back and slapped the truck twice, sending us on our way.

As we drove away Holly said, "Julien Dufay is starting to grow on me."

From my rearview mirror I watched Julien standing alone on the old Karankawa campsite, waving goodbye. "Yep. I know what you mean."

———

CHAPTER 33

Miguel picked up the sack of fresh shrimp I had placed on the countertop and eyed me suspiciously. "What's this?"

"That, my felonious friend, is a sack of fresh shrimp."

"The hell am I supposed to do with it?"

"I promised Holly that I would bring a couple of delicious po'boy sandwiches out to the cofferdam for lunch today, and nobody makes a shrimp po'boy better than you. I thought that maybe . . . ."

He released the sack and it dropped to the countertop with a squishy thud, and then he returned to the top-water popper he was rigging up at the other end of the counter.

I sighed loudly. "Or, I guess I could just do it myself. You got any Creole mustard for the remoulade sauce?" I walked around the counter to look in the pantry.

"Keep the hell outta my kitchen, *cabrón*," he said without looking up.

"Alright, alright. *Cálmate*." As I headed out back, I grabbed a beer from the cooler. Notwithstanding Miguel's churlish performance, I knew that in a few minutes he would amble into the kitchen and begin preparing the remoulade slaw and the cornmeal fry mix for the shrimp. Because I'd mentioned that the sandwiches were for Holly, they were sure to be tasty.

It was Monday and a little early for lunch, so the place was empty. Out on the deck, Hinkie had pulled the crab traps out of the bay and was filling the bait holders with chicken necks. He was bent over the traps, absorbed in his task.

I sat on one of the picnic tables and let the sun bathe my face while I breathed in the crisp morning air. There's nothing like a near-death experience to make you appreciate the simple things in life.

On the far shore of Powderhorn Lake, I saw hundreds, maybe thousands, of birds wading or floating in the mudflats and marshes. In the still morning air, I could hear the chugging diesels of a bay shrimper trawling the muddy floor of Matagorda Bay. Laughing gulls squawked in the distance. I closed my eyes and enjoyed the moment. The big freeze earlier in the month seemed like ancient history.

A few minutes later I heard the kitchen sounds of battered shrimp being dropped into hot grease, and cabbage being chopped for slaw. *Atta boy, Miguel.* He would, of course, keep the balance of the ten-pound sack of shellfish for his own use, an unspoken part of the deal.

When the po'boys were ready, I pulled out my wallet and asked Miguel what I owed him.

"Hers is free. Yours is ten dollars."

"*Híjole*, Miguel. I'm not sure I can afford to eat here anymore."

"Then sell that catch-me-fuck-me boat you got outside."

"Out of the question. That boat's a timeless classic. Unlike you." I added two Dr Peppers, a bag of Fritos and a couple of fried pies to the total. "What do I have to give you for these? A kidney?" Miguel fingered a fillet knife thoughtfully.

"I heard you almost lost more than that the other night. Heard that little Frenchman had to save your skinny ass."

I raised my eyebrows. Any time a crime was committed within a hundred miles, Miguel always seemed to know about it. "That little Frenchman is a regular Bruce Lee," I answered. "Who knew?"

We settled up and I left the marina, balancing the drinks and bait store delectables in my arms. I had to pivot around and open the screen door with my back. "Don't worry about the door, Miguel. I can get it."

The screen slammed shut, and as I headed for my boat I heard Miguel yell from inside.

"She's too good for you, *cabrón*."

"Gracias, amigo!" I yelled back, gratified that I'd been able to skip the tab on the beer I'd drunk. It would be the first time ever.

Through the window I heard, "And you still owe me for that beer, asshole."

Damn.

—

As I motored up to the cofferdam, Steve, the guy with the stud earring I'd met at the THC warehouse in Palacios, happened to be standing on the wall. He caught my line and tied it off to a cleat. I grabbed my sack of goodies and climbed onto the dam.

"You brought lunch. Awesome!" he said.

The breeze was brisk off the bay. Steve was wearing a long-sleeve pullover that read "Intelligent Design Makes My Monkey Sad."

"Sorry, Steve. Maybe next time. Is Holly here?"

"In the pit," he answered cheerfully.

I pulled on a pair of rubber neoprene boots ("Cajun Tony Lamas," Dodo called them), climbed down the scaffold steps and found Jim photographing the shipwreck, front to back. Holly stood inside the hull, her feet on the keel and her body leaning across one of the timbers. She appeared to be nailing a bright orange tag into the wood.

"Are those ear-tags, Jim?" I asked. There were hundreds of the numbered tags fastened about the ship. They appeared to be the tags stockmen used to mark and identify their sheep and cattle.

He lowered his camera and turned around. "Oh, hey, Charlie. Yeah, that's exactly what they are. They hold up great against the mud and saltwater. You should've seen the feed store salesman's face when we explained what we needed them for."

Jim told me that after all the timbers were tagged and oh-so-carefully removed—a two month process he hoped—they would be packed up and shipped to Texas A&M. There, they would reassemble the *Belle* in a specially made concrete pool designed just for her.

"The university will study the artifacts for years. And millions of dollars will be spent to preserve and then reassemble Mr. La Salle's *barque longue* for its public unveiling. I think this ol' shipwreck will be transformed into a magnificent exhibit once it's completed. What do you think?"

"I think archeology is a royal pain in the ass."

"It is if you do it right."

"You think normal folks will find all these 'treasures' as exciting as you guys do?"

"They will if we tell the story in a compelling way. Remember," he said in his lecturer's voice, "it's not about the artifacts we find. It's the knowledge we gain *from* the artifacts—where they came from, how they were used. Archeology is basically the study of people, Charlie. And I believe *that* is something folks *will* find interesting."

I thought of Julien's clumsy excavation efforts at the Port Lavaca site under the guidance of Antoine and Reginald, and of the rag-tag band of laborers they had assembled for the project, the missteps and fuck-ups that followed. That was a story about people, too. Maybe that's what had kept me so interested all these months. It was a good thing that Jim and Holly would be running the show at the Garcitas Creek project. If all went well, it might actually produce something that everyone could be proud of, most of all Julien.

Holly climbed out of the hull and walked over. "You remembered our lunch date." She had to raise her voice over the sound of the generators that powered the lights, pumps and pneumatic tools.

"Of course I did. And believe me, this will be the best lunch experience you've ever had inside a muddy cofferdam. Ever."

She peeked inside the sack. "Miguel's po'boys?"

"Yes, ma'am. Plus Fritos and fried pies—one cherry, one apple."

"I don't know, Charlie," she said, shaking her head solemnly. "This isn't near enough."

"What do you mean?"

"You told me you were going to bring lunch for the entire crew. We were kind of counting on it."

I remembered Steve's comment up top and wondered if I had screwed the pooch on this one. Seeing the pained expression on my face, Holly began to laugh.

"I'm just teasing you. Let's go up. We've got an improvised picnic table away from the noisy generators. It can be halfway pleasant when the weather's nice like it is today."

I wasn't used to this kind of levity from Holly, and I kind of liked this side of her. She was even more beautiful when she laughed, even if she was wearing mud-covered coveralls.

Jim looked over his glasses at us. "I'm crushed you didn't bring me one of those sandwiches, Charlie." A goofy grin appeared on his face; I knew another one of his lame jokes was coming. "But then, that's been the story of my life ever since I became an archeologist." He sighed dramatically and shook his head. "My life in ruins."

Jim bent over laughing at his joke and his glasses fell into the mud. He continued to chuckle even after he picked them up and began to wipe them off. He'd probably been waiting years to deliver that one.

Holly rolled her eyes and headed toward the scaffold.

"Good one, Jim," I said.

Up on the wall, I watched Holly eat her sandwich contentedly.

"My God. Where did Miguel learn to cook like this? Did he apprentice at a fancy restaurant or something?"

Holly obviously didn't know much about Miguel's criminal past. It was not something he shared with other people—so I couldn't tell her it was most definitely not from the Huntsville Prison Culinary Institute of Swill & Salmonella.

"He's just got a knack for it I guess."

"No kidding." She took a drink of her soda pop and burped daintily, her eyes dancing merrily when I pretended to be shocked.

"Where did you go to finishing school, girl?"

"Texas A&M."

"Well, that explains it."

We unwrapped our pies and savored the sugary, deep-fried delicacies. Gastronomically indefensible, but delicious all the same.

As we ate, we watched a motorboat approach from the direction of Port Lavaca, two men standing behind the console. Probably more archeo-tourists, as the crew called them. Jim had told me that over twenty thousand people had visited the project since they'd opened it for public tours five months ago.

I turned to Holly and saw her eyeing me thoughtfully. "You know, Charlie, I haven't actually told you how impressed I am with the way you handled the Fort St. Louis thing. I'm not real good at giving compliments, but, well, you really knocked it out of the park."

"I'm just glad it all worked out."

"And the good guys won," she added.

As we finished lunch and cleaned off the table, I noticed with a bit of a concern that O.B. Hadnott was aboard the boat that had nosed up to the edge of the cofferdam. It was unusual to see O.B. out on the water. Fourteen years living on the coast, and he still retained his native West Texan's aversion to open water and small boats. My anxiety increased when I realized that the other man was a uniformed sheriff's deputy. I thought we'd finished with that business the other night. I wasn't really in the mood to talk about Monroe again, especially in front of Holly.

Holly had seen the law officers too, and we both waited as they climbed the ladder and walked toward us.

"Miss Hardin," said O.B. in greeting, tipping the brim of his Stetson. "Charlie."

"Hello, Captain Hadnott," said Holly. "How are you?"

"And what brings you out here to the middle of Matagorda Bay?" I asked.

"Is Julien Dufay out here?" he asked straightaway. O.B. regarded small talk as a frivolous obstacle, like putting a dish of sorbet in front of a chicken-fried steak.

"Mr. Dufay? Why, no," answered Holly. "I haven't seen him since Saturday morning, at Mr. Sutton's ranch."

"How about you, Charlie?"

"Same here. Holly and I were together at the Lavaca River site. Before we left, he told us he was going to walk cross-country to the future dig site on Garcitas Creek. He said his pilot was going to meet him there with a car and then take him back to Houston in his airplane. What's going on, Captain?"

"The pilot *did* show up at the pick-up spot, but he said Julien never arrived."

I felt a weight growing in my belly as I searched for a logical explanation. "Are you sure the guy went to the right place? Maybe Julien gave him bad directions, or the pilot misunderstood."

O.B. shook his head. "He said he followed Mr. Dufay's directions and drove to a place on Garcitas Creek that was staked out with survey flags. He waited there until dark and then went back to town and called the sheriff, who called me."

"Do you think Julien got lost?" asked Holly.

"Maybe. But it's unlikely that six people did."

"Six? Who was with him, Captain?" I could hear the apprehension in Holly's voice, and I shared the feeling.

O.B. looked directly at me when he answered. "Clifton Sloan, Vincent Toussaint, Omar Camacho, that Cajun cook, and the boy, Hoyt Archer. None of them returned to camp."

Holly and I peppered him with more questions, suggesting other places he might look, but the Ranger had already crossed them off his list.

"We've put the word out to local law enforcement from Corpus to Victoria to Bay City. So far there's been no word of them. This cofferdam was one of the last places I could think of to look. I'd hoped maybe he shipped over here with Mr. Brannan, or with one of you two."

"Captain," I began. "Have y'all started searching Mr. Sutton's ranch?"

"We've got a small team out there right now. But the governor—thanks to a couple of phone calls from some powerful people in Houston—has authorized the deployment of a bigger, better-equipped team. I'm meeting them this afternoon in Port Lavaca."

"Was it Mrs. Dufay," I asked, "who called the governor?"

"Both of them. The wife and the mother. As you can imagine, the governor's taking it personally."

"What can we do to help, Captain Hadnott?" Holly asked.

"Miss Hardin, I would be much obliged if you'd talk to Mr. Sutton. He knows his ranch a lot better than any of the deputies we've got traipsing around out there. I asked for his assistance last night, but it was late and he was pretty deep in the bottle. He declined to volunteer. And this morning . . . . Well, let's just say he wasn't in any shape to help out."

"I'd be glad to talk to him," said Holly.

"Be careful," I warned her. "He can be touchy if he's been drinking." Then, I asked the Ranger what I could do.

He removed his hat and scratched his head. "I've got people looking for them on land, and in a little while, from the air, too. But nobody's searched the water yet."

"I can start right now," I said. "If they got lost yesterday, and then night caught 'em before they found their way out, they could've headed for the lights of Port Lavaca, or maybe just followed the river down to the bay. I just might find them wandering into town, tired and hungry and wondering how the hell they got so turned around."

"You just might," said O.B.

He sounded about as unconvinced of that as I did.

One of Holly's crew volunteered to take her back to Palacios on the *Anomaly*. As I was unlooping the lines to my boat, O.B. called down from the edge of the cofferdam. He squatted on his haunches to talk.

"I got a call from Houston today," he began. "They found Antoine Gillette floating in the Ship Channel early this morning."

I winced at the news. "How'd he die?"

"The body had been in the salt water for a good while, and they'll have to do an autopsy, but the preliminary report said it looked like strangulation. He was dead before he went in the water."

———

CHAPTER 34

My search efforts along the shores of Lavaca Bay proved fruitless, as were those of Captain Hadnott and his team. I borrowed Hinkie's ancient Rambler and drove back to Fulton Harbor after dark. I visited Raul and Sammy to inform them of the situation, and they both volunteered to help me continue the manhunt in the morning; three boats would be better than one. Come sunup, we'd search the riverbanks and bayous.

On the way home I picked up a broiled chicken and a six-pack of beer, hoping that a full stomach and a mild buzz would help me get a few hours' sleep before I continued my grim task early the next day. If Julien and his crew had lost their way—a remote possibility at best—they would have been found by now. Sutton's ranch was big, but it wasn't that big. A chopper, two tracking teams and a shore patrol (me) would have spotted them.

Something bad had happened. I could feel it, the way you feel a storm coming. Why in the hell did Julien let those three miscreants accompany him on his cross-country trek? Men that he knew were troublemakers. Men that he'd just fired, without their full bonus. I thought I'd made it clear they were a threat to him and his project. Hadn't I?

But then again, his naïveté wasn't so hard to understand. For all his genius and drive, Julien was terrible at reading people. Most people he never noticed at all. To him they were mostly extras in the ongoing drama of his life. Folks like Jim and Holly, and me too I suppose, were his supporting actors. When you always put the spotlight on yourself, it's hard to see what's happening around you.

I worried about Hoyt and Dodo, too. I should have put Hoyt in the cab of my truck and taken his happy ass back to Sugarland the day I found out he'd been roughed up by Clinton . . . or by Omar, or Vinny, take your pick: any one of them could have done it, and one was as bad as the other.

What's more, Dodo had pulled a gun on Omar when we'd had our scrape back at the camp. Omar Camacho didn't strike me as a guy to forget something like that. And if he came for you, he'd wait until your back was turned.

Dismal thoughts swirled inside my head as I opened a beer and went out to the porch. The wind was picking up and I saw dark clouds moving in from the east. Tomorrow would be rough and overcast, making it that much harder to find a body in the bay. I shivered. It was a rotten end to what had started out as a beautiful day.

I heard rustling in the oleander bushes below me. I held my breath and listened. When I heard the sound again, I went quietly inside and retrieved my shotgun, pushing a couple of shells into the chamber as I turned off the interior lights.

"Who's out there?" I yelled down from the deck.

I saw movement behind the bushes, so I clicked off the safety and brought the shotgun to my shoulder. "You better identify yourself or I'm sending a load of lead shot your way."

"Charlie, it's me, Hoyt."

I lowered the gun. It sounded like Hoyt, but the voice was weak, strained. "Come around. I'll let you in."

I heard footsteps coming up the stairs and I peeked through the window to make sure he was alone before I opened the door.

"Hoyt, it is you!" I said, happy to see him. "Is anybody with you?"
"No."

I switched on a table lamp and gasped when I saw him in the light. His clothes were filthy and ripped, and his face and arms were lacerated with scratches. He looked like he hadn't slept in a week. "Bloody hell," I muttered. "Sit down over here."

I steered him to the couch and he sat down heavily.

"How did you find me? And how the hell did you get here?"

"Walked."

"From the camp? That's almost fifty miles from here."

"Can I have some water?" he said feebly.

I retrieved a glass from the cabinet and filled it with tap water. Hoyt emptied the glass and I filled it again. After he drained the third glass, I handed him a beer.

"Here, kid. This might help too."

I sat on the other end of the couch and waited until he drank a few gulps of beer. "Hoyt—"

"He's dead," he blurted.

"Who? Julien? Julien is dead?"

Hoyt nodded. "And Dodo. They killed them."

"Who killed them?"

"Them—Clifton and Omar. They were going to kill me, too. They came after me, Charlie. They're still after me."

His eyes teared up and he began sobbing.

I put my hand on his shoulder. "Hoyt, when's the last time you ate?" I shook his shoulder. "Hoyt!"

"I don't know. Yesterday . . . breakfast."

I set two plates and some silverware on the kitchen table, poured a tall glass of milk, and forked the still warm chicken onto a wooden cutting board. Hungry, wrung out, traumatized, and scared shitless. No wonder he couldn't hold it together.

"Go wash up and then come over here and take a seat, buddy. First you get some food in your belly, and then you tell me the whole story." I locked the front door and made sure all the blinds were closed. *They're still after me*, he'd said. I got a box of shotgun shells out of a cabinet and set it on the floor by my chair.

The kid ate at least three quarters of the chicken by himself, plus a slab of bread covered with butter, and half a package of stale Oreo cookies. It was all that I could offer from my paltry bachelor's larder. I cleared the table and motioned for him get up.

"Over here," I said, pointing to the couch. I dragged over a kitchen chair and sat down in front of him, resting my arms on the chair back. "Start at the beginning."

Hoyt took a deep breath.

"Before Mr. Dufay left the camp yesterday, he told Pablo, Ernesto and Chuy to finish striking the tent . . . ."

"Wait, who?"

"The Mexican workers. He asked them to take down the camp tent."

"Okay, right. Go on."

"Then he told Clifton, Vinny and Omar to gather up some tools: shovels, pickaxes, survey equipment—those kinds of things. When he told them where they were going, where they were *walking* to, they started arguing, saying it was stupid to walk so far, and that they should wait for the truck. They didn't want to carry a bunch of heavy stuff cross-country.

"Then Mr. Dufay ordered them to go with him. He said that if they wanted their bonus, they better pick up the tools and follow him. I don't know why he had to say that. The guys were already mad at him. At the last minute, he told me to go too. I don't know why."

"What about Dodo?" I asked.

"Dodo volunteered to come along. I think he was worried to see me and Mr. Dufay going off with Clifton and them, so he said he needed to go too, so he could find the right spot for his kitchen, or something like that."

"What time did y'all leave the camp, Hoyt?"

"Right after y'all left."

I nodded for him to continue.

"We started walkin' . . . just following in a line behind Mr. Dufay. Then pretty soon Clifton starts telling Mr. Dufay that it wasn't fair they weren't gettin' their full bonus, and that he was sure they could find a lawyer who agreed with them. Mr. Dufay ignored him, and then Vinny started in, too. They kept at it for a while. Dodo tried to tell one of his funny stories to break the tension, but they made him shut up."

Hoyt closed his eyes and winced, as if what happened next was replaying in his mind. I waited patiently for him to resume.

"After we'd been walking for a ways, we stopped in a dry creek bed. The gear we were carrying was pretty heavy, and Vinny kept saying he had to rest. Finally, Mr. Dufay stopped. Me and Dodo and Mr. Dufay were sitting together on a dead tree that had fallen across the dry creek. Vinny and Clifton were sitting on a rock in front of us, and Omar . . . Omar just stood to the side, not saying anything.

"When Clifton started complaining again, Mr. Dufay finally let him have it. I mean he just exploded, you know? Like he does sometime. He told Clifton that they'd be lucky to get a penny. He accused them of trying to sabotage his project, and said they were worthless workers, dishonest—that kind of thing.

"Then Vinny mentioned again that they were going to get a lawyer, and Mr. Dufay dared him to do it. He said that he'd hire some of the best lawyers that money could buy and he'd make sure they lost everything. Vinny said something else, I forget what, and Mr. Dufay stood up and told them he might not pay 'em at all . . . that they could try and sue him but they'd get nothing. After that . . . ."

Hoyt trailed off and stared at the floor, seemingly in a trance.

"After that, what?" I asked.

"Omar."

"Omar what?"

"Omar all of sudden pulls out that knife he keeps around his neck and he . . . *stabs* Mr. Dufay. Here." Hoyt reached behind his head and touched the base of his neck, tapping the upper vertebrae of his spine.

I felt a wave of pain and anger surge through my body.

Hoyt looked up curiously. "It happened so fast, Charlie. The knife seemed to come out of nowhere. Mr. Dufay fell to his knees and his eyes got really big, like he couldn't believe it, you know? And then the life just . . . left his body. It was terrible."

I stood up and pulled a bottle of rum out of the cupboard, pouring a glass for each of us. "What happened next, Hoyt?" I asked quietly. I handed him his glass, trying to keep my own hand from shaking.

He took a sip. "Dodo was moaning and shaking his head, asking Omar why he did what he did. The rest of us just stood there watching. Stunned like. And then Omar walks over to Clifton and hands him a pick-ax. 'Finish it,' he says.

"Dodo is down there holding Mr. Dufay in his arms, and then Clifton . . . ." Hoyt faltered and took another drink of rum. "And then Clifton walks around behind Dodo. And he raises that pick-ax and . . . buries it in Dodo's head. I mean he just *buries* it there."

Christ almighty, I thought.

The boy was staring into space again so I prompted him back. "What did you do, Hoyt?"

He looked at me. "I ran, Charlie. I ran. As fast as I could. Vinny chased me and even tackled me once, but I got loose and kept running. When I couldn't run anymore, I hid in a mesquite thicket. I could hear them coming after me. All three of them. They stopped to catch their breath—they were close by me, right next to the thicket where I was hiding. They couldn't see me, but I could hear them talking." He closed his eyes and shook his head.

"What did they say?"

"They talked about killing me. Clifton started gettin' on Vinny for letting me get away—for *not* killing me. He said they would all get the death penalty if they got caught and I was alive to tell what happened. Then Vinny told Clifton that he wouldn't get the death penalty, 'cause he didn't kill nobody—that the other two might have to worry about that, but not him.

"Vinny kept talkin' like that, and then Omar . . . again, with that knife. I see the blade flash and all of sudden Vinny's got blood shootin' out of his chest. I . . . I almost got sick, Charlie. None of it seemed real. None of it seems real now."

He leaned back and looked at me, exhausted. "They dragged Vinny's body away, back to where the others were, I guess. When they were out of sight, I started running again. When I got to the edge of the next ranch over, I hid until nightfall, and then I started walking toward Fulton."

"Why Fulton, Hoyt?" I asked. "Why not flag down a car on the road and go straight to the police?"

"I was scared, Charlie. They were after me. They could've stolen a car. What if it was them on the road, looking for me? You were the first person I thought of that could help me."

I understood his point of view. Eighteen years old, alone in a hostile environment—his buddy and three others had died out there—with a couple of cold-blooded murderers on his trail. Hoyt sought out the only semi-rational person he'd met these last six months. Me, God help him.

"I made it to the other side of Copano Bay this morning," he continued. "And tonight, when it got dark enough, I crossed the bridge and came here."

"How did you know where I lived?"

"There's a phone booth outside the Texaco station near the highway. I found your name and address in the book. I've been waiting for you to come home for a couple of hours."

I left Hoyt on the couch sipping his rum while I paced around the living room, trying to sort out what had happened and what to do next.

Those murderous sons of bitches were still out there. I struggled to control my anger. As much as I wanted to jump in my truck and go after them right then, I knew I needed to call Captain Hadnott and let him handle it.

"Hoyt, listen to me." I turned the chair around and sat down. "Do you remember that Texas Ranger who visited the camp?"

He nodded.

"Well, he's the man that captured the guys who killed your friend, Judson. And he's caught other men, too, men even worse than Clifton and Omar—I've seen him do it. In a minute I'm going to call him, and he's going to want to talk to you himself. And you're going to have to tell your story all over again."

Hoyt closed his eyes and shuddered. I could tell he wanted to keep them closed.

"He might even insist that you go help him find the bodies of Julien and Dodo. Maybe even tonight."

Hoyt's eyes popped open. "I don't want to go back there."

"Believe me, you won't have to worry. There'll be plenty of fire-power around you. And you'll be helping us find the bastards that killed our friends."

I moved my chair back to the kitchen table and looked at Hoyt slumped on the couch, his eyes at half-mast. "Hey Hoyt, it's going to take Captain Hadnott a little while to get over here once I call him. I reckon you can get about two hours of sleep in the meantime." I put out my hand and pulled him to his feet, leading him toward my bedroom. "Try and get some rest, son. You've sure as hell earned it."

Hoyt collapsed on the bed and I think he was asleep before I left the room. I went to the kitchen and rested my hand on the telephone receiver. I would have several tough calls to make over the next few hours, and I dreaded every one of them. I thought of Julien, smiling, waving goodbye from the road, happy because his dream was finally within reach. That image was displaced by another—him staring straight ahead with wide, disbelieving eyes, a fixed-blade neck knife buried in his spine.

I picked up the receiver and started dialing.

CHAPTER 35

Dodo Desmarias and Julien were both buried on Thursday—Dodo in Louisiana, Julien in France. DeBergerac paid for both funerals.

Dodo's employment file at the company recorded no first name besides Dodo, and his birthplace was listed as "Atchafalaya," which wasn't specifically a town, but instead a huge basin in Southern Louisiana where the Atchafalaya River drained into the Gulf of Mexico. The area covered eight parishes and almost a thousand square miles of bayous, bald cypress swamps and densely wooded wetlands, with a few strips of farmland clinging to the high ground. I drove there myself to try and locate his next of kin.

I finally found a Desmarais in Morgan City who thought there might be other folks with that last name living near Cote Blanch Bay along State Route 317. Although I was unable to locate any living Desmarais down there, I discovered a little cemetery near Burns Point where dozens of them had been buried.

Dodo's body had been cremated in Texas, so during the three days I spent making preparations for his burial, Dodo rode around with me on the floorboard of my truck, his ashes packed loosely in a bronze urn. The funeral director in Morgan City who helped me make burial arrangements thought I was touched in the head. And maybe I was, because I frequently found myself talking to Dodo while we were in the car together, laughing out loud as his wacky coonass stories ran through my mind.

Dodo Desmarais ended up at the overgrown little cemetery at the edge of a swamp at Burns Point. I was his only mourner, but at least his grave was among other Cajuns who shared his name. I was hopeful that some, if not all, of the souls residing there were his kin. I placed the boxed-up urn into the open grave and tossed a handful of dirt into the hole.

"*Reposez en paix, Dodo.*"

Earlier in the week, Julien Dufay's remains were carried home to France in the company Gulfstream, accompanied by his immediate family. The newspaper said he was buried at their estate near the Rhone River in southern France. It was a private ceremony.

His Houston memorial service, however, was a much more public event, attended by enough politicos, industrialists and top-tier socialites to put a dead pope to shame. The mourners filled St. Anne's Catholic Church to capacity and then spilled out the door into the foyer and even onto the portico. Most in attendance were there out of respect for Monique Dufay, the influential matron of the family and Chairman of the Board at DeBergerac Corporation. Many of them, however, were associated with the museum or with the arts community in which Julien had been so active.

Since it was standing room only, I stood along the wall near the back of the sanctuary. I spotted the white bouffant of the ex-governor near the front, seated next to the new governor, their political differences evidently put aside for this occasion. Laurent sat in one of the pews further back, surrounded by other dapper men, many of whom were weeping unashamedly. He caught my eye and waved sadly. I lifted my chin in response, sharing his sorrow.

When the priest began the service, my mind wandered to the night Hoyt stumbled across my threshold and recounted his appalling tale. After I had phoned O.B., Ranger Hadnott immediately drove to Clyde Sutton's ranch house and rousted him from bed, insisting that he help the law enforcement team locate the dry creek bed where Hoyt said two of the murders had occurred. Clyde complied without objection.

Before dawn, they located the corpses in a sandy wash under a shrub-covered bank. O.B. said the bodies of Dodo and Vinny were found together in a shallow hole, along with Julien Dufay's clothes. Julien's partially nude body was found a short distance away. It had not been buried. O.B. said that coyotes, feral hogs and other opportunistic beasts had found the body long before the search party had. Cremation was the only option. I was thankful that O.B. hadn't insisted that Hoyt accompany them on their grisly search. The kid had seen enough already.

After the service, I queued up in the long receiving line of people who waited to pay their respects to the grieving family. As ready as I was to drive back to Fulton, I felt I should at least offer my condolences to Marguerite. When I finally entered the large reception room adjacent to the sanctuary, Marguerite spotted me from a distance and hurried over. She embraced me with surprising emotion.

"Oh, Charlie," she whispered, and begin sobbing in my arms.

I was not prepared for the depth of her grief, or for the wave of feeling that washed over me as well. I struggled to hold back my own tears. Say what you want about our fling, there was nothing insincere or calculating about Marguerite's love for her husband. It was as deep and real as any I had ever seen.

She held me tightly in the crowded room while people looked on curiously. Finally she released me and pulled herself together. I handed her a handkerchief and she dabbed at her tears. Even with puffy eyes and a simple black mourning dress, she still looked regal.

"Thank you for being here, Charlie. You meant so much to my husband. He adored you, *mon cher*, he really did." She caressed my cheek with her palm. "You were a wonderful friend."

Some friend, I thought, knowing that I might have prevented his death had I thought the situation through before I drove off with Holly that morning. All week I had been brooding about what an idiot I'd been. I had left Julien at the camp with three violent and disgruntled employees; I left him knowing full well his tendency for making rash, careless decisions. I knew about his quick temper and his *obliviousness* when it came to sensing a threat. It was an explosive situation that I failed to anticipate.

Adding insult to injury, I had forgotten to sign the foundation papers before he died. I was pretty sure that by now Jean-Marc and his legal opportunists had figured out a way to block the La Salle state park deal, especially with a new governor in charge—

one who never saw an oil well he didn't like. I felt as if I had killed Julien and his dream.

My self-flagellation was interrupted when Marguerite grabbed me by the hand and pulled me toward the other side of the room. "Come," she said. "*Je veux vous présenter à la mère.* She wants to meet you."

We pushed through the crowd and the next thing I knew, I was standing in front of Monique Dufay, Julien's mother, a petite, elegant woman whose erect posture and sparkling eyes belied her age. Marguerite said something rapidly in French and then, for my benefit: "This is Charlie Sweetwater, *ma mere*, the man I have told you about. He was a beautiful friend to our Julien."

"*Toutes mes condoléances*," I said—a phrase I had made a point to memorize and practice just for today. Madam Dufay looked at me with surprising intensity. Even with her slight stature, she radiated power and purpose. I hoped to God I hadn't offended her with my Tex-Mex French.

"*Je vous remercie pour vos aimables paroles, monsieur*," she replied with a weary but honest smile. "Thank you for your kind words."

She must have been exhausted—the shock of the gruesome death, the trip back and forth from Europe, and now the public spotlight. No mother should have to bury her child. Yet she seemed to be holding up well, exhibiting remarkable grace under the circumstances. She grasped my hand warmly and squeezed it.

"You saved my son's life, Mr. Sweetwater, when you rescued him at sea."

"He also rescued me, ma'am."

She inclined her head and looked at me curiously. She probably didn't know about the fight with Monroe, or about her second son's relationship with the would-be killer.

"And you also helped him realize a dream that was very dear to his heart," she continued. "The La Salle project was his passion."

"It would have been something to be proud of," I said.

"Oh it *will be*," she asserted. "You and I will make sure of it."

"We will?" I was stunned.

"*Absolument.* I will expect you to call me next week so we can discuss how to proceed." She leaned closer to my ear. "I don't care what the rest of the board thinks. My son will have his museum."

I heard someone clear his throat behind me and turned to see a large man in a shiny black suit and a bolo tie waiting impatiently to pay his respects to the powerful matriarch of the DeBergerac family. I seemed to recall that he owned the city's NFL football team.

I returned my attention to the DeBergerac women. "I will look forward to that call, ma'am," I said. I hugged them both and received kisses on both cheeks in return.

I noticed Jean-Marc standing in the receiving line a few paces down. I stopped in front of him. "Your brother is going to be remembered long after both of us are dead," I said, and then I bent down and whispered in his ear. "And so will you. But not the way you think."

Jean-Marc looked at me with utter disdain.

"Get out of my sight," he said a little too loudly.

His mother's head leaned out from the reception line and fixed him with a disapproving glance. I held my tongue and walked away. *You and I will make sure of it,* she had said. As impolitic and unchristian as it may have been under the circumstances, I savored the thought of shoving a 300-year-old French ship timber up Jean-Marc Dufay's tight ass.

Having arrived late at the church, I was double-parked in the back near the service vehicles and limos. Before driving home, I sat in the car and closed my eyes for a few moments, wanting to empty my head of a very bad week. I must have dozed off, because I was awakened by insistent tapping on my window. I looked up to see O.B. Hadnott standing outside my door. Surprised, I rolled down the window.

"Captain Hadnott," I said, rubbing my eyes. "What are you doing here?"

"Workin'."

"Security?"

"Sort of."

"That's good. I was afraid you were gonna bust me for double-parking."

"Nah." He was focused on the side entrance to the church where people were beginning to come out the door. He glanced down at me. "In fact, you're in a good spot. You should hang around a few minutes."

Several of the limos started their engines, and O.B. straightened up. I saw Marguerite exit the building, linked arm-in-arm with her mother-in-law.

"Gotta go," he said.

Marguerite and Monique Dufay climbed into their limo first, followed by three or four people who must have been Julien's uncles and aunts. Next I watched Jean-Marc Dufay exit the church and walk toward his limo. Oddly, O.B. was standing beside it, holding open the passenger door for the mourners.

After a word from O.B. to the driver, the limo drove off without Jean-Marc, who stood behind on the pavement, gesturing angrily at the Texas Ranger and jabbing his finger into the lawman's chest. *Not a good idea*, I thought.

O.B. Hadnott smiled a wintry smile and put his big hand around the little man's bicep, ushering him insistently toward an unmarked car parked nearby. I could see him leaning down, speaking into Jean-Marc's ear. Whatever he said, it caused Jean-Marc's posture to go slack. His face was pale as a ghost shrimp by the time O.B. helped him climb into the back seat of the vehicle.

———

FROM THE JOURNAL OF PÈRE POISSON

I feel a weariness, weariness deep into my bones. Almost a year has passed. Where is La Salle? Where is the help he promised he would send? I rarely sleep more than four hours. Last week, I stood guard shortly before dawn. Although I could not see them, a party of the savages gathered in the darkness to strike me down and raid our settlement. As one of them was about to draw his bow, a musket shot pierced the darkness, and I saw the flash of the powder. My friend, my trusted friend Jacque Denier fired upon him, scattering the rest of his party.

Père Poisson
WINTER 1688

CHAPTER 36

I drove back to Fulton in a reflective funk, contemplating the crazy events of the past hours, weeks and months. Around Bay City it started drizzling, a fitting backdrop for my pessimistic outlook concerning the human species. How did Poe put it? "Man is neither happier nor wiser than he was 6000 years ago; only more active." Or something like that. When I got home, I left a message for O.B. Hadnott, asking him to call me.

The phone rang thirty minutes later.

"What was that all about after the funeral, Captain? That French-man looked like you popped his soufflé."

"Hey, Charlie. Hold on a second." I heard the background noise of a busy police station, followed by the sound of a door closing. "Turns out Monroe Chambers was more than willing to give up his boss," said Hadnott. "He's already struck a deal with the DA, looking for a lighter sentence."

"Wait. back up. What sentence? Give his boss up for what?"

"Yesterday we booked Monroe Chambers for the murder of Antoine Gillette. I thought you already knew that."

"No, I didn't. Most of the week I was in Louisiana, burying Dodo Desmarais. I was out of touch."

"Oh, right. I forgot. Well, a parking lot security camera caught Mr. Chambers going up to Gillette's room; he was at one of those extended-stay hotel deals in Houston. It also captured him leaving the room a few minutes later and stuffing a sheet-wrapped body into the trunk of his car. The video tape was kinda blurry and might not've convince a jury, but forensics were able to place the body in Monroe Chamber's car trunk using DNA evidence from one of Antoine Gillette's hairs."

"All that from a piece of hair?"

"Yep, it's a whole new ballgame now."

"Look out, bad guys. So Monroe was careful, but not careful enough. And once he knew he was caught he was ready to deal, is that it?"

"Pretty much. But he *was* careful about documenting all his correspondence with Jean-Marc Dufay. My guess is that his evidence and testimony against his boss will probably knock about ten years off his sentence."

O.B. heard the silence on my end of the line. "Don't worry, Charlie. We'll both be dead by the time he's out, and if we're not, he'll be too damn old to hurt anybody."

"Considering what happens to crooked cops in the joint, getting out might not be on his dance card," I said.

"I don't have a problem with that." There wasn't a lick of empathy in the Ranger's voice. "As far as I'm concerned, he still has to answer for that soldier boy back in Houston."

"Hey, one other thing," I asked. "Did Monroe say why Jean-Marc wanted Antoine dead?"

"No. Maybe Dufay was afraid Antoine would mess up his drilling plans. You know, disgruntled employee, that sort of thing. In the tape recordings with Jean-Marc, Monroe never asks for a reason. Just when and how much."

"I appreciate the update, O.B. While we're talking about bad guys—y'all had any luck finding Clifton Sloan and Omar Camacho?"

"'Fraid not. We've had a statewide manhunt in effect for five days, but there's been no sign of 'em. Nothing. By now they've probably escaped into Mexico. Sorry," he said after the pause. "I want to catch those two as bad as you do. We'll keep looking."

O.B. Hadnott had never accustomed himself to deferred justice. He would turn the State of Texas upside down to shake out those two assholes.

Next I phoned Jim Brannan and told him about Monique Dufay's pledge to support the La Salle projects—the excavation and the museum.

"That's great news, Charlie," he said.

"Do you think it's enough to keep this thing from derailing? It's still got to get through the Lege."

"Well, there may be some good news on that front, too. Our chief-of-staff buddy says the ex-governor's found an unlikely ally for the project in the governor-elect, who may have made his fortune in the oil business, but it turns out he's also a history buff and a closet conservationist. He's doing what he can to help push through the emergency appropriation."

"Looks like you'll be digging again soon."

"Looks like it. I was just getting ready to call Holly and tell her the news. She'll want to hear about Mrs. Dufay's pledge, too. You want to tell her, or you want me to?"

"You do it, Jim. I think I'm going to shut my eyes for a few months."

"I don't blame you, Charlie. It's been a hell of a week."

I collapsed on the couch and fell asleep instantly. Sometime later—a minute? an hour? a week?—I noticed a ringing in my ears, growing louder and louder. When I finally came to my senses I realized it was the phone. I staggered toward it, trying to decide whether to answer it or jerk the cord out of the wall.

"What?" I answered groggily.

"Oh damn, I woke you up, didn't I?" said Holly.

"It's okay. I was just . . . ." I rubbed my eyes and yawned. "What time is it?"

"Six thirty."

I looked out the window and sure enough, it was dark outside.

"Which one? A.M. or P.M.?" I asked drowsily. I probably would have slept straight through to Tuesday if she hadn't called.

"P.M., dummy. I'm calling to invite you over for dinner tonight."

"Dinner? Where are we going?"

"To my place in Palacios. Everyone's off this weekend, so I've decided to cook for you."

"That's unlike you."

"To cook?"

"To give your crew a weekend off."

"We decided to do it because of the funeral, out of respect for Julien. And also because . . . well, honestly, we all just needed a break."

I could relate. I needed a break, too. "Wait, did you say *your* place, Holly? I thought you were staying—"

"Okay, yeah, it's the THC headquarters, the warehouse, but . . . . It'll be fun, Charlie."

"Are we having microwave popcorn?"

"Something better. Come on over. I'll be expecting you."

Two hours later I pushed open the door of the THC building, holding a bottle of wine in one hand and a single long stem rose in the other.

"Charlie, is that you?" Holly yelled down from the second floor.

"I have a reservation," I shouted.

She told me to come on up. "Be careful on the stairs. There's no handrail."

To get to the staircase, I had to snake my way through the huge soaking vats and hundreds of packing crates that crowded the warehouse floor. Chain hoists hung from the rafters, and in the shadows I noticed numerous cats draped across the packing boxes, like Dali's surrealistic soft watches. They followed me with their watchful eyes. The space was quiet but also oddly disquieting—the mysterious THC laboratory where mad scientists brought ancient remains back to life. I loved horror films as a kid, but *The Mummy* scared the crap out of me. I hoped we weren't having dinner downstairs amidst the relics.

Upstairs, the ambiance was much cheerier. Holly had set a fine-looking table, with a white tablecloth, real crockery and flatware, and proper wine glasses. Light from a half dozen candles danced on the reflective surfaces of the crystal. I searched around and found an empty Coke bottle to use as a flower vase. Something wonderful was baking in the oven.

"Did you bring wine, Charlie?" Her voice came from behind a flimsy partition that separated a semi-private latrine from the rest of the room.

"Of course. What am I, a crabber?"

"Open it. I'll be out in a sec."

As I twisted a corkscrew into the top of the wine bottle, I surveyed the big room. The college intern I'd met at the dock last month was right about the lack of privacy. Cots were scattered all around, some with makeshift curtains tacked up around them, and others out in the open. Personal possessions were stored in footlockers or open boxes near the cots. Pegs were nailed into walls for hanging coats, scarves and backpacks. A stable of horse stalls had more privacy.

I popped the cork, filled the two wine glasses on the table, and then carried my glass to the short wall facing the open warehouse below. The room was cool away from the oven. I supposed the gas heaters I'd seen on my last visit were only used to prevent the THC embalming fluids, or whatever they were, from freezing during the occasional cold snaps. I had not seen any AC units upstairs, only large industrial fans here and there.

The warehouse must've been hotter than the ninth ring of hell in summer. But I guess it was more comfortable than the muddy cofferdam they worked in all day long.

Outside the high-set warehouse windows, I could see Palacios Bay. A street lamp at the end of the jetty cast its glow upon two slickered fishermen who sat slumped in folding chairs in the light rain, long fishing rods jutting out from their laps.

"Nice place you've got here, Holly," I shouted into the cavernous warehouse.

"We archeologists are a tough breed," she said right behind me. "We shun comfort."

I turned around and whistled softly. "But sure clean up nicely." Holly wore a black, form-fitting dress with long sleeves, a short hem and a deep neckline. Her thick auburn hair had been wound into a relaxed bun at her neck. She also, I noticed with surprise, wore makeup for the occasion. She looked beautiful.

"You're staring at me funny, Charlie," she said self-consciously.

"God, I'm sorry, Holly. It's just that you look gorgeous."

"It occurred to me that you've only ever seen me in my work clothes. So . . ." she struck a fashion pose and laughed, "I went out and bought a party dress for tonight."

"Nice choice. It compliments . . . everything."

The meal was delicious: fresh Matagorda Bay oysters followed by Beef Wellington with roasted vegetables and a garden salad of wintergreens, cranberries and pistachios. She produced another bottle of wine after we drank the first.

After dinner, I rose to help her clear the table. "Sit," she said. "We're not finished yet."

I watched her standing barefoot in front of the counter, stacking dishes in the sink. "Why are you being so nice to me, Holly? I mean, don't get me wrong, so far this night has been sensational. But, still."

"It's my way of thanking you for all you've done." She returned to the table with two forks and a single plate containing a pair of small, strawberry-covered cakes. "Jim told me what Monique Dufay said. So we're celebrating that, too." She sat down and smiled at me. "Also, I've decided that I like you."

Before I could respond she handed me a fork. "Let's eat dessert."

I took a bite of the creamy cake and nodded my head appreciatively. It tasted very familiar. "Are these—?"

"Okay, yes, dammit, they're Twinkies. I had to improvise a little. But if you dress them up with some raspberry preserves and add fresh strawberries—"

"They aren't half bad," I said, finishing her sentence. In two minutes we'd cleaned the plate. But the surprises weren't over yet. I noticed that Holly had placed a little box on the table. She pushed it toward me, her eyes sparkling in anticipation. "What's this?" I asked.

"You'll see."

I opened the box and found myself face to face with Louis XIV— the Sun King. The heavy gold ring was set with a shiny *Louis d'or* coin. "By the grace of God, king of France," I murmured. I put it on my right ring finger. It fit perfectly.

"What do you think?" she asked.

"It's . . ."

I must have looked confused for an instant because Holly wrinkled her brow. "It doesn't mean anything . . . traditional. It's just a gift. And it's just . . . *because.* I believe gifts should be unusual, personal and unexpected."

"I agree. And this is all of those things. I love it." I wasn't much of a jewelry guy, but this ring was a keeper. "Hey, what was all that about the coin being a 'priceless archeological treasure' and me being a 'looter' for holding on to it before?"

Holly shrugged. "I made an exception."

I shook my head in wonder. "Well, thanks, Holly. It's the coolest gift I've ever received. I don't really know what to say."

Holly looked at me strangely, intensely. What now? This girl was full of surprises.

"You don't have to say anything. In fact, let's not talk for awhile."

She stood up and grabbed my hand, pulling me to my feet, and then she led me away from the flickering candlelight toward one of the cots in the corner of the room. When we stopped, she held my face and kissed me lightly on the lips as if to seal my silence. Next, I watched speechlessly as she removed her dress in one quick movement and wiggled out of her panties.

"Now you," she whispered, unknotting her lion's mane of hair from behind her neck and shaking it out.

Holly was a lioness in bed, too: adventurous, playful, sometimes aggressive and completely voracious. After the first round of spirited sex we fell back onto the cot, panting heavily. Before tonight, I could never have imagined the fun two people could have on an army surplus cot—lying in it (upside down and backwards), arched over it, hanging onto the side of it for dear life.

But Holly could, and apparently had.

"Can we talk now?" I whispered.

She giggled. "Sure. If you can."

"I bet that's the first time that's happened in the ol' THC barracks."

"Are you kidding? It happens all the time."

After a pause I responded. "Really?"

"Really."

"That's shocking." Although, I guess it shouldn't have been. A bunch of college kids and young professionals on an exciting archeological adventure, all thrown together in the same bunkhouse in a podunk town, miles from home—using the same showers, sleeping side by side. There were only so many archeology jokes you could tell after awhile.

"But it's the first time *for me* in the THC barracks," said Holly, patting me on the leg. "More than once I fantasized about us making love here. Especially when my crewmembers started going at it under the covers, thinking nobody could hear them, or else not caring if we did."

"The secret life of archeologists? If only I had known."

"Don't spread it around. Because then everyone would want to be one."

"My lips are sealed."

"Good," she said, climbing on top of me. "And hold your tongue, too, until I tell you exactly what to do with it."

CHAPTER 37

Holly's head rested on my chest as I lay under the covers listening to rain fall on the tin roof. The candles had burned out and it was dark inside the warehouse, except for the glow of the harbor street lamps that shone through the windows. I inhaled the scent of her hair and listened to her soft rhythmic breathing, perfectly synchronized with the rise and fall of my chest.

I assumed she was asleep, but we both tensed up at the same time when we heard the sound of the downstairs door opening.

"Uh-oh," she whispered, followed by a nervous giggle.

"I thought everyone was off tonight," I whispered back.

"They were. They are."

She rose silently and gathered her clothes. Before she tiptoed off to the bathroom, she smiled and put her finger to her lips. "Shhh."

I smiled too, imagining how surprised her crew would be if they discovered a naked man in her cot. I reached down and located my boxers.

Holly was in the bathroom when I saw a flashlight beam move across the ceiling and heard a cat yowl as if it had been kicked or stepped on. And then I heard a voice that froze my blood.

"Fuck me!" Clifton Sloan snarled, his grating voice sending a chill up my spine. "Goddamn cats."

The cot creaked when I stood up to put on my underwear, and the warehouse was dead silent for a few seconds.

"Probably another cat," I heard him say. Flashlights continued playing off the inside of the warehouse and I heard Clifton stumbling around below, moving closer to the staircase. "I hate cats," he added.

Who was he talking to? I hoped to God it wasn't Omar Camacho.

"Vinny said he saw 'em load the coins into the station wagon," Clifton continued. "Look for a blue tub. That's our ticket across the border."

An overhead light clicked on in the bathroom and Holly appeared from behind the partition, fully dressed. She walked resolutely toward the stairway, intending, I guessed, to head off her supposed colleagues and stall them while I found my clothes.

"Somebody's here!" Clifton yelled. I heard him rushing up the metal stairs and I sprinted toward the landing, hoping to arrive there before him.

"Stay there!" I yelled at Holly.

But Clifton got to the landing first, and when he saw me he hesitated momentarily and then came at me in a mad bull's charge, planting his hard head into my chest and driving us both backwards over a row of cots. We grappled ferociously on the floor, each of us trying to pin the other.

"Can't sucker punch me now, can you, fucker?" he hissed. At one point Clifton had me on my back and began to pummel me with his fists. I raised my legs over his head and scissor-crossed them around his neck, jerking him backwards. We both jumped up and went at it again.

Holly watched in fear as we began throwing punches and kicks at one another, our fight moving slowly toward the stairwell. My reach was longer than his and most of my blows were connecting, but Clifton got his licks in too. He was quite a few years younger and outweighed me by thirty pounds—and he was scary strong. I wasn't sure if I could outlast him.

When we neared the stairs, I positioned myself in front of the open door and waited for him. He paced in front of me in a low boxer's crouch, panting through a bloodied mouth, searching for a weakness, waiting for an opening. He reminded me of a hyena circling a wounded prey.

"Come on, you stumpy little fuck-wit," I taunted.

His eyes flared and he ducked his head and rushed me again. Anticipating his charge, I pivoted my body and shoved the back of his head and shoulders forward, using his own momentum to send him flying down the flight of stairs. He rolled and tumbled halfway to the bottom, his head ringing off the metal steps, and then he flew off the edge and crashed into a stack of wooden pallets below.

"Holly, turn on the lights." She hurried to an electrical box and clicked on the switches, flooding the big warehouse with fluorescent light.

I looked down at Clifton, curled in a fetal position on top of the shattered pallets. His head had been shattered too; I could see blood seeping out of a gash at his temple, and his neck and arm were bent at an awkward angle. Clifton Sloan was finished—as lifeless as Dead Bob resting on his coil of anchor rope on the *Belle*.

But Omar Camacho was still very much alive, standing next to a toppled pile of plastic tubs, watching me with an expression that was, if anything, mildly irritated, or maybe slightly amused, it was hard to tell. Lids had been pulled off the plastic containers, and he held a small wooden box under his arm. He bent over slowly and placed the box on the ground. I heard 299 gold coins rattle around inside.

As Omar walked toward the stairs, he took off his jacket and casually tossed it onto the pallet next to Clifton's dead body, never even glancing at his late partner in crime. I realized with a jolt of fear that he had removed that fucking knife from the sheath on his neck chain. He began climbing the stairs, slowly, deliberately, one step at a time, with that same inscrutable expression on his face.

Standing there on the landing in my skivvies, I had never felt more exposed. Where should I fight him? What could I fight him with? The knife blade glinted bright and lethal in his hand.

"Where you goin', wetback?" said a familiar voice. Miguel Cantu Negron stood just inside the warehouse entrance, wearing a glistening yellow slicker, the hood pulled low over his face. His forearm rested casually on the curved head of a stainless steel gaff hook, the four-foot shaft rising up from the floor like a conquistador's pike.

When Miguel pulled back the hood, Omar eyed him curiously. "*Esto no es asunto tuyo, 'mano.*"

"I'm making it my business," Miguel answered in English. He leaned the gaff hook against a soaking vat and methodically removed his raincoat.

"Just let him go, Miguel," I said. "So nobody else gets hurt."

Neither one of them seemed to hear me. Omar descended the steps and Miguel picked up the gaff hook and began moving too. They walked steadily toward the center of the warehouse, toward each other.

"Miguel!" I yelled. "No!"

In an explosion of violence the two men collided and began thrusting, slashing and kicking at one another. Metal clacked against metal, and at one point Omar's knife flew to one side, knocked away by the butt of Miguel's gaff. Omar moved in close and managed to get partial possession of the gaff-hook. Both men grasped the weapon at once—four rough brown hands clutching the stainless steel shaft, fighting for their lives, fighting to take the other's life.

Miguel pushed Omar against a tall vat and, using his brute strength, forced the staff across the other man's neck, trying to crush his windpipe. With his back to the wall, Omar kicked wildly at Miguel's ankles, vainly trying to knock his feet out from under him. But a roundhouse knee delivered into his kidney *was* successful.

Miguel groaned and Omar twisted away, bolting for the knife that lay on the floor near the staircase. I saw the knife, too. As he picked it up, I took three quick steps down and launched myself at Omar. He ducked under my flying body, boosting and directing my trajectory with his long arms. The blade of the knife caught the leg of my boxers as I flew past, slicing my leg and catching on my underwear. But I had knocked the weapon from his grasp and it fell to the ground. I landed with a crash on a stack of plastic tubs and thrashed about in a jumble of containers, struggling to extract myself.

But I couldn't move fast enough to prevent Omar from retrieving the blade. He moved toward me, adjusting the knife in his hand, changing his handle hold from a hammer grip to an icepick grip. Still buried in the cases, I was off balance and immobile. I tried to stand.

"*Esta vez, te mato*," he said, coiling to strike. *This time, I kill you.*

At the edge of my vision, a bright object flashed into view and Omar lurched and then seemed to freeze in place, a stunned look on his face. Belatedly, I noticed a glinting barbed hook protruding through the side of his neck. Miguel yanked the gaff again and Omar jerked backwards. Blood began spurting from his jugular and the knife clattered onto the concrete floor. He raised his hands to his neck in shock and disbelief, delicately touching the cold hard steel with his fingers. He was dead within seconds.

Miguel let go of the gaff-hook when Omar fell lifeless to the floor, then regarded me with a wry grin. "I wish I had a fucking camera."

I was still spread-eagle in the pile of containers, and in the commotion, I realized that I'd lost my boxers.

"Miguel, what the hell are you doing here?" I said, my voice raspy with emotion and adrenaline.

"He was fishing on the jetties with Rosie," said Holly tonelessly. She sat down heavily on a stair step above us, her eyes distant and unfocused. Her head dropped and she held her face in her hands, trying to assimilate what had just happened.

"Holly, are you okay?" I asked.

"Just . . . give me . . . a minute," she stammered.

I struggled to my feet and looked at Miguel. "That was you out on the jetties?" I recalled the two yellow-slickered figures I'd seen out the window, and Holly telling me before that Miguel often frequented the spot with his girlfriend, but I hadn't put two and two together.

He shrugged. "I heard the commotion. You owe me for a black drum, asshole. I almost had him up to the rocks."

"Shit, Miguel. I'll catch ten of 'em for you, and then I'll clean 'em, cook 'em and serve 'em to you on a silver platter." I started to say something else but I heard Rosie calling from the door.

"Miguelito? Is that you?"

Miguel glanced down at me and then shook his head disgustedly. "Put on some fucking clothes." He kicked the boxers toward me with the toe of his boot.

I slipped on my shorts and began climbing the stairs, taking one last look at the bloody bodies of Clifton and Omar. My adrenalin surge was subsiding, and I began to feel the bruises and sprains that I'd received in the fight. When I reached Holly, I eased her to her feet. "Come upstairs with me," I said softly.

I helped her into a kitchen chair and she wrapped her arms around me, holding me tightly. "God, Charlie. That was awful. I was so . . . ." her voice trailed off.

"It's okay. It's over now. The good guys won, like you said before."

I extricated myself from her arms and lit the burner to make some hot tea. Maybe that would calm her. As the water heated, I rummaged around in the cupboard for a first aid kit. After I'd cleaned the slice on my leg and taped on a bandage, I located my clothes and struggled into them, examining my battered body to determine if anything else was broken or bleeding.

Downstairs, I heard Miguel talking to Rosie, explaining to her why there were two dead bodies at his feet. He recounted what had happened as calmly as if he were describing a tune-up on a V-8, or how to grill a perfect cheeseburger. It began to dawn on me how lucky I was to be alive.

I prepared Holly's tea and set it in front of her. "This will help," I said.

"You called the cops, yet?" Miguel yelled from below.

"No, I'll do it now." I put my hand on the receiver to dial and then hesitated. I walked to the landing and looked down at Miguel. Rosie's head was pressed into his chest. "You sure you're okay with me calling the cops right now?" I asked, remembering that he was very skittish about the police. "You don't have to be here, you know."

"I got no more beef with the law."

"I could say it was me. That I killed 'em both—self defense."

Miguel snorted. "Yeah, right . . . . Tell 'em the truth, *cabrón*."

FROM THE JOURNAL OF PÈRE POISSON

Last night, I found myself in a remarkable dream. While I was standing watch, a figure approached from a distance. Even from far away, I could see his simple robes and recognized that it was our patron, St. Francis of Assisi. I ran out to meet him, and he told me that he was coming to make his home with us, and that he would remain with us. I awoke with a feeling of great peace and my spirit was much uplifted. God have mercy on our souls.

Père Poisson
FINAL JOURNAL ENTRY,
WINTER 1688

CHAPTER 38

Skipping over the surface of a glassy bay on a clear winter morning can have a wondrously restorative effect on your attitude. For the second day in a row I'd had trouble getting out of bed, partly because I couldn't sleep worth a damn (the bloody fight two days ago kept replaying in my head), and partly as a consequence of diving twelve feet down into a pile of plastic tubs. At a NASCAR event in Atlanta, I once met a retired Hollywood stuntman who said he'd had to do fifteen consecutive takes of a forty-foot high fall because the cameraman kept screwing up the shot. I told him I guessed it was all in knowing how to fall. He said it was that, and Percodan. Today I could relate, because Advil wasn't cutting it.

Apparently Holly was having trouble bouncing back, too. Jim had called me that morning to suggest I take her out on the water for some R&R. She only agreed to go after Jim pulled rank and insisted.

I docked the Riva at Miguel's marina and found Holly waiting patiently on the restaurant deck.

"I see we're still trying to impress the neighbors," she said, looking at the fancy wooden runabout.

"Actually, I thought we'd take the sailboat, if that's okay with you."

Holly looked perplexed. "What sailboat?"

"I thought you might drive us to Fulton in your car, to the harbor, so we can take the *Li Shishi* out in the Gulf."

"What are you going to do with this?" she asked, pointing at the Riva.

"Hide and watch."

I strolled into the marina and slapped the boat key down on the counter. "Here you go, *señor.*"

Miguel leaned out from the kitchen and saw the boat key. It was tied to a cork that had a fancy "R" for Riva stenciled into the surface.

"Park your own damn boat," he growled.

"It's your boat now, meathead. The title is in the glove compartment. It's already been changed to your name."

Miguel blinked his black, lizard eyes. "I don't want it," he responded, and walked back into the kitchen.

"Too late."

"You leave it here, I'm charging you thirty bucks a week for the slip fee," he said as I made for the door.

"No can do, *compa,*" I yelled as I slammed the screen door. "It's not my boat."

I'd finally gotten the last word.

Out in the parking lot I put my arm around Holly and we walked to her car. I could hear Miguel grumbling away inside the marina.

When we drove off she looked at me, grinning. "What do you think he'll do?"

"Who knows with Miguel? Sink it, burn it, tear it apart and turn it into a wet bar? Honestly, I don't have a clue. Maybe he'll give it to Hinkie."

"What he *should* do is sell it to some rich jet-setter and use the money to build a nice little stilt house for him and Rosie." She thought about her idea some more and nodded her head decisively. "I'll talk to him about it."

Later that morning, we motored the Chinese junk through the Port Aransas channel and unfurled the red sails after we passed the third sand bar. Hardly a swell disturbed the surface of the Gulf, and the wind was so light that I had to continue running the engine to get where I wanted to go. A junk rig sail doesn't work worth a damn in light winds because the battens keep it from billowing out to fully capture the breeze. But on the other hand, they're easy to operate and are really, really cool-looking.

When we lost sight of land, I killed the diesels and gave Holly a short lesson in sailing, showing her the ropes, so to speak. She learned quickly, and before long was handling the boat like a pro. I sat nearby and sipped my beer, enjoying watching her enjoy herself. For stress reduction there is nothing better than day sailing in fair weather. It could put psychiatrists out of business.

"I'm getting hungry," I said after a few hours of going nowhere in particular.

She pursed her lips in disappointment. "Does that mean we have to go back?"

"*Au contraire, mademoiselle,*" I said, jumping up. "You've got the helm. I'll tend to chow."

"What are we having?"

"Hardtack and gruel—an old family recipe."

I returned with a plowman's lunch and we ate contentedly in the warm sunshine, chatting about sailboats and shipwrecks and such.

When the platter was almost empty, Holly balanced the last piece of cheese on an apple slice and slipped it in her mouth. "Tell me this, Charlie," she began. "That was the first night in months the warehouse had been empty. How could they have known?"

I took a deep breath, adjusting my head to the abrupt change in the conversation. Apparently, *that* subject was still in the forefront of her mind too. Might as well talk about it.

"O.B. Hadnott told me that Clifton and Omar had been lying low in a seedy little motor court in Palacios that was within sight of the THC building. They'd persuaded a migrant worker living in the unit next door to bring them groceries and booze all week while they waited. I suppose that once they saw the crew drive away in their cars—"

"They thought they'd help themselves to the box of *Louis d'ors* and head for Mexico."

"Bingo."

She shook her head in disbelief. "I know that motel. They were a block away from us for a full week. I swear, sometimes I feel like I understand the dead people I study more than I do the live ones."

"I know what you mean, I think."

Holly gingerly touched a large bruise on my arm. "How are *you* doing? I noticed that you're moving around a bit slow on the boat today. Anything that won't heal?"

"No, everything's healing fine. And if you disregard the knife fights and dead bodies, I thought our date was pretty terrific."

Holly laughed. "It was, wasn't it?" She looked at me with a gleam in her eye. "You know what's good for a sore body, Charlie?"

"Tell me," I answered, wondering if she was thinking what I was thinking.

"Swimming!" she exclaimed. She jumped up and stripped off her clothes, leaving them in a heap at her feet. "Come on!" She sprinted across the deck and dove headlong into the sea.

That girl could shuck her clothes faster than anyone I'd ever known.

I hurried to lower the sea ladder and then threw off my own clothes. Balancing on the rail, I looked down at her floating languidly on her back, smiling up at me. The water beneath her was as clear as a swimming pool.

"Come on, jump!" she yelled.

The February seawater was chilly but invigorating; it was just what the doctor ordered. We swam out a distance from the boat and looked back at the handsome junk floating like a—how did Julien describe it?—like a "magnificent anachronism" on the surface of the Gulf. We splashed about contentedly until Holly stopped suddenly and looked at me with wide eyes.

"Do you hear that?"

I stopped splashing too and heard the *pufff* of a nearby dolphin surfacing for air, followed by a whoosh from another dolphin, and then the rippling sound of their sleek, massive bodies arching over the water.

"Over there, two of them." She pointed toward the bow of the *Li Shishi*. "I think they're coming this way."

The pair of eight-foot bottlenose dolphins made a wide ring around us as we gently dogpaddled in the water. They watched us attentively and curiously, gradually narrowing their distance, closing the circle around us. A couple of times they swam directly beneath us, almost brushing our feet. Holly giggled with delight.

We kept expecting them to move on but they stayed near us, watching us, occasionally resting on the surface and rolling onto their side to observe us, looking directly into our eyes. Holly and I were silent, mesmerized by the creatures. It seemed as though they were trying to communicate with us, to connect with us in some mysterious way.

Suddenly I thought of my brother, who drew his last breath in this same patch of sea many years ago. Were these animals there with him when he died? Did they try to lift him up? Give him peace in his last moments?

The curve of the "smile" on the darker-colored dolphin vaguely reminded me of Julien, especially when he was aboard the *Li Shishi*, uncomplicated and happy, simply glad to be alive.

"What are they trying to tell us, Charlie?" asked Holly in a whisper.

"I don't know."

A few minutes later the two dolphins slapped the water with their tails and glided away from us, further out to sea. Holly and I swam back to the boat and dressed. I poured us a pair of stiff bourbons and we sailed back to Fulton in an easy silence. Back at the harbor, after we'd tied down the boat, we embraced on the dock, holding onto each other for a long time.

CHAPTER 39: EPILOGUE

SEPTEMBER 1997

On a hazy morning on Matagorda Bay, Nu Dang was dragging for brown shrimp when his trawl net snagged on the bottom. The stringy little fisherman walked to the stern of the shrimp boat and cursed in Vietnamese, removing his conical *nón lá* hat and whacking it against his thigh in anger. The bay floor was littered with obstacles that could hang up a trawl: pipe casings, waterlogged trees, discarded crab traps, broken boat rigging. He shouted at his wife Lua Xuan to throttle the diesels down to idle.

The winch unsuccessfully labored to free the nets, so Lua Xuan backed the *New Hope* directly over the snag. They fastened the try-net winch to the main cable and ran both winches simultaneously to gain more torque, nervously watching the rigging strain against the burden. Finally the cable jerked, and the object began to rise slowly from the mud.

The butt end of a barnacle-encrusted cylinder breached the surface and the two shrimpers exchanged puzzled looks. Nu Dang used the lazy line to guide the heavy object through the air and down onto the boat while the winches groaned under the load. When they lowered it to the deck, it landed with a clunk.

They unwrapped the net and stood over the object, scratching their heads. A section of heavy drilling pipe? A creosote piling? A cannon? After a thorough inspection, accompanied by a long and vocal discussion, they concluded that it was indeed a brass cannon, and a very old one at that, encrusted with barnacles and calcified concretion. Part of the object had been buried under the mud and was relatively clean, allowing them to make out the French words inscribed on the surface. Nu Dang and his wife were old enough to recognize the writing of their former colonial rulers when they saw it.

They both knew about the French shipwreck that had recently been exhumed from the bottom of the muddy bay, too. The curious-looking structure that, until recently, had surrounded the wreck was less than a quarter-mile away. They'd had to navigate around the damn thing for almost a year, as well as around the boatloads of tourists that flocked there to peek inside the big steel vat. Nu Dang had never been curious enough to look. He had no interest in archeology.

But even so, he had a pretty good idea about what he'd found. He knew it was rare and valuable. And he knew exactly what he was going to do with it.

When Nu Dang presented Charlie with the brass cannon on the docks of Fulton Harbor (it took ten men to heave it onto the pier) he did so with a solemn declaration that all his obligations to his friend were hereby satisfied. The slate was clean—the gifted brass cannon counterbalanced Charlie's rescue of his nephew sixteen years ago. Charlie accepted the 800-pound cannon graciously, pleased that the old rooster could now live out the rest of his life in peace and harmony, having paid his debt to karma.

Soon the coveted archeological prize traveled to Texas A&M, where it received a thorough mechanical scrubbing, an electrolytic bath and a professional spit shine. 17th century French records and journals listed four bronze cannons on La Salle's final expedition. Three of them had already been found inside the *Belle* shipwreck and would later be prominently displayed in museums in Austin, Victoria, and, of course, the "La Salle Historical Museum" on Garcitas Creek.

The graceful new Garcitas complex rested on a rise above the creek, surrounded by the natural flora and fauna of the La Salle State Park. Visitors could stroll about the wild gardens that wound through the foundations of the original French settlement, walking in the footsteps of the 17th century colonists who lived and died there. Inside the sunlit interior, thousands of artifacts were displayed, telling the tragic story of René-Robert Cavelier Sieur de La Salle and his followers.

Encased in the wall, a bronze relief portrait of Julien Dufay greeted visitors. It had been created by a noted Parisian sculptor and commissioned by Monique and Marguerite Dufay. A French quote from Marcel Proust was inscribed beneath it; the English translation read *"The only true voyage of discovery, would be not to visit strange lands but to possess other eyes, to behold the universe through the eyes of another, of a hundred others, to behold the hundred universes that each of them beholds, that each of them is."*

Nu Dang's cannon was the last of La Salle's four bronze cannons. At Charlie's request, and with Jim Brannan's pull as Director of the Texas Historical Commission, the fourth cannon found a home in the Rockport Maritime Museum, just three miles from Fulton Harbor.

Charlie would sometimes visit the museum and stand in front of the beautiful brass cannon displayed in the center of the rotunda. The new museum curator, a retired archeology professor from Indiana, found it strange that the rangy shrimper occasionally talked to the two leaping dolphins that formed the intricate handle holds on either side of the long barrel, addressing the dolphins as his *"amigos."*

But what the hell, the curator thought. The Texas Gulf Coast attracted all manner of odd fellows, adventurers and cranks. Truth be told, she realized the place was starting to grow on her.

———

FIN

ABOUT THE AUTHOR

Miles Arceneaux is the storytelling alter ego of Texas-based writers Brent Douglass, John T. Davis and James R. Dennis. Miles Arceneaux is also the author of *Thin Slice of Life*, which, like *La Salle's Ghost*, is set on the salty Gulf Coast of Texas.

CPSIA information can be obtained at www.ICGtesting.com
Printed in the USA.
LVOW06s1420270713

344946LV00002B/7/P